KELTIC DREAMS

DOUBLE KELTIC TRIAD 5

LIZZIE STARR

Dokopot
Books

The Friday Night Critique group took me in, listened in wonder, and discovered fantasy. I listened in awe to their comments and suggestions, and in taking their words to heart, learned much about my writing and myself.

*Thank you for helping dreams--
Keltic and otherwise--
come true.*

Sparkles!

PROLOGUE

H is breechclout and leggings lay folded beneath a scrubby bush.

He had cleansed his body in the icy, snow-melt waters of the stream.

The circle of power had been cleared and outlined with colored stones laid out in a precise pattern. The worn, tattered blanket--the only earthly item allowed within the dream circle--was spread north to south to follow the path of the sun. Used by the fathers of his fathers, the blanket carried the essence of every quest that had come before, and soon, would guide him to dream worlds, as it also bound him to the earth while his spirit sought answers.

Taking a swallow of water from a hollowed gourd, he rinsed his mouth and spat the tepid liquid on the dry ground. He turned in place to acknowledge the cardinal points, ending to the south where the first rays of sunlight sparkled across the flat horizon. He took two deep breaths, stepped into the circle and sat cross-legged on the blanket.

Slowing his breathing, he silently chanted to the sun, asking the Seven Guardians for passage.

William Bard Stonefeather, last of his line, faced the unknown and awaited his destiny.

CHAPTER
ONE

K aelea slipped into the tiny pantry when she heard voices approaching the kitchen. Tired of the celebration, and aching to return to the quiet of her scholarly investigations, she needed a little alone time before she faced the family gathering again.

Not that she begrudged her sister or her niece the joy of their joint announcements. The increase of the family with the coming births brought the family together for the happiest of celebrations, and she would welcome each child with love. But the growing family crowded her need for solitude.

Kae frowned as she carefully shut the narrow door, cocooning herself in dim light and the aroma of fresh herbs. The questions that had haunted her for days assaulted her in the silence. She hadn't known about Nanceen's pregnancy. As twins they had shared feelings and often knew how each other felt in extreme situations.

Nanceen had known when she had broken her arm a few years ago. How had she not recognized the flutter of life she now accepted as a faint communication from her twin's unborn child? But she had missed the flow of Nanceen's happiness filling her. Perhaps she did shut herself away from others to much.

Leaning against the door, Kae hoped the intruders would

leave soon so she could force herself from her self-imposed pantry exile and rejoin the family in time for the presentation of gifts. A tiny grin tickled her lips. She didn't want to miss that part of the celebration.

The voices, a man and a woman, sounded close to the door. Kae held her breath. *Don't open the door.* Their voices carried loud enough for her to hear without straining, and Kae tried to block out the discussion on the other side of the door. Eavesdropping was not something she approved of, accidental or not.

"So, Carrie, what is it you need to tell Nightshade? You're not thinking about coming back to work, are you?"

Kae bit back a chuckle. Carrie, recently married into the family, had a rather sordid past--to some minds--as an exotic dancer. Kae hoped Nightshade's teasing question wasn't hitting the truth. Bryce would never be able to deal with other men ogling his wife's body.

Kae didn't blame him a bit.

A tiny bite of jealousy made her wince and she held back a deep sigh. She was deliriously happy for all those in her family who had found mates. It just wasn't in the stars for her to leave her solitary life. Trying to convince herself, she shrugged. She was happy as she was.

"No. Nothing like that. I wish it was something so easy." The pain in Carrie's muffled voice drew Kae's attention and she realized her curiosity wouldn't let her ignore the conversation--she would be an eavesdropper.

"Nightshade, I'm pregnant."

The rustling sounds had to be the exuberant man enveloping Carrie in a hug. Her grin grew wide. Another child. The family was really growing.

"Carrie, honey, that's wonderful. How does Bryce feel?"

"I haven't told him yet."

"Carrie. Shame on you, girlfriend. He should be the first to know." Nightshade laughed. "Well, maybe the second--after you. This is wonderful." A long pause stretched heavily before he continued. "Isn't it?"

The silence drew out again until Kae reached to turn the

knob and announce her presence, if only to end the uncomfortable waiting.

Undecided, she nibbled on her bent knuckle. Something was wrong. Terribly wrong.

"I'm twelve weeks pregnant, Nightshade."

"Three months. That's..."

As she imagined Nightshade doing, Kae mentally counted on her fingers.

He cleared his throat. "That's..."

"We've only been together about five weeks, Nightshade. What am I going to do?"

"The rape? Oh, honey."

"That's not the problem. I can deal with that. I think, for the most part, I have. And you know, I personally could never have an abortion."

"Carrie, Bryce is such a loving man, I can't believe he would condemn a child--or you--because of how the child was created. You know his past, how he was abandoned."

Kae nodded. Nightshade was correct. Bryce would love the child without reserve. As would the rest of the Zeroun clan. Carrie had nothing to worry about.

"I know. But, Nightshade... the rapist... he's trying to destroy the family. He's the one who kidnapped Tommy. He's tried to ruin Jaye's business. Who knows what else he's done, or may be planning even now."

"Carrie--"

"This child's father is the evil faerie who wants... wants..."

Carrie's voice broke and her soft sobs tore at Kae's heart. She pressed her palms to her cheeks. Not Feidhlim. Carrie carried a child fathered by the faerie who had tried to kill her brother and tried to send her and Nanceen into separate pasts. Oh, God.

"Carrie?" Nightshade's voice dropped to a low vibrating pitch, commanding attention. "Listen to me, honey. You have to tell Bryce. Now. I know this family. There'll be some anger, but it won't be at you. There'll be shock, but eventually everyone will stand behind you. Carrie, look at me. Carrie."

Kae blessed Nightshade's presence and his knowledge of

her family. Correct in his estimations, Kae knew he would help Carrie, and once she told Bryce, a fierce circle of protection would form around her.

Kae sighed and closed her eyes. Part of her, some part she really hated to recognize, ached to leave the solitary life she'd recently chosen for herself. In the past she had been so gregarious, always ready for adventure and sensual delights. Why had that changed? Why couldn't she find what she was looking for? She didn't even know what she was looking for? She didn't know, only that whatever it was lay beyond her reach.

"Carrie. We'll get through this, you'll see."

"I'll have to believe in your confidence, Nightshade. I don't have any of my own." Dejection and hopelessness thrummed through Carrie's softly spoken words.

"Honey, let's get you to a bathroom so you can wash away those tears. I'll find Bryce--"

"No! Not during the party. I'll tell him tonight. I promise."

The conversation moved away and Kae took a deep breath. Eavesdropping always turned out to be a bad thing. You always found out something you didn't want to know. Carrie needed to tell Bryce--and the family--about her pregnancy so they could protect her. Kae dreaded to think what might happen if Feidhlim discovered he had fathered a child, and a cold shudder traveled the length of her spine.

If Carrie didn't say something soon, she'd have to face Bryce's wife and admit what she'd overheard.

Pressing her ear to the crack around the door, Kae held her breath and listened. Only the distant sounds of the celebration drifted to her, so she cautiously opened the door, peered around the kitchen and stepped from the pantry.

Nanceen's voice rose above the chatter from the living room. "Where's Kae?"

"Coming," she called. Squaring her shoulders and forcing her unwelcome knowledge to a place where she could think about it later, Kae pasted a smile on her face and hurried to rejoin the family celebration.

. . .

T he silence of the surrounding desert filled Kaelea's ears when she stepped from the portal into an oasis garden. Tall palms whispered as a gentle breeze stirred the long branches. A tiny waterfall, little more than a trickle, dripped over a path of smooth, golden stone to the surface of a deep, dark blue pool.

She hurried from the pool to an outcropping of smooth stones hidden by tall dunes. She paused before the entrance to the underground library; the iron gate rusted and twisted as if crushed by a giant's hand. Kae took a long, deep breath of the hot, dry air and a fraction of the tension tightening her shoulders eased.

The rest of the family celebration had gone by in a blur. She'd watched Carrie, but except for a haunted dimness to her eyes, the woman gave no indication of the pain she carried inside her along with the new life. As soon as she had been able, Kae said her farewells and escaped back to the ancient Fey library. There might be something here to help in the coming battle. Feidhlim would stop at nothing to destroy her brother and her family. And now...

A new worry assailed her. What if the new babe carried the father's evil? The age old battle of nature verses nurture remained unsolved. Kae paused before crossing the threshold into the library.

Nurture would prevail in Carrie's case. It had to.

Tiny sand dunes shaded the corners of the shallow stone steps leading down to the library proper. No matter how the caretakers tried to keep the steps clean, somehow sand slipped past both the magic and the brooms. Luckily the ancient magic still kept the sand from the fragile books and scrolls hidden so long ago by the fey archivists of Alexandria. The recent discovery of the library hidden in the deepest desert seemed to have only marginally disturbed the protective spells.

Kae returned to the broad table where she'd spread the texts and parchments for her current project. She'd nearly completed reconstructing the history of Korin's fairy folk and the ancient split with the gentry. The history would be part of her gift to Nanceen's child--a complete heritage.

A small stack of scrolls lay to one side. The discovery of part of Iain's faerie heritage had been a pleasant surprise. So perhaps Lara's new child could also boast a complete family tree.

Kae sat and reached for a quill. She grinned at the archaic writing instrument. Using a computer might speed her compilation of research, but somehow it didn't seem right. So she used a writing instrument of ages past to record those ages anew. After dipping the tip in a tiny pot of ink, she held the long feather over a sheet of newly made parchment.

What about the third baby, Carrie's child? Tracing Feidhlim's line as well would now be of infinite importance. Perhaps there would be a clue to--what? The nature of a child barely formed?

Or perhaps why the babe's sire chose the path of evil.

Sighing, Kae lay the quill aside without making any notations, braced her elbow against the table and rested her forehead against one palm. If fear held Carrie's tongue, how long should she wait before she brought the situation to light herself? This secret should not be hidden from her family.

The stroke of warm hands across her shoulders momentarily tightened her muscles further until the soft touch increased in pressure, paused and returned to knead the muscles at the base of her neck. "You are very tense, my love."

The lilting, musical cadence of the voice delighted her ear.

"Did you not enjoy your family's celebration?" The low tones, modulated to seduce, merely made her smile. Kae lay her palm over the hand that rested just under her ear.

"It was a wonderful gathering. I was just thinking about how much I need to do before the babies are born."

The lean body behind her shifted and her friend pulled out a chair and slouched next to her. She glanced sideways and he straightened, reached for her hand, and stroked her fingers. "Would that you would allow me to give to you such a child."

Kae chuckled and snatched back her hand. "Gowthaman," she chided.

Elegantly shrugging his shoulders, he gave her a grin bright against his light-brown skin. She marveled at the slight angle of a broken tooth. Few Faerie would let such an injury mar their appearance. Along with the golden hoop high on one ear, he had a rakish, wild appearance. As if knowing the effect of his appearance, Gowthaman's grin broadened and his dark brows lifted over chocolate brown eyes.

"You should not think so hard, my love." He stroked one of his fingers under her eye. "You are tired, I can see it in your eyes. Come to bed and I shall sing to you of desire--"

Kae grasped his finger and shook it lightly before releasing the digit. "Stop that. I like you, Gowthaman, I really do."

He sighed dramatically, so reminding her of Nightshade she had to bite back a grin. "I understand, my love. But, how can I not hope my presence at your side may change your delightful mind so you shall see me as more than a friend."

His voice sang light and teasing, but a strange glint shone in the depths of his eyes. She'd seen the look before, in the days when she, too, took pleasure for pleasure's sake. Now, the thought of a casual relationship, no matter how willing and attractive the partner, made a painful lump settle heavily in her stomach. She wanted more, and until she discovered what that more was, she would remain alone. It wasn't a big deal.

"You never give up, do you?"

"I do not." He stroked her cheek with a curled finger then leaned back in his chair. "One day, perhaps, I shall discover the key to your heart, my love."

"I wish you wouldn't call me that."

Gowthaman bowed his head. "As you wish it to be, so shall it be, sweet one."

"Not that either. Call me Kae--or don't say anything to me at all."

He dipped his head again in reluctant acknowledgement. "As you wish. Now, Kae, you must rest. I do not tease when I say you are tired. Your eyes express much to me."

"I'm not so--"

"Ah, but you are, my... Kae. The eyes, they do not lie. Go, I will not permit you to return to the library until tomorrow."

Kae narrowed her eyes and glared at Gowthaman. "What right--"

Innocence mixed with determination filled his expression. "By the right granted to the Guardian of the Fey Library of Alexandria." He rested his palm flat against his chest. "The honor granted to me."

"But--"

"I understand you have much to study here, and much to discover. But, if you are fatigued, you may miss the smallest of important clues in your search for history."

"I suppose you're right." To her horror, Kae yawned, eliciting a grin and soft chuckle from Gowthaman.

"See? Now go. If you do not wish to sleep, at least relax at the oasis. The cool waters may refresh you." At her frown, he smiled softly. "There are none about. All have returned to their homes but for the two of us. Set personal wards if you wish, but I give you my word, I shall not disturb your peace."

"That does sound wonderful, but there are so many documents..."

"That shall remain where they lay until the morrow. How long have these scrolls and texts lain in waiting for you? A single night will not matter. Do not make me ward the library. I do not wish to forbid you anything."

Kae laughed at Gowthaman's forlorn expression and leaned to plant a quick kiss on his cheek. His almond-shaped eyes grew wide and a shudder coursed through his body, but he remained still and tipped his head to one side.

"So, you think to turn me from my purpose, by distracting me with promises you don't intend to keep? It shall not work, my sweet Kaelea. Not this time."

"All right, I'm going." Kae rose and scanned the crowded tabletop. There was too much she didn't know.

Gowthaman stood beside her, gently grasped her shoulders, and turned her from the table. He marched behind her to the steps and gave a careful shove to keep her moving. She climbed three steps then turned.

Gowthaman chuckled and moved his long, graceful fingers in an intricate pattern. "It is not that I do not trust you, Kae."

Testing his magic, Kae stepped down and encountered an invisible wall that oozed around her hand. She pushed and whispered a short phrase. The warding remained intact. When she glanced at Gowthaman, he stood with his hands resting at his hips, a tilted, half smile upon his face.

"The ward against your entering remains until the sun rises, Kaelea. As I shall remain here and not disturb your relaxation." He bowed slightly. "I wish you the peace of the night, the pleasure of dreams, the rest of the weary, the power of my love." Before he straightened, Gowthaman lifted his hand in apology, then peered at her from under his long, dark eyelashes.

Kae shook her finger at him, but grinned before turning to climb the remaining steps to the iron gate.

T he painful jerking of his muscles on his return to full consciousness sprawled Bard face down on the hot sand. He groaned and, without lifting his head, gathered a handful of the burning grains and threw them to one side. The temptation to yield to frustration nearly tore a forbidden curse from his lips. Unwilling to sully the sacredness of his power circle with words, he pounded a fist against the ground.

He'd asked the Seven Guardians for passage, for a vision, an answer, even a question. He'd received nothing but the agony of a body held too long motionless and a mouth full of sand. Lifting his head slightly, he spit the dry grains from his mouth and licked his lips, trying to pull moisture to his mouth to ease the painful cracks. How long had he remained frozen in supplication?

With another groan, he flopped to his back and shielded his eyes against the glaring sun. Intense heat burned his tanned body so he tugged a corner of the blanket to cover the paler skin of his groin. A frown tugged his lips down and he opened his eyes behind the protection of his arm.

The sun, even the air was too hot. Even high in the desert mountains, the sun did not shine so fiercely. He lifted his arm slightly. The brightness surrounding him was different; the faint colors he was accustomed to had disappeared, replaced by a stark white glare.

His vision, then? Had the Guardians truly granted him...?

Bard sat with a jerk, blinked, and tried to see clearly through the intense glare. Instead of the scrub brush covered place of visions, bounded by the stream and the higher moun-tains, the entire world was now sand. White--gold and rising in dunes like waves upon an angry sea. A shimmer of heat rose from the earth, a visible tremor in the air disrupting his vision.

A hot breeze caressed his bare skin, leaving behind a gritty residue he couldn't brush away. The powdery substance coated his tongue, filled his nostrils, and brought tears to his eyes. Bard struggled to his feet and wrapped the tattered blanket about his waist. There were some places it was better the strange sand did not infiltrate. A blast of the sandy air blinded him and he turned from the sun. With the wind at his back, the swirl of sharp, miniscule particles lessened, and after long moments of blinking behind the palm of his hand, he was able to peer about and study his surroundings.

This was like no vision he'd imagined, either in his own earlier seekings, or in the tales of the quests of his forefathers. Even when he'd been an active participant in those visions, there had always been a barrier, a veil that kept him apart from the world he looked upon. Unless the heat shimmer served that purpose now, there was no veil. Bard reached to the edge of where he imagined his power circle ended and met no resistance.

No confining force surrounded him.

What had the Guardians done to him? A rise of panic started just below his heart. Where in the name of the Seven was he? He scrubbed one hand over his face and winced at the scraping of minute particles against his skin. First, he needed shelter from the sand, else he would have no skin remaining upon his body. His dry chuckle rasped in his throat, scratching as the sand scratched his skin, reminding him of the need for water.

The shade of his hand was enough to allow him to squint

into the distance. Nothing but sand rising and falling until reaching the blurred line of the horizon. Behind him was also sand. He turned to the side. More glittering dunes. Blowing out a long breath along with a prayer the Guardians grant him direction, Bard turned to face the final horizon.

His shoulders slumped and he gnawed on his dry lower lip. Sand.

Nothing but waves of sand. He spread his arms in supplication, straightened his spine, and threw his head back to stare into a sky so filled with heat the color was nearly leeched away.

Standing silent, frozen in supplication, Bard waited for a sign from the Guardians.

And waited.

His arms shook from holding the unnatural position. His eyes burned from staring into the bright, cloudless sky. His thoughts turned inward to find--doubt.

Had the Guardians sent him to a place where they had no control, where he could not reach them? What was to be his fate? Was his destiny the end of his line here in some forsaken place--alone--unmourned--easily forgotten? Despair filled him and his arms lowered a fraction.

A soft sound, the slither of sand against sand halted his failure.

Something near him moved. With tense, short jerks, Bard lowered his arms and looked down. A creature, no larger than the giant biting flies of his homeland, burst from beneath the sand and scurried over his foot. The dry press of tiny, sharp nailed feet tickled and he bit back a chuckle. The creature, a rodent, paused in the shade cast by his body and carefully preened its large ears and miniscule pointed snout. Entranced by the dainty actions, Bard relaxed and watched and, for a brief moment, forgot the strangeness of his situation.

With a rumble rising through the soles of his feet, the dune shifted. The crest slid down around his ankles, startling the creature into a frightened dash across the moving sands.

Swinging his arms to maintain balance as the dune

shifted, Bard slipped and slid into a valley nestled between three tall, windswept dunes.

Landing heavily on his back, he slid a few more feet before coming to rest. He winced as he moved, sand covered places where it definitely shouldn't. He stood and shook, then brushed at his lower body with sandy hands. The clear sky mocked him as he rolled his eyes at the foolishness of trying to displace grit with sand.

Tiny prickles circled his foot. Before he kicked the irritant away, he looked down. The small rodent stood on its hind legs, pawing at his ankle. Once it gained his attention, the creature scurried away, weaving a zigzag path over the motionless sand.

About to dismiss the creature's antics as insignificant, Bard jerked his gaze back to the shallow trail left through the sand. He stared and blinked twice. The path. The rodent scurried, leaped, and darted, leaving an odd pattern across the smooth sandy surface.

Bard shook his head in amazement. The father of his father's father created the same design after a vision, and commissioned the woman who was to become his wife to weave it into a blanket. It was that blanket, or rather the dream of the weaving, that first led the old one to his life path. That blanket, aged and worn, now covered his loins. Bard sank to his knees and pressed his palms to the sand.

"My thanks." The words rumbled from his dry throat. The Guardians granted him the way. He had no idea where that way would lead, but he would follow.

When he looked up, the small guide had disappeared, but even though the wind whistled between the dunes, no sand covered the zigzag path. The way before him remained clear, as clear as the intent of the Guardians. He would follow the winding path through the sand.

Confident now, he wrapped the blanket tightly about his hips and tied the ends in a thick knot.

The hot sand burned through the tough soles of his feet as he tried to keep his strides long, loose, and easy on the shifting dunes. His gaze alternated between the distant horizon and the rambling path he followed. He stopped once to turn and look behind him. Even as he watched, sand shifted to cover the creature's path and fill his footsteps. If he desired to return the way he came, he would soon become lost in the repetitive dunes and featureless landscape.

Bard nodded once and his confidence grew. He turned back to the path, clear in the golden-white sands. He nodded again and tried to draw moisture to his parched mouth. Hopefully the guide's path would lead him to water, for without the life-giving moisture, death would soon claim him. Chasing the debilitating thought from his mind, Bard cleared his throat and began a low chant, perfect in rhythm for pacing the sands, a chant to remind him of the unquestionable power of the Guardians. Water would be provided when the need was the greatest. In that great need, in the wisdom of the Guardians, he would find answers.

His steps faltered. Where in the five hells was he?

TWO

The heat and relentless rays of the sun sapped what little energy Bard could muster without the regeneration brought to his body by water. The dunes sucked at each step, threatening to draw him down, making it harder to continue with each agonizing stretch of his muscles. The chant had long ago faded from his lips and the tattered remnants floating through his brain offered no comfort, no encouragement. How easy it would be to stop, to sit upon the hot sand, to let the sun dry the final moisture of life from him. Even if he hadn't been weakened from his fasting and the preparations he'd made to meet the Guardians, this strange desert would still drain the determination from him.

Halting and shading his eyes with the ineffective cover of his hand, Bard squinted. He could no longer judge time or distance, and for all he knew, he trudged in an endless circle over and between the towering dunes. Ever the tiny footprints of the scurrying creature led him forward, and never did his own large footprints remain behind him to show him a way to return.

Hope drained from him.

But he could not stop setting one foot before the other. As he trudged onward, he tugged the blanket from his hips and covered his head. The action offered a minute coolness to his scalp and seemed to lessen the shimmer of heat around him. It didn't matter now where on his body the swirling sands settled. It didn't matter if the sun blistered the paler skin at his groin. It didn't matter that his muscles screamed protest and tightened to knots at every step. All that mattered was following the path.

He would not crawl. If it meant he would die in the middle of a Guardian forsaken land far from his home, then die he would. But he would not crawl upon his belly, nor admit the defeat such actions would prove. He would walk upright, as a man walked, until he collapsed.

Bard chuckled to himself, then bit his cracked lip at the hysterical sound echoing around him. Had he made that sound... or was it the wind? Insanity would not be the last thing he heard.

As if answering his internal question the wind died, and silence shrouded him. His muscles twitched, trembled, and folded in upon themselves, collapsing him to the ground. Bard groaned and struggled to rise.

He wasn't ready to die.

He lifted his body to his hands and knees then slowly straightened. Sand grated in the sensitive folds of skin at his groin, the prickling of pain a reminder he still lived. He dragged the blanket from his head, wiped at his body, then covered himself. He would die cloaked in modesty, as befit a man, not naked and tortured as a wounded animal.

The struggle to move one leg in preparation to rise was nearly more than his abused body could tolerate. He rested his crossed arms on the top of his thigh and panted, the breath wheezing from his lungs. He would stand. Bard lifted his head.

The painful widening of his eyes made him blink and glance away from the sight before him. When he looked again, tears blurred his vision until he blinked the dampness away. There had been nothing there before--had there? Where once had been nothing but sand, and sand upon more sand, now hovered a spot of lush green. Where once he had heard nothing but the wind scraping sand from the dunes, was now the faint tinkling of water upon stone. Where once there was despair, he found a rising hope.

If the vision were only that--a vision--a trick of his exhausted mind... Bard didn't care. If it was cool, if there was shade to shield him from the sun, if there was water...

A word of praise burst from his lips, breaking open a deep, dry crack and releasing a trickle of warm blood. Brows drawn close over his eyes, Bard licked the salty blood, winced at the stinging pain of his tender lip, and rose awkwardly to stand. He stared at the grove of trees.

He took a step. Then another. Until he ran mindlessly. Fully expecting the trees to fade from sight as he neared them, he could not tear his eyes from the splotch of green and stumbled over the smooth sand. Flailing his arms, Bard regained his balance, paused, then ran again. The trees were still there. His heart sang with the joy of discovery, of hope. The trees were still there.

Beneath his feet the sand gave way to more solid ground. The softness of patches of grass tickled between his toes, the bruised blades giving rise to a fresh, green scent. Bard smiled and slowed, listening, following the crystal sounds of water bubbling over rock.

His soul surged with the promise of renewal. Soon his body would experience the renewal as well. First, he would drink. Then, if there was enough water to allow it, he would cover himself with moisture. Then, he would drink once more.

The siren's call drew him closer and he silently thanked the Guardians before asking forgiveness for his doubt. He inhaled deeply. Damp air caressed his nostrils and the lush scents provided him the Guardians' response. He would not doubt again.

Rising over the sounds of the water came a new sound. Bard frowned. Singing? He stepped from under the trees onto a grassy knoll beside a wide, clear pool. The water called to him, urging him recklessly forward, but the bare back and flowing dark hair of the woman singing in the center of the pool froze him in place.

• • •

T he tingles coursing across Kaelea's neck stiffened her spine. Someone watched her.

Gowthaman.

She sank below the surface of the water. Even though the clear pool would hide nothing from an inquisitive gaze, it gave her a small sense of protection.

"Gowthaman, you promised."

There was no reply, but the prickles continued. She crossed her arms over her breasts and turned, her mouth forming the words she hoped would sting the librarian and send him away to remember his blithe promises.

Her lips parted and the breath died in her lungs. It wasn't Gowthaman. It was... She sank lower until the water touched her chin. "What do you want?"

Dark brows lowered over even darker eyes. Confusion tilted the man's head to one side and he ran his fingers into the hairline at his forehead and back through a length of wind tossed blue-black hair. With a shake of his head, he pointed at her. "Tkoh-ha."

"I don't understand." Where had he come from? While ancient desert legends spoke of the fey library, none of the nomadic tribes ventured far enough into the sands to visit this oasis. Kae squinted. He was no desert nomad.

The man's long nose had a bump half way down its length, evidence of a break. His high cheekbones stood out in sharp relief under his golden-brown skin. Black hair hung limp and straight about his face and over his shoulders. Dark smudges under his eyes made her ache to comfort him and ease the strain tightening his full lips.

Nor was he dressed as a nomad. The desert men wore full robes and head coverings to protect themselves from the harsh sun and biting sands. This man wore--nothing but a narrow blanket. Tied low at one hip, the strip of material dipped almost to his knee at one side while the full length of his leg showed below the knot. A slightly paler patch of skin at his hip held her attention until he collapsed to his knees, lifted one hand and, with his eyes wide and pleading, spoke. "Tkoh-ha."

"I don't understand."

The man shook his head, his eyes rolled back and he slumped to his side.

"No!" Awkward in her haste, Kaelea splashed from the pool. She swiped up her robe and shrugged the cotton over her damp skin as she raced to the stranger's side. She stood over him for a long moment, staring at broad expanse of smooth chest. She tried to convince herself she was merely checking to make sure he breathed, but the odd dryness in her mouth and the overly rapid beating of her heart spoke of other interests.

The man drew a long, shuddering breath, then the air escaped in a low moan. Her gaze fastened on his lips. Dry, cracked, bloody. He was dehydrated, he needed water.

Kae returned to the pool and dipped the trailing hem of her robe into the water. Carefully, she pressed the dripping mass to the man's lips. He shook his head and mumbled, the words odd and unlike any language she'd ever heard. He definitely wasn't one of the desert nomads. Unless he had been banished from his camp...

No, there was nothing about him to suggest he ever dwelled upon the surrounding sands. Even the golden-brown color of his skin was subtly different.

Finally his lips parted and she squeezed a few drops of water between them. The mumbles turned to a sigh and a faint smile broke another crack in his dry lips. He needed more, but she had no cup, nothing to carry water to him. And, as long as he remained unconscious she could not get him to the water.

Unless she called Gowthaman.

That thought froze in her mind, then burned with rejection. She could not submit this stranger to Gowthaman's questions, his suspicions. His jealousy.

She blinked. Why would Gowthaman have cause to be jealous of this man?

Kae let her gaze roam over the man and gasped. She trailed her palm over his chest without realizing her actions. She

gnawed on her lip and stared at her hand as if it had a mind of
its own. Tingles rose from her palm and snaked up her arm.
Prickles of awareness lifted fine hairs at the back of her neck,
then traveled to merge with the tingles. When she lifted her
gaze, the man's eyes were open and staring at her.

"Who... who are you?"

Blank confusion swirled in his eyes. He licked his lips.
"Tkoh-ha."

"I don't understand." Kae closed her eyes and called upon
a magic Lara had taught her, but she'd never had the occasion
to use. She opened her eyes and reached her hand toward
him. He started to draw away, but after his long probing look,
held himself still. As she spoke the words, she touched her
middle finger to his forehead, his ears and the center of his
lips.

Kae cleared her throat and spoke slowly. "Who are you?"

"Water first." He blinked, the surprise at understanding
her words registering as he attempted to sit.

"Let me help you."

Dark, dark eyes bored into her, reaching deep into her soul.
Refusal sparkled in his gaze, then faded and he loosed a long
breath. "Where am I?"

"An oasis in the Sahara desert."

"Sahara?" He pronounced the word strangely, the accent
wrong, a guttural hitch before the last syllable. The spell had
given him understanding and the ability to speak so she could
understand, but he still retained the patterns and flow of his
native tongue.

Kae asked again, "Where are you from? Who are you?"

The woman asked logical questions, questions to which he
would demand answers, were their places reversed. He
wanted to answer, but when he tried to form the words, his
throat closed, choking off his speech. The Guardians wished
him to keep silent. He would honor their desires.

"I'm Kaelea." She had pressed her palm to the fair skin
highlighted in the low opening of her robe. Above her hand, a
tiny pulse beat frantically at the base of her throat. Below her
hand, the swell of her breasts... Bard closed his eyes to block

the tempting sight, enough to tantalize yet not enough to satisfy the sudden rise of his curiosity.

The warmth of her fingers caressed his arm. "What's wrong? Are you okay?"

Okay? What was this word, okay? Bard bit back the question and said, "I have walked long through your Sahara. I need water."

"I have no cup." She spread her hands.

Bard shrugged away the odd concern. "If I may drink from you pool?"

"Oh, yes, of course. Can I help you?"

When she reached for him, Bard nearly forgot his need for the cool, healing touch of water upon his dehydrated skin and parched lips. The woman's touch would sustain him.

Deranged. He had gone mad. The time on the sand under the blaze of the sun had stolen his mind. "No," he said with more force than he intended. "I am able."

"Uh, okay."

There was that strange word--okay. Somehow the Guardians granted him understanding when the woman spoke the strange words and touched his face, but that understanding didn't extend to the okay word. No matter. He needed water, and he would obtain it without her touch. He couldn't risk--the distraction of her touch.

The water would clear his mind, yet still he sat, his gaze locked with the woman's. For a brief flicker of thought he wondered what she saw when she looked at him so intently. When she made a movement to reach toward him again, he shook his head and forced his unwilling muscles to lift him to his feet. The world spun and he lurched to the side. One step. Take one step. The whisper of a chant curled through his mind and he focused on the sound, not the agonizing pain that had once been his legs. The scent of water rose to him as he neared the pool and he eagerly stumbled forward.

The woman's presence was warm at his back, but although she hovered like a granny over a misbehaving child, she did not touch him. He was confused, but grateful.

Bard reached the edge of the pool, but instead of kneeling

to drink, he continued forward. A gentle slope took him from the bank and into the pool. He didn't stop until the water lapped at his chest. The liquid was warm and cool at the same time and he imagined the cells of his skin greedily absorbing the moisture.

In a swift motion, he ducked his head below the surface and gulped large draughts of the life-giving water. The woman called to him. Bard lifted his hand, but kept his face in the water. After a dozen gulps he paused and lifted his head. It was not enough, but if he forced too much liquid into his empty belly he would become ill.

Already the water worked both to refresh his dehydrated body and to calm the heat shimmering against his skin.

"You. Man. Stop, or you'll get sick."

The joy of living surged through him and he laughed. "Yes, I know. I've had enough for a short time. Perhaps we can find your elusive cup before I must drink again." The waterlogged blanket slipped from his hips. He gave it no mind, until the woman's eyes widened and she took a quick step back. Then he looked down and realized he could see each stone at the bottom of the clear pool and how much of his body was exposed to her. Ruddy heat covered his chest and crawled with agonizing slowness to burn his face.

When he returned his gaze to her, she stared at a spot over his head and held out a large square of cloth. "Uh, this might be okay instead of your blanket. Until we find you some clothes. Uh, you do wear clothes? Don't you?"

That word again. Okay was the first thing he would learn.

"Man. Oh, I can't keep calling you that. Surely you have a name."

Bard waited for his throat to constrict, for the Guardians to deny him speech. But, nothing happened. Perhaps he could tell the woman his name. His call name would suffice.

"Bard."

"Okay..."

"And you are Kaelea."

Finally a smile broke over her features and his chest tightened. "Yes, I am. Good, I guess you'll be okay now. Are you ready to... umm, leave the pool?"

Bard ducked below the water to retrieve his blanket and held it before his groin and moved from the center of the pool. Kaelea kept her eyes averted as she held out the soft, dry material, and he found her embarrassment intriguing.

"I'll take you back to the library and let--" A frown stole the light from her face and the ache to bring back the smile centered in his chest. His heart skipped another beat before she continued, "I can't. He won't let me in." She took a deep breath and the opening of her robe gapped wider, exposing the full valley between her breasts. As though the pool hadn't refreshed him, Bard's mouth dried in that instant.

"Bard? I guess it will be okay--if you come to my dwelling."

THREE

While the library remained buried under the sand where it had been hidden when the human library at Alexandria was destroyed, living quarters for those who studied there had been constructed not far from the edge of the oasis. Shaded by the tall, exotic palms, the small dwelling provided for Kaelea's use was spacious and amazingly cool. Built of rounded stones chinked with a sandy mortar and faced with a wide canvas overhang, the cave-like house was a delight to her eye. Kae led the stranger, casting a concerned gaze about her in hopes they wouldn't meet any of the few who remained at the oasis. Not wanting to examine her motives for keeping the man's presence secret a while longer, Kae chatted nervously.

Bard answered her comments in a series of emotionless grunts, until they reached her dwelling. Then he reached over his head to run his fingers along the edge of the fluttering awning and sighed. "Ah. Clever." Then he turned to look her square in the face. "Where is this Sahara?"

Kae shrugged, so he didn't have a grasp of geography. She looked into his eyes and became lost in the black depths as she tried to determine where his pupils ended and the iris began. His eyes widened slightly, then narrowed. His brows lowered to a scowl that brought a rise of fear to her chest. This man was formidable.

"Where?" He reached out as if to shake her shoulder, but with a soft, mumbled curse, let his hand drop back to his side.

"The northern part of Africa."

"What is Africa?"

Kae took an involuntary step back. He didn't recognize one of the major continents? Even the Fey in the Faerie Otherworld had a minimal understanding of the human world beyond their portals.

She hesitated, then asked, "Where do you come from?"

"Ashga-al."

"I... I don't know where that is."

A hint of a grin twitched one side of his mouth. "Then it appears we have something in common." He paused for a moment, staring out over the desert sands before he let the smile completely control his mouth. "Have you a map?"

His dazzling smile halted the breath low in Kae's throat.

He watched her expectantly, one eyebrow lifted slightly into his high, smooth forehead. When she didn't answer, the brow lowered, creating a double wrinkle over the bridge of his nose. "A map?"

"Oh, of course." Kae shook herself, both mentally and physically, to dispel the strange lethargy overtaking her when he smiled. "Come on inside." She led the way so she wouldn't have to look at him. Once they entered the building's cool interior, she rushed to the shelves where she had sheaves of notes, maps, and the odd book she had been allowed to remove from the library.

The intensity of his gaze heated her, and she knew the exact moment he looked away, probably to survey the room. She had a feeling he was normally acutely aware of his surroundings, and not knowing where he was must eat away at him. If showing him a map would help clear the confusion, she'd show him every map in the library. But for now, she searched for a large, flat map the Fey had drawn of the human world. Granted, the map was thousands of years old, but the basic features of the land hadn't really changed that much.

Making a small sound of triumph, she tugged the rolled map from the bottom shelf and waved it in the air. "Here it is. Now, I'll just spread it out on the table and show you exactly where we are."

After clearing the table of several piles of books and papers, she suited actions to her words and stood back until he moved to stand by her side. When his gaze drifted from her face to the paper, she leaned and pointed. "This is the Sahara desert. We're in the center of--"

"This is not my world." Bard swiped his hand angrily across the map. "None of these lands are of my world. What games do you play at, woman?" He folded his arms over his chest and leaned back to glare at her. Yet, even as his expression darkened, there was doubt, and a tiny spark of fear in his eyes.

Kae hastened to reassure him. "This is a map of the Earth. It's an old map so maybe some of the coastlines have changed since it was drawn. This is where we are. I wouldn't keep the truth from you."

He snorted. "Where is Ho-ohchah?"

"I've never heard of Ho-ohchah. What continent is it on? Or, is it an island?"

The struggle to understand her questions was visible in Bard's face. Kaelea watched the flow of emotions with fascination until acceptance and resignation settled in the taut downward turn of his mouth and the tight narrowing of his eyes. "The Guardians have sent me far from my home. I don't understand why--or how. Or what lesson they wish me to learn." His shoulders slumped. "I don't know what I am supposed to do."

Did the stranger have some form of amnesia? Kae studied him, somehow understanding an offer of compassion and comfort would not be welcomed. When the warding was removed and she could return to the library, perhaps she would be able to find something to help. Until then, he might feel better if he kept busy at something.

"Could you draw me a map of your lands?" Kae asked softly. "I have plenty of paper."

Although the frown faded, his lips only managed a straight line. He nodded, a single up and down motion of his head. "Perhaps that would help."

Kae indicated a chair and watched as he adjusted the towel at his hips and sat. He needed clothes--even more than that, she needed him to be in clothes. She'd get him started on his drawing then slip out and find something for him to wear.

She offered Bard a cup filled with different types of writing instruments and slipped a few large sheets of paper before him. As she watched him search through the cup, the thought of asking Gowthaman for a robe and telling the librarian about Bard made her stomach churn. Tomorrow would be soon enough. For today, she would return to her part of the Faerie Otherworld and visit the clothiers.

The decision made, she rested her palm on the page before him. "I'm going to leave you to your mapmaking, Bard, and find you something other than a towel to wear."

"That would be appreciated. How does this work?" He held a mechanical pencil out to her.

Kae took the pencil and showed him how to click to advance the lead. Then she took off the metal cap, exposing the eraser. His brows rose high and the smile returned. "Amazing. I may use this?"

"Yes, of course. Use any of the pens or pencils you want. I won't be long."

His head already bent over the soft lines he made in one corner of the paper, he lifted his other hand. Whether it was a farewell or a gesture of dismissal, she didn't know. "I will not leave. I have nowhere to go."

Before she left, Kae placed a bowl of plump fruit and a flagon of water at the edge of the table. Bard drank deeply, directly from the flagon, and grunted his thanks as he reached for the fruit. Kae bit back a chuckle. She didn't need to worry about him, she doubted if he'd even know she was gone.

Bard stared at the white paper before him as he munched on the fruit. Acutely aware of the woman's movements behind him, he forced his focus from her, trying to direct his thoughts elsewhere, but had little success. When she had leaned over him to place the fruit on the table, he'd inhaled deeply, tasting her scent. And was glad he was sitting, his groin hidden beneath the tabletop.

She had rustled around in the next room and spoken a short farewell before she passed outside. Once she was gone, Bard leaned back, tossed the fruit pit into the bowl, and loosed a long breath.

Though he'd had a hand's count of willing partners since traveling the path to manhood, none affected him as swiftly as this unknown woman. Perhaps the intensity was due to the exhaustion of his body, or the strangeness of his surroundings.

After shoving back the chair, Bard rose and paced the circumference of the room. He glanced into a side room and jerked to a halt. A low bed, little more than a thick mattress upon the floor, lay covered with brightly colored, silken throws and fat pillows. Gauzy material draped like a tent from a fastening in the ceiling to surround the bed. A breeze from the windows stirred the fabric and Bard shivered. It was a sensual room, too much a match for his underlying thoughts to be comfortable. He backed away, turned and stalked to the table.

He shoved the clean page to one side and studied the map the woman had originally shown him. When he leaned closer, he noticed an interesting similarity to his world. Tracing a long coastline with the tip of his finger, Bard studied the path he made across the paper. Yes, it was similar and different both. If he could create a map of his own, in the same scale, it would be easier to compare. He returned to the chair, closed his eyes and pictured a physical rendering of his world.

His world. Bard took a deep breath. He no longer stood upon the land he knew, he was almost completely sure of the fact. After another long breath, he picked up the amazing pencil and began to draw.

• • •

K ae hoped the bundle of clothing tucked under her arm would fit the stranger. Bard. She smiled as she whispered his name, then shook her head. She knew nothing about the man, except that just thinking about him delighted her mind and body. A curl low in her belly twisted tighter. Oh, yes, she'd love to explore the possibilities.

Kae rolled her eyes to the clear blue sky. As far as she knew, he was crazed, at least addled by the heat of the desert sun. How long had he been wandering the sands before he found the oasis? She knew she shouldn't be away long, but took a moment to stop at her cabin in the Faerie Otherworld. She'd spent little time there since Nanceen had married Korin; it was lonely without her twin's presence. If she was going to live in solitude, the quiet aloneness of the library in the desert was much more to her taste.

Especially with the stranger there.

Oh, that insidious voice. Kae chuckled at her inner voice, then smiled broadly when she saw her brother nearing her cabin from the other direction. Maybe this was why she felt compelled to return.

"Jaye," she called and he lifted one hand in greeting, quickened his pace, and drew her into a fierce hug when he reached her side.

"Hey, sis. Glad I caught you."

There was a smile on his face, but worry drew fine lines at the corners of his eyes. The normal sparkle was dull with concern.

"What's wrong, Jaye?"

"I need you to do something for me, Kae."

"Of course. Research?"

"I need to know anything you can find out about Feidhlim's family line."

She'd been expecting his request. "Ah, Carrie?"

Jaye gave her a puzzled look. "Yes," he drawled with the rise of a question at the end. "What do you know about this?

Heat rose in Kae's face. "I, uh, happened to overhear Carrie and Nightshade at the baby shower."

Jaye angled forward on to the balls of his feet. "And you didn't say anything?"

"It wasn't my place. But, rest assured, if she hadn't told Bryce--and the family--soon, I would have admitted to my eavesdropping."

"You knew she's pregnant with Feidhlim's child?"

Kae nodded. "Yes, that's what I overheard. She's really concerned about the family's reaction."

"So far, only Bryce, Tommy, and Derrik and I know. And you, sis. For the time being, there's no reason for anyone else to be privy to this information."

Kae grinned at Jaye. "How much were you going to tell me?"

"Uh, only that I needed the information to give to the Alastriona to aid in their search for him."

She folded her arms across her chest and tapped one foot. "I see."

"I'm glad you know the whole truth, Kae. That should make it easier if you find anything that might be of use."

"How's Carrie doing? And Bryce?"

"As well as can be expected. She's terribly frightened the family will disown her."

"That will never happen."

"You and I both know that. She hasn't been part of the clan long enough to have confidence in our acceptance of her, no matter what. Not surprisingly, Bryce, Tommy and Derrik have closed ranks around her. Nightshade as well. Both for comfort and for protection. When Feidhlim finds out--and I doubt it will be long--I hate to think what he will try."

Kae rested her hand on her brother's arm. "I'd already planned on looking into his line. There might be some clue we can use to finally and completely defeat him. He's a slippery snake."

Jaye chuckled. "You shouldn't demean a poor snake that way. How soon can you get started? I hate to ask you to put aside your other searches, but this is important."

Kae gave him a look of mock disgust. "Anything else loses importance when it comes to protecting family and clan." A mental picture of a nearly naked man bent over her worktable flashed across her vision. She had to blink to keep her focus on her brother. Even the stranger, with a story she ached to know and understand, would have to wait.

But not too long, her heart whispered. *Not too long.*

Gowthaman paused at the edge of the cluster of dwellings, a thin volume cradled in one hand. He discovered the illuminated history a week earlier, and had withheld it from Kae, hoping for a time when presenting the book to her would be the most advantageous to him. Perhaps now, when she was rested and relaxed from her time at the oasis pool, the gift of knowledge would turn her gaze lovingly toward him. There was little movement of air around the dwellings, and even though he had lived long in the hot, dry climes of Faerie, a light sheen of sweat covered his forehead. He used a square of cotton to blot the moisture from his face, then tucked the cloth under the wide sash tied at his waist.

Gowthaman twisted the ring in his ear before crossing the sand to stand under the awning at Kaelea's door. He cleared his throat and swept his hand over the chimes hanging to one side. After announcing his presence, he stepped into the cool interior, smiling broadly, with the book held out in front of him.

The smile froze, then disappeared as he stared at the bare back bent over the table in the center of the room. For the space of a breath his heart soared, then plummeted as his mind registered the masculine width of the shoulders and the dark hair falling loose only to the center of the shoulder blades.

Gowthaman leapt forward, fist upraised. Before he had taken two steps, the man sprang to his feet, tipping the chair to one side, and whirled to face him. A dangerous satisfaction glinted in the man's eyes, a calm smile twisted his lips.

Skidding to a stop, Gowthaman dropped the book and stared. Then the moment of startled caution disappeared and he puffed out his chest and straightened his spine. "What are you doing here? What have you done to my Kaelea?"

One of the man's eyebrows jerked upward. "Nothing."

Gowthaman wondered for a moment which question he answered. So he asked another. "Where is she?"

The man gave a negligent shrug. "I don't know. She said she would bring me clothing. I'm busy. Go away."

Gowthaman's mouth dropped open at the imperious, commanding tone. He sputtered, then gained control of his emotions, lifted his chin, and returned the attitude. "I shall not. Not until Kaelea returns."

Another shrug. "You will, of course, suit your own purposes. If you will pardon me, I'll return to my drawing." Without another word, the man righted the chair, angled it toward the table, and sat. He remained still for a few moments and Gowthaman narrowed his gaze at the tense shoulder muscles and proudly canted head.

With a third shrug, Bard reached for his abandoned pencil and leaned over the paper to make a few careful strokes to complete his map. He let his mouth twitch in a grin as the power of a gaze heated with anger burned into his back. His presence had surprised the Other, and Bard's refusal to acknowledge his primal claim upon the woman had made him bristle. The reaction pleased Bard, but he ignored the possible reasons.

He heard the Other move to the door and step outside. Sitting on a low bench under the awning, the man moved no further. Ignoring his presence, Bard set the pencil aside and picked up his map to study the drawing by the light of the setting sun shining through the window.

It was as accurate as he remembered from his studies as a youth. A quick glance at Kaelea's map brought a nod of satisfaction. He'd kept the scale the same, or nearly so.

He laid the maps side by side and placed the tip of one finger to the place the woman had indicated this location in the desert Sahara. With the index finger of his other hand, he found the sacred spot in his world, the spot where he had created his power circle and begun his quest for answers.

Lightly dragging his map over the first, he matched the two spots. Bard canted his head to one side and stared. Squinting and keeping the maps together with the press of his finger, he inched his drawing in a circle around the point of joining.

Dreading what he might discover, the temptation to wad his map into a tight ball and toss it through the window opening grew strong. But losing the map would not change the facts. And he needed facts if he were to return home. He chewed on his cracked lip, winced at the pain, but kept the page moving.

The east-west lines of Kaelea's ancient map met the south-north indicator he'd placed at the edge of his drawing. His eyes drifted closed and he released the breath he hadn't realized he'd been holding. Compared at the ninety-degree angles, the maps were now nearly identical.

FOUR

B ard stared at the strangely aligned maps. So very similar, yet still different in fundamental ways. He turned his head to glance out the window-like the passage of this sun from east to west. A moment of worry seized his mind, unless somehow the Guardians had taken his ability to accurately gauge directions. He closed his eyes and felt the pull of each of the cardinal points. That felt the same. Slowly, he looked again at the arch of the setting sun. West. The sun fell in the west. Not the north as he was accustomed. The directions matched the skewed map placement.

Bard straightened with a jerk, then leaned against the back of the chair and ran his hands through his hair, wincing at the pull of dried tangles. This discovery might prove the ancient legends of his people. Shaking his head did nothing to clear the sudden, uncomfortable thought from his mind. Legends were only that--legends and tales meant to instruct or entertain around a nightly fire. There may be some kernel of truth upon which the first storyteller built his tale, but most of the tale had to be elaboration--didn't it?

Bard shifted uncomfortably and shoved at the maps with one finger so they were no longer aligned. The legends claimed his ancestors--the Old Ones--had come to their world through a magical passage provided by the Guardians. Their original world was said to have suffered from drought and wars over what arable land and pockets of water remained. An entire people had suddenly appeared and settled the new land. So long ago, even the elders knew only the legend.

But, what of his mother's mother? She had been scorned as a crazed, delusional old woman. She had claimed to come from another place, a world only slightly different from the one she came to love. Bard let a single snort of laughter pass his lips. She had been a dear woman, full of life and loving all around her even as they turned their backs on her. He missed her and her crazy tales.

What of the book Grandmother claimed to have carried with her from that other place? A large volume, filled with plays and poems by one man. He hadn't believed her until one day, just before his passage into manhood, she had shown him the book in effort to explain the strangeness of his name.

His grandmother had read the plays to his mother, who fell in love with the characters of fantasy. To recall that love, she had given her son a name to honor the one revered as a bard in that other world. The man's name was said to have been William, so William he became as well. His strange name had provided much amusement for the other young men, and only the power of the Stonefeather name kept the boys from physically showing their disdain.

William Bard Stonefeather now took pride in his name and his family.

He missed them.

That loneliness had driven him to create the power circle and attempt the ancient rituals to call upon the Seven Guardians. Maybe he had been more successful in his quest than he ever imagined possible.

Bard rose, adjusted the towel, and paced a circle around the table. The cloth slipped and he hitched it higher. Although the towel wasn't much more than he normally wore, he was uncomfortable and hoped for Kaelea's rapid return. Even one of the odd robes she wore would be better than this sliding cloth. He yanked again and the knot worked itself loose, dropping the towel to the floor. Tempted to leave it where it lay,

Bard stared at the pile of cloth at his feet. The memory of a faint, pink blush infusing Kaelea's face brought tightness to his groin and the unmistakable evidence of physical interest. He shook his head at a body that responded to his simple thought. He needed clothing--no matter what kind--before he truly embarrassed himself.

He retrieved the towel with a quick swipe and loosely tucked the ends together. His blanket would provide more modesty and, with the heat and wind, should be dry. Before entering the patio beyond the door, Bard peered around the doorframe at the man perched on the edge of a bench, staring at a spot at the edge of the trees. A grin eased Bard's discomfort.

He strolled across the patio to the low, stone wall where Kaelea had spread the blanket. Now dry and warm to the touch from captured rays of the setting sun, the blanket was comfort to his questing fingers. He kept his back to the Other, smiled at the desert beyond the wall, and dropped the towel.

A sharp intake of the Other's breath slowed Bard's actions. He reached for the narrow blanket then turned to face the man as he carefully wrapped it about his loins and tied a tight, secure knot.

He didn't think about his strange actions or the reasons behind them. Unaccustomed to exhibiting his body, Bard paused, an apology rising to his lips. But the man's narrowed gaze and the return of his expanded chest increased Bard's desire to taunt him.

Having been the brunt of such taunting, Bard understood the pain that could be inflicted and quickly discarded the idea. Yet the possessiveness of this man toward Kaelea raised his hackles. He turned away before action preceded thought.

The sound of the Other settling back to the bench made him smile.

The man must not honestly wish a confrontation. However, the heat of an unfriendly gaze upon his back made Bard straighten his spine and fight the urge to clench his fists.

A faint shimmer, different than the rise of heat from the desert, drew his attention from the Other. His eyebrows rose high into his forehead at the surprise of seeing Kaelea, backed by a lush green forest, stepping through the shimmer. She waved one hand over her shoulder and the tantalizing view beyond her blinked out of existence.

Kae stepped from the soft grasses of Faerie back to the Sahara, the blast of heat barely registering. She kept her gaze lowered in thought and followed the path toward her home away from home. While there were many much more intriguing projects demanding her attention, the need to discover as much as she could about her family's antagonist weighed heavily in her heart. They desperately needed any information she could uncover. With any luck, once she found something useful and gave the findings to her brother, a way would be found to finally stop Feidhlim.

Kae's world felt like it was closing in on her and exploding at the same time. She'd never experienced the helplessness of not being able to handle everything thrown at her. Funny how just a little knowledge, information she didn't want anyway, made such a difference.

Now there was the added concern of the strange man who appeared at the oasis with no knowledge of where he was. At least he knew his name, so she didn't have to deal with a case of complete amnesia. Maybe the Faerie healers would be willing--

"Kaelea, who is this man?"

Kae jerked to a stop and reluctantly lifted her gaze to Gowthaman. He stood before her, arms crossed over his chest, his hands clenched into white-knuckled fists. Her shoulders slumped and she drew in a soft breath. She really didn't need this.

"Hello, Gowthaman." Maybe a dry, casual tone would diffuse his anger.

Gowthaman pointed over his shoulder. "What is he doing here?"

"Bard is my guest." There was no need for the jealous faerie to know more, although from his expression he wouldn't drop the issue.

"Where did this guest come from?" Accusation stole the

normal, lilting music from his voice, giving him a harsh, fierce tone.

No one used that tone with her. Kae mimicked his pose by widening her stance and hugging the bundle of clothing to her chest. "What difference does it make who I might have as a guest?"

Gowthaman's glower deepened and ruddiness crept under his coffee-colored skin. His breath came in sharp, staccato bursts. Kae took a step back. She'd never seen him so angry. The physical expression of the raw emotion frightened her.

Then the rise of her corresponding anger and the rush of adrenaline startled her. Kae leaned forward and hissed through clenched teeth. "What I do is not your concern. You do not own me or my thoughts. I will invite anyone I choose to visit me. My decision, Gowthaman. Not yours."

Gowthaman reached toward her, but the movement was far from consoling or apologetic. Possessiveness rolled from him in waves, the force of his emotions rocking her back on her heels. She took a step to the side. "Don't touch me."

A quick jerk returned Gowthaman's hand to his side. His brows remained lowered, a tense frown carved deep lines around his mouth. "I only wish what is best for you, Kae."

"Best? How dare you think you know what's best for me?" Her voice rose and she barely caught herself before shrieking at him. Kae took a deep breath and continued in a harsh whisper. "I don't tell you what to do, do I? I don't tell you I know what's best for you, do I? What right do you think you have--"

"I'm sorry." A deep voice from the patio froze her speech. "I don't mean to cause a lovers' quarrel."

She turned to Bard in amazement. The contrite expression on his face brought a spark of humor to the tense air and Kae laughed. At her chuckles, confusion altered his expression.

"Oh, we're not lovers."

Eyes blazing with remnants of anger, Gowthaman stepped in front of her, blocking Bard from view. "You need not tell him anything."

"Get out of my way, Gowthaman." She gave a gentle shove to the center of his chest. "Go back to your library and I'll see you there in the morning. Or, if you can be civil, stay and share the evening meal with us." She pushed past him and stood before Bard.

"I've brought you clothing. Hopefully it will fit and be more comfortable than that blanket." Damn, if heat didn't fill her face, a telltale sign she was blushing. She never blushed, but there was something about the glint in Bard's eyes--a satisfaction that appeared and remained when she'd said she and Gowthaman weren't lovers--that tickled a place of innocence she thought she'd lost long ago.

Part of her hoped Gowthaman would refuse her invitation and leave. Soon.

But the faerie hovered at her shoulder as she handed the bundle of clothing to Bard. Her fingers brushed Bard's palms when he took the bundle, the lingering impression of his warmth more intriguing than the familiar heat of Gowthaman at her back. She lifted her gaze to Bard's and couldn't look away. The expression touching his dark eyes compelled her closer, so she fought to remain an arm's length from him. She compared the glistening darkness of Bard's eyes to the softer black of Gowthaman's. Their skin color was similar, yet Bard's showed a harsher life through the weathered skin and slight wrinkles at the corners of his eyes, as though he'd spent long hours staring into the distance, searching for something. She idly wondered what he needed, what he wanted. A tremble deep inside her angled her closer.

"I shall stay for the evening meal."

Kae jerked, blinked, then turned her gaze to Gowthaman. "What?"

One eye narrowed even more and he glared at her through the bare slits. "You invited me to share the evening meal with you--and Bard."

The growl of Bard's name made her completely regret the spontaneous invitation. She forced a smile. "Of course. Let's go inside." She glanced over her shoulder at Bard. He hadn't moved, still held the bundle of clothing before him and watched her with tentative curiosity. A sigh passed her lips before she could bite it back. "You can use my bedroom to change into those clothes. I'm anxious to see how they fit."

He lowered his head in acquiescence. "As you wish."

Wish? Oh, she constantly discovered wishes centered on the strange man, wishes she had no business having. And certainly no business pursuing.

Gowthaman wrapped his hand around her elbow and gave a tug that indicated his disapproval. She allowed him to lead her into her house, then shook away his possessive gesture. She turned to direct Bard to the bedroom, but he had already stepped into the dim room and lowered the tapestry over the doorway.

Gowthaman stood close to her side, and ran his palm up her bare arm and under her loose sleeve, caressing her skin. He leaned his head close to hers and touched his lips to her earlobe. "Who is he?"

Kae's eyes drifted closed and she tilted her head to one side as the warmth of his lips heated her skin. The tension in her shoulders faded and...

"Why is he here?"

"No!" Kae leapt away from Gowthaman's seduction, lifting her hand to protectively cover her neck. One man attempted seduction, while her mind placed another at her side. What was she doing? What was Gowthaman doing? Turning a fierce glare to him, Kae fisted her hands at her waist. "Actually, you know as much about him as I do."

Wrong thing to say. Gowthaman's frown deepened, turning his smooth, handsome face ugly. "You do not know anything about this man? Kae, what are you thinking?"

She couldn't answer that question, for the same thoughts had been hiding deep in her mind since meeting Bard. After thinking of little but the stranger, she was no closer to understanding what compelled her to think she could help the lost, confused man. But, she wasn't going to admit that fact to Gowthaman.

The rustle of the tapestry saved her from her attempts at forming a response. She turned toward the bedroom and

Gowthaman stalked to the doorway. The breath died in her lungs when Bard entered the room.

The loose, cotton drawstring pants she'd selected hung low on his hips. He'd forgone the shirt and wore the vest hanging open, exposing the muscles of his chest and abdomen. Kae licked her lips, found her breath, and released it slowly.

"You are going to answer my questions, stranger." Gowthaman lifted one fist and held it, hovering before Bard's face. "You will answer to my satisfaction, or--"

Kae couldn't take Gowthaman's superior, possessive attitude any longer. "Stop it. If you can't be civil, you will leave. Do you understand me, Gowthaman? This is my house." Kae crossed to his side and shook his arm. "Do you hear me?"

He ignored her until she shook his arm again. Then he slowly turned his gaze to her and she waited while he visibly controlled his expression. He spoke through clenched teeth. "I understand."

"Good. Now, you sit over there. Bard, will you clear the stuff off the table while I find us something to eat?" Expecting the men to do as she ordered, Kae turned away and reached for the bowl and flagon on the corner of the table.

She held up the bowl and twisted back to show the container to Bard. "Did you eat all the fruit?"

He ducked his head. "It had been long since I'd eaten."

"Not a problem." Kae chuckled, "Good thing I've got more. I'll have the meal ready in just a few minutes."

She entered the tiny side room that served as a kitchen, hoping she did the right thing leaving Bard and Gowthaman alone. Even though she really didn't know Bard, she was convinced he could be trusted. However, Gowthaman had never shown such a strong anger toward another. Especially not such unreasonable anger. While he continued to profess his love for her, she'd never taken his gentle seductions seriously. She liked him, but had never felt a stronger attraction to the librarian. Maybe she should have laid down the law to him long ago. But now, when forced to admit it to herself, she had enjoyed the attention. Having a man dancing in attendance made her feel feminine and desired. A thing she supposed every woman wanted.

She refilled the fruit bowl and set it on a tray. A loaf of bread and a small platter of thinly sliced cheeses followed. She debated what type of beverage to serve, then decided on fruit juice and water. Wine would further dehydrate Bard, and she didn't want to fuel the thick power of testosterone with alcohol.

After a deep breath, she felt ready to face her guests. There had been little sound from the room, so at least they hadn't beaten each other senseless. Kae gave a soft snort of laughter at the whole ridiculous, male preening issue.

Bard rose from his chair at the table when she entered the room. In three strides he was before her and took the heavily laden tray from her hands. He graced her with a smile before he returned to the table, set the tray in the center and stood slight to one side, waiting.

After completing his requested task, Bard had pulled his chair to face the doorway where Kae had disappeared, and studiously ignored the Other. As the Other ignored him. He thought he understood the man's anger, but if it was true as Kae said, and they were not lovers, then why did the Other work so hard to make it appear so?

When Kae stood by the table, he pulled out a chair for her and was rewarded with a bright smile that tugged at his heart. Maybe that was why the Other acted as he did. Bard acknowledged the desire he felt for the woman, a desire he would keep hidden. If this truly wasn't his world, he should form no attachments. He returned to his chair.

The Other sat, then slid his chair closer to Kaelea, who frowned at him. Bard ducked his head and grinned. Even with the logical decision to strive for no attachments, he was pleased Kaelea didn't seem to care for the Other's advances.

CHAPTER

FIVE

W hy the same number of hours in a night could seem so much longer than usual didn't bother Kae so much as the round of questions whirling through her mind to keep her awake during those hours. When normal calming rituals didn't work, she gave up, propped her back against a thick pile of pillows, and attempted to order her thoughts.

There were too many priorities. While finding the information Jaye needed was the obvious top of her list, concern over Bard kept inching its way higher.

Kae replayed the awkward meal over and over, searching for some new insight. Although Gowthaman plied him with questions, Bard smoothly avoided all but the most innocuous basics. In return, he had asked no questions, but Kae experienced the desire, the need to know, almost physically thrumming from him. She'd tried to keep the conversation going with light and general topics, but had failed miserably. Finally, and thankfully, after a long period of uncomfortable silence, Gowthaman had risen, tucked a thin book under his arm and, without speaking, stalked from her house.

Just as silently, Bard stood and cleared the table. She'd watched the homey action with a sharp pang of longing. She tried to tell herself it was only the wish for companionship, and unsuccessfully ignored the fact it was his companionship she now sought.

How had it happened? He'd appeared out of nowhere, claiming to have walked through the desert. In truth, he had looked like the wind, heat, and sand had taken their toll on him, but rest and water had done wonders for him. What wonders.

Kae stretched, then hugged her arms about her knees. Her palm tingled with the memory of the feel of his chest after he'd collapsed. She rubbed her palm against her silken bed coverings, trying to capture the sensation. But it wasn't just the physical attraction that confused her. She ached to know more about the man himself.

After he'd cleared the table, he'd gathered the map and drawing he'd completed. He looked as though he wanted to talk, but after a minute shake of his head, had rolled the pages together, tucked them again into the corner of the bookshelf, and turned to her.

"I shall sleep under the awning before your home."

"You don't need--I mean, that's okay, if it's what you want." A piercing disappointment shot through her.

"There is a question I've been meaning to ask you."

Kae chuckled at the memory of his earnest expression. She had expected, and hoped for, some deep, perhaps personal question.

"What is okay?"

She sputtered in surprise for a moment, then struggled to contain her laughter at the swift change of his expression. Dark and stormy, with deep hurt shining in his eyes, his expressive face made her realize his question was in earnest and her initial reaction had somehow caused him pain. "Okay means all right or fine. Sometimes we use okay as an agreement instead of saying yes. Sometimes it can be a question, if you're prompting someone to give you more information. The word is used in many ways."

"Ah. I believe I understand. It is a common expression. Yes, I'll be okay sleeping outside."

"Okay." And they had laughed together. She'd given him a

thick cushion, pillow, and a blanket against the cold of the desert night, though he had glanced at the cushion with disdain as he took it. Later, she had peeked out her window and grimaced. The cushion lay to one side, but he had used the pillow. She'd watched him, hands folded behind his head, as he'd watched the stars.

When the first faint light of the rising sun filtered into her small house, Kae rose, dressed in jean shorts and a loose tee shirt, and tiptoed into the main room. She rolled her eyes at herself--Bard was outside, so she doubted he'd hear her movements. She brought a flagon of juice from the kitchen and, with it tucked under her arm, reached for a pile of her research materials.

She glanced at the rolled maps, shrugged, and turned away. But after she'd arranged her books and papers on the table, her gaze kept drifting back to the bookshelf. When her curiosity could no longer be denied, she moved to the bookshelf and stood before it, one hand reaching toward the maps. She glanced outside, but there was no evidence Bard was awake.

With a sharp exhale of breath, she snatched the papers to her chest and returned to the table. If she was going to help Bard regain his memory and find his way home, she needed clues. Perhaps his drawing would provide some elusive information.

But when she compared his drawing to the ancient map, she found no similarities. Frustration huffed from her lips and she tossed the pages to one side, returning her focus to a volume of Fey genealogies.

S oft sounds from within the dwelling alerted Bard to Kaelea's movements. He knew she'd had a restless night and he'd found little comfort, for sleep had eluded him as well. He counted each time she'd turned upon her bed and pretended to sleep each time she'd risen to peer through her window. Had the same thoughts kept the blessings of dreams from each of them? Disturbing his meditation, the unaccustomed longing to be close to someone, to her, vibrated through his being. Very disturbing, like no other woman had ever affected his calm. That thought was disturbing in itself. Why her?

And in this odd location. The Seven Guardians brought him here, to her. Why?

Bard shook away the questions and sat, folding his legs into a comfortable cross-legged position. His gaze found the spot where Kaelea had stepped from another place. He pictured the shimmering oval in his mind, the fresh, green forest imprinted deeply in his memory after just the brief vision. He ached to go there.

But the Guardians brought him to this Sahara instead, led him to this oasis, and filled him with questions. He should have been clearer in his desires when he formed the power circle. At that time he'd known the importance of answers to enable him to determine his destiny.

But, he'd not known the questions. He glanced at the rising sun. He'd asked for questions and received more than his fair share. The Guardians continued to withhold the answers.

A soft scrabbling of sand drew his attention to the edge of the stone patio. A tiny, pointed nose peeked over the thick cushion he'd tossed to the side. Bard held himself frozen, eyes widening as the creature he recognized as his guide climbed onto the cushion, lifted itself to sit upon its hind legs, and daintily cleaned its face and ears.

Bard closed his eyes. There must be many times many of these animals in the desert. When he opened his eyes, the animal had stopped preening and stared at him with eyes expressing wisdom uncommon in such creatures.

Silently, Bard asked forgiveness of the Guardians. Once again he had doubted, this time, to be put in his place by a desert animal small enough to fit in his palm.

The tiny guide leapt from the cushion and ran in a tight circle before bounding toward the trees. To the exact place he had been staring. To the place where Kaelea had appeared.

Contemplating the meaning of the message, Bard rose and

folded the blanket. He held the silky cloth against his chest for a moment, comparing the smooth weave to the rougher texture of the blanket of his fathers. Then he dropped the covering to the cushion and turned toward the house. After the long night, cool fruit juice would revive his dry throat.

Bard froze in the doorway and gripped the rounded frame as though his life depended upon anchoring himself in this reality.

Perhaps it did.

Kaelea leaned over the table, studying her old map and his recent drawing. The short garment she wore exposed nearly the full length of skin where her long legs wrapped around the chair legs. The slow, leisurely pace of his appreciative gaze stalled at the tight, blue material covering her shapely bottom. The rungs of the chair back were narrow and widely spaced, affording him a perfect view of the muscles of her back, softly stretching under her clothing as she moved. Her clothing was scandalous, but he liked how the material covered her. And didn't cover her.

With a frustrated sound, she tossed the pages to one side. Bard forced himself from his study of her, adjusted his own clothing, and stepped inside. He stopped behind her and, even though it would have been easier to circle the table, reached over her to gather the maps. He felt a slight hitch in her breathing when his chest brushed her shoulder and his body woke to full realization of the woman. He nearly dropped the maps to turn her to face him. Aching to explore the taste of her, Bard cleared his throat. Could he keep no promise to the Seven for more than a brief moment? He couldn't become involved with this woman, no matter her appeal. He would not lower himself to taking pleasure, when he knew he could not offer the permanence such actions demanded. No matter what world the Guardians brought him to, he was still himself. And would remain so.

He had been hanging over Kaelea's shoulder, silently holding the maps for far too long. She pressed back minutely, increasing the contact between them.

"Let me show you my map and my discovery." His voice

rasped as though he had spent another day wandering the sands. His tongue felt thick and cumbersome as he attempted to form words.

"Pull a chair next to mine. That'll be easier for both of us. I'll get a crick in my neck trying to look back at you."

Moving away was one of the more difficult tasks he'd ever attempted, and it left his skin cold, an unusual feeling while the air around him heated and the sun rose higher in the sky.

After he moved the chair from the other side of the table, Kaelea poured a tall glass of juice from the flagon and set it before him. He drank greedily. She smiled when he lowered the glass.

"You need to make sure and drink a great deal today to make up for yesterday's trek though the desert."

"Yes, I know. Thank you. The juice is refreshing."

"I'll fix some breakfast in a bit, if that's okay."

He grinned at okay and nodded. Then he pointed at his hand-drawn map. "I attempted to make my map in the same scale as yours. I believe I came close."

Kaelea held the two pages side by side. "Looks good. But, I don't see any similarities. Do you remember where you came from or how you got here?"

He nodded and waited for the telltale closing of his throat. But the Guardians didn't forbid his speaking so he nodded again. "First, I shall show you what I discovered about the maps, then I'll tell you my tale." He glanced at her books and papers. "If you have the time to spare from your duties."

"Oh, I can spare the time. Especially if I learn something new in the process." Excitement brightened her face at the prospect of a new discovery.

She would learn something new, a thing he found difficult to understand or believe. Yet, she had come through some sort of a gateway from a place filled with an ancient, lush forest. A place he could believe in for he witnessed the vision with his own eyes.

"In my world..." Bard paused and let his gaze slide sideways to Kaelea. She glanced up from the map, interest and anticipation filling her expression. He took a deep breath and continued. "The sun rises from the southern horizon and follows a path to the north."

Her eyebrows lifted but she remained silent.

Bard took his drawing from her hand and smoothed it on the table. He pointed to a mark he'd made on one side. "This is the registration for the cardinal points. There is a similar registration on your map. Yet, if you lay one map upon the other, there is no similarity."

"I know. I tried that."

"Ah. But if you rotate one map so that my south matches your east..." As he spoke he made the ninety-degree alteration in his map then placed the drawing over the older map. The paper he'd used was thin, so the heavily drawn lines on the ancient map shown through enough to show the near perfect match of landforms.

"This is amazing. But, I don't understand."

Bard shrugged and pointed to a spot on his drawing. "This is where I made the power circle for my quest. In my world, this is the place I was last."

"If the maps are correct..." she leaned over the table to study the maps and made a measurement with her fingers, "... you walked over twenty miles through the Sahara to reach the oasis." She stared at him with wide eyes and her mouth parted in astonishment.

Such a trek was normally not a hardship for him, but after days of ritual fasting and deprivation... Bard reached for the juice and poured another tall glass. Kaelea touched his arm when he lowered the empty glass. The contact burned his skin as the sun had never done. The refreshing moistness the juice brought to his mouth disappeared. He should pull away, but the gentle touch held him prisoner, a willing captive of the woman's caress.

Her hand moved along his arm and he wondered if she realized she stroked him, or how the caress affected him. It was agony to breathe. When she tugged her lower lip between her teeth, he forced back a groan and tore his gaze from her face.

And dropped it to the material pulled tight across the fullness of her breasts. Tiny peaks pressed against the fabric, evidence to the effect of his visual caress. By the Seven Guardians, despite his promise, he had to kiss her.

As if sensing his thought, Kaelea's hand slid up his arm to his shoulder. When he ripped his gaze from the fullness of her breasts and looked again at her face, her lips had parted with soft invitation. Her breathing altered subtly. She leaned closer and her eyelids lowered until thick, dark lashes lay like crescents upon her flushed cheeks.

By the Seven. The silkiness of her hair against his fingers surprised him. When had he lifted his hands to cradle the back of her head and pulled her so close?

The air hummed between them. He carefully touched his lips to hers. She tightened her fingers on the back of his neck, encouraging more pressure, a deeper kiss. Unable--and unwilling--to resist, Bard slanted his lips over hers and touched the pout of her lower lip with his tongue. He teased, nibbled, soothed until she clung to his shoulders and gave a soft whimper. Only then did he fully accept her invitation and allowed the mating of their tongues.

The leisurely dance, the thrust and withdrawal, stroking and twining together, dazed him and he pulled her closer, settling his hands at her waist and lifting her so she straddled his lap. Then he cupped her bottom and pressed until her heat flowed through their clothing. She squirmed against the fierceness of his arousal and he growled his pleasure into her mouth.

Kae took his groan, greedily letting the vibrations pour through her. She rubbed the twin aches of her breasts against his bare chest and pressed her hips to his. He splayed his hands over her bottom and held her there. Every inch of his expanding length, captured between them, throbbed in time with the rapid beating of her heart.

Oh, God. She'd never wanted a man this quickly, this much, this... hard. A faint tremor of concern, ringing like distant chimes, warned her that Bard was too much of an unknown. The louder humming of her heart, the blood pounding in her ears quickly drowned out the concern, filling her with a sensual haze.

She arched her hips against him, bumped the table with her elbow, and heard the distant thunk of the flagon hitting the wood. A quick glance before she returned to Bard's expert kisses showed a thick rivulet of deep orange juice spreading toward her papers and the tattered, ancient genealogy. A split second later, she realized what she was watching and jerked from Bard's lap to sweep the book into her arms. Panting, she stared as the juice touched the edge of the hand drawn map and absorbed into the paper, spreading like the unreasonable desire recently infiltrating her body. Bard's hand appeared in her vision, a cloth clutched in shaking fingers. He sopped up the juice then tossed the rag into an empty bowl.

Horror at what might have happened filled Kae, and she took a step back, the book held against her chest like a shield. The book could have been damaged through her careless actions. There were so few of the precious, ancient volumes, the chance of ruining or losing one struck her to the core. She shuddered and stared at Bard.

He stood beside the table, hands spread, a bit of juice dripping from his finger to stain the hem of his pants. Despite his contrite posture, his body remained hard, tenting the soft cotton. "I... did not mean for... I don't..." He fell silent, dark eyes begging her for understanding.

She did understand. She understood that he thought she leaped away from him because of the intensity of the budding passion between them. He thought he had pressed too quickly. Kae shook her head. She was the one who let herself be lifted willingly into his lap and rubbed against him like a cat in heat.

"Bard, I do understand."

Relief flooded his expression, followed by a sadness that broke her heart. "Thank you."

"No, Bard, listen. I understand what you think. Don't you realize I wanted that as much as you? Maybe more." Kae caught her lip between her teeth and stared at him; amazed she'd just admitted how much she wanted him. Confusion knotted his brow and she reached toward him, intending to smooth the tension with her fingertips.

Bard took a step back. "I don't understand."

"The book." Kae held out the thin volume. "It's very old and irreplaceable. My actions, my desire, nearly caused damage to this. If I had ruined the information I might find in here, my family could be destroyed."

His spine straightened and he assumed a warrior's alert pose. "Who would dare?"

"That's a long story, and though important to me, it's not really something you need to worry about." After a quick glance at the table, she placed the book on a chair.

"I..." He paused, rotated his shoulders and visibly relaxed. "This, then, should be a time of tales, not of passion, for you wish to learn of me. As I wish to learn of you." He cast her a dazzling grin. "I shall move my chair to the other side of the table. For now, distance between us is a good thing."

"Yes."

Bard dragged the heavy chair to the opposite side of the table, sat, grimaced, and reached below the tabletop. Kae ducked her head, grinning as she imagined him adjusting his pants to accommodate his arousal. Maybe later, after they talked...

CHAPTER
SIX

L eaning back and resting one arm over the back of the
chair, Bard attempted to ease the pressure at his groin.
It was a welcome pressure. One he hated. No, he didn't
hate the feelings the woman evoked in him. He hated the fact
that such feelings were inappropriate when he did not know
where the next day, the next hour, would find him.

Somehow he would summon the control he needed.

He reached for the maps, aligned them, and pressed his
fingertip against the spot of his power circle. "There is little in
my tale that is important prior to the creation of my power
circle. I was compelled to seek answers from the Seven
Guardians."

"Guardians? You mean, like gods?"

"No, for the higher powers of gods are present in my world
as well. The Guardians are intermediaries, beings who are
more than human but less than gods."

"Like angels?"

"I do not know of angels. But, if you say they are, then it
must be so. In order to properly come before the Guardians, I
prepared with fasting and cleansing rituals. Then with body
and mind naked and open to the words of the Guardians, I
formed the circle and spread the blanket. Come to me from the

fathers of my fathers, it is the only earthly item allowed within the circle. I sat upon the blanket, faced the south and the rising of the sun, and waited."

"That sounds like a Native American vision quest."

Bard shrugged. "It is a quest. Often a search for vision. I should have entered the circle with a precise question, a need held within my mind. But I didn't even know what question drew me to the circle. There is nothing left of my family, my father long dead, my mother more recently. My people... ah, my people. They turned their backs upon me. The reasons are unimportant and I accepted it long ago."

"Have you?" Kaelea gave him a look so filled with under- standing he almost blurted out the pain of rejection, the agony of his confusion. What good would that do? If the Guardians didn't see fit to give him answers, what more could he expect from a woman?

"Perhaps there was some pain behind my decision to seek the Guardians," he admitted slowly.

"I can tell, from the look in your eyes." She gave him a soft smile. "I also see that you're not willing to talk about it. Tell me what happened when you entered the circle."

"I tried to clear my mind. I don't know how long I sat. It was long beyond when discomfort settled in my muscles and the chanting had dulled the pain. Without warning, I lay face down in the sand of your Sahara. The Guardians sent a guide to lead me to the oasis. The rest you know."

"A guide?"

Bard scrubbed his hand through his hair. He expected laughter if he admitted how the small rodent drew him forward when he had lost hope.

"Bard? Can you tell me?"

He hesitated then continued. "There was a tiny creature, a rodent, which ran before me to show the way."

"You were very lucky."

"I don't believe in luck."

"No?"

"That is the tale of how I arrived here in your world. How

do I return? I thought long on the problem during the night. Will I be able to return from any place on this world? Or do I have to be in the exact place where our worlds are joined?" There it was, the question. If he had to return to the middle of the desert, he would never find the same location. Every dune looked the same.

He glanced at Kaelea's half smile. She hadn't immediately laughed at him. "Do you believe me?"

Her smile grew wide. "Of course I do. How could I not? Let me tell you about my world."

Hope surged in his chest. Maybe she would tell him about the strange gateway and the forest beyond the shimmer. At his nod, she continued.

"It's easy for me to believe in a parallel world because I'm from one, too. You see, this isn't the world of my birth, although now I probably spend more of my time here than I do at home. I am Faerie. I'm able to move between the Faerie Otherworld, and the human world through magical portals."

He leaned forward eagerly. "The shimmer you came through yesterday? Is the forest I saw a part of your Faerie?"

"Yes and yes," Kae chuckled.

"And these portals can take you anywhere?"

"Pretty much."

Bard drew a long breath and let it out slowly. If the portals allowed her to travel from one of her worlds to another, there might be one to his home as well. The possibility was more than he dared to hope. "Show me how to use this portal."

Kae's eyebrows and her anger rose at his demanding tone. Even if she wanted to show him, his imperious attitude pushed her to cross her arms over her chest and glare at him.

Immediately, he lowered his gaze and spread his hands flat on the table. "I was hoping... perhaps there would be a way for your portal to reach my world."

"Oh, I'm sorry," she whispered. Her anger dissipated, and she covered one of his hands with hers. "I understand how important this is to you. It's just... I don't know, Bard. I don't know if I could form a portal to your world."

"Show me how to use the portal and I will find my own way."

"It's not that easy. The portal is magical, and I don't know if you have the ability."

"I can learn."

"Magical ability is innate, something you're born with. If you don't have that talent--"

"Kaelea, I must try."

"It's not something I can--"

"Kaelea!" Bard jerked his hands from under hers, stood, and gave her his back, stiff and unrelenting.

Kae rose and faced the other way, planting her fists at her hips. "This is not the way--"

"Then tell me what is. I don't see many options. To sit back and make no attempt to find my way is unforgivable failure. Show me how to use the portal."

"No." Maybe if she had more time she could, but not now, not when danger threatened her family's existence. She stared at the far wall.

"Show me how to use the portal." Bard's voice hissed low and menacing. She didn't think he actually threatened her, but his frustration made his voice rumble through her. Still, there was only one answer she could give, but she was unable to face him as she spoke. "No."

"I must learn to use the portal."

"I shall teach you."

Kae whirled to face the door. Gowthaman leaned against the frame, casually inspecting the nails on one hand. He glanced up. "If he really wishes to learn."

A strange, hard glint sparkled in Gowthaman's soft, dark eyes. Gone was the gentle librarian. She peered at him, but couldn't determine what emotions her friend hid behind a false exterior. She lifted one hand in denial. "No, you won't. It's not safe."

Bard stepped forward. "I'm willing to take the chance."

Gowthaman pointed at Bard but directed his words to Kae. "If he truly desires it, then he should be allowed to go wherever he wishes. Whenever he wishes. We have no right to deny him."

"The Alastriona will not allow it."

A wicked light glowed in Gowthaman's eyes. "There are ways around the Defenders."

Kae took an involuntary step back. The shock at Gowthaman's words held her silent for a long moment. Bard turned to stare at her, his expression unreadable.

There was no way to bypass the Defenders of Mankind. Her uncle Derrik, leader of the Alastriona, had created additional safeguards after Korin's attack. She didn't think any beings used the portal without the Alastriona's knowledge.

"No." She shook her head. "You won't do anything like that, Gowthaman. I'll talk to..."

With both men glaring at her, Kae let her words die. From their fierce expressions she knew there would be no reasoning with either of them. Testosterone flared thick and high in the room, distending her nostrils and lifting the tiny hairs on the back of her neck. This was more than she would to tolerate. She stomped her bare foot, spread her arms, and dismissed them both with a wave of her hand.

"Gowthaman, go away. Bard, sit down and we'll continue our discussion."

"There is no discussion. If you will not help me, I'll find someone who will. Kaelea, this is important." His tone was hard, unrelenting, desperate.

"I know, Bard." She softened her voice. "I know." She swung her gaze to the faerie silhouetted in the doorway. "I said go away."

With a low growl at Bard, Gowthaman spun on his heels and stormed from the house. Kae breathed a sigh of relief, for much of the thick, uncomfortable tension followed him.

She and Bard stared at each other in silence. Bard didn't move and she matched his frozen pose. A standoff. Tension trembled in the air between them, prickling across her skin. Kae licked her lips, tasting the power of his determination. It was a heady taste and she savored it on her tongue. She had no idea an emotion could have such a physical presence. But then, she'd never met a man like Bard.

The intensity grew palpable, the discomfort deepened to a vicious throbbing and she longed to turn away. Damn it. She didn't want to be the one who gave in.

The chime at her door sent sweet music tinkling into the room.

"What?" she shouted. "If that's you, Gowthaman..."

"Nope, sorry, Kae."

The tension shattered. She blinked then turned toward her nephew. "Jayse, what are you doing here?"

"Family business. We're gathering at Granda's to discuss the latest development."

"Development? You mean about Carrie? Pretty harsh word."

Jayse winced at her tone. "You know the family's behind Carrie one hundred and ten percent."

"Everyone knows?"

Jayse took a deep breath. "Yeah, we all know. After she told Dad, it was like a dam broke and she had him tell us all. She's dealing okay, I guess. But you can see how hard it is for her. God, Kae, I can't imagine what's she's feeling."

Sorrow flowed through her. "And on top of everything, to think we would turn our backs on her."

"There are many families who would do just that." Bard spoke softly, drawing the attention of the others. "Sometimes for even the smallest of imagined reasons."

Jayse jerked his thumb toward Bard. "Who's this?"

"A complication," Kae muttered. Bard must have heard, for his eyes dulled and he drew back with his shoulders slumped. Before she could apologize, Jayse stepped forward and held out his hand.

"I'm Jayse, Kae's nephew."

"Bard." He glanced at the offered hand, then wrapped his hand around Jayse's wrist. Jayse grinned and returned the grip.

"Not from around here, are you?"

"I am not. My world, from what we can determine, is parallel to this one. Like your Faerie Otherworld."

Jayse's eyebrows lifted high in his forehead. "Uh? Okay?"

Wearily, Kae sank into her chair. This was great, just great. She'd wanted to keep Bard's origins quiet--at least for the time being. Now--now she didn't know what to do.

"Cool." Jayse had processed the information. "How did you get here?"

"I'm not sure. I have been trying to convince Kaelea to teach me how to use your portal. Perhaps I can use that means to return to my land."

"Great. I'd love to visit another world."

Bard snorted. "But, I cannot even attempt to return, for she refuses."

Jayse gave her a sideways glance. "Well, it is a magical ability. Do you have magic?"

Bard's brows drew lower over his eyes. "Tricks such as a charlatan uses on the unsuspecting? No."

"Better not let Bryce hear him say that. He doesn't take well to being called a charlatan," Jayse stage-whispered to Kae.

"Magic such as a shaman would use when contacting the Seven Guardians?" Bard paused in thought. "I don't know. But," he brightened, "I did appear in this world when seeking the Guardians, so maybe magic was involved."

"And you'd use the portal to return to your world?"

"If I could. I think, however, first I would explore this world. I have questions that need answers. I think I might find the truth here."

Jayse rested one hand on the back of a chair and leaned into the support. "There's part of the problem. In order to move from one place to another, you have to be able to picture where you're going, you have to have some knowledge of your destination."

The air left Bard's lungs in a loud whoosh. "Then I may never return home, for I don't wish to attempt such a trek without gaining the needed skill, without adequate practice."

Although he hid the emotions behind a calm expression,

Kae experienced a welling of pain and hopelessness that could only have come from Bard. Only a fleeting pain his eyes showed the sadness. She wanted to help, physically ached to help him, but there was no time. If she was to assist her family, she had to stay focused and able to concentrate. No matter what, that would be difficult with Bard nearby.

"I know," Jayse said as he tapped Kae's shoulder. "You'll be really busy with research for Dad. But, I'll have some time and I'm pretty sure Iain would enjoy the chance to do some exploring as well. Maybe Bard will be able to control the portals."

Kae frowned. She wasn't ready to turn Bard over to anyone else, even if they were family. The faint green haze covering her vision faded when she acknowledged she would be jealous of the time others would spend with him while she was stuck in the library.

Stuck in the library? When had her studies and research become something of dread? Only yesterday she'd had to be forced from her studies. A horrifying thought crawled insidiously into her mind. If Gowthaman hadn't made her leave the library, someone else would have found Bard. The green haze tickled the edges of her sight. Someone else might have helped him, might still help him. At least if her family surrounded him, he would be safe. And, she could see him any time.

She studied Bard from under her lowered lashes. She wanted to see him, to know more of him. And, she admitted, her academic curiosity was piqued by his claims of a parallel world. To visit such a world could be the height of learning.

Slowly, she realized both men were staring at her, waiting for her delayed response to Jayse's suggestion. When he caught her eye, he gestured toward Bard with a sideways nod. "We need to get going, Kae. Dad wanted everyone there as soon as possible."

"Oh, right. But what about Bard?" He stood taller when she spoke his name, defiance strong in his stiff, unyielding posture.

"He can come along. Might as well get started showing

him the portals and Faerie. Right, Bard? Can you wait long enough for us to get through this family gathering?"

The defiance fled his expression, his shoulders relaxed and he smiled, his strong, white teeth flashing. "I can wait."

F ollowing Kaelea and her nephew at a short distance, Bard scanned the surrounding desert and the tall palms of the oasis. He didn't want to admit to himself, but he was looking for a sign that his choice of actions was correct. The small creature had given him hope in the early hours of the morning, but now Bard questioned leaving the oasis to discover yet another world. Yet, he was curious and chuckled softly to himself. No doubt Kaelea was just as curious about his world.

Beyond that, he was curious about her family and the apparent tragedy and danger that drew them in a tight, protective circle. In hopes of helping them, he wanted to ask the details, but didn't know if such questions would be proper--or any of his business.

He needed to find a way to return to his home, not settle into this strange place. However, if he could help Kaelea, perhaps she would look kindly upon him.

At the edge of his vision, a man hovered. The Other. Bard ignored the fierce glare twisting the man's face. Once away from the oasis, he wouldn't have to think of him or be concerned with the odd, misplaced jealousy.

Ignored by the man, a small rodent bounded around the Other's feet, leaping high and rolling in the grass. Bard turned his head to watch. The creature looked like the one sent by the Guardians, a tiny white spot centered on the top of the small head glistened in the sunlight.

The animal moved away from the Other--Bard refused to dignify the man with the use of a name--toward where Kaelea and Jayse had turned to wait for him. A sign? He expected so.

Hurrying toward them, Bard apologized, then stood to one side as Kaelea spoke a short phrase and the shimmer opened before her. She glanced at him, took his hand, and tugged until, holding his breath, he followed her.

A faint, electrical tingling surrounded him before he encountered the portal, but disappeared when he took a step into the shimmer. Another step brought him from the portal into the forested world he had glimpsed the evening before.

Kae turned a wide grin to him. "Welcome to Faerie, Bard."

CHAPTER
SEVEN

Bard sat at the edge of the clearing before a small cabin and studied the gathered people. He had offered to watch the children while the adults talked and, after the mother of a set of precocious twins stared long into his eyes, she had agreed. An older, sightless boy sat quietly at his side while the other three chased each other in a rough and tumble game of tag. Once the shrieking and laughter died down, Bard told a story, a favorite tale of wild animals from when he had been young. Now, the three youngest slept, and the boy watched him with sightless eyes.

"My angel says you'll help."

Startled, Bard stared at the boy. Angel--Kaelea had mentioned angels. "I don't know angels, David."

He grinned. "Everybody knows angels--sometime we just call 'em by other names."

So, perhaps the Guardians of his world were like these angels. "You are very wise for one so young."

He shrugged. "Maybe. My angel is a guardian for my new family. She's the one who brought me to them and helped me to stay."

Sadness filled his eyes and Bard wondered for a moment at the expressions. Once before he had met a sightless man, but those eyes were blank, as if without sight there was also no emotion. The boy's eyes, however, conveyed much.

"She hasn't been around much lately. And we need her."

"She is the one the adults are discussing?"

"Sorta. There's a bad man, even worse than Reverend Templeton, the man who kept me before Tommy saved me. For a long time, this bad man's been trying to destroy my new family." David leaned close and gestured so that Bard bent nearer and he whispered. "He raped Carrie."

"What?" Bolting upright, Bard tensed his muscles to stand but David's hand on his arm held him in place.

"Shh, don't wake the little kids. They don't understand."

"And you do?" Bard's soul twisted. The boy was so young.

David nodded. "I know I shouldn't, and I wish I didn't. But, I learned lots of bad stuff with Reverend Templeton."

"I'm sorry." Bard closed his eyes and took a deep, shaky breath. A child should never be subjected to such knowledge, such evil.

"That's okay. I have a good home now with Tommy and Derrik. They love me, and I love them. And my new brother Bryce, too. And Carrie." David pointed in the direction of the youngest child, a blonde girl. "I'm not so sure about Bree, though. She can be a real pain in the butt."

Bard chuckled, then laughed outright when David giggled.

"We're family," David continued, "so it's okay to think she's a pain."

"Yes, we can put up with much if we have family, can't we?" The two fell silent for a short while and Bard listened to the rise and fall of voices from the adults. They were far enough away that the overhang of thick, leafy branches muffled the words and made them unintelligible, no matter how he strained to hear. With a shrug of one shoulder, he turned his attention back to David.

"Tell me more about angels."

"I suppose I don't know a whole lot, because what Reverend Templeton taught was wrong. But I know my angel, my guardian. Her name is Searlait."

"She has a name?" He'd never heard of a Guardian having

a name, in his world the seven beings were simply called Guardians. Perhaps individually they once had names.

"It's a long story. Maybe I can tell it to you sometime." David patted Bard's arm. "They're done talking."

Bard cocked his head and stared at the boy, then, as his eyebrows lifted in surprise, turned to face the men sauntering toward them.

David giggled. "I hear pretty good, huh?"

"That you do. I'm impressed."

David puffed out his thin chest. "Yep, I can do lots of things nobody suspects."

Before Bard could respond, the boy jumped to his feet and unerringly found the arms of a tall, blond man. Bard rose and, recognizing the wary stance and piercing gaze, faced the warrior.

"Da," David pulled the man forward. "This is Bard. I like him."

The man ruffled the boy's hair. "I ken that ye do. Now I must speak with him. Why don't ye take Bree an' find yer pop?"

"Okay." The men watched in silence as David woke the other children and the group headed toward the cabin. Then Bard turned expectantly to Derrik.

The warrior smiled. "Jaysson tells me ye wish to travel the portals in this and the human world."

"Yes." Perhaps it was best to not yet divulge his ultimate desires. A flash of Kaelea's smile burst across his inner vision. He blinked the delight away and focused on Derrik.

"I am Derrik, leader of the Alastirona, the Defenders of Mankind. Part of the duties of the defenders is to assure the safety of the portals." In the silence following his statement, Derrik studied him.

Holding himself still, Bard returned the steady gaze and recognized the moment Derrik acknowledged the warrior within him. Before the scrutiny became uncomfortable, Derrik gave a sharp nod. "I shall give permission fer ye to travel the portals with Jayse or Iain. If ye are able to learn the magic, have the ability and accept the responsibility, ye may use the portals freely."

"I thank you." .

Derrik clasped him on the shoulder. "'Tis a pleasure. One thing I would ask of ye."

"Okay." Bard bit back a surprised smile at his use of the word. It was an easy word.

"While ye travel, would ye watch fer signs of my cousin? She dwells in a place between worlds an' if--when we find her, mayhaps we can return her to this world. To the place she belongs."

"What can you tell me of her so I'll recognize her?"

"'Tis said we are alike in appearance, though she is much fairer than I." Derrik gave a sad chuckle. "Her name is Searlait."

"Like David's guardian? His angel?"

"Oh, aye. Searlait has appeared to many in the family in time of trial."

"This is a time of great trial for you."

"Aye." Derrik glanced back over his shoulder. "Come, ye can meet the clan now. I believe Jayse is eager to begin yer instruction."

Bard held back a moment when Derrik made to move toward the cabin. "Defender?" he said softly. Derrik paused until Bard stood beside him. "I understand a little of what your family faces. I will help as I am able. Be assured, your family is safe with me."

"I ken. I understand," Derrik amended. "I dinna doubt yer life has been entwined with this family fer a reason. What that reason may be, we shall see in time. If ye have questions, dinna fear to ask. As I'm sure we shall be askin' ye many things."

"I understand, I ken," Bard replied. With a broad grin, Derrik led him forward to introduce him to the entire family.

Bard tried to associate names with faces but the rapid introductions left him confused. Kaelea's parents seemed hardly old enough to have grown children. He was drawn to Kaelea's sister, Nanceen, identical except for the length of her hair and the softly rounded bulge of her belly. She was beautiful in her pregnancy, and Bard imagined Kaelea filled with a child.

No, not any child, his child.

Bard closed his eyes. He would stop thinking of her in such ways. To entertain these notions served no purpose. The sooner he learned to use the portals and began his search for a way home, the better he would be able to deal with the strange, uncomfortable thoughts of Kaelea.

Excusing himself, he turned away, intending to look for Jayse. The sooner--

"Oh, I'm sorry."

Bard glanced down at the young woman who'd bumped into him. She stumbled as she moved away and he caught her about the waist to steady her.

She glanced about nervously and pulled a loose shirt down over her hips. "I'm not usually so clumsy. I'm... Carrie."

"Ah, Carrie. I am pleased to finally meet you."

"And I wanted to meet you. As the newest member of this extended family, I think I probably understand better than the others how overwhelming this all can be."

Bard chuckled. "I must admit, I have difficulty keeping names and faces together."

"I've finally gotten everyone straight, so if you have any questions, just ask me." Even though there was a smile in her voice, her eyes remained wary. Longing to ease her discomfort, Bard took her hand.

"I don't understand why this family has agreed to help me when it appears there is much trouble surrounding you. Why take time to help a stranger?"

Bard was leery of her answer. In his world, helping others was often limited to the amount of gain a person would achieve. Even without tales and legends, he knew it had not always been that way. The comfort of acceptance here in this world confused him to the point where he strove to ignore the feeling.

Although a haunted light remained in her eyes, laughter bubbled from Carrie's lips. "Get used to it. Once this family accepts you, you're stuck. And, since you're here right now, I'd say you're stuck. It's not such a bad thing."

Bard glanced to where Kaelea spoke quietly with her sister and pressed her palm to Nanceen's belly. "No, I don't believe it is." When he turned his gaze back to Carrie, she also looked at the twins and unconsciously rubbed her own abdomen.

Taking a deep breath, Bard stilled her restless hand by covering it with his palm.

Startled, she stared at him, her eyes wide and filled with fear. "What are you doing?"

"I'm sorry." He quickly drew his hand away. "David told me of how your child was conceived."

"David? How does he know?"

"He sees much."

"But he--"

"He sees with his heart, Carrie. I believe the rest of this family does as well." Bard swiped his hand through the air to indicate those gathered around the clearing. "No one here will ever turn their back on you for something you had no control over."

"That's what everyone says, but it's so hard to believe. My father turned against me when I was a child and hadn't even done anything."

The sadness in her eyes and the trembling of her lower lip filled Bard with a surge of protectiveness. If by default he had also been accepted into this amazing family for a short while, he would do all within his power to aid them. Perhaps as he traveled, he could add the evildoer to his search. For now, he could offer comfort.

"I have also experienced a family who faced away. I understand the fear within you. But, there is nothing here to indicate displeasure with you, Carrie. Hold your head high, sweet woman, and carry the life within you proudly. The child will be as you raise it, full of love and joy."

A young man wrapped his arm about her shoulder and gave Bard a grateful nod. "Haven't I told you that, over and over?" He tipped her chin with a finger and pressed a light kiss to her mouth. "Are you going to listen to a new friend over me?"

"Bryce, I--"

He silenced her with another kiss. "As long as the meaning's the same, I don't care who you listen to. Bree's clamoring for tacos tonight, so we'd best go feed her before she gets cranky." After Carrie nodded, Bryce held out a hand to Bard. "Thank you. I appreciate you talking to Carrie."

Bard wrapped his fingers around Bryce's wrist and smiled at the returned gesture. "My thanks to you, and your family as well."

"I understand Jayse is going to take you through the portals. I hope you find what you're looking for."

Bard gave a short nod. Bryce and Carrie turned away as Kaelea stepped to his side. A slight frown marred the smooth lines of her face. She crossed her arms and shook her head. "I'm still not convinced this is a good idea."

His huffed out breath stirred the hairs around her face. She wanted to believe learning how to use the faerie portals would help him find a way home, but after just one day, she didn't want him to leave. Not just yet, anyway.

"I have to do this, Kaelea. Unless I am able to find the exact spot in your Sahara where our worlds are conjoined, this may be my only chance to return home. If I choose an incorrect spot in the desert, I may find myself in yet another world. Perhaps one not so congenial to my presence."

Kae remained silent a moment. "I hadn't thought of that. Still, I don't like the idea of you running around, who knows where, with Jayse."

"You don't trust your nephew?" A smug, grin tugged at his lips.

She hated that look--that condescending, male look. Of course she trusted Jayse. Maybe she didn't trust Bard. Kae turned her face from him and stared at the trees surrounding her parent's clearing. No, she trusted him, too. Probably a foolish action, but she couldn't seem to help herself. Usually a fairly good judge of character, she found nothing about Bard to mistrust. Except perhaps her intense feelings for him.

She spoke without turning her head. "Of course I do. Can't I worry about what might happen if you go traipsing off through worlds you don't know?"

His hand rested lightly on her shoulder. "You would worry?"

"I--of course I would. I feel... feel responsible for you."

The warmth of his hand dropped away and she knew she'd said the wrong thing in a moment that could have been-- what? Special? She closed her eyes and gnawed on her lower lip.

"There is no need to feel responsible." Cold and hard, his voice chilled her heart. "It is my responsibility that I have come to your lands. And my responsibility to find my own way home."

Waves of his anger tumbled through the air, blasting against her skin, heating what his words had cooled. Slowly, she faced the fire in his eyes. "Why are you so angry?"

He growled at her. Growled. The sudden rise of Kae's angry response momentarily surprised her, then overtook her surprise and she bit back a growl of her own. She spoke between clenched teeth. "I'll feel responsible if I want to." She blinked. Well, that was an adult response. She ought to tell him that she wanted the time to get to know him better, time to explore the fierce sensual aura surrounding them. She ought to tell him that she cared about what happened, because, despite her better judgment, she did care about him. She ought to tell him how much she cared.

Bard's chest rose and fell rapidly as he visibly fought to control the anger simmering in his expression. Kae reached one hand toward him, but he backed away before her palm made contact with his chest. His head shook back and forth and his eyes narrowed to mere slits.

Kae frowned. This reaction wasn't normal; she couldn't see any reason for him to be furious with her, or anyone else. Weren't they doing all they could to help him?

A low rumble sounded from him. Another growl. He turned away.

"Well, fine then. Act like a big baby to get your way. Go

ahead, wander all over, do whatever you want. I don't care. Do you hear me? I don't care." Kae winced after she stomped her foot and glanced around the clearing. The rise in her voice had attracted the attention of her family and heat flared in her face at their mixed expressions.

Especially painful was the tolerant humor filling her parents' faces.

"Ooh!" She stomped her other foot, whirled, and stormed from the clearing, anxious for the peace and solitude of the desert library.

B ard held himself stiff, his back straight. He longed to chase after Kaelea and beg forgiveness for his stupid pride. But before he could give into that need, Jayse sauntered toward him, clasped his shoulder, and grinned. "That was a touching farewell."

Resisting the urge to shrug the young man's hand from his shoulder, Bard settled for a noncommittal grunt.

"That's what I thought." Jayse laughed until Bard relaxed and gave him a wry grin. "Don't worry about it, Bard. You'll find that tempers flare very quickly in this family, but die down just as fast." He shrugged one shoulder. "None of us stays angry very long when we care. And she does. A lot."

Bard doubted that fact, but didn't voice his opinion. He didn't need to alienate another who might be able to help him find his way home.

Jayse peered intensely at him for a moment, then shrugged again. "Let's go talk with Iain. He'll be helping with your instruction, but we've got to be careful how long to keep him from home. He wasn't here when Lara was pregnant with the twins and they both insist he 'share the experience' this time. She won't let him out of her sight for very long." Jayse chuckled. "My sister can be really demanding at times."

Watching the couple as Jayse led the way toward them, Bard couldn't blame either one. Iain rested his hand against her belly as he leaned close to whisper in her ear. Lara laughed and patted his cheek.

Bard released a long, slow breath and the rest of his anger. If Kaelea carried his child, he'd be near at all times. Loving, protecting, caring. Shaking the words from his head, he amended his thinking. If he ever found a woman to share his life--not Kaelea. Somehow, he had to keep such inappropriate thoughts at bay.

But a smile softened his lips and his mind whispered, *Kaelea.*

CHAPTER

EIGHT

One month. Thirty days. Kae didn't even want to consider adding up all those minutes. For one month she'd been hard at research into family lines and she didn't feel one iota closer to an answer.

One month. He'd been gone for one month. Thirty days and an equal number of unusually long nights. Kae rested her chin in her palm and, not for the first time, wondered if time was measured the same in his world.

Drawing an invisible doodle with her finger on the page before her, Kae attempted to force her attention back to a nearly unreadable scroll. The information she needed had to be there somewhere. Her finger stalled. Somewhere. Bard was somewhere...

She'd gotten brief reports on his progress from Iain, but only after she'd badgered him unmercifully after Jayse had only grinned and shook his head. Men. The three of them seemed to have formed some sort of an agreement to shut her out. She tucked an errant strand of hair behind her ear. Maybe she should cut her hair short like Nanceen's.

Damn, she couldn't keep her mind on one topic for even half a minute. She let a smile soften her lips as she released a slow breath. Unless she was thinking about Bard.

Iain told her Bard had been able to learn how to manipulate the portals, at least for simple transfers. Pride in his accomplishments swelled in her chest as though she had something to do with his success. Then the swell shrank to a tiny, hard, heavy lump. She'd denied his request for instruction and forced him to turn to another.

Even though that other was her nephew, it still hurt. But what hurt even more was knowing that she had caused her own pain.

How difficult would it have been to take a few hours each day, leave her research behind, and go with him on his explorations? She needed to take breaks from the studies in order to keep her mind sharp; she could have been enjoying the time off. Enjoying Bard.

With a long, drawn out sigh, Kae reached for a scroll half hanging from the edge of the table. As she stretched she sensed the presence of someone behind her then felt the warmth of a hand smooth the length of her hair to one side before stroking across her shoulders. She arched into the sensation and the hand moved to press firmly into the tense ache at the base of her neck.

"Ah." Pressure at just the right spot eased the tension and she let her shoulders slump. The smooth, even movements of two hands massaged her shoulders. Her heart beat swift and hard in her chest singing with the fleeting hope Bard had returned.

Common sense told her otherwise. The wards against discovery would never allow him access to the library, even if he could find the entrance. Besides, she didn't believe he would be so bold as to touch her in such a way. Especially after the anger at their parting.

The pressure of the massage eased, but soft strokes continued, inching toward her neck. A lover's touch.

"Gowthaman!" Kae jerked away from the pleasure and twisted in her chair to stare at him. His chest rose and fell heavily while, with sensual slowness, his eyes opened. He swirled his robes in a wide flourish as he bowed. "Your servant."

"You shouldn't--"

"What? Assist in relieving the tension of a friend who takes little time for herself?"

Kae couldn't argue with his statement for he had often rubbed her neck after a long day of study. However, she did take issue with the light burning in his eyes. She'd seen a similar glint far too often in her own eyes over the past month when she glanced in a mirror after thinking about Bard. Now, both her head and her heart agreed, Gowthaman would never be more than the friend he claimed to be.

With a sudden movement, Gowthaman knelt before her and took her hands in his. Silent, he looked deeply into her face. Desire swirled through his eyes. "Kaelea."

She slipped her hands from his. "Don't say anything more. You know how I feel."

"He will not come back to you, Kae. His kind never do."

Hot with the realization Gowthaman voiced her inner thoughts and the whispers she'd tried to deny, pain settled around her heart. She caught her lower lip between her teeth to stop the denial--of his words or of her dreams, she didn't know.

A bright, fierce fire burned in Gowthaman's eyes. "He will never love you. Not as I do. Once you realize the truth--"

"I realize more than you think, Gowthaman. He's not the reason I don't love you. There just isn't that special spark, that tingle when I see you or think of you. I want you for my friend."

"Friends have often become lovers."

She could deal with this argument. "How many times must we have to rehash this? You're special to me, Gowthaman, as a friend. But, I don't love you in a romantic way. No matter how often you declare--"

The firm, hot pressure of his mouth smothered her words. His forward lunge pressed her deep in the chair. Shock held her still for a moment before she tried to twist her mouth from his.

Intent upon his purpose, Gowthaman captured her face between his palms, then slipped one of his hands into her hair to hold her still under the assault of his mouth. With a muffled cry she arched back, breaking the kiss. Before she could speak, he'd claimed her mouth again, sliding his tongue between her parted lips. Kae slapped at his shoulder, then clawed her fingers into the soft underside of his arm.

He grunted in pain, but didn't release her, or end the kiss.

Kae pounded her fist at the top of his shoulder joint and wedged her hand between them to shove against his chest. Panting, he drew away.

Slowly his dazed expression faded. His eyes cleared, widened, then closed. "By the gods of the desert, Kae. I am sorry."

Kae touched her slightly swollen lips in disbelief. Gowthaman stretched one hand toward her. Fear made her shove the chair back, putting a small distance between them. "Don't touch me."

When he made a sharp movement as if to rise, she cried out and he froze. "Kaelea?" He stared at the floor, arms hanging loose at his sides and whispered harshly, "A thousand devils take me. What have I done?"

She shook her head. He'd tried to force... God, was this what Carrie felt? Terror at an act meant to be beautiful? "No," she whispered. No, not like this. Gowthaman was her friend, had been a friend...

She stared at him. When he lifted his head, was the pain in his expression real? Or another attempt at seduction? She couldn't be sure. How would she ever trust him again?

He slid back on his knees, increasing the space between them. Carefully, keeping his eyes fixed on hers, he rose. "Kae-lea, I..."

"No!"

Shoulders slumping and arms spread in supplication, he ducked his head and backed away. "Forgive me."

When he was gone from sight, Kae wrapped her arms about herself and shuddered. Could she? He'd only kissed her. "No," she whispered. He'd kissed her without preamble, without permission or welcome. He'd refused to stop when she denied him. Oh, God. She couldn't stay here.

Nearly blinded by hot tears, she gathered her papers and

clutched them to her chest. A quick glance around showed her an empty room. She released her breath and stumbled from the table, through the oasis and across the short expanse of sand, only feeling safe once she reached the cool interior of her small house.

T hirty-eight days. How many hours, how long the minutes?

Thirty-eight days of longing for Kaelea with an intensity, a need Bard didn't understand. Learning to use the faerie portals consumed his time and his thoughts through the daylight hours--until the nights left him alone. Refusing the offers of beds both within the human world and the Faerie Otherworld, Bard lay under the stars each night and searched out constellations both familiar and yet somehow strange. He'd adapted to the eastern rising of the sun, but somehow the colorful setting in the west still disconcerted him.

He lay sleepless once again, his head cradled on his crossed palms, staring into the clear night sky. There, just above the horizon lay a sprinkling of stars, a pattern that had no name in his land. In this world, the sparkle, the shimmer, the shape of the stars reminded him of Kaelea's eyes. Bard drew a deep breath as the familiar longing settled low in his body, liquid heat filling him, tightening his groin.

Every night had been the same, and every night he would rise and pace through the darkness until the longing came under control. Each night his pacing took him farther from the spot he'd spread his blanket, each night it became more diffi-cult to temper his desire with thoughts of anything else.

Bard tossed his covering to one side and rose, letting the night air cool his heated flesh. By the Seven, the nearly constant arousal was uncomfortable. Yet he welcomed the pain as a sign he still lived. Sliding his loose trousers over his hips was delightfully unbearable and Bard growled low in his throat. He slipped on the soft, faerie-made shoes and took the first steps in his nightly walk.

After the first mile, he was able to pull his thoughts from

Kaelea and concentrate on the coming day. After two miles he shifted to a slow jog-trot that carried him far with little effort. He grinned and the exhilaration of the movement filled him. As a youth, he'd often outrun the others of his age group, and once had traveled one hundred units in a single day. He wouldn't go so far during the night, but he could use the time and the rhythmic pounding of his feet to prepare for the coming challenge.

Days and days of practice under Iain or Jaysson's watchful eyes had brought him to this point. At sunrise he would be allowed to create a portal by himself. His smile grew wide and he laughed into the wind.

The magic had come easily to him, the tingle of power reminiscent of when his grandmother had insisted his grand-father teach him the simple chants of an apprentice shaman. He'd not thought he'd had the ability then, and when Grand-father died, there was none willing to continue his training.

Bard jerked to a stop on a slight rise, turned to the north, and found the single, unmoving star. The star held a similar place in his world. He associated the shine with his grand-mother--steady, unchanging, yet twinkling with life and power. He lifted his arms, threw back his head, and whispered a chant of honor. After he repeated the short chant four times, he kept his arms raised and lowered his head. "Thank you, Grandmother, for you must have seen within me more than I still can see myself."

An unusual rustle in the grass made him open his eyes. Moonlight from the pale half moon surrounded him, casting a silver glow to the hilltop. The mystical haze stole his breath, replacing air with wonder. The rustle sounded a second time and Bard followed the sound.

Highlighted by the silvery glow, a tiny white spot on the top of a small creature's head sparkled as it grasped the stem of a tall plant, reaching for the flowering tip. Bard knelt to peer closely at the animal. Unconcerned by his presence, the rodent nibbled daintily.

"Little guide," Bard said softly. The creature paused,

looked at him with soft, dark eyes and dipped its head as if nodding. "What do you wish of me?"

The tiny head tilted to one side, then lifted until the sharp nose pointed to the sky--and the stars of Kaelea's eyes.

"I do not understand."

Bard received a look so filled with disgust, he leaned back, amazed to feel such emotion from a rodent. The guide ran in a tight circle then skittered away.

The guide. Of course, the animal was no mere rodent. "Shall I continue to follow you then, little guide? What do you wish me to do?"

The creature turned its head back over its shoulder and blinked at him. Then it faced the horizon and the stars of Kaelea's eyes. The tiny head bobbed up and down and the animal looked back at him again, nodding.

"Do you wish me to go to Kaelea?"

After turning in a triple, tight circle, the guide bounded into the underbrush. Bard chuckled, the sound rough and unused to his ears.

For once, the Guardians had given him a clear answer, and he would be a fool not to respect the wishes of the small one.

Taking a deep breath, he turned from the horizon and loped back into the surrounding Faerie forest. The run exhilarated him and his doubts concerning the coming day vanished with the pound of his feet upon the grass-cushioned path. He would make his first solo transfer through a portal of his own making to the desert Sahara. And Kaelea.

His lungs tightened and he frowned. Had he lost conditioning in his pursuit of the portal magic? At his tiny camp, he stopped and gauged his breathing. His intake of air was heavy but unlabored, typical after the length of his run. But as he rolled his blankets, he thought of Kaelea and the tightness returned. Ah... he began to understand.

The electric tingle of an emerging portal tickled his back and Bard faced the shimmering oval. Jayse and Iain stepped through, followed by the warrior, Derrik. Bard kept his face impassive but was surprised at the presence of the leader of the Alastriona. Beyond the initial testing for magical ability, Derrik had left the others to instruct him.

Perhaps there was some other rite of passage involved this day. Bard squared his shoulders. Whatever might be placed before him, he was ready.

Derrik grinned. "Aye, I dinna think ye would be able to control our portals, an' I'm glad to be wrong. Where yer talent may come from I dinna ken, but it resides within ye. If yer challenge today is successful, ye shall have the freedom to go where ye wish, provided ye dinna abuse that right."

"I shall not."

Derrik extended his hand and Bard wrapped his fingers around the thick wrist. "Then, m'friend, let's begin."

Bard turned to Jayse and Iain in turn and, with the firm grasp of his hand, silently thanked each for their patience and instruction. Iain remained somber, but Jayse grinned broadly and gave Bard a wink.

"So where're you going?"

"I decided during the night."

"And?"

"Since I must accurately picture the place I wish to go, I shall return to the place I entered this world. I remember it well."

"The middle of the desert?"

Lost for a moment in the vivid memory of Kaelea's smile, Bard didn't respond until Jayse asked a second time. He shook his head. "No, the changing sands are free of land-marks. There would be no guarantee where the portal would open."

"Guid," Derrik said. "Ye must have a clear an' precise picture in yer mind before ye enter the portal."

"I shall travel to the oasis."

Jayse laughed, then sputtered to silence when all eyes turned toward him. He spread his hands and widened his eyes in a gesture of belabored innocence. "Sorry," he said, but his expression was far from apologetic. The man had the spirit of the trickster coyote in him and if Jayse suspected his need to see Kaelea, he would face the brunt of good-natured joking.

Bard gave the young man a stern, thin-lipped look before facing the space where he would create his portal.

"After ye arrive at yer destination, I'll follow to determine the accuracy of yer portal creation."

"I understand."

Bard took a step forward, lifted one hand and, after taking a deep breath, sketched the sign, and clearly spoke the first of the words. From the corner of his eye he caught a movement that stopped the flow of his spell. The tiny guide waited beneath a bush, its bright gaze focused intently upon the spot where his portal would form. He didn't question how the rodent had reached his camp so quickly, but the presence gave him courage and support in his decision to return to the desert Sahara.

Completing the spell, Bard held his breath until a shimmering oval hovered steadily before him. Without glancing at the men who waited behind him, Bard confidently stepped forward, felt the power surround him, caress his body, then push him through to his destination.

The breath whooshed from his lungs. The deep green oasis stood before him as it appeared when he had run from the burning desert toward the relief offered by the cool shade. In the silence following his exhalation, he could discern the faint sounds of water flowing over the rocks into the deep pool. The urge to run, to rediscover the pool, burned hotter than the sand beneath his feet. Shaking with the effort of remaining still, he waited until he felt the presence of the others behind him. He let satisfaction show in his smile as he turned his back to the temptation of the oasis.

Derrik clasped him on both shoulders. "Well done. Ye have earned the right of passage within the portals. D'ye remember the call should ye have difficulties?"

Nodding, Bard answered, "I do, though I do not expect to have need of that spell."

Derrik chuckled. "Nonetheless, m'friend, dinna hesitate to use it. 'Tis no shame in neeedin' the occasional assistance."

"Agreed." He faced Iain. "You have been a calm, tolerant instructor. I thank you."

Iain silently clasped his wrist, nodded, and returned through the portal.

Jayse chuckled and moved into the space Iain had vacated. "Lara must be having a tough day. Or maybe I should say, Iain's having a rough day dealing with his wife's raging hormones. I remember all too well how her first pregnancy affected us all."

"Aye," Derrik agreed. "Iain is a buffer fer the rest of us this time. I, fer one, am pleased."

"What's next?" Jayse gave Bard a look full of meaning.

He ignored the thinly veiled speculations. Let the young man think what he would. "Since this is where I first entered your world, I believe I shall remain here a short while. From here I'll begin my search for a way to return to my world." Hoping to divert Jayse's curious interest, Bard shaded his eyes with one hand and peered out into the desert. He ignored the low chuckles behind him.

"Enjoy your time here." Jayse slapped Bard's shoulder. "Hey, you still interested in going to those ancient Native American sites?"

Glad of the change of subject, Bard nodded. "After reading the books you provided, I wish to visit the mesa dwellings, the places where the homes were created high in the cliffs."

"It's been awhile since I've been to the Southwest, but whenever you're ready, I'll take you there the first time. Agreed?"

"Okay." The word still felt foolish to his tongue, but he'd found it effective in conveying many meanings.

Waiting the few moments until Jayse and Derrik left strained his patience. Wondering where he might find Kaelea, he watched the portal blink out of existence. He remained staring into the depths of the desert, searching through the white-hot air and golden sands. He wasn't looking for anything, for he believed the answers he sought lay in other directions.

Turning on his heel, he strode swiftly toward the welcoming shade of the oasis. And Kaelea.

NINE

K ae slipped down the library steps, pausing on each riser to listen, but no sound carried to her to indicate the presence of the other scholars. She breathed a soft sigh of relief. Eight days away from her primary source of reference materials put a serious dent in her search. But, until late the previous night, she'd been unable to put Gowthaman's deplorable actions into perspective.

Although she could never condone how he--attacked--she thought she understood the emotions behind his actions and hoped they could return to a place of friendship.

She had to swallow her fear before she could cast a glance around the silent library and take the final steps to her table. The scatter of her research remained untouched, just as she'd left it when she ran away.

Except...

A thin volume rested at the center of the table. Kae tilted her head and peered at the book as she sat. Deep in her heart she knew Gowthaman had left the book there. A peace offering.

Kae bent close to the thin volume and studied the cover. The tooled leather cover was unusual, the lines and curves similar to the ancient Pict designs she'd become familiar with since Lara married Iain. But, there was something--otherworldly--about the swirling knots and shapes. Finding it odd that she would consider something otherworldly, Kae chuckled softly to herself.

She stroked the leather; even the feel of the tanned skin was different than the oldest of volumes she encountered in her studies.

Otherworlds. Could this book be familiar to Bard--something from his world? Or was it merely that much older, so that it appeared foreign? The touch of her questing fingers became a caress. If she knew where Bard was, she'd show him the book, ask his opinion.

Startled by her thoughts, Kae leaned back in her chair. Too many times lately she'd wanted to ask Bard a question or discover his views on some interesting bit of information she'd found in her research. Or even to explore something as simple as what shapes he saw in the rare clouds flitting through the Sahara sky. She didn't dare ask herself why his opinion was so important to her. It wasn't as if he would have some impact on her search for answers to help her family.

Helping her family. Saving her loved ones from the evil power of another, from a faerie who, despite his loss of powers, continued to haunt and strive to destroy her brother. Along with the entire family.

What had caused Feidhlim to hate them so much?

Her aunt, the queen of their clan, had every right to choose whomever she wished as her heir, not that any thought she would soon release that rule to Jaye. Although, her brother did play an increasingly prominent role in the guidance of the clan and their place in both the human and Faerie worlds.

Kae shook her head and straightened. This need helped her overcome the fear raised by Gowthaman's advances and brought her back to the library. She had to discover the whys of the past--the reasons Fiedhlim turned evil in his quest for more power. She reached for the book and sighed. But, wasn't that often the way it was? Ultimate power became ultimate corruption.

She pushed aside the fear that Gowthaman may have been

somehow corrupted by his actions toward her. He was a gentle man, and had never before pressed his desires beyond where she stopped him. No, once they talked, once they worked out what had happened, she was sure he would return to being her kind, helpful friend. Despite her fear and concerns, she'd missed him.

Gathering a parchment and quill, she set them beside the small book. But, before she eased open the cover, a skittering of sound drew her gaze to one side. Shocked at the appearance of a tiny, desert rodent within the boundaries of the library, she stared open-mouthed as the creature climbed the supports of a shelf, then sat on its hind legs and returned her stare.

Remembering the dismay she'd felt at the discovery of a pile of scrolls torn to shreds by mice making nests, she knew she had to get the small animal away from the library before any of the librarians or caretakers discovered its presence. If any of the librarians found the small animal--Kae shuddered and sympathy welled inside her for the innocent creature.

Leaning toward the shelf, she whispered, "You should leave, little one. Don't let anyone see you."

The animal cocked its head to one side and wiped a paw over one ear. Then it tilted its head to the other side and cleaned the other ear.

"Go on. Shoo." She waved her hand but the animal only rubbed its tiny, pointed nose and watched her. "Run away."

She stared at the animal for long moments, then finally decided it wasn't going to move. She'd have to chase it from the library, but feared if she moved, it would run further into the stacks of books and be lost. She couldn't allow that to happen. Maybe she could catch it and let it go somewhere far from the library entrance. Now, as long as the rodent didn't run when she stood.

Slowly, the movement of each muscle a torment, she straightened then rose to her feet. The rodent sat motionless. Kae inched one foot forward. No movement. She took another step. The animal watched her calmly, only the long, brown whiskers twitching. A third step. The tiny black eyes blinked.

She reached out her palm, intending to gently scoop the animal into her hand before it could scoot away.

Instead, the small creature walked onto her palm and sat.

Frozen with astonishment, Kae stared at her hand. Whiskers tickling her palm, the creature curled into a tiny ball. She lifted her hand and stared, nose to nose, at the animal. "You're a strange little thing."

The whiskers quivered as it took a deep breath.

"If I take you away from here, do you promise not to come back?"

The animal blinked.

She curved her hand and held it close to her stomach. "Where shall I take you?" She reached toward the table and snatched up the thin volume. "I'll take this and look at it at home. How does that sound to you, little one?"

With the book in one hand and a tiny animal in the other, Kae made her way carefully from the library. She paused at the rusted gates and glanced around the oasis. Where could she take the animal in order to prevent its return? It was a cute thing, and she thought for a moment about taking it home with her. She chuckled at herself. Just what she needed, a mouse. There was never just one mouse, and she had too many precious papers and scrolls to chance a rodent's gnaw fest. She didn't want to let it go in the desert, even though she supposed the animal was well suited for survival. Something about the diminutive creature made her feel protective, like she needed to guard it somehow from the dangers of the vast expanses of sand.

The faint sounds of water drifted through the surrounding palms.

The pool--she'd take it to the pool. That should be far enough from the library to prevent a return, yet with safe places where it could hide. With her decision made, she cupped her hand securely about the creature and turned toward the clear oasis pool.

Awkwardly tucking the book under her arm, she hesitated, then gently stroked the pale spot on the center of the animal's head. "I think you'll like the area around the pool. Lots of grass and underbrush to hide in. Plenty of water. I don't know what you like to eat, but I'm sure you'll find that there, too."

Kae smiled at herself. She was talking to a desert animal as though it understood her words. Oddly enough, the expression on the furry face, and the way it watched her, gave an impression of intelligence.

"Am I being silly, little one? Sometimes I don't think I can tell any more. Almost there."

Kae stepped from under the overhand of a twisted palm and gave the animal a small grin as the memory of the last time she'd been at the pool assailed her. She hadn't returned since the day Bard had stumbled into her life. Well, maybe not into her life, but into her world. She scanned the open area, letting her gaze linger on the pool's smooth surface. Closing her eyes, she pictured how she had turned at the first soft noise he'd made.

The animal squirmed and her eyes popped open. "I'm sorry, little one. Do you wish to explore your new home?" Kneeling, she stretched out her arm and rested her hand on the ground. After giving a tiny squeak, the animal bounded away and disappeared under a leafy, low growing palm. Kae chuckled and lifted her gaze.

Her chuckle died with a squeak not much louder than the one the animal had given. A shadowy form stood to one side, just beyond where the light filtered through the high palm branches. Tall, broad shouldered, it was a form Kae had dreamed of for thirty-eight nights.

She rose from her crouch and took a step forward. "Bard?"

Moving into the light, he spread his arms slightly, but said nothing.

She rushed forward, his open arms an invitation her heart accepted, but before she foolishly embraced him, her head found a way to slow her body and she stopped before him. "I... I'm glad to see you."

The light left his eyes for a moment before he smiled and the odd expression disappeared. "I'm pleased to find you well."

"How else would I be?" She shrugged away the need to

press close to him. Needing to touch him, she rested her hand on his arm. "How did you get here?"

His smile broadened. "I created a portal. It was my challenge, my test. Now, I am able to travel the portals as I wish." His smile faltered. "Though I still must ask assistance to go where I have not been before."

"That's true for any of us. Except maybe Lara. Her talent's different."

"How so?"

"She's able to create portals through time, as well as from place to place. No one's sure how she does it." She rambled on nervously, even though she really didn't want to talk about Lara. Or anyone else.

No one except the man before her. The force of missing him assaulted her and she took a step back. At his frown, she hurried to explain. "I'm so glad to see you."

"So you have said." His smile returned and he reached to take her hand in his. "Yours is the familiar face I've longed to see, but I needed time to learn if I could control the portals."

"Can you... stay for a while?"

Kae held her breath as she waited for his answer. He stared past her shoulder and a double line marred the smoothness of his forehead. "What was it you brought to the pool?"

The question surprised her and it took a moment for her to form an answer. "A small desert rodent found its way into the library. They've been known to gnaw at the books and make nests in the scrolls. There've been wards placed around the library, so I don't know how this one got in. I couldn't see the adorable animal being destroyed just for being in the wrong place. I was able to capture it, so..." She was rambling again and curious why Bard was so interested in a rodent, she let her speech fade.

"What did this animal look like?" His fingers tightened around her hand.

Kae shrugged. "Like any of its kind, I suppose. Though, this one was really cute, with a tiny white spot on the top of its head."

"Ah. I understand." With his slow nod the intensity left his expression and he gave her a hopeful smile.

What did he understand? Why did he seem to think the animal was important?

Bard stroked his thumb over the back of her hand. "Yes, I shall stay a short while."

"What?" The soothing touch distracted her from his statement.

"You asked if I would stay and I shall. I would like to see how your research is progressing."

A flare of guilt centered at the base of her throat at the subtle reminder she should be working. But, at Bard's soft chuckle, she joined him in laughing the guilt away. "Oh, my brother got to you, huh? Wants you to check up on me."

He ducked his head and his grin turned sheepish. "He did ask."

"Don't worry. I've been immediately sending him any information I discover. Though, there hasn't been much. Will you come back to my house?"

Subtlety was obviously not high on her list of current priorities.

She tried to turn away, but he caught her cheek in his free palm and held her rapt attention in his steady gaze. "I was hoping you would ask."

"Oh." Kae stared at him, drinking in the angles of his face and the soft, kissable fullness of his lips. It would be dangerous taking him home, being close to him. Alone. She let loose the breath tightening her lungs. Ah, but this danger she wanted, and had wanted for many weeks.

"I'm sorry. I was angry with you and your need to use the portals. I was wrong." There, she said the words she'd practiced every day, almost since the moment she'd stormed away from him, leaving him to learn from Jayse. He had returned to the oasis, so hopefully he'd forgiven her.

"You were concerned for my safety. Even more for the safety of your family. I understand. There is nothing to forgive you for, unless it is for that caring. I find no fault in that." After a long pause in which he simply looked at her, he continued.

"I've not... mmm, for some time I've not had to be concerned with how my desires may affect another person. I should not have been so insistent."

A hitch in his voice, a low catch when he spoke the word desire, tingled a response low in Kae's belly. Again her head and heart warred. Her head knew he spoke of his desire to learn the portals, her heart demanding another, more personal desire. Every bit of that desire, every thought and feeling she'd tried to squash over the past month flared to vibrant life. If he touched her, she'd explode. She wanted him to touch her. She closed the shallow distance between them. "I understand."

When she slid her hand along his arm, Bard shuddered. Then she moved closer and her heat rose to him. He inhaled deeply. Her palm was cool against his skin as her other hand slid around his waist. The tips of her breasts brushed his chest. She sighed and rested her check over the pounding of his heart.

As if with a will of their own, his hands settled at her waist and inched her minutely away from his body. She lifted her face to him, questions forming on her tempting, parted lips and in her dark expressive eyes.

Pressing his mouth gently over hers, he inhaled her sigh. *Yes*, his mind shouted. This was why he returned to the desert Sahara. There was no other reason, but the woman. He deepened the kiss, nipping and teasing her lips, his male pride satisfied when she responded with soft cries and the gift of her tongue.

She pressed closer, rubbing sinuously against the rise of his passion, of need, of a desire long unfilled. He slipped his hands from her waist to cup the full, womanly softness of her bottom and held her tight against him. He could not restrain his low, vocal response and moved his kisses from her mouth to the arch of her neck.

High pitched squeaking, then the prick of sharp pain at his ankle tore him from the pleasure of Kaelea's kisses. He stared in disbelief at the small creature digging long scratches in his ankle. Kae backed away and stood trembling, staring toward his feet. He reached for her, but the tiny guide squealed, gave his ankle a vicious swipe with needle-sharp claws, then scampered away.

The noise of approaching footsteps filtered through the hazy combination of confusion and desire clouding his brain. Kae gasped, squared her shoulders, then grabbed his hand and pulled him closer to the pool. She pressed on his shoulders to make him sit on a large stone facing the pool, effectively hiding his arousal from any who approached. Smoothing her clothing, she sat beside him and faced the intrusion. He silently thanked the Guardians, his guide, and Kae's swift thoughts as he willed his breathing to calm and his rampant body to relax.

The breathing he managed.

"Kae?" Gowthaman's questioning voice preceded him into the clearing. "You barely returned. Why did you leave the li--oh."

"Look who's here." Bard wondered at how easily she spoke and how natural her voice sounded when her body quivered with strange tension. He wasn't sure he would be able to speak without vocalizing the want still evident in his body.

"Yes. I see. Kaelea, what did I--"

"Don't start with me, Gowthaman. Just don't even start."

There was meaning to her words that went beyond her simple denial of the Other's dislike of him. Bard felt the Other's gaze bore into his back so he angled the upper half of his body and gave the faerie a grin. "Good day, Gowthaman."

Gowthaman's eyes narrowed briefly. "Have you mastered the portals then?"

"Mastered? I do not believe so. However, I have been given leave to travel as I will, and as I am able. Permission granted by the leader of the Alastriona himself." Mentioning Derrik after the faerie had previously claimed to know ways to circumvent the Defenders would irritate the Other. By the way Gowthaman schooled his features, he had been correct in the assumption. "Derrik was kind to offer additional instruction."

Before Gowthaman could speak, Kaelea rose and stepped between them, her arms crossed over her chest. "Were you looking for me for any particular reason?"

"No... yes."

"Well, which is it?"

Gowthaman stared at her, his face expressing a rapid array of emotions. He looked about to speak, then turned and stomped away.

Kaelea faced Bard. "This is much too public a place. Come home with me?"

She held out her hand and Bard wrapped his fingers about hers, rose, and tugged her to his chest for a quick embrace.

Her smile brightened the world around him and lightened his worried heart. Her lips formed words he felt rather than heard. "I really am glad to see you."

T rying to choose a name to accurately portray his new identity took longer than Feidhlim anticipated. His last two identities had proclaimed him king, king of the elves. Elves, Gentry, Faerie--whatever mortals chose to call his race was of no consequence. But the accurate meaning of his new name would bring him added power.

He needed to inspire fear in the usurper's heart. A name to bring him victory.

"My lord?"

Feidhlim glanced up from the book of names and lifted his eyebrows. The slender faerie before him bowed slightly at the waist then stood waiting.

"Yes?"

"There is much news, my lord."

Feidhlim pushed the book away and leaned back in his chair, straining the hydraulics until the chair creaked in warning. He nodded for the faerie to continue.

"Despite the Alastriona's additional binding spells, we have been able to move the urn. The container now stands where we are able to increase the flow from the crack without detection. Soon, my lord, your magic shall be returned to you."

Satisfaction burned through Feidhlim. To once again feel power, to experience again the rush of control, of his true nature. Despite the desire to leap to his feet and dance, he nodded calmly. "Good. And what news of the ursurper?"

"Word of a happening, of a great thing, has come to us. Though Zeroun strives to hide this knowledge, keep the secret from us."

Useful fool. Feidhlim experienced a brief flash of loss. Torquil had been no fool, rather a faerie worthy to share in his plans and his glory. He would have given the news in sharp, concise statements, as befitted his lord's power. "Enough with the posturing. You do your job, and you do it well. What is this great thing?"

"The one who most recently joined the family--"

"Ah yes, the human dancer." Feidhlim's groin tightened. He'd not felt such desire for a human since Allyn. Unlike the witch, this one he'd had--and had taken the astounding power of her virginity. This one he still savored in the darkness of his imagination. He let the anticipation show on his face as he leaned forward. "What of her?"

"My lord, she is with child."

This was important news? That the Zeroun clan bore yet another brat to taunt him? He growled low in his throat and slumped back in the chair.

The faerie took an eager step forward. "Lord Feidhlim. She quickened *before* she joined the cursed family. She quick-ened..." He paused until Feidhlim growled again. "We have confirmed she quickened with your seed, my lord. She bears your child, none other. Think on the glory of your child, my lord. Your child."

Silent, Feidhlim watched the messenger until he shifted nervously. Outwardly calm, inside Feidhlim shook with the absurdity of it all. His child, to be born within a clan destined to be destroyed. His child.

Laughter burst from him. "By my powers," he forced out between the laughter. "This is wonderful news."

The messenger relaxed.

"Have her watched even more closely. I will know of anything, no matter how seemingly trivial, concerning my child. Am I understood?"

The faerie nodded.

"Double your efforts upon the urn. I will have the return of my power before the child is born. Then I shall time the power of my return, and take the child as well. The usurper shall experience the pain of witnessing his complete downfall before he and his clan are destroyed. Once and for all. Then I will return to my rightful place in Faerie. Go now, do as I proclaim."

Alone, Feidhlim chuckled, pulled the book before him and carefully turned a page. Yes, he needed a name worthy of his rightful place in Faerie. It must be a name to create fear in the hearts of the humans. A name filled with pride--a name he would share proudly with his son. For what else could the child be, but a son?

TEN

K ae tugged at the thick tapestry, trying to pull the weaving down to cover the doorway. She'd seldom sought the solitude and privacy indicated by the simply blocked entrance, so the ties holding the material were stiff and unresponsive. When she growled in frustration, Bard moved behind her and reached over her shoulder. Two sharp tugs loosened the rolled material and the thick weave covered the doorway.

Fanning away the resulting dust, Kae coughed and backed into the solid mass of Bard's body. She leaned heavily against him, hoping he would wrap his arms about her and they would continue what they'd begun at the pool.

He stroked the length of her hair and she was inordinately pleased she had worn it loose. But after the one caress, his touch was gone, as was his presence at her back. Slowly, she calmed the beating of her heart and turned.

Bard held a single, large sheet of parchment toward her. "A tracing of family history? Is this one of the histories Jayse says you search for?"

Kae nodded and sat in a hard-backed chair. "I wanted to recreate Korin's family history as a gift to Nanceen's and his first child."

She remained silent a moment while he sat and studied

the intricately drawn family tree. Then he smiled and took her hand. Kae returned the pressure of his fingers and spoke softly. "Oh, Bard. I've got to find something in my family's history to help eliminate the danger facing my brother. Facing all of us. I've got to."

The agony of the responsibility she'd taken upon herself echoed through Bard, bringing a rise of protectiveness. He would find some way to help. Cupping her cheek with his palm, Bard tilted his head to one side and gave her a tentative smile. "And so you shall. I believe, and if you doubt, I shall believe for you."

Kae gave a small, sarcastic chuckle laced with the sparkling tears hovering on her lower lashes. "You can't believe for me."

"Then I shall believe in you. And, if there is a way I can help--"

"I'll let you know. It might help now..." Dare she ask? "Help if you kissed me."

His deep, honest laugh made her smile. "Precious Kaelea, I fear that would be more of a distraction than a help. However..." Leaning closer, he claimed her lips with a kiss both gentle and demanding, a possession that lingered but was over far too soon.

When he eased back, Kae grasped the seat of her chair with white knuckled fingers. He lifted one eyebrow. "Did that help, Kaelea?"

"You were right," she gasped. "Very distracting." Then she dipped her head and glanced at him coyly through her lowered lashes. "I rather enjoy being distracted."

He opened his arms and wiggled a finger to invite her closer. She took a deep breath, moved to his lap and snuggled against the firm warmth of his body. The rise of his arousal pressed along her hip and twitched when she squirmed closer.

"A short distraction," he mumbled against her neck, knowing in his soul she would be nothing less than a lifelong distraction. The promise he'd made to the Guardians after he entered this world, the unthinking promise to form no lasting ties, had burst into a myriad of jumbled thoughts the moment he'd seen Kaelea at the oasis. The physical attraction and insistent needs of his body surprised him, and he knew that was why he had returned to the desert Sahara. The sleepless nights spent running to ease his pain had done nothing but increase the ache to be with her.

Bard trailed kisses along her neck to her soft, feminine jaw line, then back to her ear. "Distraction."

"Yes. Oh, I..."

Bard leaned to the side and looked into her face before exhaling a rough chuckle. "Don't speak while I'm distracting you." He crushed his mouth over hers, slanting the pressure first one way then another.

Her lips parted, inviting, tempting. For a fleeting moment he wondered how he had fallen so easily into the role of lover despite his easy vows to the Guardians... by the Seven... what she did to him. The press of her warm lips at his temple shot white-hot desire straight to his already straining erection. He tried to focus on something else. He hadn't been ripped from his world merely to love a woman. "Kaelea," he groaned. Had he?

"Umm, Bard. Don't stop distracting me. Please don't." She held his face between her palms and touched the tip of her nose to his. It was a simple gesture, yet one that touched more within him than he thought touchable.

"If it weren't for that desert mouse..." She kissed the tip of his nose, then rained swift, tiny kisses over his face.

"Kaelea, precious. Stop."

"I don't wanna." She continued her sensuous assault and he nearly surrendered and let her continue. It was pure agony to pull away, to span her waist with his hands and lift her from his lap. She wobbled and he held her until she gave a quizzical nod then collapsed back into her chair. "Bard?"

Resting his forearms on his thighs, he groaned at the sensations shooting along his erection, tightening the sack at its base. He shifted but the movement only increased the torment.

"You look like you could use a cold shower." At Kaelea's light statement, he jerked his gaze to her.

"As do you." Flushed with passionate excitement, her face glowed. Her lips were slightly swollen and she touched the fullness of her bottom lip with the tips of her fingers and sighed. He followed the rise and fall of her breathing, the strain of material over her breast, and the engorged tips poking against her clothing. What was he doing, stopping? He should finish this. A fever bright light grew in her eyes.

"I don't think a shower, cold or otherwise, would do any good."

"What about sharing the shower?"

By the Seven, the image shooting through his brain--why *had* he stopped?

"Why did you stop?" Her softly spoken question echoed his thoughts. "Did I do something wrong? Is there a prohibition?"

"I'm not sure. No and no." He smiled to ease the tension in the air. There was only one thing that would ease the tension in his body. But first, he had to slow the moment or he wouldn't be able to love her as he wished. Trying to cool the ardor, he reached for a second large sheet of parchment.

"Another genealogy?"

Kaelea took a few long, slow breaths and he ached to kiss away the confusion, to return the dreamy longing to her eyes, to make her his. To distract her, he spread his hand over a blank space. "Why is there nothing here?"

"Nothing?" Kaelea's gaze moved from him to slowly sweep across the page. "Oh, I haven't been able to discover any sources to explain what happened before that time."

Lifting her fingers, he kissed the soft pads at their tips. Unwilling to lose the tingling, he let his lips linger against her skin. "What time is that?"

"This genealogy is supposed to be for my sister." She swallowed heavily after he touched the tip of his tongue to her finger. "Korin's... umm... line stops here at the time just after the split between his kind and mine--the fairy and the gentry."

He moved his kiss to her inner wrist. "And..." His lips lingered then at the crease of her elbow.

"B--before that time our races existed together. In fact there was even a human playwright many, many years ago who wrote of the time when Gentry and fairy were ruled by one pair of rulers. Oberon and Titania--"

Startled by her use of names from a tale his mother had often told him, he stared at her and whispered, "I know the tale. I know of Shakespeare."

Laughter bubbled from Kae, a deeply sensual sound sending tremors coursing across his skin and flowing deep inside him. "So, the family got to you, huh? My brother's always been fascinated by *A Midsummer Night's Dream*."

Slowly, Bard shook his head. "None in your family mentioned Shakespeare."

"Then, how do you know?"

"Perhaps, I'll tell you later." He needed to sort through the references in this world to the playwright Shakespeare. Later. Now was the time to satisfy her sensual needs. And his own.

But, despite the flush covering her skin, Kae had warmed to her subject. "If the children of Titania and Oberon became the rulers of the different gentry clans, wouldn't it make sense that the one chosen to lead fairy would also be a child of the pair? Or, since there was the separation, perhaps this ruler was a child of only one. Despite what Korin's fairy text's say I'm not sure Puck wasn't the child of one of them. It's said that Oberon did not cherish fidelity, though he loved Titania to distraction."

The heat in his groin leaped at her use of the word. Distraction.

The last distraction had--

Kaelea took his hand, played with his fingers and lifted his hand to kiss the tips as he had done. "I wonder if Titania had lovers of her own. It would make sense, don't you think?"

His precious Kaelea had added the word lover to his distraction.

Thought processes stalled then fled completely when she stroked her hand along his arm to his shoulder. "Bard?"

"Yes, it's possible," he growled. He didn't care about other lovers, or who desired whom. Only that he desired her. He cast a quick glance out the window. The dish of the sun nestled on the horizon and soon dark would flood the desert. A breeze, cool with the coming night, curled through the opening and stirred the hair about his face. Instead of cooling his need, the caress urged him to capture her hand. "Kaelea?"

Silently, she stared into his face. It was all the encouragement he needed to follow her to her bedroom and lower the tapestry to cover the arched doorway.

Kae stood at the bedroom window, staring into the dusk. When the tapestry fell, she had reluctantly let go of Bard's hand and tried to put a bit of distance between them to calm her racing heart by lighting a few candles. She wanted time, a great deal of time, to experience the joy of Bard's body, but feared her current state of arousal would take them too far, too fast.

Silently, he moved behind her and stroked his hand from her shoulder to her elbow. "Kaelea?"

Besides the question in the speaking of her name, there was a bright note of fear. And the underlying rumble of barely controlled passion. She turned and leaned her hip against the wide window ledge.

No words were necessary, and she doubted she could have spoken anyway. She touched the backs of her fingers to his cheek, the feel of his heated skin chased tremors up her arm. This feeling, this delightful pain of desire was what she'd been thinking of, somewhere in her brain, even as she'd turned her outer thoughts to her research. This is what she'd been waiting for all those thirty-eight long days.

"It was a long month. I believe some destiny brought us to this moment." His words vibrated the fingers she'd rested against his lips and she gasped as what he said finally registered in her clouded mind.

"Destiny?" Kae gave a ragged chuckle.

"You do not believe in destiny?"

"No. I mean, yes. I mean... Oh, Bard. Stop talking." She stretched up on her toes, barely brushing her lips over his, until the contact wasn't enough and she wrapped her arms about his neck and kissed him with a voracious need. He held himself still for a few moments, then captured her face with the gentle cupping of his palms and returned the fervor, plundering her mouth with gentle ruthlessness.

She cried out in denial when he pulled away, but caught her lower lip between her teeth at the dazed expression of wonder on his face. He stared wide-eyed at her until heat rose to color her skin.

"By the Seven Guardians," he whispered, "this is what I've dreamed of."

"So... so you're saying dreams can come true?"

"Only if you let me give you pleasure, precious Kaelea. Only then."

"I want... nothing else, Bard."

"Then come."

She had no doubt of that. One more touch, one kiss like the one that just branded her lips, and she'd shatter like an exploding star.

Stepping carefully backwards, he drew her the short distance to the bed, then tugged her into a tight embrace, gifting her with the feel of the length of his hard body. He stroked a few stray hairs back from her face and looked down on her, his eyes so black she was lost in the sensuous void. When he finally kissed her, the darkness exploded, shattering her vision into prisms of blinding colors. She clung to him, arching her hips to his, the low, moaning rumble of her release vibrating through the joining of their mouths.

When the shuddering calmed, Bard ended the kiss and drew back, surprise filling his face. Kae cupped his cheek with a trembling hand. "You did say come."

A tiny frown turned down the corners of his lips, marring the potent kissability of his mouth. Bard's brows lowered. "I don't understand."

Trying to slow her breathing, Kae paused. Another word her aunt's spell couldn't translate. "The use of the word come?"

He nodded.

"Oh." This was embarrassing. "Sometimes that word is used... it means... well, when someone has..." She couldn't believe she was so flustered just trying to explain. Blowing out a long breath, she smoothed her fingers over the wrinkles in his brow and made the explanation in a rush. "It means to obtain a release. An orgasm."

"You are embarrassed?"

She ducked her head. "A little."

"So, it is allowable to 'come', but not to speak about the experience?"

"No... Yes..." Kae glanced at him and he grinned mischievously.

"So, precious one, will you always do as I say in these matters?"

Kae lifted her eyebrows to match the arch in his. "Depends. Will you also do what I say?"

"If it brings you pleasure." The impish expression faded and pure desire sparkled in his eyes. The response low in her body caught her by surprise, only a look and she was ready...

With slow, deliberate movements, Bard stripped her shirt from her. Just as slowly, he ran his hands over her bared skin. The heated pressure at the juncture of her thighs grew unbearable and she reached to undo the snap of her jeans. But Bard stopped her hands with one of his and shook his head at her confusion.

"Kaelea, lay upon your stomach for me. Please?"

Silently, he waited while she searched his face. On her stomach--a position of trust. She found nothing in his steady gaze to create even the merest glimmer of distrust or reason to fear. But before she gave him her back, she stroked her hands up his arms and over his chest.

Catching the neck edge of his loose vest in her fingers, she shoved the material from him so that the upper portion of his body was as bare as hers. Then she touched him as he had touched her, slow, lazy, a dancing of pressures over his skin. He let his head fall back, arching his neck, and she kissed the hollow just below the slight lump of his Adam's apple. The vibration of his response against her lips resounded through her.

She gave him a smile, inched from the heat of his body,

and lay face down on the bed. She curled her arms under a pillow, hugged it, and held her breath.

The mattress dipped, rolling her slightly to one side and against Bard's hard body when he stretched on his side beside her, hip to hip, to begin his soft, stroking exploration of her back.

Stretching and sighing, she arched to follow the path of his hand and he chuckled at her purring moans. His own breathing came harsh and heavy, stirring her hair where he'd pushed it to one side.

The sudden, hot, wet trail of his tongue down her spine made Kae jerk and give a breathy yelp. One of his large hands, splayed over her bottom, held her in place as he drew intricate patterns on her skin with his tongue, awakening her body to new, heady desires. She lifted her bottom against his palm but he held her steady, until, with a flick of his tongue at the narrowest curve of her spine, he slipped his hand between her legs to cup her denim clad mound.

"Bard, oh God."

"This is... okay?"

In answer she ground against the heel of his hand and cried out wordlessly. She crumpled the pillow and tossed her head from side to side. Using the side of one finger, he pressed hard against the denim seam just below the zipper, then groaned himself and eased her to her back.

Kaelea opened her arms to him but before he entered her embrace, he knelt and stripped the jeans from her, then stood and wiggled out of his cotton trousers. He settled into the cradle of her thighs, his belly pressed to hers, his chest cushioned on the softness of her breasts. Not wanting to restrict her breathing, he tried to ease up on his forearms, but she held him tight, raining hot, wet kisses along his jaw.

He twisted his head away then returned to crush her lips with his, nibbling, devouring, chasing her cries with the slick dance of his tongue.

His erection twitched, the swollen head unerring in its mindless search for her heat. She adjusted herself beneath him, stroked her hands restlessly over his back, then cupped his face to hold him still.

"Don't wait, Bard. Please... don't make me wait."

He wouldn't, couldn't--not much longer. But there was something yet needed, something he was compelled to do.

"Precious Kaelea." He kissed her deeply and rotated his hips, inching closer to their bodies' shared goal. Nearly mind-less with need, he broke the kiss and gazed down into her face. He could not join with her until... "Kaelea," he whispered harshly and waited until she lifted heavy lids and questions rose in her eyes. "Kaelea, my name... I must give you my name..."

"I know your name, Bard." She smiled and lifted her head to touch his lips with hers.

"No." Fiercely, Bard shook his head, twisting the length of his hair around her slender fingers. She didn't understand the power he offered her--the power of knowing his name and how he trusted her with that knowledge. He didn't under-stand why, but he could not love her without giving her that honor. "My name... William Bard... Stonefeather."

At the last syllable of his full name, he sank deep into the tight, welcoming heat of Kaelea's body and held himself still as her inner muscles clutched to draw him deeper.

Her soft, amazed sounds of delight spurred him to action. He withdrew all but the tip then eased back, deep into Kaelea's body. He watched her face and he increased the pace of his thrusts, adjusted the angle, played his fingers over her face and breasts. She was beauty in passion; he would willingly watch her like this for the rest of his life.

Hips pressing hers deep into the mattress, he froze. The harsh, throbbing realization that he loved her, loved her far beyond the pleasure she brought his body, tore through him. The flare of his despair blazed through his vision, momentarily clouding his sight. How could this have happened? He rested his forehead against Kaelea's and groaned, a deep sound, drawing pain from his soul.

Kae shuddered as Bard's groan seeped under her sensuous haze and registered. The sound was different than passion, making her think of pain when she didn't wish to think--only to feel. To increase the feelings, she planted her feet firmly against the mattress and lifted her hips against his still body. She found a rhythm and increased the already unbearable tension within her, branding her with a spiral of nearing release. Expanding. Encompassing her entire being.

She gasped and moaned, her hands splayed on Bard's sweat damp skin, encouraging him to join her urgent movements.

Finally, he lifted his head, returned to devour her mouth with desperate passion then angled up on his extended arms and matched her pace. She wrapped one calf over his tense, thrusting buttocks and, opening herself wider to him, encouraged a new, deeper angle of penetration.

Sounds of passion's music filled the room and Kae closed her eyes, letting her other senses fade until all became feeling, of him sliding, slick and hot within her, the dampness of his skin against hers, the burst of his harsh breath against her face.

Feeling exploded, the sudden shattering of the tension wrenching a sharp cry from her lips.

With a mighty groan, Bard held himself tight against her and shuddered violently. The intensity shot another wave of shattering release through her.

Bard lowered himself slowly to rest on her body and, welcoming the weight to keep the waves of her orgasm captured between them, Kae wrapped her arms about his shoulders. He touched his lips to the tip of her nose then angled their bodies so they could remain joined but more easily calm their ragged breathing.

An aftershock rippled through Kae and Bard gasped. She giggled and he gasped again. Then her breath caught as he expanded within her. With a wicked chuckle, Bard rolled to his back so she sprawled over him--and began again.

ELEVEN

B ard cradled Kae against his side, letting the night air cool their heated bodies. Sated, yet exhilarated, he was unable to relax. Perhaps now was the time to learn about her family. Perhaps it would relax them both so they could find sleep. He propped himself on one arm and smiled. "Tell me what you have discovered in your research this past month. I have learned some from your nephews and your brother, but I would understand more."

Giving him a lazy grin, she nodded and sat, pulling the light covering over her breasts. Disappointment flared through him and he moved to lean against the wall beside her. Her slight frown indicated this wasn't how she wanted to spend the time. She glanced at his lap--nor what he truly wanted if the bulge were any indication.

He lifted her chin with a crooked finger. "Later, precious scholar. I will not disappear." He touched her lips with the pad of his thumb and tried to let the reverence and promise he felt shine in his eyes. "Tell me of your family."

"L... long version, or short version?"

Delight sparkled through him. "A shortened tale would be welcome." He replaced his thumb with his mouth and kissed her softly. Then, using his finger, he angled her face and kissed her earlobe. "The very short version," he whispered.

The sooner she started her short--short history... Taking a deep breath, she held tightly to Bard's hand and began. "Before my brother Jaye was born, the queen had named a high-born faerie of her realm as successor. Then, she changed her decree and named Jayezer. Needless to say, Fiedhlim wasn't happy. He began a crusade to banish any taint of human blood from Faerie, and like me, Jaye is half-human. So, Da and Mother sent Jaye to the human world when he was just a baby. It wasn't until he was an adult, and a successful businessman, that he discovered his Fey heritage. That's the time when Nanceen and I were born, too."

She glanced at Bard. A smile relaxed his lips and he stroked the back of his fingers over her cheek. "A blessed day, precious scholar."

Heat rose in her face but she couldn't tear her gaze from Bard's. Ignoring the goosebumps dancing across her skin and the puckering of her nipples, she continued. "Even though Jaye didn't want to believe he had Fey blood, he came to the Otherworld when Fiedhlim kidnapped Allyn and captured my family. Fiedhlim tried to send Nance and I through time portals to God knows where. We were only babies, Bard. We would have died."

He squeezed her hand. "I have heard the tale of how the black canine, Noid, saved you."

"Yeah, somehow Fiedhlim's magic didn't affect him and Noid forced the bastard through one of the portals he'd created for us. The family thought that was the last of him-- until Lara went back in time."

"To the place when she found Iain?"

"And a wandering storyteller named Aubrian. Who was really Fiedhlim. He tried to use her to get back to this time. It took all the power Jaye and Derrik had, augmented by magic Iain didn't know he possessed, to capture Fiedhlim. Iain's half-faerie, you know."

"I did not. Is this one of the histories you search for?"

Kae nodded. "Like the one I'm doing for Nance and Korin, I wanted to recreate his family history as a gift to their new child."

"A gift to treasure." A wistful look passed over Bard's face. "There is much comfort in understanding your past and the family you belong to. I wish... never mind. Now is the time for your tale, not mine. Please, go on."

Kae set her curiosity and questions aside. Eventually she would discover what made him so sad when he spoke of family. Maybe he missed them terribly since he transported to this world. A frightening thought flashed into existence. Did he have a mate in his world? Was this who he missed and why he was so sad? They'd just made love. Did she have the right to desire him if he had another?

A tightening of his fingers around hers brought her wandering thoughts speeding back. "There is no one who waits for me, Kaelea."

It was as if he'd read her thoughts.

He tucked her more securely against his side. "With the exception of cousins who care not if I live or die, I have been alone since my mother's death. I am a bit of a... pariah among my people. I doubt there are few who have even noticed my disappearance."

"I can't believe that." How could they not miss him?

The soft pressure of his lips on her hair was comforting. "I speak truth, precious Kaelea. Yet, I would find the way to return. But, we were not speaking of my life."

She remained silent a moment then spoke softly. "The queen stripped Feidhlim's power and made him mortal--one of the humans he hated so fervently. Then he was banished. We'd thought to some other time, but he still had followers, and somehow they thwarted the Alastriona's plans. Feidhlim ended up in the here and now of the human world. He took the name Titus Avery and tried to destroy Jaye's business. He was also behind Tommy's kidnapping and of course you know what he did to Carrie."

Bard's fingers fisted and tensed on her thigh. Turning her head, she stared as anger burned in his eyes.

"How could a man use a woman so? I don't understand."

"For power more than anything else. Power and control-- the two things Feidhlim seeks to have returned to him. He's very dangerous. I'm still amazed that what seems to have been a random assault--he'd attacked other dancers, too--has such a deep effect on my family."

"No one knows where this monster is?"

"No. The Alastriona continually search for him, but his followers have been able to block their attempts. Human law enforcement is also looking for him because of the rapes and kidnapping. They haven't had any luck either. Oh, Bard. He's gonna show up when we least expect it. I just know it." She leaned forward and covered her face with her hands.

He inched her closer, trying to offer comfort, protection. Love.

Her shoulders shook but she made no sound as she wept. Finally she drew in a long, shuddering breath, lifted her head and stared toward the doorway.

"Oh, look!"

Confused, Bard followed the motion of Kaelea's outstretched arm and pointing finger. Just inside the lowered tapestry, a tiny desert creature preened, unconcerned by their presence. One tiny paw moved over its head and the candle-light caught the white spot centered between its alertly held ears. "Bard, I think that's the same animal I took from the library. The one that alerted us to Gowthaman's coming to the oasis."

He closed his eyes. And the guide sent to him by the Guardians. "Kaelea, I know this animal. It is a guide to me. This one led me from the desert when I first found myself in this world. I have seen it many times since then, usually when I am searching for answers. When I don't understand. I believe the guide was sent to me by the Guardians."

Kaelea nodded. "And now, twice it brought us together at the pool. I think that's important. How about you?" She leaned against him, her arm brushing his side, her hand resting upon his upper thigh.

Before he could react to her innocent touch, a low, rumbling noise startled the guide and it ducked under the tapestry. Kaelea chuckled and rubbed her belly. Bard followed the movement avidly then swallowed past the dry lump in his throat.

The noise sounded again. "I missed breakfast this morning and now it's past nightfall. Guess I must be hungry. How about something to eat?"

A sensuous menu filled his mind, the need to taste her again nearly overpowering any need for other sustenance. Acting on the thought became impossible, however, for Kaelea rose and started toward the kitchen. "I don't have much but some fruit and cheese."

"It will do. Shall I come to the table?"

Flashes of making love on the table, scattering books and papers, burst into her mind at his innocent question. Then she caught his grin and the wicked glint in his dark eyes. She pressed his chest to hold him in place. "No, don't. I'll bring the food back here. We can have a picnic in bed."

Kaelea chucked softly at Bard's soft denial when she drew her hand across his groin and left the bedroom. Leaning on the tiny, stone-topped kitchen counter, she took several long, slow, deep breaths. Her legs shook with the effort of holding her upright, her insides still churned with desire and a longing she'd never experienced. Oh, what the man did to her.

She shook her head. Maybe it was just that she'd thought so much about him in the past month she'd built her desire for Bard way out of proportion. With automatic actions she piled a platter high, filled a flagon with juice, and returned to the bedroom.

Bard stared at the doorway as if he hadn't moved his gaze in the time she'd been gone. After setting her burdens at one end of the bed, Kae crawled across the resilient surface to his side.

His brows lowered over his dark eyes and a thoughtful expression tightened his lips. "Was there any significant event during the time you spoke of earlier? At the time when there is no information for your family histories?"

Kae hugged herself and shivered at the intensity in his expression.

He relaxed and smiled in response. A smile full of promise. She licked at the sudden dryness of her lower lip and he straightened, gaze intent on her mouth. Even as she leaned forward, the logical part of her mind screamed for her to stop. But, she could no more ignore the call of her body than give up breathing.

With only a gently brushing of their lips, Bard kissed her then angled back. The promise in his smile deepened, merging with the heat building deep within her. Again.

"A significance?" he repeated.

Kae blinked. Significance? To the kiss? Of course there was. Didn't he feel it?

With a loose shrug, he rotated his shoulders. "To the time when there is no more history?"

Oh, that's what he meant. Heat burned in her face and moved down her bare chest. Her hand trembled and she reached for a glass. He took the tumbler from her, poured the juice, and handed the cool liquid to her. Then he layered cheese on a round of flatbread and placed it on a napkin on the bed before her.

"You have expended much energy. Eat. It will revive you and make your thoughts clearer."

She doubted that, not as long as he sat close enough their thighs touched and he bumped her arm with his. Not as long as he was in the same room, or the same desert, or even in the same world.

Kae closed her eyes, hearing an echo of the words she'd said to her sister not that long ago when they sat at Korin's bedside, 'You've got it bad'.

And she did. From the musky scent rising from Bard and the hitch in his breathing each time they touched, she expected he did, too.

He set his bread aside and angled slightly to face her. "Tell me about this time when there is no history. In my world there is also a period such as this, a time before it seemed my people simply appeared in our world." He fell silent and pensive, an odd look settling upon his face.

"What is it?"

"What? Nothing, precious one." He smiled and the

unusual seriousness was gone. "Tell me more of your family's history."

Kae moved the platter and flagon to the floor and cuddled to his side. "You've met Korin?"

"Yes, your sister's mate."

"I've been trying to chart his family history as well. You know he's a fairy." Expecting confusion she waited, but Bard nodded.

"The differences between your Faerie world and his have been explained to me."

The rise of painful jealousy hovered as a thick lump in her throat. Everyone in the family seemed to have talked to him over the past month. Everyone but her. Why hadn't he come back to her sooner? *Sure, like I'd go visit someone who ranted and raved like a madwoman before turning her back.*

"Kaelea?" He took her hand. "I've spoken with many in your family in my quest to master the magic of the portals. I've gathered bits of information from each. Now, I've returned to you to tie these tales together. Will you do that for me?"

How could she resist such a plea? She couldn't--not any more than she could resist the man himself. Using one finger, she drew a circle on the covers bunched at her side. "So much seems to revolve around the time of the split between the Fey such as I am--"

"As Korin calls the gentry?"

"Yep, that's right. Between the gentry and the other fairy folk--like Korin and his kind."

Bard's dark brows lowered over his eyes. "Though I've been told there are differences, he seems no different than you."

"He chose to remain this size. But, when Nance first met him, he was hardly bigger than her hand. And he had wings. Beautiful blue and silver butterfly wings. Lara's kids still call him b'fly man."

"He has no wings now."

"No, they were damaged when he was attacked while going through a portal."

His brows lowered further and he scowled. "I was lead to believe there is minimal danger."

"Somehow, a creature was loosed there by Korin's king just to destroy Korin. Later, when the Bocan escaped the portal, it was destroyed by Derrik's cousin, Searlait."

"Yes, the woman he asked me to watch for."

"She was banished to a place between worlds as punishment for killing another faerie--even though he was in league with Feidhlim. Now, somehow, she's able to watch over the family and has helped us in a number of dangerous situations."

"Like a guardian angel, as the boy David names her."

"Yeah, sorta like that."

Bard shook his head and a few strands of hair fell over his forehead. If only just to touch him, Kae longed to brush back the soft hairs.

Before she acted on her desire, he shook his head again. "Even with a simple telling, the stories of your family make a complicated tale."

"I suppose they do. I'll give you a quick rundown of what else I'm looking into." Quick, yes--for she wanted to make love with him again. "Like I said, it looks like much of what I need to discover hinges upon the time when there was the split between gentry and fairy. It was then that the different gentry clans set up autonomous rules. And the tribes of the fairy folk passed into myth, even to the gentry. It took Korin's loving my sister to reunite the two worlds.

"And gave me lots of new information, new scrolls, new stories to study."

Before she finished speaking, Bard eased her to her back and wrapped one long leg over hers, pressing the evidence of his need against her side and said, "I have learned enough, for now."

. . .

The deep velvet night cooled the sweat from his body. Kaelea curled against him, sated and murmuring sleepily. Bard stroked his hand languorously along her back until she quieted and slept. Still he touched her, the hours spent memorizing her body and learning her reactions were still not enough.

His skin thrummed, vibrating like the tight skinhead on a drum.

And despite the many times Kaelea's body had drained satisfaction from him, he was still drawn as tight as that drum. Physically exhausted, he tucked Kaelea closer to his side and tried to ignore the not so subtle questions denying him the peace of sleep.

For over a month he'd avoided the needs of his body, the desires running rampant through him whenever he thought of Kaelea. Desires far surpassing what he'd believed the most important need in his life--to return to his own world.

Easing from the temptation of Kaelea's body, he turned to his back and scrubbed his hands over his face and into his hair. He lay with his elbows pointed toward the ceiling and attempted clearing his mind.

Thirty-eight days full of questions--or rather, he admitted to himself--more than a month of the same questions, had led him no closer to answers than when he had first appeared in this world, naked and drenched with sand. He covered his eyes with his forearm. Now, even more questions tumbled through his mind, all beginning with the single word why.

Why was he brought here, when answers could have been shown him in his own world? More specifically, why here? Why this desert, this oasis, these people?

These people. This family helped him, took pride in his accomplishments, and encouraged him, when his own family cared so little. A flicker of anger corrected his thought. His family didn't even care a little for him--since his father's death they cared nothing.

Alone, he had cared for his mother in her last days, and alone, had sent her spirit to the Seven Guardians. Alone, he had struggled to find his way in a world where the family unit was stronger even than the minimal governments and their attempts at lawmaking. A world slow to forgive differences and so had remained turned from him because of his grandmother's claims of coming from another place.

His lips twisted in a grimace. While a young boy, he'd loved her stories. But when others had begun to tease him for his strange name, he had turned from her as well--at least when the other boys were near.

The tightness in his expression faded. Grandmother had been understanding, even reproving his mother when she called him to task over his behavior. Now, when she was gone, he realized what an amazing woman she had been, and hoped his prayer for forgiveness somehow traversed the space between the worlds of life and death.

A soft noise at his side made him turn his head and open his eyes. He smiled at the satisfaction on Kaelea's soft, pouty lips, the sensual tangle of her hair on the pillow. She still slept so he returned to the darkness of his thoughts.

Here, in this world, he'd experienced the acceptance he'd given up hope of finding when barely past the ceremonies of manhood.

Here, in this world, he found a family who cared for him, was concerned for his well being, even requested and listened to his opinions. But, this wasn't *his* family. Here, in this world, he could return the caring and concern, using the skills he'd honed on his world, to discover the man who strove to destroy his friends.

His friends. Yes, friends are what he'd found in this world. Not those who only wished to befriend him until their own goals were achieved, or those who used a supposed friendship to belittle another. These friendships asked nothing in return.

With a start, Bard realized, the less asked of him, the more he wished to give. There was much he could give to Kaelea's family. To Kaelea, if she would allow him.

He turned carefully to his side and leaned on one arm to watch her. The covers, once pulled up under her chin, had slipped to the full curve of her breasts, barely hiding the darker circles of her nipples. He leaned his head against his fist and simply looked at her.

Here, in this world, he'd found a reason for the passion burning deep within him. Kaelea.

The sheet slipped further, exposing her nipples to the cool night air and his avid gaze. They puckered and grew firm. The breath died in his throat. The sheet inched lower until the creamy skin of her breasts was fully exposed to him. He couldn't swallow past the lump caused by lack of breath.

"Like what you see?"

He snapped his gaze to Kaelea's face and she gifted him with a sultry smile. "Well?"

In answer he buried his face in the valley between her breasts, then ran light kisses over the fullness and took a nipple deep into his mouth, swirling his tongue over the tip. She arched to his mouth and he sucked firmly.

"I... I'll take that, oh... as a yes."

"Yes," he mumbled, barely lifting his mouth from her body.

Pleasure burst through Kae and she expressed her delight with soft moans and by tangling her fingers through the coarse silk of his hair.

He kissed, laved, stroked and encouraged. Kae nearly forgot the plan she'd formed when she woke to discover him staring at her. Until the hot length of his growing arousal pressed against her thigh.

Gently, she encouraged him to lift his head from her breasts. The loss of heat and sensation brought a whimper from deep in her throat and Bard bent back to his task. But she held his face between her palms and when he lifted his confused gaze to her, she shook her head. "My turn now. I just want to look at you."

His eyebrows rose and delight twinkled in his dark eyes. "If that is what you truly wish."

With a slow nod, she released his face and he rolled to his back with his fingers interlaced behind his head. She mimicked his earlier pose and lay on her side, head propped against her fist. She started at his face and caressed him with her gaze. He held his breath when she lingered at the fullness of his mouth. She loved his firm, amazing lips, and what they did to her.

Her gaze inched lower, past his square chin, over the bobbing lump of his Adam's apple, to the broad expanse of his chest. His nipples puckered to tight nubs and she licked her lips.

There was another, stronger hitch in his breathing. Kae delighted in a surge of power. She was doing this to his body, doing this with nothing but her eyes. She couldn't wait to touch him. But, not quite yet.

The ridges of his abdomen quivered and her gaze slipped over them to pause at his navel. An outie. She grinned.

"Precious Kaelea, please. No more. Let me--" He held out his arms, reaching for her.

"No. This is my time, William Bard Stonefeather."

His arms fell loose to his sides, then he supported his upper body with them and gave her a look so serious, she paused. Time froze and they simply stared into each other's eyes. There was some special meaning for him when she used his full name, something she only marginally understood. She did realize, however, how important it had been for him to give her his name before he gave her his body. At that time, she hadn't thought much about the importance, hadn't really thought at all. Only experienced what he gave her along with his name.

He gave a short nod and the spell was broken. But not the spell of her need of him, for him, to him. She turned her gaze back to his body, to the soft nest of hair at his groin. He watched her avidly, so she tossed her head to hide her grin behind the curtain of her hair.

Now that was definitely an outie. Soon to be an innie as well. Kae bit back a chuckle. But first...

"Like... like what you see?" The harshness of his voice told her he also liked what she saw. Would he like what she planned?

In a swift, graceful movement, she angled next to him,

wrapped her fingers around the base of his erection, and took the swollen tip into her mouth.

Bard collapsed onto the bed with a wordless cry. His hips jerked, and she took more of him, lowering her mouth as she stroked upward with her hand. With each jerk of his body she repeated the action, swirling her tongue, then blowing her delighted sighs over him.

Peeking over his side, she grinned at the way he'd crushed the bedding in his fist. She moaned low in her throat when his other hand cupped the back of her head and the rhythmic caress of his fingers directed her movements. Breathless, she lifted her head, rubbed her cheek against his velvety skin, and cast him a crooked smile.

"Kaelea," he croaked, using gentle pressure to draw her up his body. "Precious one, come."

"If you insist."

TWELVE

Sated exhaustion finally drove Bard to the arms of sleep. But as physically tired as his body was, his mind churned, actively, directing his dreams. Visions of his home, the pinkish-orange sky streaked with high clouds, the rocky landscape dotted with twisted trees and scrubby plant life, flashed through his dreams. Favorite places, the few places he'd found comfort and solitude crowded his mind.

Restless, he woke for a moment and smiled when Kae snuggled closer to his back, and draped her arm over his stomach. He tucked his arm over hers and returned to the dreams.

His world turned gray, indistinct, bleak. He stood in the center of a broad plain, surrounded by ranges of tall, craggy mountains. Turning in a slow circle, he surveyed his world, his entire world, spread out like a map before him. His dream self waited for the pull, the feeling deep in his chest, the contentment of home.

Echoes reverberated in his chest, now a hollow container with only the beating of his heart, empty of any feeling.

The dream refocused, his attention drawn to a single point partway up a mountainside. There he looked down onto a pile of tiny, tear shaped stones. The black, glass-like stones shimmered in the pale light cast by an opening faerie portal. Though he strained to see, there was nothing beyond the pulsing oval, no destination, no new place to discover. He reached out one hand, felt the tingle of magic--then nothing.

Struggling to draw breath past the panic squeezing his throat, Bard jerked awake and stared into the darkness. Kae shifted then her hand touched his cheek. "Jus' a dream. Sleep, darlin'."

She rolled so her back warmed him, her breathing soft and steady.

Bard eased from her warmth and rubbed his eyes. Even in her sleep, she tried to comfort him. But he found no comfort, for the dream images continued to swirl through his waking mind. He followed the swirls, tracing the spirals of meaning he knew must be hidden there. This dream could only have come from the Guardians, a dream for him to decipher, to under-stand. A dream to guide his future.

What future? One in his own world or had he discovered his place here, in the world he now believed to be his beloved grandmother's? He didn't know. He couldn't think. Not here, not with the temptation of Kaelea so close. Not with his love for her clouding any thoughts.

He loved her. The initial insight had surprised him, shocking him to stillness while buried deep within her body. The truth of his feelings did not. Now he would consider her in any decision he made.

What was the correct decision for him, for them--to continue his search for a way back to his world or remain here?

Bard moved to the edge of the bed and sat, leaning forward with his head in his hands. The decision should be simple and uncomplicated. No love waited for him in his world, and now that he loved Kaelea and believed she loved him in return, he would not be able to ignore the lack. Yet, such was his world, and this place was not.

Both sides of his dilemma clamored for prominence. He couldn't reason with himself. He had to leave. He closed his eyes and a series of pictures formed, pictures he had seen in a book. The southwestern states were similar to his world. Perhaps there he could find refuge from the confusion.

Having made a nominal decision made it no easier to act.

Bard stood in the shadows at the foot of Kaelea's bed--
watching the way her even breathing lifted the sheet covering
her chest. The way her hair spread over the pillow, seeming to
reach for the place where he had lain. The way her lips pouted
then curved in a soft smile so full of sensuous promise, he
nearly crawled back to her side and began yet again. The way
the rising sun speared dancing shafts of light through the
room, highlighting that smile.

He shouldn't leave without explaining his decision to her,
but knew if he tried, he would never leave. It would take only
one smile to hold him there at her side. Then he would always
wonder. If he didn't leave now to discover answers, he would
always wonder if she loved him or only took pleasure
with him.

Finally, steeling himself against the want of her, Bard
backed from the room, then from the small dwelling, silently
lowering the door coverings. He paused, lifted his hand to the
smooth curve of the opening and bent his head, beseeching
the Guardians to watch over her. If love had power, she would
be well protected.

Understanding how he could come to love a woman so
completely was easy, for he had witnessed and benefited from
that kind of love between his grandparents. How he could love
a woman of a world different from his own was not so difficult
either, for his grandfather had loved the strange woman who
said she came from this same world. He lifted his head and
turned from the house. The Guardians brought the Stonefeather family and this world together--again, but he could
find no reason, no purpose to his being placed in the desert
Sahara. He paused, glanced back, then formed a portal and
stepped through.

Derrik would track his path, for that was the duty of the
Defenders of Mankind. But, he needed solitude, so made two
additional portals, moving quickly from one place to another,
hoping, not to confuse or unnecessarily alert the Alastriona,
but to give notice of his desire to remain alone. As he formed
the third portal, he held his breath. He had never actually been
to this place, but had seen a glorious picture in a book at

Jaysson's home. This place called to him, a place where he knew, at one time, searchers such as he had always gone. A place of long ago, a place of beginnings.

The remorse filling Gowthaman pressed him to his knees in the dank, dim recesses of the oldest section of the library. He hung his head and bent forward until his forehead nearly touched his knees.

Wrapping his arms over his head, he rocked, the motion, once a comfort, kept him from crying out his pain. He'd been foolish, forcing his attention upon Kaelea. He leaned back, stretching his neck until he stared at the high ceiling. He didn't see the ornately carved corbels, nor the intricate mosaics. He saw Kaelea's eyes. The horror on her face. The fear rising in her expression. Each long day she stayed away from the library, from him, had been the same. Yet the darker sections of the library brought him no comfort.

He didn't mean for her to fear him, only to notice him as more than someone to fetch books for her. Scrubbing his hands over his face, he closed his eyes in defeat. Deep within his heart of hearts, was no true belief that she would ever love him as more than a friend. His insane pride made him act the fool. The attacker.

"Aiiiyeee," he wailed softly. He had assaulted her, and in doing so, destroyed the friendship they already had.

He slumped forward again. And now, before he could face her and apologize, the stranger had returned. A twitch at one side of his lips brought a small, sad grin. In following Kae to the oasis, he'd hoped to offer an apology she would accept. Now he knew, he understood, another held her heart in the way he had wished to experience.

Another had earned her love. Without effort. Without force.

Gowthaman pressed his fingertips against his eyes. Beautiful, as she was beautiful, an image of the aura surrounding her when the stranger touched her hovered behind his closed eyelids. He could not fight the soulfire, for the faint aura filled with twinkling amethyst proved to be a visible beacon to those who would see. Kaelea had discovered the mate of her soul.

But, Gowthaman thought with a rise of determination as he stood, he could still be her friend. If she would allow grant him the honor.

Slow, deliberate steps took him from the library and into the desert. Night was far gone, and soon heat would rise before the sun. Mayhaps with the new day, Kaelea would look upon him, not with fear, but with forgiveness and understanding.

He turned back toward the living quarters, but paused when still distant from her small house. The tapestry had been lowered, blocking the entrance, indicating a desire for privacy. From the flare of soulfire he'd seen at the oasis, with those private moments there would be much desire. Desire in which he had no part.

Except for chasing her into the stranger's arms.

"No," he said aloud to the fading stars. "She would still find his arms. Soulfire does not show false attraction."

A scrabbling in the sand made him drop his gaze. A small, brittle bush, barely close enough to the oasis to find sufficient water for life, rustled. A tiny creature climbed through the stiff branches and stopped to peer at him with black, sparkling eyes. The desert rodent lifted a front paw and touched the white spot between its ears.

Surprised, a genuine grin filled Gowthaman's face. He bowed and touched his forehead in return. "Greetings, little one."

The animal chattered at him, a high-pitched song that made him feel he should understand. Gowthaman shook his head. Imaginative foolishness. The chittering grew louder, harsher, as if the animal chided him for not listening. He chuckled. "I beg your pardon, but I do not understand what it is you try to tell me."

The creature paused in its tirade, fluffed out its fur, then shook itself and leaped from the bush to run a zigzagging pattern across the sand. Gowthaman followed the path toward Kaelea's dwelling with an interested gaze, then lowered his brows in confusion at the sight before him.

The stranger--no, he would use the man's name. Bard backed from Kaelea's dwelling, silently returning the tapestry to the lowered position. His actions seemed stealthy and out of place. Deep sadness etched lines in Bard's face, and even with the faint light of nearing sunrise, Gowthaman recognized pain and defeat in the tall man's shoulders. A faint hope blossomed. Had Kaelea turned him away?

Bard bowed his head and rested one palm against the doorframe.

Gowthaman cocked his head to one side and let the false hope die a peaceful death. There was some reason Bard left in the still of the morning, an unknown reason but painful in evidence.

While Gowthaman pondered what to do, Bard turned and strode a few paces from the building. After a long look at the bedroom window, he formed a portal and disappeared.

Slowly, Gowthaman lowered his raised brows. He felt a voyeur, yet the feeling he was meant to see Bard leaving hovered stronger, purpose wiping away the discomfort. Without considering the possible consequences of his action he drew on a long hidden talent and mentally touched the remnants of the dissipated portal. With his mind's eye, he followed Bard through three rapid transitions and frowned in confusion at the man's final destination. Then he filed the knowledge away and turned back to the library, whispering words to hide his mental presence from those who guarded the portals.

Long ago he'd discovered the talent within him, but had never wished to become Alastriona. If the Defenders had discovered the skill, and perhaps other of his well-hidden magicks, he would never have been allowed to retain his guardianship of the library.

The library... The love of his heart that would never forsake him.

He took a deep breath and paused at the rusty iron gate. Mayhaps he could once again gain Kae's trust through the books they both cherished. Sad determination took him past the main library to an inner room housing manuscripts and scrolls so ancient he believed they may have been written at the formation of the world. He would find something there, and give the knowledge to Kaelea. If she forgave him for his thoughtless passion, then they would be friends. If not... He refused to think on that possibility.

W aking with a yawn that turned easily to a smile, Kae snuggled deep into the messy bed and pulled a light cover up under her chin. Her body ached of pleasure and completion, and she yawned again. This would be a good day to stay in bed. But not alone. And not for sleep.

The room was too silent, so she turned on her side to face the empty side of the bed. Trying to straighten the wrinkles, she smoothed her hand over the sheet. The cotton felt cool to her palm and she wondered how long ago Bard had risen. And when he would return.

Rainbows of satisfaction pulsed through her mind, remnants of the joy he'd given unselfishly. Her lips twitched at the memory of his surprise and surrender when she'd taken the length of him into her mouth, loving the response of the velvety steel to her kisses. Later, much later, he'd whispered his awe to her, and admitted her intimate kiss was not a form of lovemaking in his world. She'd giggled and offered her condolences to those who missed so much.

Now, with the tingle of memory pouting her lips, she wondered again where he was hiding. No sounds came from the other rooms, and only the morning breeze scratching across the sand came from the exterior of her home. If he didn't return to bed soon, she would be forced to find him. Maybe she'd deny him kisses for leaving her alone for so long.

A long sigh ended in a full body stretch that rubbed her body deliciously against the bedding. Or maybe she wouldn't.

She rose and tugged a silk caftan over her head. The material caressed her sensitized skin, but the feeling was nothing compared to the many ways Bard had touched her. At times reverence and adoration filled his caress. At others, nothing but pure, blatant passion exploded between them. She tried to choose between the two delightful feelings, but could not, loving any touch of his skin against hers.

The tapestry over the outer door was still lowered, but the inside of her home felt cold and strangely empty. She stepped outside and faced the rising sun. Nearly the entire ball hovered above the horizon, and heat waves rose from the sand to chase the chill of the desert night. She turned in a slow circle to scan the immediate area. No tall, broad-shouldered man. In fact, there was absolutely no activity. Ah, it was still early, so perhaps the other scholars were asleep. That suited her, for she wanted Bard to herself. For a long, long time.

An odd sense of discomfort made her frown. Where was he? She glanced toward the oasis. He might have gone to the pool without her. A grin replaced the frown. Maybe he needed refreshing before... Kae trotted barefoot across the warm sand, but slowed to a casual pace when she entered the shade of the trees surrounding the pool. If he was relaxing in the pool, she didn't wish to startle him--until she joined him.

No sounds of splashing came from the pool, and only the soft tinkle of water upon the stone filled the oasis. Concerned, Kae pushed through the undergrowth and froze. The small clearing and the pool were empty.

The frantic thought he had gone twined into her mind. He couldn't have left. Wouldn't have disappeared without telling her. Not after the night and all they'd shared. He couldn't-- wouldn't. He promised.

She whirled in a circle, stubbed her toe and sobbed. Not in physical pain, though her toe throbbed and sent sharp jolts of burning agony up her leg. However, the pain in her chest, deep in her heart, soon became physical. She ran, blindly stumbling in her haste.

Scenarios flashed through her mind, sudden panicked thoughts she fought to ignore. She'd missed him somehow. He'd left the oasis by a different path. Or he'd wandered into

the sands and had been hidden behind a dune. He'd returned
and was undoubtedly wondering where she'd gone.

Oh, she'd give him a piece of her mind for frightening her.
Then, she'd forgive him and keep him in her bed for a long,
long time. Holding thoughts of the delights of his body at the
front of her brain, she swept the tapestry to one side, leaped
through her door, and skidded to a stop on the stone floor.

If possible, the house was quieter than when she'd rushed
away.

Immobile, she strained to hear any sound, any indication
of Bard's presence. *Bard?*

Nothing. Not even the breeze answered her silent call. She
collapsed to a chair. Not even the wind. She called upon her
fey skills, the magic she seldom used, and expanded her senses
as Derrik taught her long ago. There, the barest hint of faint
electricity left behind by a faerie portal. Kae kept her gaze at
the doorway, staring past the rapidly disintegrating remnants
of the portal's power.

"Where are you? Why did you go? You promised you
wouldn't disappear. You... you told me your name," she
sobbed. How could he do that then disappear?

Resolutely, she straightened. She could go to Derrik, ask
the Alastriona to track his movements through the portal.
Then she would follow Bard and find the answers to her whys.

Despair forced her to close her eyes. What was she thinking? She wasn't one who ever went chasing after another. If
Bard wanted her to know where he was, he would have told
her. Maybe, despite his words, he only used her to ease his
physical discomfort. Despite the pain welling fresh and sharp
within her, a teary smile eased her lips from a quivering pout.
He'd eased her longing, too. And if he truly meant to leave her
alone, at least she would have the memories, for she couldn't
imagine anyone else taking his place. Not in her bed. Not in
her heart. Not now. Not ever.

Fuzzy and dulled, she let her thoughts fade to incoherent
bits she released to float away. As if her mind no longer
directed her body, she made sure the tapestry covered the door
and returned to her bedroom. She sprawled on the bed, pulled

the cover over her head, and curled around a plump pillow. Dry-eyed, she stared straight ahead, recognizing nothing, not caring if she ever saw anything again.

A fter his first transfer to the place of dreamers, Bard realized his clothing, while comfortable in the Faerie Otherworld, was not now practical. He wished for his breechclout, leggings, and a soft buckskin shirt, but instead visited the faerie clothiers and was satisfied with worn denim jeans and a soft shirt of a similar lightweight material.

The clothiers also offered him currency from a small coffer, insisting the money was provided to those who wished to visit the mortal world where such things were important.

The first day he'd visited a place where those called Native Americans lived. Reservation was a cold word for a dismal place, yet he felt a comfortable familiarity that went far beyond the similar landscape of his home.

As he wandered apart from a small busload of tourists examining the cluster of square block buildings, the residents watched him with a mixture of curiosity and startled recognition. Soft whispers followed his path, much like the children who hid each time he turned. Bard grinned. He'd often played hiding games as a child and remembered his pride the first time he touched his grandfather's arm without the older man recognizing his presence.

Lost in the memories, he didn't notice the sudden silence until a small body leaped beside him, slapped his elbow, then dashed away shouting, "*Khuda*--got him. *Khuda*."

Hands fisted at his hips, Bard watched the gamboling children, then joined in the laughter of the others visiting the village. A chant of children's voices rose from the far end of the short road between the buildings. Bard's laughter died and he furrowed his brow. He knew this chant, although the words rang with a slight difference. The chant whirled through his mind. Occasional syllables, spoken in a deeper, whispered tone, rumbled from his throat.

Trying to shake away the discomfort of knowing, Bard

turned away and returned to the area designated as the place for tourists. Confusion battled the questions already crowding his mind. So much of this world, this place reminded him of his own. He glanced into the cloudless sky. Change the color and there would be no noticeable difference. How did he recognize chants and games here? How did he know, when he'd never...?

Another mystery to ponder with another answer to discover.

Intending to leave the village, he paused, his attention captured by a shaded stall dominated by a wild profusion of colorful blankets. He moved closer and studied the weaving, drawn to a zigzag pattern much like the design on the blanket of his father's fathers. For the first time in many weeks, he thought of the blanket, his only connection to his home. He'd left the blanket folded in a corner of Kaelea's bedroom when she first gave him clothing and took him to the Otherworld. Did she still have the ancient piece of cloth?

Cold settled over him and he rubbed his palm over his arm. She wouldn't understand and wouldn't know of the importance of the tattered blanket. Bard scrubbed at the side of his face. She wouldn't dispose of the blanket... she could not. Closing his eyes, he released a long breath. Kaelea was a scholar who valued history--and seemed to value him as well. She would not dishonor the blanket.

The elderly woman selling the blankets watched him through slightly narrowed eyes. He felt exposed to her gaze, as if his thoughts were emblazoned above him. Using a strength of will he was surprised to discover within himself, he forced his thoughts from Kaelea and returned his attention to the weavings spread across the low table.

The old woman chuckled. "It's not that easy, *Hisatsinom.*" She turned away and moved to a small stack of crates where she drew out a bulging pack. She held it against her chest until Bard chose two blankets and held out the currency to her.

Grinning, she took the money and placed a loop of the pack's strap over his extended palm. "For you, *Hisatsinom.*"

Bard frowned and tried to hand the pack back to the woman. "I did not pay for this."

"Money's not needed, but you will need this." She shook her head and tugged at the end of one of her long, gray braids when he made to leave the pack on the floor. "No. It is for you, for your time of searching. My granddaughter... well, just you take that pack, young man." She turned her back. "Our business is concluded."

"But..." The straight, square set of her shoulders indicated she would listen to no argument, reminding Bard so strongly of his grandmother he had to blink furiously to cool the burning of his eyes.

He would get no further response from the woman, of that he had no doubt.

"My thanks then..." He paused, then smiled and offered an honorific. "Grandmother." The woman stood taller, but did not turn to face him. Bard hadn't expected otherwise.

Quickly, he rolled the blankets together, slipped the pack's strap over one shoulder, and turned back to the desolate landscape. The land might appear dry and forsaken, but from the sounds of simple industry and the noises of playing children, the lives of these people were not. He strode toward a rocky outcropping, planning to form a portal unobserved, but felt the woman's eyes on his back.

She had been so insistent he take the pack. He couldn't imagine what the bulging canvas contained. But mostly he wondered the meaning of her word *Hisatsinom*.

For the second time that day, Bard wandered the plateau along with masses of tourists. He avoided the larger groups, but listened as those in uniform, those who had been set to guard and guide, explained the history of the area. Again, the sense of familiar threatened to overpower him. The shape of the circular ruins, the way the walls had been constructed, reminded him of an ancient site on his own world. A site he'd visited often, for it was the place his grandmother claimed to have entered his world. His lowered brows shaded his eyes from the late afternoon sun when he peered over a deep canyon with wide bands of striations of light and dark rock.

Visible from his vantage point, one of the abandoned dwellings had been built into a broad underhang in the stark cliff face. The lush foliage of short, twisted trees and long-needled pines topping the cliff stretched to the horizon. The burnt-orange dwellings fascinated him, giving him a destination for the next day's exploration. He sat cross-legged on a bench, watching the shadows grow longer as the sun settled low on the horizon at his back. An announcement was made and the visitors began their slow, reluctant movement toward the exit from the fenced area. The extent of his intended transgression pushed to the recesses of his mind, Bard waited until the guards were occupied at the gate, cast one final glance over his shoulder and, taking the pack the old woman had given him in hand, moved to the split wood fence.

He swung over the low double-railed fence, slipped through the closely spaced, scrubby trees until hidden from sight. The guards scanned the plateau then moved through the gate and latched a padlock securely. Bard nodded to himself, stepped out of his soft leather boots, tied the laces to the backpack, and scrambled over the cliff edge. Stretching, reaching his toes lower, he searched for tiny indentations barely visible in the shadows. The pack weighed heavily on his shoulder, threatening to throw him off balance, and he curled his toes tightly into the shallow depression.

The breath escaped his lungs with a whoosh and he pressed his forehead against the cool stone. Rock climbing was not his favorite activity, but it was the only way he could quickly gain the canyon floor. He would not attempt a portal, for he realized he'd been lucky thus far in successfully finding passage to places he'd never been. He hoped to find a sheltered area where he could camp.

Fingers curled around a narrow outcropping, he carefully slid one foot lower. His action froze at a strange indentation in the smooth cliff face. Carefully moving one hand, he found a grip near his waist. A second grip was near the same level slightly to the other side.

Brow furrowed in concentration, he secured his grip at his sides and slid his higher foot down over the stone.

Another crack captured his toes, seemingly placed perfectly for a smaller man's use. The afternoon's lecture had mentioned how the original inhabitants of the area had built the cliff dwellings and provided ways to reach those dwellings--if one knew how to look for them. Was this what he'd discovered? A ladder carved into the rock itself?

The holds were close enough together, his muscles ached to stretch further making Bard scramble awkwardly down the nearly vertical rock face.

When his feet touched the ground, he still held to the rock, leaning into the cliff, thanking the Guardians for the safe passage. He let his head fall back and peered at the sky. The sky had turned a deeper blue and night would soon shroud the canyon; he needed to find a place to camp.

He didn't walk far along the cliff base before he found a tiny alcove with narrow open area before the rock fell away in another, much shorter cliff. The space was not much more of than an indentation in the rock, but with the surrounding plant life he'd be hidden from casual observation. After committing the site to memory, Bard rapidly created a portal, retrieved the supplies he'd gathered earlier and returned. He stored the small cache under the overhang, took a bottle of water, and moved to the edge of the man-high cliff.

With his legs hanging over the edge, he sat, took a long drink, and stared out over the canyon. The golden sun hovered low over the western horizon, coloring the sunset with the pinks and oranges of his home sky. Deep blue, tinted with streaks of purple followed and when he glanced to the east, the first faint outline of the rising moon and a single bright star captured his attention. The previous night had been long and lacking rest. He would not change a moment of that time, even though being with Kaelea had brought him the need for more answers. And the need for more time with her.

He could not offer her any of that time until he understood

himself and his place in whatever world he chose. Questions
slurred together and danced through his tired mind. The
stretch and pop of his jaws when he yawned made his face
ache. Perhaps if he slept--if he could sleep--the questions
would make more sense in the light of the next day.

But even the promise of sleep didn't dampen the curiosity
when he turned his face to the alcove and the dying light
flashed upon the pack given to him by the old woman. He
narrowed his gaze and stared. The shaft of light remained
upon the bulging canvas long after the brightness fled the
ledge. Before night was completely upon him, he'd look inside
the strange gift.

By lying back, he reached the pack without rising and
wrapped the ends of his fingers around the strap. He tugged
the pack to him and scooted back enough to place the bag
between his thighs. A deep breath filled his lungs as he pulled
on the string tie at the top. Despite his nervous curiosity, he
needed to hurry, or he'd not be able to see, for he could not
build a fire and risk discovery.

Bard chuckled, then broke into a full-throated laugh. The
first item he pulled from the pack was an artificial light. He
touched a button on the side of the long tube as Jaysson had
once shown him and laughed again at the light dancing over
the canyon trees. He angled the beam of light into the pack.

A stack of slick, folded papers reflected the light. He took
them from the pack, spread them on the ground next to his
hip, and arched one eyebrow. Each pamphlet described a
place--many of the cliff ruins, a mountain, the old woman's
village, the site high above him on the plateau. Bard shrugged
and stacked the papers together before he reached into
the bag.

The cloth packet he pulled out next was created from a bit
of weaving with a pattern like one of the blankets he'd
purchased. He unfolded the packet and shone the flashlight on
a glistening black stone. Another mystery.

A second cloth packet revealed a bowl the size of his
cupped hands, decorated with zigzags of paint and colored
similarly to his new blankets. He turned the bowl over and

over in his hands, then tipped the stone into it and set it with the papers.

He struggled with the next item, placing the flashlight on the ground in order to use both hands to pull the small drum from the pack. The sides were plain and undecorated, the skin head drawn tight to give a low, pleasing thrum when he rapped it with a bent knuckle. Thin hide strips stretched to hold the head to a smooth, shallow cylinder. The bottom curved and fit well in his hand. He gave a nod of appreciation, set the drum by the bowl and reached for the final item in the pack.

He frowned at the thin stick, twice as long as the spread of his fingers. Four colors, a single wrap of wide leather each, tipped one end of the lightweight wood. He ran his fingers over the smooth wood and contemplated the colors. In his world, colors had meaning, and from his short visit to the Native American village, he'd learned of a similar importance here. But, he had no idea what these colors signified to the woman who'd placed the stick in the pack.

Most of the items appeared to have some symbolic mean-ing--for both worlds. He glanced at the pamphlets. Perhaps these locations did as well, and if he visited them he would come to understand.

Another wide yawn popped his jaw. There would be no understanding that night. After replacing the items in the pack, he pulled a sweet from his pocket. Before he turned out the artificial light, he unwrapped and studied the red and white swirled disk. He'd developed a passion for the mint candy, deliciously different from the offerings of his world.

But as the flavor curled through his mouth, another passion spiraled lower in his body. He closed his eyes and shook his head. This world was filled with passions. It would be too easy to ignore his need for answers, return to Kaelea's bed and the comfortable forgetfulness he found in her arms.

He rose, placed the pack next to the small pile of supplies, then brushed at the ground with his foot. Clearing small, loose rocks from a space before the cave provided a place to spread his bedroll. He used one of the new blankets to cushion his head, the other he laid nearby. The night would grow cold as well as lonely.

K ae remained in bed for a day, trying not to replay the previous hours and the wonder she'd discovered in Bard, of Bard, about Bard. Ignoring the physical sensations, she searched each word she'd said, each of her reactions, then examined his words and reactions, looking for whatever she did to make him leave. Without even telling her why. If he thought... no, she couldn't imagine what he thought.

Exhausted, she knew she should sleep, but she couldn't control the dreams, her very physical dreams. Awake she could direct her conscious thought and when the twisted pathways of her reasoning brought her no closer to an answer--any answer--she turned her thoughts to her research, to the library. To Gowthaman.

Now, hot tears burned and filled her eyes. How could Gowthaman do what he did? She curled into a tighter ball and gnawed on her lower lip. She understood how. Her passion for Bard was as strong--stronger--and at times during the night, reason had left her and only passion directed her actions. Why should it be different for her friend?

Her friend. Kae sighed. She needed Gowthaman's friendship, now more than ever. Had too large a wedge been driven between them, a wedge they wouldn't be able to overcome? In order to solve the mysteries her brother had set before her, she needed his help. With both of them working, maybe she'd quickly find what she needed, a way to save her family. The problem facing her now was how to talk to him, how to explain that she understood, and tell him how much she valued their friendship.

A second dawn rose and she groaned as she rolled from her cramped position and stood. Ignoring the tangles as she divided the length of her hair into thirds, she finger-combed and plaited it loosely. Wearing the wrinkled caftan, she passed through her home into the desert heat and blindly made her way to the library.

The cool interior welcomed her. When she faced her research table, some of her lethargy and confusion lifted. Here was work she needed to do, work to keep her mind and body occupied, so she wouldn't have to think of him. Work to give her a purpose, a reason to leave her home.

The dim haze still filled her mind, yet she felt someone watching her. Kae pressed her lips together in a thin line to keep from gasping out a startled cry. It had to be Gowthaman. Though she longed to clear the air between them, she wasn't sure if she was ready to speak with him and renew their friendship. So much depended on his feelings--and how he expressed them.

The prickly feeling of being watched dissipated and she shrugged away the odd disappointment. Research and hidden answers awaited her, so she sat, rearranged the pages and books before her, and began.

Drawn, wrinkled, and puffy-eyed, Kae looked terrible. Gowthaman accepted the entire blame for her discomfort upon himself, but a flare of anger at Bard made him catch his breath. How dare the man leave her in such obvious pain? The flame died as quickly as it had risen. The stranger had not caused her pain. He had.

His actions opened a wound Bard might not have been able to heal. Gowthaman watched Kaelea settle into her chair, then backed further into the recesses of the library. He should not judge the man, or Kaelea, for he didn't know what had transpired two nights previously.

He could, however, judge himself. Had judged himself. And found himself unworthy.

Shoulders rounded with sorrow and care, he returned to the chamber containing the oldest of the library's materials and unlocked the door. He'd studied long to learn the ancient languages, yet only understood a little of what these scrolls and volumes contained.

Normally, his time spent with the musty, ageless volumes would be exhilarating, and he would easily become lost in the words of ages past. But today, without Kae's smile, the effort became effort. Only the possibility she would forgive him kept him at his table.

"Both physical and magical guards were placed outside the chamber. 'Tis nae other entrance. I dinna ken how this happened." Derrik's confusion mirrored Jaye's and he clasped his friend's shoulder.

"Whatever the cause, we must be wary. I'm sure Feidhlim is behind this."

"Without doubt. We must inform the Queen."

The sound of soft footsteps turned both men toward the Faerie Queen. She stopped before them and smoothed the flowing silk of her gown. A frown drew the normally merry tilt of her lips to a thin line. "The Queen knows, good defender. But, like you, I do not understand."

The trio turned to face the large, heavily sealed urn that had moved of its own volition from the center of the chamber to one corner. The other storage containers were now grouped in the opposite corner, crowded together as if they feared the solitary urn.

The Queen sighed. "At least the others no longer appear to pay homage to Feidhlim's contained magic."

Jaye made a non-committal sound in the back of his throat. Not that long ago, every other storage urn lay on its side, the stoppered tops pointing toward the urn containing Feidhlim's magic. Just the thought of the macabre scene sent shivers creeping along his spine. If only they knew why, or could find those few who still followed Feidhlim, maybe they could thwart his current plans--and end the threat to his family and clan once and for all. Even though Kae voiced disappointment in her efforts to find information in the ancient texts and records, he believed the key was there some-where. And that his sister would find at least enough they could piece together some answers and find success.

Derrik moved closer to the urn and eyed the stone container critically. Then he turned back to Jaye and the Queen and shrugged helplessly.

A clamor, the sound of rapidly approaching feet, chased the somber expression from the Defender's face. Jaye smiled as Derrik's granddaughter skipped through the squared entryway. She rushed toward Derrik, who stopped her advance by lifting one palm. He shook his head and gave a short, jerking nod toward the Queen. "Breanna."

The girl's eyes widened as she turned and her small, rosebud mouth formed a circle before she smiled and executed a curtsy before the Queen. "My lady Queen." She repeated the curtsy to Jaye. "My lord."

Jaye returned her smile and knelt, holding his arms open to her.

Bree giggled and rushed into his embrace. "Hi, Unca Jaye." After a wet kiss on his cheek, she ran to Derrik and hugged his legs. "Granda, here you are."

"Aye, here I am, darlin'. But, ye shouldna be here."

"I know, Granda. I was lookin' for you. And I founded you."

"Ye found me. But, why were ye lookin' fer me, darlin'?"

She snuggled happily into his arms. Jaye chuckled at the sight and promised himself he'd soon visit his grandchildren. Maybe he'd take them home for a visit with Allyn and give his daughter a break from the rambunctious twins.

"I just wanted to see you, Granda. Because I love you."

Derrik touched the tip of his index finger to her nose. "I love ye, too, ye little minx. Where's yer da?"

"He's talking to Unca Iain." Bree leaned close to his ear and whispered loudly. "About my pony."

"An' ye have been a guid enough child that ye believe ye deserve such a beastie?"

Bree patted his cheek and he caught her fingers between his lips, making her giggle.

Jaye placed the Queen's hand at the crook of his elbow and spoke to the royal faerie. "So, my lady aunt. Shall we investigate this business of providing mounts for the youngest of the clan?"

Her brilliant smile glistened up at him and her eyes twinkled merrily. "Aye. I have had enough worry for this day."

Jaye heaved a mental sigh. It was difficult for many of the Fey to remain serious for any length of time, their love of gaiety and dancing often overshadowed any sense of responsibility. The Queen had willingly given him the majority of burdens of responsibility in governing the clan, responsibility he had accepted just as willingly.

Yet, in matters surrounding the continued threats by Feidhlim, he wished he could impress upon her a stronger need for serious consideration to keep the clan and extended family safe.

As they strolled from the chamber, the Queen chatted happily, the problems of the urn's strange movements forgotten. Jaye sent a mental plea to his sister. *Hurry, Kae. I fear this is more serious than we ever imagined.*

Behind him, Bree spoke. "Granda?"

After Derrik's rumbling, "Hmm?" she continued. "Why is that jar in the corner leaking?"

THIRTEEN

G iving up on sleep as the sun lightened the sky, Bard
rose and gathered his belongings. His stomach
rumbled, but during the night he had decided to
fast, hoping the inner cleansing of his body would assist the
clearing of his mind. The meanings of the items given him by
the old woman would come with ritual fasting. When he
returned to the ledge that night, all he would bring with him
would be the pack and the new blankets. Although he feared
to undertake a quest--for what if it opened the passage to his
world, or some other, and threw him there without warning--
such a quest was his hope of answers.

After he hid his belongings in the Faerie Otherworld, he
scanned the pamphlets and planned his day's journey. He
placed a single piece of candy in his pocket with the black
stone and, after a longing gaze at the rest of the sweets, turned
his back on mortal concerns and focused on the answers he
sought. First he would go to the place where the pamphlets
stated the glass-like, black stone was found.

His portal opened some distance from a square-topped
ridge of clay-red mountains. He knew the distance was
deceiving and the walk would be long but he relished the
physical exertion. Bard knelt to retie one of his boots as he
studied the mountain. Legends told of a defeat of the native

peoples, a defeat that led many to die by riding over the cliff edge, rather than being killed by those who fought them. He straightened and fingered the stone in his pocket. Stones such as this represented the tears shed for the brave warriors.

There was no similar story in his world, and in the light of so many, overwhelming similarities, that fact itself fascinated him. The old woman obviously pointed him toward a spiritual quest, so what meaning did the stone have for him?

His long, easy strides carried him swiftly toward the foot of the mountain. The walking chant hummed through his mind, covering his jumbled thoughts and easing his heart. It was good to forget--even for a short while.

He skirted the town cradled at the base of the mountain and found a secluded place to rest. The small stone became heavy in his pocket, so he removed it and rested it on his palm. One side of the oval stone was rough, the black surface spotty with a soot-like white stone. A flat, shiny surface greeted him when he turned the stone over. Dark and smooth as glass, the surface warmed under his fingers. He held the stone up to the sun and gasped.

What had appeared to be a solid black stone became smoky yet clear enough the light brought out darker swirls within the stone.

Shadows from the unpolished side blocked the light as Bard turned the stone one way then another, catching the light. Fascinated by the subtle movements within the stone, he let his gaze lose focus.

Beyond his outstretched arm, the mountain sharpened, the colors intensified. The blue sky burned his eyes, the red of the stone vibrated with suppressed power. Bard shuddered, but could not tear his gaze away. His arm lowered as a shimmer surrounded the mountain top.

Closer, drawn close to the flat plateau, Bard accepted the vision. From the plateau, the land around blazed with heat, the town disappeared into the heat waves. He viewed the past.

The black stone burned in his hand and he pulled his fist back against his chest to feel the warmth encompass him and surround his heart. He closed his eyes briefly, then opened them and peered over the cliff edge.

Stark white bones lay scattered at the base of the cliff, while some littered the rocky outcroppings halfway down. Weeping sounded behind him and Bard turned from the gruesome sight to face the wavering specters of crying women. Tears slipped between their fingers to drop to the stark white sand at their feet. The tears shimmered for a brief moment before turning black. A single tear-stone rose, hovered before his eyes, then disappeared into his fist.

The increase in heat forced him a step back. He gave a short, surprised cry, blinked...

And found himself back on the plain, still far from the mountain, returned from the land of his vision.

Weak kneed, Bard sank to the ground. Never before had he experienced a vision without the ritual preparations--and even then the Guardians had seldom chosen to speak to him. This time, he hadn't even been asking, merely studying the stone.

The sorrow of the mourners surged through him, followed by a swelling of pride. The men had chosen to sacrifice themselves, dying as the brave warriors they were, rather than succumbing to a way of life that would have murdered them anyway.

Bard searched his mind for the reasons he had been shown such a sight. One word shimmered like the sun through the tear stone.

Sacrifice.

Did this mean he must make a personal sacrifice? He gazed into the clear, blue sky. Of course that's what the vision told him. But, what sacrifice was required of him? He could think of only two choices--his duty to his home world, or his love for Kaelea.

Bard rose and turned from the mountain. Neither was an enviable choice.

He lifted his hand to form a portal and realized he still clutched the stone. His stiff fingers opened slowly to reveal his stone and three additional, tiny, perfect teardrops of the same shiny, black stone. A slow smile stretched his lips as he cupped the stones in his palm and lifted them to the sky.

"By the Seven, I give thanks. I begin to understand."

The stones slipped easily into the small cloth bag and Bard slipped as easily through a portal to his canyon ledge.

T he intensity of her frustration forced Kaelea to throw her pencil far across the library. As the thin wood clattered against the stone floor, she propped her elbows on the table and hid her face in her hands. She ached to cry, but she had no tears left. Even if there were, what was the use?

She felt as though she could count every single hour since she woke and discovered Bard gone. Although she drifted occasionally into uneasy sleep, those hours had drained her.

Like the magic drained unchecked from a nearly invisible weak spot in the urn of Feidhlim's disgrace. The message from her brother had been curt and to the point. They had found no way to stop, or even slow the leak. And since they knew the banished faerie lived, shared this time in the human world, there was no doubt a way had been discovered to return his magic to him. Jaye hadn't voiced his desperation, but she knew the strength of the feeling, a deeper pain than her personal loss.

She'd attacked her research with renewed vigor, but the enthusiasm for her work faded much too quickly in the face of dead end after dead end. She had to find something--some little bit of information--anything to help her family. Kae rubbed her forehead with her fingertips. She had to do it alone. Somehow, she'd chased Bard away and although she thought she might be ready to talk to Gowthaman, he'd remained apart from her and others, deep in the oldest parts of the library.

"What am I going to do?" she whispered to her palms, then stared blearily down at the polished wood table.

Her pencil rolled into view. Kae held her breath and, in the silence, a chair scraped across the stone floor. There was a rustle as if someone sat in that chair, then the silence returned to surround her.

She lowered her hands, slowly lifted her gaze, and stared across the table. Gowthaman gave her a tentative smile. "You seemed to have lost your pencil, Kaelea."

"Gowthaman, I--"

He lifted his hand, halting her speech. "No, Kae, let me speak. I ask--no, I beg forgiveness of you. I have acted shamefully toward you as my friend and toward you as a woman. I claim no excuse, but that of male stupidity. A stupidity that believed I could make you feel--as I wished you to feel. I was wrong, and wronged you in my error. If I must pay for my actions by the loss of your friendship, so be it."

"Gowth--"

"No! I must finish while I maintain the courage. I was also wrong about the stranger. About Bard."

Kae shook her head fiercely. "Don't mention him, please."

"I do not wish for him to stand between us, if it is possible to regain your friendship."

"Gowthaman, I've missed your company." Kae watched him carefully. In the past such statements would bring a flare of life to his eyes, a glitter of desire. But only sadness and remorse held sway over his expression.

"As I have missed talking with you, assisting in your research."

Extending her hand across the table, Kae asked, "Truce, then?"

Gowthaman stared at her hand. Forgiveness couldn't be that easy, could it? Dare he believe how easily she appeared to accept his apology? "You forgive me then?"

"You know I'll never be able to forget--"

He rose with a jerk and turned from her. He should have listened to his inner voice and stayed away. If he were in her position, he would never be able to forgive either. As he could not forgive himself for building that wall between them. That cursed wall. He would bring her the information he discovered, then would leave the library, leave this part of the world, until her research was complete and she had returned to her family.

"Where are you going?"

Her simple question froze his muscles and Gowthaman only shook his head. "I should not be here."

"Why?"

Trying to hide his anguish, he faced Kae. "You do not need the reminder of what I have done."

"No, I don't. But, I do need your friendship. I need your help." She gestured to the mess of papers and books before her. "The situation has gotten worse. Feidhlim is getting his magic back."

He dropped back into the chair. "How? The urn is impenetrable."

"Yes, we thought it was. But somehow, there's a weak spot, a tiny crack, and his magic is oozing from the urn. I'm sure it's flowing right back to him."

Forgetting his personal sorrows, Gowthaman leaned over the table and spoke urgently. "We must double our efforts."

"We?" Kae smiled and his anguish returned full force. Just as suddenly, the pain dissipated, leaving him with an amazing sense of warm acceptance. She extended her hand once again. "Truce?"

After hesitating only a moment, Gowthaman took her hand in his. "Do friends need call a truce?"

"No, they don't. There's no need. Now, I listened to what you had to say, please listen to me."

"Yes, of course."

"Your friendship is very dear to me,"

He tried to pull his hand from hers, but she clasped his fingers between both of her hands.

"And while it is true I won't be able to forget what happened, I believe I understand how you feel."

Shaking his head broke their eye contact. She could not understand the depths of his pain, his--humiliation.

"Yes, I do, my friend. Trust me, I do. Now, that said--now listen to me--we've gotten past that pain. Maybe our friendship will be even stronger for it. I don't know. That's something we'll have to work on as we go. Okay?"

She winced when she said 'okay', and he wondered at the flash of sorrow. If it was within her to tell him later, then he would listen. If she never told him of her sorrow, he would not question her. In his heart, he knew her emotional state had more to do with Bard than with the evil facing her family. Or his transgression. She waited for his response so he nodded, covering the tensing of his muscles with a tight smile. There was still anger within him that he would deal with privately, anger that the stranger had gone, leaving her with such sorrow.

"Right, then. Gowthaman, I'm really glad we can still be friends."

"If I do anything to—"

Kae chuckled soberly. "Oh, don't worry. I'll let you know. Now, will you help me?"

He pressed his palm to his chest and bowed his head. "As you wish." The smile Kae bestowed upon him lightened even the deepest, darkest chambers of his heart, and he let a true smile relax his face. "I have something to show you in the old library. Will you come?"

Again the flash of pain, followed by a glistening of tears upon her lashes. What had he said to bring her such pain? A moment of guilt cornered his conscience. He knew where Bard had gone and could take her to him. Or, go there himself and insist the man return and make explanations.

"Yes, I'll go with you."

Gowthaman paused for the space of a panicked heartbeat. Had he spoken his knowledge of Bard out loud? Kae stood and stretched. "I need a walk to loosen up, anyway."

A faint, light purple glow hovered just below her denim-covered navel. Gowthaman jerked his face from her to hide the shocked widening of his eyes. Lighter than the soulfire that surrounded Bard and her at the oasis, the pale color and placement of the aura could only mean...

If the man did not return soon, Gowthaman vowed he

would physically drag him back. Even at the cost of exposing his long hidden talents.

Bard sat cross-legged on his ledge, one of the blankets spread before him. Upon the blanket lay the four stones, the small bowl, and the leather wrapped stick.

After his vision at the mountain, he'd thought about visiting the old woman, but even as the thought crossed his mind, he knew he'd get no answers from her. This was his quest, the difficult answers his to discover.

He took the stick and lay it across his palms. The wood was light and even with the strips of colored leather around one end, well balanced in his hand. He obviously held a supplication stick and wondered what the people of this Southwest called the ritual creation.

Now, he would make the stick his own by adding things needed for his personal search.

He lifted the stick to the afternoon sun. The colors of the four wraps held his attention for a long moment. Colors and the meanings of the colors were important to him. Red, yellow, white, blue--colors of nature, colors of knowledge, wisdom, and the healing power of all things. He wished to add additional colors. Purple for spirit, orange for life, and turquoise for protection. He drew a deep breath, released it slowly, and placed the stick back on the blanket. First, he would attach the small items he gathered over two days of visiting places in both of Kaelea's worlds. He emptied his pockets of small treasures.

A downy feather, five green-blue beads, a short, leafy twig from the Otherworld and one of the red and white swirled candies joined the teardrop stones. He rearranged the items and was satisfied. It should be enough.

But, he had no leather thongs. Hating the thought of waiting, Bard tried to think of a way to attach the items to the supplication stick without leaving the ledge.

The soft skittering of tiny claws over the stones made him look toward the sound. His guide sat upon its hind legs, preening the white spot between its ears. Bard smiled and spoke quietly, "Little guide, where have you been the past two days?"

Dark eyes shining with intelligence, the rodent looked around.

"There is no need to answer. I understand your guidance has led me to this point and without such guidance I would have been lost long ago. Alone in a strange land that is not so strange. Now that I'm here, I must find my own way. But, I'm glad you are here with me. It is a comfort, little guide."

The creature bounded from its perch and paused at the edge of the blanket. With its tiny paws, it scratched at the small cloth packet that had held the first black stone. The animal picked up the edge of the flap and gnawed at the weaving.

Bard held his breath as the guide struggled to carefully pull a single thread from the weaving. Holding the long, orange thread in its mouth, the guide scampered to Bard, dropped the thread, then backed away. At the edge of the blanket, it rose again to its hind legs and tipped its head to one side.

Bard lifted the nubby string and peered closely at it. When he didn't move, the small animal returned to the pouch, gnawed, and pulled a purple string loose and dropped the length before him.

Realization settled over him and Bard grinned. "You've solved one of my problems. I thank you." The guide chattered once then turned and ran into the scrubby brush at the cliff's edge.

Bard hummed tunelessly as he picked apart the woven pouch and stacked each color in a separate pile. The majority of threads were in the colors he'd wanted to add to his supplication stick: purple, orange, and turquoise. He didn't question how, he simply took a purple thread, one of the small teardrop stones, and began the process of binding the stick and adding his treasures.

FOURTEEN

L ibrarians in the past kept the oldest sections of the
library ruthlessly restricted and, to Kae's eyes, it
appeared they didn't even frequent the area. She held
back a sigh of delight. If she were given unlimited access to the
most ancient of texts--oh, the wonder of the possibilities filled
her, and she released the sigh.

Gowthaman turned his head and gave her a lopsided
smile. "I knew you would find this interesting."

"Interesting? This is far more than interesting,
Gowthaman." She twirled in a slow circle trying to take in the
dusty piles of books, the scattered heaps of scrolls, and even
older, painted hides. "This is amazing. After we find what I
need, will you bring me back here?"

The smile crept to the other side of Gowthaman's mouth.
"I shall do better than you ask, Kae. I shall allow you unlimited
access to this room."

"You... would do that?"

"It is within my power. Now, sit and I shall retrieve the
volume I wished to show you."

Kae perched on the edge of a chair, hands clasped tightly
in her lap. She ached to touch the books, run her fingers over
the pages, smooth the wrinkled scrolls across the tabletop,

and discover how much she could actually read. Excitement trembled through her and she twisted her fingers together. An answer had to be here somewhere, and with Gowthaman's help, she'd find it.

He returned, a large, thick-paged book held carefully before him. At his nod, Kae cleared a space on the table. He set the book before her, stepped back, and waited.

She stared at the simple leather binding, fear of what she might find warring with the thrill of discovery. "What is it?" she whispered.

An elegant shrug lifted Gowthaman's shoulders. "It is written in a dialect that appears to combine our Faerie gentry language with that of the wee fairies."

Her eyes widened as she turned her head to look at him. "Korin's realm?"

He nodded. "I know you have translated some fairy documents and hoped you would be able to read this. From what I am able to decipher, this is a history--a history of the time that pre-dates the split between the Fey races."

Kae gasped. "That's the time I've been looking for."

"Yes, I know."

"How long have you known about this book?" Kay rested her palm possessively on the cover.

His tolerant, understanding grin answered her. Then Gowthaman said, "Only since late last night. I might have found the volume sooner, but I had much... on my mind. If you will forgive me?"

Kae leaped to her feet and wrapped him in a tight hug. When she drew back, his almond eyes were nearly round with shock. She kept her hands on his shoulders to hold him in place when he tried to step back.

"There is nothing to forgive, my friend. We both needed time to come to terms with what happened." Trying to keep her thoughts centered on Gowthaman, rather than letting them slip to all that had happened with Bard, she paused. "I'm glad it didn't take too long."

Past disbelieving her words, he shook his head. "But--"

"Let me tell you something, Gowthaman." Kae waited until his attention focused on her. Then she let her hands drop to her sides and returned to the chair. When he remained frozen, she gestured toward a second chair. "If you hadn't made the first move and talked to me first today, I would have come looking for you. I really do value your friendship too much to let it slip away because of a misunderstanding."

"Misunderstanding? Kae, I--"

"Hush. We need to put the past in the past, except for what we find in this book." As she patted the leather binding, she fought the pain of the past days and grinned up at him. "Can you do that?"

"I shall try, Kaelea."

The look he gave her made her think he could read the anguish in her mind, see the unanswered questions, as if he knew about Bard. About Bard's leaving. How could he know anything? She tried to maintain the grin. "I can't ask for anything more. Now, can't we take a look at the book?"

"As you wish."

Gowthaman sat back as Kae leaned over the book and caressed the worn cover. While he barely understood the feelings she hid from him, he did understand and share her delight in scholarly pursuits. Although he had studied the book through the night, he still felt the rise of vicarious excitement as she carefully opened the front cover and gently ran her fingertips over the aged, yellow page. The paper was handmade, slightly rough and thick with a torn appearance to the outer edge. There were hints of gold along the edges, as if the gilding were rubbed off by the many hands that had turned the pages.

She turned to the second page, a page with a large illuminated letter, the remainder of the page filled with cramped, narrow writing. He imagined the scribe had created the decoration without giving thought to the amount of text to also occupy the page and had been forced to squeeze the words together. Or perhaps that was the way of writing at the time the book was created. An adventure awaited them.

"You're right," Kae stated as she pointed to a word. "Some of this is fairy writing." She turned her face to him. Her expression glowed, she glowed. Gowthaman closed his eyes. It was not only the discovery that made her appear so, it was the child cradled within her womb. She hadn't yet recognized the minute presence and he feared for her the moment she did.

The possibility of bringing Bard back to her blazed through him again. He released a long breath as he opened his eyes. Kae bent over the book, tracing words with her finger, mouthing the syllables. She shook her head, moved further down the page, then nodded. Silently, he rose and brought paper, quill, and ink from a cubbyhole. Kae accepted the tools without looking at him and immediately began a list of words down one side of the page.

Gowthaman stepped back and watched for a few moments. More than anything else right now, he believed Kae needed to accept the child. Any new life in Faerie was a joy to be treasured and care given to ensure the rare birth. Kae would think little of herself as she worked, and he couldn't mention the child to her. Confronting the man if he didn't wish to be found would not bring happiness to the situation. Gowthaman decided to enlist the assistance of Kae's sister, Nanceen.

He paced from the chamber, sealed the door against interruption, and hurried from the library. He doubted Kae even realized he had gone. He would use this time to contact Nanceen.

The achingly slow return of his magic angered Feidhlim. Without remorse, he took his frustration out on his underlings, yet still the fools fawned over him and begged for more. The promise of power held sway over those few faerie who still followed him and claimed to cling to his ideals. Amazing progress had been made in his return to his rightful place as the leader of the Faerie clan--of all Faerie.

Feidhlim concentrated and a ball of pure magic formed between his palms. He rotated one palm over the other and the magic deepened, concentrated, pulsed with energy. Spreading his hands, he let the energy leave his fingertips to form a weak portal. It wasn't much, but it was a beginning. Soon, the fools had promised him, soon he would feel the return of all his magic.

But for now he would be content with a secret return to the Faerie Otherworld. An underling stepped in front of him before he could enter the portal. "Wait, my lord. We must form the protection. With this concentrated spell, none of Faerie will ascertain your presence in the Otherworld. Until it is too late." The faerie laughed, but the laughter died on his lips when Feidhlim remained stoically silent.

He scowled at the underling and the faerie scrambled through the portal. Feidhlim felt the overflowing power of the building magic, crossed his arms over his chest and tapped one foot. They should not keep the portal open long, for despite the assurances of his followers, each moment the portal existed increased the possibility of Alastriona discovery.

"Now, my lord." The faerie gestured broadly, then bowed. "Welcome, and glory upon your return to your rightful world."

Head held high, Feidhlim took long, confident steps and felt only a slight resistance as he entered the portal. The rush of fresh Faerie air upon his face, the mingled scents of his home, the clarity and brightness of the colors around him made him pause as the portal dissipated at his back. How long? How long had he waited, planned, and fought for this moment? Although this was not the fully triumphant return he had anticipated, it would do--for now.

His followers had chosen a place far removed from any Faerie clans. The bleak landscape held no interest for him and he turned his attention to the large, stone castle hovering at the edge of a high, sheer cliff. At one time this had been the center of Faerie rule, in a time ages upon ages past. He felt the truth of the knowledge in every fiber of his being. And so would be again. Soon.

"Chambers have been prepared according to your specifications, my lord."

"Good. And my powers?"

"The return should hasten, my lord, now that you are within the Otherworld."

Feidhlim stretched his arms over his head, fisted his hands and let the partial power flow through him. Striding toward the castle, he spoke, knowing the underling followed close on his heels. "Come, there is much to discuss."

"My lord, as always, my pleasure to serve you."

Feidhlim led the way down a narrow path. Others of his followers hovered by the arched, wooden gate. He held back a smile--after completing the preparations, they would not enter without him. Good. That was how it should be. How his life should have been honored since before the usurper was born. Damn the usurper. Damn Zeroun to all the hells.

"My lord?"

"Hmm?" Feidhlim looked down upon the faerie maid who had spoken. She was lovely, a delight to the eye and his body tightened. Too long had he denied himself.

"If there is aught you wish, my lord?"

His easy smile brought a flush of pink to her cheeks. "Perhaps later, my dear. Perhaps later. First, call my council to chamber." He stroked the backs of his fingers over her cheek, down the length of her neck to the swell of breasts nearly exposed by her low cut bodice. "Do it now," he whispered fiercely.

The young female licked her lower lip and brazenly met his gaze. "Yes, my lord. I shall await your... pleasure."

After an imperious glance around, Feidhlim's long, measured strides took him into the castle, along the halls to the room that had once held the throne. He paused and let satisfaction flood his senses. Soon. Soon there would be a throne here--his throne. For now he sat in a high backed chair at the head of a broad table. Moments later the remainder of the chairs were filled with his followers. The best of those who believed the taint of human blood must be removed forever from Faerie, the best of those who acclaimed him leader.

When the gathering grew expectantly silent, Feidhlim pushed back his chair and rose. "My compliments. The return of my magic progresses apace with our plans to rid Faerie of the cursed Zeroun clan, down to the last child. Except," he paused and rubbed his hands together. "Except for the wench who carries my child. She shall be spared, for the time being."

"A child? My lord, your child?" Incredulous voices rose and chased each other around the table. Feidhlim waited until the amazement died away and raw admiration shone in every face. A flicker of doubt settled in his mind. The child was half-human.

After the usurper was destroyed and he firmly held the rule of all Faerie clans, then would be soon enough to deal with the problem of human blood. He would be king, and would make and remake his own laws. If his over-exuberant followers were unable to comprehend, it was easy enough to dispose of any dissidents.

The niggle of doubt returned. Perhaps there was a sad irony in the fact that his seed had only taken in a human wench.

"My lord?"

Called from his thoughts, Feidhlim returned to his seat. "What plans, then?"

A dark haired faerie stood. "Watchers at the ancient library hidden in the human desert send word that the keeper of the library has discovered an ancient text that may expose unre-membered history. Of the time before the supposed split of the fey races, of gentry and fairy."

Pompous ass. "Go on. Of what importance do you consider this information?"

"My lord, I do not know. But Zeroun's sister seems to take great interest in what the book contains."

"And that is?"

The faerie stared at the center of the table. His voice lowered to the barest whisper. "I have not been able to ascertain that information. There are strong wards on the library, even stronger around the area containing this book."

"How did you come by this information?" Only mildly curious, Feidhlim gave his underling a benign smile.

Evidently relieved at his lord's lack of anger, he sneered. At the ugly twist to his lips, Feidhlim frowned. "The librarian does not guard his thoughts well. He believes they have found something to be used to defeat you. Fools."

Feidhlim gave a soft snort. More likely, the fools surrounded him and he marked the speaker as one to be watched. Still, if the Zeroun clan believed the importance of some bit of information, then he would know as well.

"Bring the librarian to me. Perhaps a... visit within the castle will relieve him of the information. Take him so the Zeroun bitch is unaware, no need to tip our hand at this time."

A breath of perfumed air caressed his senses and he turned as the young faerie maid sat on the floor at the side of his chair. She rested her hands demurely on her thighs but flashed him a look that sent jolts of desire through his veins. Feidhlim slapped one palm on the tabletop. "Bring me the librarian. Once we have the information, we will complete our plans."

Silence followed his abrupt departure, but as he reached the wide doorway, whispered conversations again swirled against his back, speculation about his child the prevailing concern. He paused with one hand on the doorframe, turned and pointed at the kneeling woman with the other. "You. Come with me."

Desert twilight lingered over the oasis, cooling the air with the promise of night. Gowthaman sat next to the pool tossing bits of torn leaves into the water. Troubled, he fought to order his thoughts. It seemed Kae had forgiven him, and unconsciously had encouraged him to forgive himself. Perhaps he could do so. He would try for the sake of friendship.

He turned his thoughts to the faint lavender aura of Kae's pregnancy. Even these few days after conception, how could she not know? Unless her sorrow at Bard's disappearance blocked her acceptance of the child.

Although three days had passed and the trail grown cold, he believed he could still follow Bard's path through the portals. He could convince the man to return. When he looked past his jealousy and doubts, Gowthaman knew Bard to be an honorable man. There had been strong reasons within him to make him leave, and strong reasons to keep him away. Gowthaman tossed the remainder of the leaf to the pond and watched the ripples travel outward from the point of impact. A stranger had arrived and the ripples of his presence had far-reaching effects. How far, Gowthaman couldn't guess.

He sent Kaelea's sister a message, asking her to come to the library. He'd not received a return message from Nanceen, but hoped she'd simply appear tomorrow as he'd requested. Kae would need help from them both.

Gowthaman grinned to himself and his sad smile reflected in the clear water. Unless Bard returned soon, Kae would need a great deal of support from her family--and her friends.

First, he would take her a meal, for she looked drawn, as if it had been long since she had eaten. Then, despite her insistence she was fine, he would insist she rest, telling her that together they would tackle the translation in the morning.

He brushed tiny bits of leaf and sand from his clothing as he rose.

A tall, dark haired faerie moved before him. Before Gowthaman could speak, he brandished a silken cloth dripping with a rancid odor. Gowthaman took a step back and lifted one hand.

The intruder chuckled. "My lord Feidhlim wishes to speak with you, librarian." Then he lunged forward and pressed the cloth over Gowthaman's mouth and nose. As darkness stole his mind, the attacker laughed again. "My lord was correct. At times, human means can be the best recourse."

. . .

B ard's head jerked up as if he had been called. His fingers
froze and his wrapping of the supplication stick
unwound and dropped to the blanket. Strange. There
was an odd tremor in the air, calling for his attention,
demanding he listen. He set the supplication stick aside,
closed his eyes and waited.

But, there was no additional movement of the air, no call.
Nothing but the evening sounds of the canyon.

Bard shrugged and returned to adding the final treasures
to his supplication stick.

F eidhlim glared at the unconscious figure slumped on
the cold stone floor of the lowest dungeon. So, this
was the keeper of the ancient library. He poked the
prone faerie with the toe of his boot. The librarian should be
awake by now, unless the drug affected fey senses differently
than it did humans.

Giving voice to his frustration, Feidhlim growled low in his
throat. He'd get no information until this one woke and the
drug cleared his system. Feidhlim brightened, he'd have more
time with the woman still chained to his bed. The anticipation
of a some what willing partner turned him from his captive.
And, one of his underlings understood his tastes, for she had
violet eyes. He smiled as he checked both the physical and
magical locks on the door.

Gowthaman waited for the count of eight breaths after the
door closed, then rolled to his back and groaned softly. So, that
was Feidhlim. By the desert sun, the man reeked of evil, the
powerful essence stronger even than the potion that had been
used to render him unconscious. Sensing that the smallest
movement would make him violently ill, Gowthaman opened
his eyes to the dark gray stone above him.

Carefully, he reached out with his mind to touch his
surroundings.

He was being held in Faerie? That meant Feidhlim had
found a way to return. Gowthaman bit back another groan as

he turned his head to the side as bile burned in his throat. Faerie gentry seldom fell ill, and he didn't know how to react to the physical discomfort. Remaining as still as possible, he willed comfort from the cool stone at his back, willed the swirling remnants of the potion to dissipate, willed the churning of his stomach to...

Lurching to his knees, he doubled over and, clutching his stomach, was violently ill. He gasped for breath, then tried to draw moisture to dull the vile, cottony taste in his mouth. Finally, he crawled from the mess, leaned against the wall, and let the strange potion return him to unknowing darkness.

CHAPTER
FIFTEEN

After an uneasy night filled with disjointed dreams, Bard wandered from his ledge to the tiny stream at the canyon floor. The flowing water invited him to drink his fill and quench his growing thirst. Instead, he pressed his lips together tightly and splashed the cool water over his face. He paced the rocky shore waiting for stones to catch his eye. Those he gathered and tossed into a bundle made from one of his blankets. The burden grew heavy with a satisfying weight, the sound of the stones clicking together a pleasing, rhythmic counterpart to his walk.

The supplication stick rested in a darker recess of the alcove with the bowl and the drum. He would use the drum when he completed the circle of stones, but he still had no idea of what use he would make of the bowl.

Bard climbed back to his ledge and surveyed the cleared space.

There would be barely enough room. He glanced over his shoulder, there might be a suitable place along the stream, but that didn't feel right. Here, on the ledge overlooking the arroyo, he would build his circle.

Using his foot, he widened the space he'd already cleared.

Satisfied with his work, he dumped the collected rocks in a small heap. He sat next to the pile and picked up the first water smoothed stone. With only a moment's thought, he placed the rock on the southern cardinal point. He set the second stone, a long, thin oval, pointing west. After quickly placing the east and north markers, he completed filling in the circle. Roughly six feet in diameter, the edges brushed the cliff face at the rear and hovered at the opposite drop off.

Bard removed the few unused stones and used them to build a small cairn just outside the circle. He blew out a long breath. Soon the sun would set and he would begin. By taking ritual from his past, information he had garnered in three days of exploration, and the feelings of his heart, he hoped his night's quest would carry his appeal to the Guardians. Without carrying him back to his world just yet.

Remembering how he had entered the desert Sahara naked as a babe, he grinned. For this night, he would not bare himself to the elements. Bare his heart and soul, yes, for that was the only way to achieve understanding, the only way to be open to the will of the Guardians.

Making a rapid decision, Bard formed a portal and returned to the Faerie Otherworld. He paused--the strange disturbance he'd felt earlier returned. Holding himself still, he concentrated, trying to discover the reason for the tremors settling like frigid chills over his body. No answer came to him, and he rubbed his arms to chase away the malaise. After the night, would he ever return to this parallel world? Then he recovered his belongings from the hiding place, took a long look around, and returned to the human world.

Bard removed his boots to better feel the vibrations of the earth. He carefully traded the boots and the small pile of his belongings for the ritual items under the overhang.

The sun touched the upper rim of the surrounding canyon and he held his supplication stick high in the air. As the sun lowered, he lowered the stick until, with the disappearance of the bright orange sun, he planted the stick in the center of the cairn. A breeze curled over the ledge, rattling the halo of treasures fastened to the stick. The pleasing sound calmed Bard's nervous energy as he placed the drum and small bowl at the northern point of the circle. Even though the sun fell into the west, he was more comfortable with facing north, as if he were in his own world. For it was his world's Guardians he would call upon. The Seven Guardians he hoped would answer to show him the meaning and way for the remainder of his life.

The soft rattling continued as he stepped into the circle and spread one of the new blankets east to west to honor the passage of the sun in this world. He spread the second blanket north to south then sat at the center, imagining it to be the point where the two worlds touched.

Leaving the empty bowl in place, he reached for the drum, set the rounded bottom in the hollow created by his crossed legs, and rested his fingers at the edge.

He pursed his lips and gave a low whistle. The sound faded into the twilight. The rattling of the supplication stick grew louder, rapid as he whistled again, long and low. Evening sounds faded with a third whistle, the air itself stilled, waiting, listening, held in a moment in time until he called it forth again. The supplication stick fell silent.

Bard tested the drum with five sharp taps. The center sounded with deep, full vibrations rumbling through him. At the edges, the sound became sharper, with less reverberation. Closing his eyes, he listened to the rhythms of his heart, of his breathing, of the song that echoed through his mind. With one hand, he tapped the center of the drum, a constant beat that varied only in the strength of his fingers against the skin. The other hand beat an alternating rhythm, fast then slow, hard then soft. He followed the song, followed the trail of his spirit, followed the sound.

Soon there was nothing but the sound of the drum. His breathing disappeared into the rhythm. The air danced around his circle, the essence of the earth rose to him, the light of the appearing stars twinkled behind his closed eyelids.

Still he drummed. Until the questions he tried to hold in his mind faded. Still he drummed. Until he became his world, became the world where he was, became the conjunction of those worlds. Echoes of another drummer rose from the earth, rattling the supplication stick and followed his beating, then formed a counterpoint. Still he drummed. Until there was no feeling. Until he had no body with which to feel. Until he was spirit.

Still he drummed, filling the night with himself--filling himself with night.

The second drum paused, then pounded a sharp, rapid continual beat, calling him to follow instead of lead. Softer. Slower. Both drums fell silent. Bard's spirit rose to hover beside his slumped physical body. He stretched out his arms, embracing the experience of every molecule around him.

"Welcome." The soft voice drew his spirit further from his body.

A young woman sat on a log beyond the edge of his circle. A drum lay at her feet. A small rodent, his guide, sat on her lap. She stroked the tiny head and spoke to it. "He looks a little surprised, doesn't he?"

She appeared to listen, then spoke again. "Yes, I understand. He doesn't. Yes, I'll help him, but you know there is another who is better suited."

The guide curled into a ball on her lap and watched him. The girl lifted her soft, dark-brown gaze. "Welcome, William Bard Stonefeather. Come, let's talk."

Surprised, his spirit found a voice. "How do you know me?"

She indicated the intense colors of the landscape around them. "Here in the middle world each spirit knows the other, *Hisatsinan*."

"But, I do not know you."

She bowed her head, but not before he saw her smile. "True. But, you met my Grandmother two days ago. She gave you the items that brought you here."

"Where is here?"

Shaking her head and rolling her eyes as if he should know, the young woman gave him a wide smile. "I just told you, the middle world. The place where the spirits of all things may meet and find guidance."

"Guidance. That's what I search for."

She stroked the tiny animal in her lap and remained silent.

"How do you know my guide?"

"He came to me in a dream and told me you would need my help to understand. I told Grandmother so she could help prepare the way. *Hisatsinom*, we have waited long for your return."

"My return? What does this mean, this *Hisatsinom*?"

"Ancestor." The young woman cradled the guide in her hand and rose. "It means ancestor."

"I don't understand."

She gave a laugh, light as the tinkling of water over stone. "No, I didn't think you would. That's why I answered the call of your drum. That's why I'm here. Will you let me tell you a story? A tale of long ago, yet of a not so distant past?"

"You will tell me a tale, but not your name?"

A faint bronze blush covered her cheeks. "Catori. You can call me Catori."

Bard nodded and she stepped into his circle. She took his spirit hand and lay it against her forehead, her palm covering the back of his hand. The guide climbed to her shoulder and chattered once. "Yes, I understand. I know what I'm doing." Then she stared up into Bard's eyes. "Your guide is concerned that even once I show you, you will not understand. Believe me, William Bard Stonefeather, what you see is the truth of the past."

"Like the sacrifice made on the high mountain?" The teardrop stones tied to the supplication stick rattled in response.

"Sacrifice? Yes. Truth? Yes, again. Come." With a whispered word, their spirits lifted, easily rising along the cliff he had labored to descend. Now he could see the sharp outline of each finger and toehold, and was amazed at the ingenuity of the simply carved grips.

The young woman chuckled. "It is also true that the Old Ones created this pathway to the plateau. For this was a center of powerful worship for them. A place of strange destinies. A place of sacrifice."

"How do you know these things?" They had risen to the plateau and settled upon the top of the stone wall. She released his hand and stepped back.

"I was very young when the spirits of this place called me. Only four when I first beat the drum and undertook a shaman's quest." A look of deep sadness and longing filled her face. "I was not a child for long. Each time I came here, to the middle world, a new guide presented itself to me. Each time, I learned more. I've been told I have the wisdom of a shaman decades older than I am." She gave a shrug. "Maybe, but I've met no other shaman, except for you."

Bard made a sound of derision. "I am no shaman."

She looked as if she fought laughter and Bard frowned. "Are you not? You felt the power of the drum."

She waited until he nodded then continued. "And, you're here, aren't you? What other explanation could there be?"

"A dream."

"An ancient tribe of a faraway land call quests such as this the 'dreamtime'."

"I..." He could think of no answer.

"Your grandfather gave you training." It wasn't a question.

"He began."

"I'm sorry for your loss of him, and the loss of your family. Why do you wish to return to a world where few even acknowledge your life force?"

"It is my world." As he spoke the words, he knew them to be meaningless. His world could be wherever he felt he belonged. Like this world. With Kaelea.

"Ah," she said. "You begin to understand. Let me show you another place and tell you of another choice--a sacrifice maybe. Maybe not."

He let Catori place his hand upon her forehead and closed his eyes against the sudden rush of wind carrying them from the plateau. When the whirling ended, he opened his eyes and they stood at the entrance to a cave. A tall, stone arch towered just beyond them. The woman tugged on his arm and backed him against the cave wall.

The wavering form of a person stood at the base of the arch watching a full moon hanging low over the horizon. As the moon rose, she, for it was a woman, stepped back, turning her head to glance at a spot on the cave floor. Bard followed the woman's gaze. A spiral had been chiseled into the stone and the moon's light appeared to follow the path to the center. When the light touched the simple pattern carved there, the woman gasped.

"There," Catori whispered. "Watch within the arch."

Tearing his gaze from the familiarity of the woman, he angled so he faced the arch. A shimmer of light shone brighter than the moon and a vista opened before him. He gasped as well. He saw his world, his home, the place he'd left behind. The place where Grandmother had often taken him to tell the stories of why she had come to that world from her own.

A man appeared beyond the circle, surrounded by the deep, orange-black sky. A man who was dressed as he had dressed at home. A man whose visage he loved well. "Grandfather."

Bard took a step forward but Catori tugged on his arm and pulled him back. "No, this is but a whisper of what happened in the past. You are not yet a part of this tale. We must return to the Sun Temple."

He shook her hand from his arm. "No. My grandfather-"

"Lives in the spirit world," she finished. "Come. There is yet more for you to see, and my time is limited. If I am away from my body too long, the middle world may not release me and, spiritless, my body will die."

Keeping his gaze fixed upon his grandfather, Bard watched until the stone arch disappeared into a fine, rainbow mist. Then he looked down at Catori.

Weariness drew deep lines in her young face, but she grinned at him. "I'll make this part of the story short. The woman at the arch saw your grandfather, and he her. Their souls met, and they loved each other." Catori gave a small sigh. "Oh, to find a love like that." She gave him a speculative, meaningful glance he didn't attempt to interpret and continued.

"But, the moonlight only follows the spiral path on the night of what scientists call a lunar standstill. That has something to do with the moon's distance from the horizon and the amount of distance between the phases. I really don't understand it at all. I do know, however, that on those nights, a gateway such as you saw was opened."

"A gateway? Like a faerie portal?" His spirit shuddered at the mention of a thing he thought better left hidden.

"Yes. Oh, don't look so surprised. There are many interconnected worlds. Some can only be reached through gateways, some only through dreams. Some gateways are ancient and have been closed. Others, I'm sure we are yet to find. But, my tale. The woman loved this man so deeply, she vowed she would leave this world to be with him. However, the lunar standstills only happen about every eighteen years. That was too long for her to wait."

"A long time when one loves."

"I would imagine. However, through her dreams, she discovered another way. A way that had been used hundreds of years before…"

Catori's voice grew weak and she slumped against Bard. "Here, at the Sun Temple."

Surprised at her comment, Bard scanned the area. They had returned to the plateau. "How?"

"I haven't been shown that. I believe that is… your vision. We must… return… to your circle."

The descent was rapid, a free fall that would have stolen his breath had he been in his physical body. A tug in the center of his chest, an irresistible force, urged his spirit to return to his body. Catori smiled as she backed from the circle, sat upon her log and took the guide from her shoulder. She touched noses with the small animal before she set it on the ground. "You feel it, too. Return. I believe we…shall… again."

Her spirit faded and reluctantly, Bard allowed his spirit self be drawn back into his body. The drum slipped from his fingers. He curled on his side and let exhaustion take him to dreamless sleep.

SIXTEEN

After a very short night, a break she took reluctantly, Kae returned to the oldest section of the library. Surprised, she was able to enter the crowded room, so Gowthaman had been true to his word and given her free passage. Before she settled onto the hard chair, she glanced at the stacks of books. This was a researcher's dream. Thankful Gowthaman had chosen to share it with her, she reached for the thick volume he'd presented to her.

Where was he? Thinking back, she realized she hadn't seen him since shortly after he'd handed her the book and she'd begun her translation. Hopefully he understood she forgave him and needed his help. She rubbed at her temples.

The translation progressed easily, pleasantly surprising her. The list of words she'd been unable to discover meanings for was blessedly short. Perhaps she'd contact the boggart who assisted her when she first began learning the fairy language and had translated Oberon's final declaration to the combined Fey peoples of his realm.

A stir of air behind her alerted her to another presence, but no one stepped forward. Kae grinned. "Don't hover, Gowthaman."

"Okay, so I'm hovering. But, I haven't seen Gowthaman today."

Kae leapt from her chair and whirled to embrace her sister. "Nance. What're you doing here?"

"Do I need a reason to come see my sister?"

"Of course not." Kae held Nanceen at arm's length and gave her a long look. "You look great. Pregnancy is good on you."

A flutter of worry crossed Nanceen's features, barely enough to light her eyes, but Kae, with a twin's understanding, caught the subtle emotion. "What's wrong?"

"Nothing."

"Come on, Nance. This is me you're talking to. What's up?"

Nanceen paused a moment, rubbed her hand softly over the small of her back, then glanced meaningfully at the chairs. "Can we sit down?"

"Of course. Have you had breakfast?"

Nanceen chuckled. "I have, have you?" At the shake of Kae's head, she chuckled again. "Didn't think so. They wouldn't let me bring anything in here, but Mother sent a basket. I left it by the pool, so let's go to the oasis and you can eat there. Umm, I think baby might be hungry again, too. Here," she took Kae's hand and pressed her palm against her rounded belly.

Kae gasped at the sturdy kick against her palm. "Wow."

"Yeah, she's an active little thing."

"She?"

Nanceen nodded happily. "We think so."

Kae gathered her sister in a fierce hug. "This is so wonderful. I'm so... so happy." She burst into tears.

Nanceen held her as she cried, stroking her back and humming a song they'd made up when they were children until her sobs faded into soft hiccups.

"I'm sorry, Nance. I don't know what got into me."

"Um--hmm. Kae, we need to talk."

She didn't like the knowing look on her sister's face, so Kae swiftly tried to change the subject. "I think I may be on to something. Gowthaman found a book." She paused and looked past her sister's shoulder. "Wonder where he is."

"I'm sure he'll show up later. Come on. We really do need to talk."

Before Kae could turn back to the table, her sister wrapped a strong arm around her shoulder and guided her from the library.

Nanceen didn't loosen her grip until they neared the oasis pool. Kae sniffed, rubbed at her nose with the back of her hand, and sniffed again. It didn't help so she collapsed to her knees, powerful sobs rising from deep within her pain and wracking her body.

Nanceen stood over her, hands on her hips. "I thought I was the one who was supposed to be hormonal." Then she knelt and took Kae's hand. "Kaelea, don't you try and hide anything from me. You know you can't. Talk to me."

Nodding, Kae dabbed at the corners of her eyes with the hem of her tee shirt. "This is where I first saw Bard."

"Yes, I know."

"And... and four days ago this is where he returned and I found him again."

"And..."

"And we had the most wonderful night." Kae ducked her head to hide the heat blazing over her face and neck.

Nanceen cupped her cheek with her palm. "Yes, I know," she said with a teasing lilt.

"You know? But... oh, God." She'd forgotten about their connection. She'd known when Nanceen had found Korin, when they'd discovered the bliss of each other's bodies. She must have projected her own joy... "Oh, God."

Her sister laughed. "Don't worry about it, sweet sister. Korin and I enjoyed the time immensely."

"Oh, God." Kae moaned into her hands. "I'm so sorry."

"Don't be. We had a great time. And don't worry, you'll learn to block those thoughts--like I have--keep 'em to yourself. While I love sharing just about everything with you Kae, there are just some things..."

"I won't have to."

"Have to what, Kae?"

"I won't have to block those feelings. Bard's gone."

A long sigh prevented Nanceen from speaking. Then, she said, "Yes, I know."

Gowthaman woke with sudden clarity and shook his head to chase away the final, clinging remnants of the human drug. Every muscle screamed with pain, every joint ached as if stretched. Cold metal surrounded his wrists, holding them over his head. His feet barely touched the floor, his ankles shackled to a ring set into the stone.

Crude, but effective, for he could barely move. Even trying to rub his sweat drenched face against his arm was a study in frustration.

He saw little in the dim light surrounding him, but supposed there wasn't much to see. A dungeon was a dungeon, and he doubted a pleasing view would be provided for any held there.

Trying to ease the dull ache in his neck and shoulders, he moved his head from one side to the other, looked down, then up toward the high ceiling. Long, horizontal openings, thin slits in the stone used to observe the dungeon's occupants circled the top of all four walls. He twisted against the chains and followed a shadow moving behind the openings. Soft footsteps paused outside his cell. After an eternity of waiting, the door creaked open.

Bright light from the hall hid the identity of the figure standing in the open doorway but Gowthaman knew whom he faced. Who had him taken from the oasis. Who kept him chained like an animal in the dark

"Feidhlim," he croaked. The movement of his dry lips split the skin. He dragged his parched tongue over the coppery heat of blood then spoke again. "Why do you hold me?"

The faerie laughed, a harsh, humorless sound that sent shards of pain through Gowthaman's skull. Feidhlim advanced a few steps into the room, motioned for a lantern to be placed on a table in one corner, then dismissed the servant. Taking his time dusting off the rough-hewn chair, he sat facing Gowthaman. He said nothing, simply gazed at his prisoner with slightly raised eyebrows.

Trying to keep his expression calm and stoic against the uncomfortable scrutiny, Gowthaman returned the appraising look. He had seen Feidhlim once, long ago, long before the first banishment. Then, the leader of what he'd called the Nechtan-Cattee had been fleshy from excess of drink, slovenly, and vile. Still vile, the faerie had regained his straight, lean form, and the glint in his eyes showed no influence of drink.

A flash of fear coursed through Gowthaman. They had underestimated the current power Feidhlim held over his followers and Kae's family. Before he could control the shudder, the chains rattled and Feidhlim smiled, a glint of straight, white teeth sparkling in the lantern light.

"A brave one, are you, librarian?" A sneer twisted his lips. "I only wish a little information from you. You are a librarian, and used to such requests, are you not?"

The hair on the back of Gowthaman's neck stood, bristling both in fear and anger. Rather than voicing the emotions, he angled his body from Feidhlim as much as the chains allowed and turned his face away.

Feidhlim spoke a harsh word. The chains shortened, jerking Gowthaman back to face his captor. His agonized muscles trembled with the strain and he bit back a groan.

"See, librarian? See how my magic returns to me? Each day, every hour sees me nearer to my restoration, closer to my goal of destroying the Zeroun clan. Including your precious Kaelea."

Gowthaman shook the chains in frustrated anger then stilled, pressed his lips together, and watched warily as the evil one circled him.

"Oh, yes. I know how you feel about her." Feidhlim lurched forward and speared the fingers of one hand into Gowthaman's hair and jerked his head back sharply. "And if you wish her to live--a little longer--you will tell me what I wish to know." He angled Gowthaman's head back further and leaned until his face was close. "Do you understand... librarian?"

Then he shoved Gowthaman's head away and resumed his circling. Like a predatory bird, he paced slowly, silently around the chained man, inching closer, then backing away, threatening then retreating.

Until sweat covered Gowthaman's body and his muscles tensed with waiting. He chewed his lower lip raw to hold back any retort, any sound.

Softly, Feidhlim moved behind him and whispered, "Isn't anticipation a lovely thing?" With a laugh, he paced from the room, pausing only to extinguish the lantern, leaving the room in cold, silent darkness.

K aelea stared at the small bowl of fruit in her lap. When Nanceen wasn't looking, she pushed the pieces around to make it appear as if she'd eaten some. And, although Nanceen hadn't said anything, Kae knew she hadn't fooled her sister.

They'd been at the pool for over an hour while Kae poured out her longing and fears. More than with their twin's connection, she knew Nance understood. Kae had remained strong and steadfast at Nanceen's side while Korin recovered from an attack that left him nearly dead and his beautiful wings destroyed. She'd never given up hope for Nanceen, and now her sister's presence at her side offered the same comfort.

But part of her refused comfort, wanting instead to wallow in the misery she'd brought upon herself. If she wouldn't have insisted on helping a stranger who appeared here, at the oasis, this pool--she dipped her toes in the cool water--if she would have turned him over to someone else immediately...

Nanceen took her hand. "Don't rethink the past, Kae. It doesn't do any good, because it never changes. I think--no, I believe--you were fated to meet Bard. And you'll be with him again. I know it."

Filled with disbelief, Kae turned her head to look at her sister. "How can you say that? Oh, sure, there was a spark between us."

Nanceen opened her mouth as if to speak, then only shook her head.

"A spark that wasn't even enough to last beyond one night," Kae finished. "How could that mean anything? No, Nance. It's not meant to be. I had my night of... wonder... glorious... of fun. Now, it's time to get on with my life, finish my research so we can finally put an end to Feidhlim and his threat to our brother."

"Kae--"

"No. Don't. Don't say anything more. I've been a fool and let my fool's actions rule my heart. Time to get down to business." She took a deep breath and squared her shoulders. "Now, we need to find Gowthaman and..."

Concern for her friend rose and momentarily took precedence over the personal pain she longed to deny. It wasn't like him to disappear, especially when their friendship was back on track and she was making progress on her research.

Nanceen stroked the back of her hand. "I have a confession. When Gowthaman sent me the message yesterday, asking me to come, he asked something else, too. I didn't know if I... but now that I'm here, I see he was correct."

"Correct about what?" A faint suspicion trembled within her like a butterfly first opening its wings. There was something she should know, a feeling much like when she found a hint in one text that led her to another, which in turn carried her to an answer. What was the answer? "Nance, what was he right about?"

Hesitating, Nanceen took a deep breath and nibbled on the corner of her lip. Kae smiled at the action, a sure giveaway there was something Nance didn't want to mention. But, this was more serious than their childhood games. "Nance? What about Gowthaman?"

Nanceen looked away, then returned to lock gazes with her. "Soulfire."

"Soulfire?" Kae chuckled. "What tales is he telling you? What did he say about soulfire to get you to come here? In order for there to be soulfire, two people have to have that special connection like Jaye and Allyn, or Tommy and Derrik. Or that flying thing you and Korin do."

Bright pink infused Nanceen's face, but she smiled. "Yep, you understand the whys of soulfire. Nobody knows the how or the reason it manifests differently for different couples. But, don't you understand why Gowthaman sent the message to me and mentioned soulfire?"

"No clue." That odd fluttering beating around her heart returned full force, denying her denial. No, she didn't have a clue. Fear of what Nanceen was going to tell her next kept the breath in her lungs.

The fingers Nanceen wrapped around hers were warm, the touch as familiar as her own skin. She looked into the face that mirrored hers and searched for answers. "Tell me what he said, Nance. Please."

After a visible swallow, Nanceen nodded. "When he came upon the two of you here at the oasis, he saw it. Saw the soulfire between you. Sparking purple..."

Kae twisted her hand away then pressed her fingertips to her lips. "No. That can't be. Only some trick of the sun," she mumbled.

"It wasn't a trick, Kae. And no mistake."

"But, that's for couples who stay together, forever. He barely stayed one night." Tears burned Kae's gritty eyes. To find a love that would spark a soulfire had always been her hope, a deep longing. But she'd never expected it to happen. Now... now she wasn't sure she wanted it. "No, it can't be."

"He'll be back, Kae."

She cast Nanceen a grimace. "Back? He left without even saying goodbye. Just disappeared into the night. Like a thief." A thief who stole her heart, a heart she'd never regain, except with him. "What kind of soulfire would that inspire? No, Nance. Gowthaman must have been mistaken. Or he just used that as a ploy to get you here."

"No ploy. But, if you don't want to talk about it--"

"I don't."

"Okay, then. Eat your lunch."

"I'm not hungry." Kae set the bowl aside and crossed her

arms. It was time to get back to work. She'd wasted enough long moments on foolishness and dreams. Nanceen's visit had proven that to her, solidified her resolve--again. "I need to get back to the library."

Nanceen's hand on her arm stopped her from rising. "Not until you eat something."

"I said I'm not hungry. Can't you let it go?"

Placing the bowl of fruit back in her hand, Nanceen gave her a gentle, sad smile. "If you won't eat for yourself, then eat for the baby."

Kae gave her sister an incredulous look, then burst into laughter. When she regained her breath, she smoothed a short, stray curl behind Nanceen's ear. "That was a low blow. Why do I need to eat for your baby? Does she want a chubby aunt?"

The sadness lingered in Nanceen's expression. "No. Not for my baby."

"Then what are you talking about?"

"Kae, look inside yourself. Feel what I feel emanating from you. From here." Nanceen touched Kae's lower belly. "There's a type of soulfire here, too. Faint, the barest of a lavender glow. But it's there, Kae. Feel it. Feel."

Kae shook her head and tried to push Nanceen's hand away. Not to be deterred, Nance captured her sister's hand and held it beneath her own on Kae's stomach.

"Feel, Kae. Don't deny what we both know is there. Don't deny the child you created."

"Child?" Kae closed her eyes and, though she fought to ignore the tiny flicker of life, a faint swirl of lavender curled behind her lowered eyelids. The swirl touched her mind and opened her thoughts to the realization. The truth. Still, she could not allow herself to believe. "He was only with me one night."

Nanceen hugged Kae to her and chuckled. "It only takes once, you know," she whispered. Then she held Kae at arm's length and searched her face. "Kae?"

"My child? It's true. Oh, Nance. Bard gave me a child."

"Think how happy he'll be when you find him and tell him."

Kae jerked away and lifted her hands in a forbidding gesture. "No. I'm not going after him--not now, not ever. And neither are you." She shook her finger at her sister. "And no one else either, so don't even think of telling Derrik or Jayse. I'll let the rest of the family know when--"

"You won't be able to hide the child. I can see the soulfire now, and everyone will be at the meeting Jaye called for this afternoon."

"Soulfire... because a child? No, that's impossible. That's never happened before. No child has--"

"Never say never, Kae. Look at all the nevers that have happened in our family. Why shouldn't the child of a great love have a visual aura of its own?"

"Great love? But he..."

"Don't say it." Nanceen waited as Kae sputtered to silence. "We don't yet understand why, but there must be a reason for him to have left so suddenly. He's too honorable to do otherwise."

This was too much, much more than she had the energy to comprehend, more than she was able to deal with, so she flattened her palms over her lower belly and accepted the life within her. Bard may have left her, but he unknowingly left her with something more wonderful than anything else she could imagine. He may have left her alone, but a piece of him remained with her--a piece she would cherish and care for like a precious gift. Their child.

An answering welling of love filled her and she grinned at Nanceen. "Okay, so where's my lunch?"

SEVENTEEN

K nowing the more he consciously thought about the dream journey he'd taken, the less he would understand, Bard spent the morning challenging his physical body. He ran many units, climbed steep rock cliffs and shorter, wind-tossed trees and spent long hours by the stream repeating ancient patterns of defense and attack. Then he bathed in the cold water and returned to his ledge.

Unable to banish the vision of his world he'd seen through the arch, he concentrated on the place where he'd created his power circle there, held his breath and formed a portal. Shocked, and surprisingly dismayed at his success, he managed to shrink the portal until it was more a window than a gateway. Then he sat cross-legged upon his blankets and stared into the bleak landscape and peach colored sky.

Chin in hand, he didn't alter his gaze when, much later, he sensed the opening of a portal beside him.

"I beg yer pardon. I ken ye dinna wish to be disturbed." Derrik's soft apology drew him from his dangerously scattered thoughts and he focused on the leader of the Alastriona.

"Welcome, defender. No bother. I hope my travels have not abused the privilege of portal use." He stretched his cramped shoulder muscles and looked up at the tall faerie.

Derrik squatted beside him. "Nay, dinna fasch yerself.

Each of us may have, at times, a need fer privacy. I wouldna intrude now, but there've been... developments in our quest against Feidhlim an' Jaye has called a family meetin'."

Bard nodded his understanding and gave a slight shrug of one shoulder.

Derrik continued, "An' he wishes fer ye to attend."

"Me? I don't understand."

The smile Derrik gave him shone bright in the afternoon sun. "An' I'm sure I dinna ken, either. However, he is heir to the leadership of my clan an' I do as he asks. Will ye attend?"

Bard was silent and returned his gaze to the small portal. A family meeting. Kaelea would be there. Could he face her, after running from her bed without explanation? Now he had even more questions, and still no explanations. "Yes," he said without looking at Derrik. "Where?"

"Stephen's cabin."

"Okay." Bard winced. Would he ever be able to say that word without filling with longing for Kaelea? He doubted... but if she wouldn't forgive him for his thoughtless abandonment, he'd know for the rest of his life.

Derrik hadn't moved so Bard gave a soft snort. "Stay awhile if you wish, defender. I am not bound to being alone." Yet.

With movements that barely stirred the air, Derrik sat, rested his forearms on his bent knees, and leaned forward. Curiosity filled his posture and Bard knew that questions had to be filling the faerie's mind. He waited for Derrik to ask.

A bird perched in a nearby tree trilled a long note then flew away before Derrik spoke. "That is yer world then?"

"Yes."

"Ye've been successful. Congratulations, m'friend." Derrik clasped his shoulder.

"Thank you."

Leaning to the side, Derrik peered at him, his bright blue eyes searching. "Yer nae happy?"

Giving the universal sign of non-commitment, Bard shrugged.

Derrik's hand remained on his shoulder, now a gesture of

comfort. The concern brought an unwelcome tightness to Bard's throat and he swallowed heavily. The hand fell away and both men turned toward the portal.

Vast, fluffy clouds skimmed over the peachy sky. Bright sunlight created deep, dense shadows trailing from each of the small rocks he'd used to create his circle. The shadows warped the circle, stretching it toward the small portal. To one side, his cast off clothing remained partially hidden beneath the bush. A mountainous backdrop reached high into the sky, as if the peaks were trying to catch the clouds. He'd thought his world a beautiful place, until the Guardians brought him to another place. The landscape of his home still touched his heart. But true beauty was here. And only realized with Kaelea.

After a long silence, he spoke. "I've been thinking about magic."

"Aye?"

"I didn't believe in magic in my world. Even though Grandfather was a shaman and Grandmother claimed to have come from a different world." He cast a sidelong glance at Derrik. "I now believe she originally came from this world."

While he didn't expect disbelief, Derrik's calm acceptance surprised him. "Aye. Such happenin's would explain much within history. Both human an' Faerie. This connection is part of what Kae is searchin' fer. But what are yer thoughts now on magic?"

Grateful Derrik hadn't continued speaking of Kaelea, Bard turned his attention back to the portal and his words back to a safer ground. "In spite of my skepticism, I discovered magic in this world. And, surprisingly, within myself."

"Aye. 'Tis a part of all livin' things." Derrik grinned. "The trick, m'friend, is to realize yer magic. Then ye must harness that magic an' make it yer own."

"That's the difficulty, defender."

"Aye, 'tis."

"I have magic here." Bard spread his hands then pointed to the portal. "But, would I still find magic within myself in that world? I have created a portal--"

"Small, dinna ye think?" Derrik chuckled. "How would ye be able to--"

With a quick flick of his wrist, Bard grew the portal to full size. He returned Derrik's grin and lifted his eyebrows. "I didn't need a full portal for watching only. Why expend the energy?"

A full, rolling laugh erupted from Derrik. "Guid. I like yer thinkin', man. But ye still dinna seem as pleased wi' yer portal as I expected ye to be."

Bard angled to face the defender. "What if my magic is only possible in this world and in your Otherworld? What if it doesn't exist in my world? What if I am unable to call upon this newfound ability there? What if I cross the portal and... am unable to create a return portal?"

"An' ye would wish to return?" Laughter filled Derrik's question and Bard lowered his brows to peer at him. The faerie schooled his expression and stared innocently through the portal.

He'd asked the question Bard had been avoiding. Once home, would he wish to return? Perhaps the question was, if he really wished to return there, once the only world he'd known.

"Or, mayhaps ye dinna really wish to return to that world."

Amazed that Derrik's statement echoed his thoughts, Bard scrubbed his hands over his face and through his hair. He stared at the ground just beyond his crossed legs. "I... don't know."

"Ah."

A low groan gave voice to his frustration and with a quick flick of his fingers, he closed the portal.

Derrik rose with fluid grace and stretched. "Ye have one human hour before we meet. Come to the gatherin'." Derrik continued as if nothing were amiss. "Mayhaps some of yer questions will be answered then as well. Nanceen has gone to bring her sister, so Kaelea will be joinin' us. The message Gowthaman sent Nanceen says Kae pines fer ye."

Conscious of the faerie's intense gaze upon him, Bard struggled to maintain his composure. The Other had said that?

Bard had been sure the slender faerie wished Kaelea for himself. Why would the Other--would Gowthaman--appear to support him? More cursed questions.

He rose and clasped Derrik's forearm. "I'll be there."

How long had he been held? Gowthaman tried to ease the muscles that had long ago ceased aching, but the short lengths of chain allowed minimal movement. With no further movements along the watch walk, few visits from Feidhlim or his followers, and with no light, he had no way to judge the passage of time. He rested his cheek against his extended arm.

If only he could sleep. The physical pain drained more than just life's energy from him. The barriers he'd erected around his hidden talents were falling, like a decrepit wall, stone by stone. How might Feidhlim use the knowledge of his... deception? His tired mind blasted him with self-incriminations, each more painful than his physical agonies.

By hiding his abilities, was he any better than Feidhlim? By not allowing others to know the truth of his talents, had he condemned Kaelea and her family? Was there some magic he'd hidden and tried to forget that could have helped more, solved the problem sooner, kept the evil at bay?

He groaned and a laugh from the observation windows answered him. Wearily, he turned toward the door. Time for another visit from Feidhlim.

A richly clad woman followed Feidhlim into the cell and stood quietly to one side as he advanced to stand before Gowthaman. Bending slightly, Feidhlim peered into Gowthaman's face.

"Are you enjoying your stay with us, librarian?"

He would not let the evil one see his pain or his despair. Gowthaman lifted his head and willed hard defiance into his expression. "What think you?"

Feidhlim smiled brightly and began circling him. Tired of the trick, Gowthaman turned his attention to the woman. She had set flame to the lamp and the light slowly filtered through the cell. The flickering shone upon her face, deepening the soft bruising on one cheek to nearly the color of her violet eyes. He'd heard the evil one had a penchant for women with violet eyes. Like Kae's sister-in-law, Allyn. He held back a shudder.

The woman rubbed at her arm, the action drawing his attention to the raw skin braceleting her wrist. A mark that matched the torn skin at his own. She didn't appear a prisoner.

"I wish for you to meet someone, librarian." Feidhlim moved before him, blocking his view of the woman.

"What you wish is of no concern to me."

The force of Feidhlim's blow jerked Gowthaman's weakened body and he hung limply from the arm shackles until he could regain his feet. Blood oozed from the corner of his lip, but he forced a grin.

Returning the grin, Feidhlim planted his fists at his waist and considered his prisoner. The defiance from the scholar surprised, and pleased him. He had feared extracting information from Gowthaman would be too easy, but now...his anticipation increased. He swung his arm toward the woman. "As I said, I wish for you to meet Petulia. I believe you shall become well acquainted."

The librarian snorted and turned his face away. Catching the stubborn man's chin in his hand, Feidhlim forced him to look at the woman. "It does not matter what you may think you believe, or how strongly you believe you can hide what I wish to know. Petulia shall discover your secrets."

Feidhlim paused at the fear shining from the librarian's eyes. So, he did conceal information. From the scent of fear rising from his captive, Feidhlim became convinced that knowledge would be useful. He would take that knowledge now, and enjoy the fear later.

"You see, librarian, Petulia is my seeker." Again he paused and held a gentle smile for the man's confusion. "You wonder what I mean by seeker, do you not, Gowthaman?"

"I won--wonder nothing."

"Oh, but you do. Petulia has a unique gift, talents she has

chosen rightly to use in my cause." He turned his face toward her. "Haven't you, my dear?"

Desire that a moment ago lay dormant flushed through her expression and she took an eager step forward. "Yes, my lord."

Gowthaman shuddered and Feidhlim laughed. He enjoyed being the object of desire, of adulation, of fear.

The laughter chased another shudder across Gowthaman's shoulders. Even the air around the evil one became dark and fetid.

What power did he have over the woman that she would accept his bondage then serve him with such... lust in her eyes? Disgusted, Gowthaman tried to twist away but Feidhlim held him fast.

"So, my fine librarian. Petulia's talent is seeking answers. Without questions, without coercion. She will seek within your mind."

Feidhlim released him and Gowthaman slumped against the pull of his shackles. There had been rumors of such a talent throughout the known history, but no faerie with the magic had ever been confirmed. If it were true, and she were a seeker, he would be exposed. His eyes closed as he struggled to hastily rebuild the walls around his talents.

But before he could mentally lift the broken stones, cool fingers pressed lightly just above his eyebrows.

"If you fight me, this will be painful," Petulia whispered in his ear.

Feidhlim leaned close to his other side. "Fight if you dare librarian. I'll have what I want from you."

Tendrils, light as the newest growth of a Faerie vine, curled inward from each of Petulia's fingertips. He saw them, felt them, as they inched deeper and deeper into his consciousness. One by one, the tendrils wrapped around the stones of his barrier, easing between the tightly mortared construction, and tore them down. With the tearing away, a scream ripped from his throat.

Each stone became a scream, followed by Feidhlim's wild laughter. Gowthaman's legs gave way and he hung by his wrists, gouging deep tears in the abused skin. He didn't feel the pain or the hot blood that ran down his arms. His shoulders popped with the strain. His throat burned. He thrashed his head back and forth but was unable to escape the seeker's touch.

The tendrils withdrew, leaving a void that filled slowly as his mind returned to him. She had taken, but somehow still left the contents of his mind intact. Panting, Gowthaman struggled to set his feet under him and ease the pain in his shoulders. He couldn't even draw upon enough energy to glare at Feidhlim.

Petulia patted his cheek then moved to Feidhlim's side. "He knows nothing more than we do of the history the usurper searches for. However, there is a book in the guarded center of the library. A book the usurper's sister studies."

Feidhlim caressed her cheek and she leaned into the touch. "Go on."

She glanced at Gowthaman as she pressed her lips to Feidhlim's palm then gave a satisfied smile. "He has talents, my lord. Talents he has hidden even from the Alastriona. Talents you shall harness and use to your glory."

"Indeed." He eyed Gowthaman with wicked speculation.

"And, my lord, he..." She stood on her toes to whisper to Feidhlim. The evil one's eyebrows rose and he smiled.

Gowthaman's heart plummeted. They knew... knew what he had done in his attempts to win Kaelea's love. No hope remained. Petulia had stolen his dishonor as she flowed through his mind. A faint hope glimmered. Perhaps they would kill him for he would be of no use now.

"He did?" Feidhlim turned a predatory smile toward him. "Perhaps there is a place for him with us after all, Petulia. What think you?"

By the gods of the desert. What plans did the evil one create? He would not serve him, somehow he would...

"As you wish, my lord."

"Yes, as I wish. Within him is a wealth of possibilities. For now, have him taken to... more comfortable quarters."

Feidhlim returned to circling him and Gowthaman stood

still, head hanging forward, his gaze focused on the drops of his blood spattered across the stone floor. There was no longer a reason to fight. The evil one knew what he knew, knew the talents he'd hidden. Knew about the book and Kaelea's studies. He sent a brief mental whisper of thanks that he'd warded the inner chamber. But, if the seeker knew...then she would also have discovered the wards he'd set and would find the way to circumvent them.

He'd failed--again.

"So, my dear. How do we get this book that you claim rests prominently within his mind? How do we make the usurper's sister hand the volume over to us? Will she trade it for the life of the librarian?"

Gowthaman jerked upright. "No. She would not."

Feidhlim chuckled. "You don't think so? This family, this clan of Zeroun is loyal to each other, to those they call friend."

"I am... am not... friend. How could I be when I..."

"Don't flatter yourself, librarian."

"My lord?" At Petulia's words, Feidhlim turned expectantly toward her. "My lord, there is someone else. Another he believes Kaelea would trade for the book. We..." she glanced at Gowthaman, "... witnessed soulfire."

"Aiiyyee!" Gowthaman wailed softly and collapsed back upon himself. He knew the paths Bard had taken. Now, the enemy also knew those paths. He hadn't thought he could sink lower into the depths of despair.

Feidhlim clapped his hands once and the shackles fell from Gowthaman's wrists and ankles. He slumped to the floor and lay in a dejected heap. Why move? There was nothing more he could do, for he'd done enough. Forgive me, Kaelea. Bard.

"Have this other being brought to me. Immediately. Then, we shall see what he shall tell us." Leaving Gowthaman to his misery, the pair exited the cell. The door stood wide open but Gowthaman couldn't even raise his head to peer into the hallway. There was nothing left.

. . .

Anticipation assaulted Bard, making him lean against the sun warmed cliff wall. Though it had only been four days, soon he would see Kaelea. And with the Guardians' blessing, he would find forgiveness. Perhaps they could start over, begin their relationship the correct way.

As he reached to replace the drum at the bottom of the pack, the tingle of an opening portal raced across the back of his neck, lifting the fine hairs. He frowned. This felt--different. He straightened and turned.

A strange, dark haired man stood before him, a satisfied smirk tightening his lips. "My lord Feidhlim wishes to speak with you."

Feidhlim? The one who threatened Kaelea's family? What devilment was this? Bard folded his arms over his chest. "I have no wish to speak with him. Go back to your lord and tell him so, if you wish. But I will not accompany you."

The faerie didn't seem threatening, but the uncomfortable twitching of a muscle along Bard's jaw told him the threat was real, none-the-less. He'd never given much credence to the odd feelings Grandfather encouraged him to follow, and now he regretted his ignorance.

"Your wishes mean nothing, human."

Bard let a tiny smile touch his lips as he lifted his eyebrows in silent challenge.

"You will come with me."

"No. You may tell your lord--"

Like the splitting of stone, a loud crack sounded above him. The swirl of a second portal opened above his head and arms reached down to him. A chain wrapped magically around his chest, arms, and legs to hold his struggles immobile as he was lifted into the portal.

EIGHTEEN

J aye glanced around the clearing at the gathered clan. The
tight knit support system was a constantly flowing
entity, moving easily to where it was needed most. His
sister hadn't needed to make a formal announcement of
her pregnancy, the evidence was there in a faint lavender glow
around the child. Only a few days after conception, and the
love that created the babe was visible. He shook his head in
amazement. An aura never seen before in his family.

His two pregnant sisters. He looked forward to a niece or
nephew, almost as much as he looked forward to the birth of
his next grandchild. The three women had clustered together,
an island of life and hope in the struggle against Feidhlim.

Carrie stood nearby, the fourth new life showing in her
rounded belly. Carrie, who suffered insecurity and fear
because her child had been fathered in violence by the faerie
who strove to destroy them all.

Lara reached out and gathered Carrie into their group. Jaye
smiled in relief. Carrie still didn't understand or believe the
unreserved acceptance by her new family.

Derrik joined him and canted his head toward the women.
"'Tis a beautiful thing."

"Yes, it is. And we have to do all we can to protect those
lives and that beauty."

"Aye. Do ye believe there may be somethin' in the book Kae found?"

"I honestly don't know, Derrik. I just don't know. Maybe we're grasping at straws. But we can't afford to overlook any possibility."

"Aye."

"I hoped Bard would be here, especially with Kae's... surprise."

Derrik stared into the distance. "He said he'd come. I dinna understand why he remains away." Eyes slightly unfocused, he concentrated for a moment. "He hasna used a portal."

"Bard didn't seem like someone who would go against his word."

"Nay, he isna. 'Tis a concern."

Jaye chuckled. "And you'll be checking on him."

"Aye, that I shall."

The men turned back to the cabin and Kae watched their slow progress across the clearing. She was probably imagining it, or maybe just hoping, but she thought she'd heard Bard's name. Maybe Derrik could find him and bring him back to her. She patted Nanceen's arm.

"I'll be right back."

Halfway across the clearing she met Nightshade, who smiled before giving her a tight hug. "Congrats, honey. Is this family growing, or what?"

Kae chuckled. How could one not with Nightshade's exuberance? "Looks like it. How's Carrie really doing?"

Nightshade sighed, a true sigh rather than one of his feigned, overly dramatic mannerisms. "She's tough. She'll be okay. Once she really believes what it means when you're accepted into this family."

"And we'll just keep on accepting her. And her child. So, where are you off to in such a hurry?"

"Business, darling. Nothing but business."

"I won't keep you then." She slid her arm around his slender waist, but jerked her hand away when she touched a hard, cold lump tucked into the back waistband of his tight jeans. She grabbed the hem of his flowing, silk shirt and lifted it to find--a gun.

"What in the world is this?"

Nightshade chuckled dryly. "A gun, honey."

"What are you doing with a gun? Nightshade, you'll shoot your foot off."

He straightened and his demeanor changed subtly. The soft, flighty expression firmed, the loose set of his muscles tightened. Kae took a step back. The man changed and radiated a power she'd never imagined could rise from him.

"This family needs protection, Kaelea. Derrik does a fine job here in Faerie and in dealing with magical concerns. But Tommy's kidnapping proved that there is human danger as well, that Feidhlim will use any means to get what he wants. And, honey, so will I. Trust Nightshade, and he'll help keep you and yours safe."

"But... but, a gun?"

"Don't worry, honey." Nightshade reached toward the gun, pressed it slightly, then tugged down on his shirt hem. "Don't worry. I know how to use this. And, given provocation, I will not hesitate."

Then he gave a loose wave and returned to the Nightshade she knew and loved. "Don't worry about me, honey."

Before she could ask him more, the chameleon-like man stepped through a portal to the human world. Jaye and Derrik had also disappeared, but her mother and Allyn had joined Nanceen and the others. Kae swallowed her sadness and returned to the gathering of women.

"You have done well."

The brown haired faerie's chest puffed with pride as he glanced at the others in the chamber. Finally, his gaze returned to Feidhlim. "It is my pleasure to serve."

"I don't doubt." Feidhlim drummed his fingers on the table, irritated that his sarcasm was lost on the preening underling. When the man sat, still accepting the quiet congratulations of those around him, Feidhlim flattened his palms against the tabletop and leaned forward. "You left no trail?"

"Oh, no, my lord. We did as you ordered. The Alastriona will not follow."

"Good." He rested back against the high, padded chair and returned to his thoughts. The monotonous drumming of his fingers throbbed through the room. If the Alastriona were able to follow... He made a mental note to have Petulia seek the librarian's mind again. If he'd been able to shield his talents this long, there might be a way the Nechtan-Cattee could harvest his skills without his cooperation.

Hiding the ability to follow another's movements through portals from a group that actively sought such talent lifted the seemingly mild librarian in his estimation. And though he fought them, Feidhlim knew, given time, Gowthaman would be his.

Time. He returned his focus to the gathered council. "You have arranged the time distortions?"

"Yes, my lord," a gray haired faerie said softly. "It is as you wish. While only a few days may pass for our... guests, in the human world, time flows more quickly. One day within your castle, three months to others."

"Good. We shall wait the length of our day before contacting the usurper's sister. If a satisfactory agreement can be made, we may trade the human for her information. Or, perhaps not. Nor will I guarantee the... condition of the human if he returns to her."

Laughter rounded the table and Feidhlim gave a slight nod of satisfaction. "In any case, the librarian remains here. There is much to learn from him." He caressed the hair of the woman seated on the floor next to his chair. "Isn't that so, Petulia?"

Blatant adoration filled her face as she looked up at him and nodded. "Yes, my lord. He does not willingly reveal his secrets."

"And that is enjoyable, is it not?"

"Oh, yes, my lord." She smiled and tasted her bottom lip with her tongue. Heat gathered in Feidhlim's groin. She was a wild wench, and useful, earning a lengthy stay at his side.

At least until he had the usurper's woman. Soon, he vowed, he would finally have his vengeance, and Allyn.

Bard paced the small space of his captivity. Three strides in one direction, turn, three strides. The only alteration was a slight side step around the narrow pallet tossed against the wall opposite the door. His captors had left him alone, and as the door closed, the chains slipped from his body. He'd kicked them into a corner and glared at them each time he passed.

He should have been more vigilant and not allowed himself to be taken. He tried the door, and it opened, but he was unable to pass through the opening. A firm, slightly elastic force kept him from leaving. So he'd slammed the door and continued his pacing.

Two small, vertical slits interrupted the smooth flow of the squared stone wall. No force hampered him when he stuck his arm through the opening, but it didn't matter. Too narrow for him to squeeze though, the windows did allow a fresh, salty breeze to clear the chamber of the taints of disuse.

Tension drew a sharp pain between his shoulder blades and his head throbbed. Wondering why he had been abducted, Bard leaned against the wall and watched the door. He had no doubt he would meet Feidhlim soon. Then he would make his escape. A wicked thought crossed his mind and he grinned. Perhaps he would take the defeated Feidhlim with him. Conquering the reason for Kaelea's fear would be a way to prove himself to her.

How would she feel when he didn't appear at the gathering as requested? The smile faded and he stopped to peer out one of the windows. A vast expanse of calm, crystal blue-green sea stretched to the horizon. A sheer rock face followed the line of the castle wall to a beach littered with sharp, pointed boulders. Wind whistled through the beach stones, and he thought he heard words: cries of pain and sounds of joy, doubts and fears and pleas that tore at his heart without knowing the cause. It was a dismal, frightening place, and he backed from the window.

The sounds of pain continued, louder as he neared one of the side walls. Sounds of abject terror and soul rending agony, though muffled by the thick stone wall, sent chills skittering along his spine. Was his to be a similar fate at Feidhlim's hands? He'd heard enough of the man's evil deeds to believe it possible. A lull in the pitiful noise let him relax and he rolled his shoulders. No matter the force used against him, his conviction should enable him to stand firm against it.

But what did they want from him?

He had no knowledge useful to either side of this conflict. His only connection was Kaelea.

Feidhlim must believe he knew of Kaelea's studies and of the reasons she searched through the old texts. He gave a soft snort. What use could a genealogy be, either for Feidhlim or in the fight against him?

The silence from beyond the wall shattered with one low groan and tension cramped his shoulders to tight knots. His stomach clenched. It wouldn't be long.

Within minutes, two figures appeared in the open door-way. At a harshly spoken word they entered, the woman following a few steps behind the man. Bard studied the man, the overconfident set of his shoulders and arrogant stride proclaimed him to be Feidhlim. He strode to the center of the tiny room. His face flushed, his eyes were glazed as though he had just come from a lover's bed. But, those hadn't been love's sounds emanating from the neighboring room.

In a flash, the look was gone and the man crossed his arms over his chest, mimicking Bard's stance. The touch of his gaze was physical, cold, impersonal.

"Where do you come from, human?"

Bard remained silent.

"You're different from the others, but I am unable to deter-mine why." He cast a quick glance at the woman. "Petulia, discover the reason."

Wary, Bard watched her advance, a smooth glide over the stone. She smiled up at him. "This won't hurt, much."

Her hands lifted toward his head. Bard wrenched away and took the three steps to the far side of the room. She followed, hands stretched toward him. He backed away. The woman attempted to appear harmless, but her eyes had lost focus for a moment, then glazed with the same cold satisfaction that Feidhlim's had held when he entered the chamber. The look chilled Bard to the depths of his soul.

"Enough." The command halted both Bard and the woman. Once he stopped moving, Bard found himself frozen in place, unable to move his feet, his arms hanging like leaden weights at his sides.

Cool fingertips pressed against his forehead, following the line of his brows. Sharp tendrils of pain pierced his skull. He bit his lip to contain his shock and his eyes widened. He saw the paths the tendrils made as they curled through his mind. Searching. Seeking. Stealing his will to resist.

A glint, the silver slash of a sword cut through the advancing tendrils and the woman gasped. Her lips firmed to a determined line and she pressed her fingers hard against his forehead.

::*No, you shall not.*::

The soft declaration, a woman's voice in his mind, cooled the heat. The sword lowered to block the renewed advance. Bard closed his eyes--and saw.

Dressed in gray, with a cloak thrown back from her shoulders, the woman turned her gaze to him and smiled. ::*Dinna worry, She shallnae seek yer mind.*::

::*You are... Derrik's cousin?*::

::*Aye.*:: She turned away and slashed at a tendril curling around her ankle.

With a force that would have sent him stumbling had he been able to move, his mind was attacked by innumerable tendrils, rising, curling from every direction. The woman in gray fought valiantly, but many passed her sword and eased with white-hot pain into his thoughts and memories. Slowly, his will drained from him.

The soft, rapid beat of a drum grew steadily louder, demanding attention. With an effort strong enough to tear his mind asunder, he focused on the drum. Each tap beat the tendrils back, each resounding thrum returned his mind to him. Bard felt his face relax in a smile, Catori had somehow known of his trial and, together with Derrik's cousin, helped to chase the invasion away. Silver fire, tinted with a pale purple glow surrounded him. With a mighty shout, Bard physically twisted from the woman, escaped the magic holding him in place, and put as much space between them as he was able in the tiny chamber. Hands planted against his knees, he gasped long, deep breaths of air.

The woman stared at her hands then sank to her knees with an undulating wail. Feidhlim opened his fist and slapped her. The wailing ceased.

"Petulia. You have failed me."

"My--my lord. I have never sought in a mind such as his. I do not understand how he fought me or how he regained the control to force me away. My lord, my fingers..." She stared at her hands and Bard leaned to the side to watch her lift her hands to Feidhlim. The tips of her fingers were blackened, as though burned to coal in a hot fire.

Eyes wide and glistening with tears, she hesitantly touched Feidhlim's hand. "I... I f--feel n--nothing."

"Get out of my sight," Feidhlim growled through clenched teeth. "Dare not appear before me without my leave." He took a step back and pointed at the doorway. "Go."

"B--but, m--my--"

"Go, while I feel generous."

Petulia opened her mouth as if to speak, but a fierce glare from Feidhlim kept her silent. Gathering her skirts, she rose and backed from the cell. With a wave of one hand, Feidhlim slammed the door.

Then, fists clenched tightly, he held his arms stiff against his side. The air around him vibrated with palpable anger. "How... did...you...do...that?"

NINETEEN

For the fifth time in as many days, Derrik opened a portal to the ledge where he'd last spoken to Bard. He stepped through and scanned the immediate area. No changes. Each stone lay in the same place, Bard's pack lay tossed in a heap, his other belongings remained stacked under the slight overhang.

Derrik stood spread-legged, hands fisted at his hips, and shook his head. There was no indication of Bard returning to his own world. In fact, no portal to that location had opened since the one he'd witnessed. The ledge was undisturbed except by his repeated visits.

And, for the fifth time in as many days, Derrik moved to the center of the stone circle. He sat, closed his eyes and after a moment's concentration, sent out his feelings, searching for some sign of Bard.

After a fruitless search he blew out a short, frustrated breath. Other than an odd wavering in the air over his head, he felt--nothing. And that in itself was odd.

The air beside him stirred. Derrik rose and turned to face the young Alastriona who stepped onto the ledge. "Anything?" he asked.

"Nothin' different than yestern. Or the day before that."

"What shall we do now, Derrik?"

"Ah, Macaire, I dinna ken. He's gone, but where? An' how? Nay, he dinna return to his world, but he has hidden well." Derrik gave Macaire a brief smile. "I dinna think he would develop such a talent."

Macaire shrugged. "Perhaps it is not so unusual in his world."

"I dinna... perhaps. This is the last time fer us to come here lookin' fer him. But, I wish to take his belongin's back to the Otherworld. When he returns..."

"These shall be returned to him. I shall place them in safe-keeping." Macarie reached for the pack, but instead took up a short stick that had been planted in a small rock cairn and held it to the light. Strips of colored leather and nubby string wrapped one end. Small stones and other objects hung from short pieces of the string. Macarie fingered a red and white candy. "What do you suppose the things on this stick mean?"

S truggling to control his anger, Feidhlim slowly unclenched his fists and flexed his fingers. The urge to wrap his hands around his captive's neck and throttle the defiant smirk from the man's face was undeniably strong. He lifted his hands, shook himself, then drew them back to his sides. His seeker had failed, indicating there was much to learn from this one. Too much damage would slow the process.

Consciously deepening his breathing and slowing the fierce beating of his heart, Feidhlim took a step back and folded his arms across his chest. Now that he studied the man, it was evident Bard didn't understand what he'd done, or how he'd rejected the seeker. Confusion lingered in the human's eyes. Feidhlim allowed himself a brief, satisfied grin.

Let the man think himself safe--for the time being. Feidhlim tilted his head slightly to one side and executed a tiny, mocking salute. "Until the next time, human."

Bard kept his face impassive as Feidhlim stalked from the room, but once the faerie was gone, he let his shoulders droop and he slumped against the wall. The ordeal exhausted him and if the seeker returned now he'd never be able to fight her touch. Even with assistance from Catori's drum and the woman's sword.

::*There be no need. She will nae touch another mind. Her seekin' is failed and he will also suffer failure. Dinna worry.*::

Bard accepted the soft lilting tones in his head and slid down to sit on the cold floor. He hung his head and rubbed the back of his neck. Why had Derrik's cousin chosen to come to his aid?

Kind, gentle laughter eased through his mind. ::*Ye have been under m' watch since ye arrived in this world. Ye jest dinna have cause fer m' interference.*::

"But why?" he whispered.

::*Ye dinna ken... ah, yer guide tells me ye do.*::

"My guide?"

::*Aye. Now, we must find the way from yer prison. There is also another held here who must be taken wi' ye.*::

Someone else was held by this evil? Of course, the cries from the other room. Monster was the only word that he could dredge from his abused mind. Feidhlim was a monster.

He thought to Derrik's cousin. ::*I tried to create a portal soon after I was brought here.*::

::*Aye, I ken. Magical wards are placed around the castle. None who dinna ken its presence may see it. None within may leave wi'out speakin' the magic. I canna hear the words fer the wards block me. 'Tis only wi' the help of yer guide was I able to come to ye.*::

Bard closed his eyes and leaned his head back against the wall. If this being, this guardian angel was unable to defeat Feidhlim's magic, what hope did he have?

An animal's soft chittering imposed itself on his doubt and worry. Behind his closed eyelids, next to the pale, nearly faded presence of Derrik's cousin, his small guide sat preening its ears. Bard smiled as relief flowed into him. "So, you are here, too," he whispered.

The guide looked at him, bright intelligence clear in the misty world between worlds. The distant echo of a drum parted the mist and ripples rolled from a thin, clear path that shone bright as sunshine. A low moan, cut short by a gasp of pain, sounded from the other side of the wall.

He understood with a clarity that surprised him and he turned his inner gaze to Searlait. ::*You couldn't enter this place alone,*:: he thought to her. ::*And I can not leave alone. I couldn't fight the invasion of my mind without your assistance. Perhaps it is only combining our abilities that will enable me to escape.*::

Searlait's expression brightened as she sheathed her long, silver sword. ::*Aye. 'Tis a guid thought. If 'tis to be, I believe we must each of us add a part to the puzzle. Yer shaman friend an' her drum must also be a part. Wi'out her, we would have been hard pressed to defeat the seeker.*::

A dull pain throbbed through Bard's head. Searlait knelt as if listening to his guide then rose with the small creature nestled in her palm. ::*Yer pardon, traveler. Yer mind is tired an' I canna stay. Rest. I shall return when 'tis time. Rest, Bard, an' be ready.*::

He nodded slowly, opened his eyes and squinted blearily at the door. He angled himself to a comfortable position where he could rest, yet watch the opening and be ready should his captors return. In moments, the vision of Kaelea's face led him to peaceful rest.

E ach day brought a fresh wave of loneliness to the desert library. When she was able to concentrate, the translation of the ancient book proceeded swiftly. She shared information daily with her family, then moved further through the book. Strangely, the text had been written backwards in time. As Kaelea delved into the pages, she found herself going far back into Fey history. Far enough back that what she translated seemed fantasy.

Kae chuckled. Even for her, a being of fantasy, what she read was difficult to believe. Even knowing Korin was the descendent of Robin Goodfellow, discovering this documentation of the truths behind Shakespeare's tale... along now, with hints alluding to Spenser's The Faerie Queene--Kae made a

note on a small pad to talk to Bryce about that work of litera-
ture and how it might help the family.

Each day brought new awareness of the life growing inside
her. At little over a month, she knew her child was barely
physically formed, however the tangible life force comforted
her in her loneliness. Often as she worked, she'd curl one palm
over her abdomen and in the silence of her mind, speak to her
child and tell him of his father. The child's spirit would
answer, the images and intelligence so reminiscent of Bard,
she knew she carried a son.

A son. Kae rested her chin in her palm and stared into the
distance. The stacks of books faded and she imagined herself
in the Faerie forest of her home, Bard sitting at her side, their
dark haired son playing nearby.

She clung to the belief Bard would return with a tenacity
that surprised her. Not only had he left her side without warning, he'd also disappeared from both the Otherworld and the
human world. The Alastriona had discovered no evidence of
his use of a portal to his own world. Or anywhere else.

Sighing, Kae twirled her pencil on the tabletop. He'd be
back. The soft rhythm of a hand drum answered her thoughts.
She'd heard drumming before, soft, distant, and yet distinct.
Once before she'd heard two drums, now only one. The power
behind the dancing, insistent beat gave her a strange, gentle
comfort.

She stopped the spinning pencil. It was time, again, for the
daydreams to end.

Each day it seemed she'd discovered some new information and each day she'd looked for Gowthaman to share her
find. But, he'd disappeared as well, leaving no word, no clue,
no trace. She missed her friend and longed for the assistance
of his logical, studious mind.

At times the library's quiet seemed to vibrate, as if with
pain. Kae wondered at the strange texture of the air and the
tears filling her eyes at imagined cries of agony. With his
guardianship of the library, his connection to the preservation
of the ancient Fey texts of Alexandria, did Gowthaman's

disappearance have anything to do with the discomfort and sadness?

Fanciful thoughts again. Such things, even in a magical world, surely weren't possible. But as a wave of nearly palpable sadness washed over her, she wasn't so sure.

Why had Gowthaman disappeared, too?

Fighting through the sadness was like clawing her way through an oozing river of mud. There were times she couldn't convince herself it was worth the fight. It would be so much easier to simply forget Bard and Gowthaman and concentrate only on her family's safety. Why should she care, when neither of them seemed...

The hope, the reason for the fight, lay quiet now in her body.

She took a deep breath and returned to the worn volume. Only a few pages remained and she studied the broad strokes of the flowing fairy writing. Maybe when she'd discovered how and why the book's timeline ran backward... When she realized the anomaly, she should have turned to the end and started there. No. That didn't feel right.

Now, at last, here she was, ready to turn the page to the final entry. Would she finally find some information they could use in their battle against Feidhlim? So far, she'd been able to trace his family, along with her own, almost back to the time of Oberon and Titania.

A flush of excitement heated her face. It was still amazing and difficult to believe that the legendary Faerie rulers of Shakespeare's play were real, and that her family descended from them.

She released a soft chuckle at Nanceen's reaction when she'd told her sister and her husband that Korin, as the Puck's descendant, and despite what the ancient fairy books had claimed, was actually a descendant of Oberon as well, from a liaison with a fairy maid. It had taken long, intense discussions for Nanceen to accept she and her husband shared an ancestor, no matter how long ago and far removed. Now, they reveled in the shared heritage.

Nanceen and Korin shared that, and so much more. What

did she share with Bard besides a night of passion? Only their child.

Mindful of the health of the growing babe, Kae snatched an apple from the bowl she kept filled at the edge of the table and scanned the page before her. But before she took a bite of the red fruit, she set it aside and leaned close to the book. Oh, God. This could be it.

The stone urn had been dragged to the center of an empty chamber and circled with Alastriona guards. A tiny crack oozed visible magic that dripped to form a small pool at the urn's base. No means had been found to slow the leak or seal the crack. All Jaye and Derrik could do was stand by and watch Feidhlim's magic form a tiny puddle only a hand span wide. Then the magic rose as a long finger, seemed to search the room, then shot through a portal that opened and closed faster than a blink.

Unable to follow the magic, Derrik paced tight, rapid circles around the urn, mumbling to himself. Just as frustrated, Jaye watched his friend's movements until the latest magical puddle obtained the usual size, rose and disappeared.

Both men stared at the spot where the tiny portal opened. Every fourth day, for the past seven weeks, it had been the same. They were no closer to discovering Feidhlim's whereabouts than they had been when Bard disappeared. Though he'd not voiced his suspicions, Jaye knew Derrik believed, as he did, Feidhlim had caused the man's disappearance. But, he dared not face Kaelea with those suspicions.

While Derrik and the gathered Alastriona studied the clear air, Jaye let his thoughts turn to his sister. Despite the overwhelming emotions of joy and sadness she carried with her each day, Kae had discovered an interesting bit of history. A history he believed wholeheartedly would be helpful--if they could only discern the way to most efficiently use the information.

. . .

G owthaman sprawled on the cold, stone floor, barely moving his head at a noise from the doorway. After the first rape of his mind, the seeker returned twice more to steal his thoughts, his dreams, his memories. The invasions took more than his mind, for his unsuccessful fight against the seeker had weakened him to the point he had no energy to cry out his agonies.

He had nothing left. Although his knowledge and memories remained, the lingering presence of the seeker's touch sullied him. His mind burned with a fever pitch and he doubted. Were his memories truly his, or had she exchanged what he was for something Feidhlim had chosen for him? Was he still Gowthaman, guardian of the Fey Library of Alexandria? Was he still Gowthaman, scholar and Faerie?

Was he? That final question plagued him and plunged through the ragged tears in his mind. Was he? Did Gowthaman still to exist within the battered mind and abused body?

The noise sounded again. The seeker hadn't returned for a lengthy time, but he expected no other. Other than Feidhlim's earlier taunting, he had been ignored by all but the beautiful woman with pain in her touch.

Movement at his side and a light touch on his shoulder caused Gowthaman to jerk away weakly. When pain lurched through his body, he wondered why he continued to resist. Eyes closed, he waited for the soft pressure of fingertips against his brow. *Please, take no more. Kill me instead.*

A sharp slap wrenched his head to one side and masculine laughter covered the sound of his surprise and pain.

"Wake, librarian... for I have a thing I wish to show you."

So. Feidhlim had returned instead of the seeker. Perhaps she had drained all she could from him. What more could the evil one desire?

Gowthaman closed his eyes. It didn't matter.

"I said wake." A second slap rolled him to his back. With a huff of expelled breath, Feidhlim dragged him closer to the wall, lifted his upper body, and propped him in a sitting position. Peering closely into his face, the evil one assured himself of Gowthaman's attention then rose to stand before him.

"So, librarian, have you enjoyed the visits from my... seeker?"

The pause before the word and the snarl to the evil one's tone told Gowthaman the seeker had somehow lost favor with her master. He released a soft sigh of relief, then tensed. His muscles twisted in agony. Would he be able to endure the next torture? Did he wish to endure? Would Feidhlim finally kill him? By the gods of the desert...let it be so.

Feidhlim chuckled. "No, there is much yet to learn from you, gentle librarian. I shall not yet order your death." He laughed again and crossed his arms. "Though your mind would be easily accessible to me now, I do not have to read your thoughts. Your hope for death rests plainly upon your face. I am sorry to have to disappoint you."

Gowthaman angled his face to one side and let his eyelids droop.

Rewarded with another slap, he returned his gaze to the evil one, wiped the fresh blood from his lip with shaking fingers and summoned the last bit of defiance within him. As he squared his shoulders, he heard a soft, feminine voice in his head. ::*Courage.*::

The distant, rapid beat of a drum lifted his heart and he managed a weak grin.

::*Aye, that be the way of it.*::

"What is it you wish this time, Feidhlim?"

The evil one's golden brows lifted in surprise, then he smiled and delight shone in his eyes. "Defiance? From my gentle librarian?"

"I am... your nothing... Leave me be." Where this spark had come from, Gowthaman didn't care. Nor did he care if swift, vicious retribution came to him. What more evil could be lavished upon him?

Feidhlim paced from one side of the room to the other, his gaze never leaving his captive. Gowthaman met his cold stare boldly.

"It's time," Feidhlim announced as he paused in the exact

center of the room. "I bestow upon you a great honor, librarian."

"Honor? I cannot see how anything you could bestow upon me would be an honor. Be done with it. Be done with me."

The arch of Feidhlim's eyebrows gave Gowthaman pause. Had he pushed his meager defiance too far? Good.

The evil one spread his arms at shoulder height and, with a smile, tipped his head back. "Behold, gentle librarian. Behold how magic returns to me. My power grows. My supremacy increases. Behold, for it is time."

Gowthaman shrank against the wall as a thin thread, a golden-orange glow, appeared from a portal the size of his hand. The glow whipped through the room, creating a streaming whirlwind about Feidhlim. The glow expanded and faded, pulsing with life power that lifted the fine hairs on Gowthaman's arms. He'd never imagined the physical presence of magic. So few willingly gave up their abilities, and he knew of no other who had been totally stripped of power.

Had been... Gowthaman's eyes widened and he fought to keep his mouth from following suit. Magic in the purest form--magic without the bounds of a physical body. For a moment, he was lost in awe and beauty.

The whirlwind tightened, wrapping Feidhlim completely in narrow orange bands. The bands pressed into his body. His breathing grew harsh. Bursts of sharp, ecstatic cries twisted his smiling lips.

Tighter, the bands sank into Feidhlim, the combination of pain and pleasure in his expression and in his cries sending wild shivers of dread coursing through Gowthaman's veins. He couldn't tear his gaze away. It was ugly, disturbing, and exquisitely beautiful all at once.

Finally, with a shout to rival passion's completion, Feidhlim sank to his knees. Panting, he stared at his open palms, then flexed his fingers as an orange glow encompassed his hands. He created a vivid ball of power and, with a wicked grin, lobbed it toward Gowthaman.

The ball encompassed him and shards of fiery agony

repeatedly pierced his body. A knifing pain, centered at the base of his throat, cut short the single scream ripped from him. He gasped, but couldn't draw breath past the pain. Darkness and, in the deepest pathways remaining in his mind, he hoped, death closed a tight fist around him.

No time--no final thought.

When Feidhlim recognized the dull lifelessness of his captive's eyes, he quickly withdrew the ball of power. Holding the orange glow between his palms, he smiled lovingly at the physical embodiment of his magic. Then he pressed the glow to the center of his chest, sighing as the final bits of magic from the latest delivery flowed into him.

Another portion of him had come home. He held his hands protectively over his heart for a few moments. He rose slowly and moved to stand over his captive's slumped body. With gentle motions, he arranged Gowthaman so he lay with his hands folded over his stomach.

"Ah, gentle librarian. Rest you well."

TWENTY

The remnants of the choked-off cry vibrating through the wall chilled Bard's heart. He sent a silent request to the Guardians to soothe the spirit of the tortured one. Following his prayer, he vowed if the man still lived, he would not be left behind when Bard escaped. If it were within his power, he would leave none to Feidhlim's machinations.

Bard stood by the narrow window and glanced out at the clear sky. The crash of waves against the rocks reminded him of a deep drum and he turned his thoughts completely to escape. How did one coordinate presences that were only within his mind?

Fleeting fear tripped through him. What if Catori's drum and Searlait's bright sword were only his imagination? How swiftly would failure come to him then? He tried to shake away the disturbing thoughts and replace them with strong belief, but the doubt remained.

He fought with himself when his energies were better spent fighting the magic. Bard shook his head. He had to believe. If his precious Kaelea could believe she would find a way to defeat Feidhlim within a stack of ancient books, then he would believe in the defeat of magic with the powers held in his mind.

Two tiny, rounded ears and a small, pointed nose peeked

over the edge of the window sill. The white spot between the ears sparkled in the sunlight before the guide skittered into the shadows at the other side of the window. Bard released a sigh of relief. If his guide was here, then the presence of the others was more tangible than just his imagination. He angled toward the desert rodent and whispered, "How did you find a way through the magic, little guide?"

The animal appeared to shrug and Bard bit back a chuckle. "If you found a way in, then there will be a way out."

The guide ran in a tight circle then paused with its head lowered in an aspect of silent contemplation. Bard tilted his head to one side and stared at the animal. "So, is now the time? I understand, little one. I shall meet the others there and plan the escape."

The guide circled again, then leaped from the window sill and ran to a spot to the left of the doorway. Again it lowered itself to a prayerful pose.

"There? As you wish." Bard took the three steps to cross the room, sat with his back against the wall, and tried to relax. He took long, slow breaths, filling his diaphragm, then releasing the breath just as slowly through his parted lips. The deep breathing normally brought him easily to the relaxed, meditative state, but this time, each breath further tensed his muscles. His body shuddered as his focus wavered.

The doubt was strong, even with the guide beside him. He clenched his fist until the tips of his nails bit into his palm, but even the concentrated pain didn't redirect his focus. He couldn't do it. He would fail.

If he failed, he would never see Kaelea again. Never touch the smoothness of her skin or bury his face against the silky length of her hair. He'd never again know joy in her arms, or the pleasure of simply being near her.

His fist relaxed and he flexed his fingers once. Behind his closed lids, he created the oasis pool where he'd first seen Kaelea, and where he'd first kissed her. A faint purple sphere rose from the pool and expanded as his breathing altered to the rhythm of his contemplation.

As the purple encompassed him, love, pure and vital,

spilled into him and his doubts disappeared with an audible snap. Kaelea loved him as he loved her. Her love would keep him strong. Laughter at the simple thought echoed through him and the joy of his discovery drew away the last of the doubts. He would be successful and soon, soon he would tell Kaelea of his love.

::*Guid, ye found the way.*::

::*The way? No, the reason.*::

::*There be a difference? I dinna have much time wi' ye. Next we meet, ye must be ready. Yer shaman friend be restin' an' when she is strong enough, I shall return to ye.*::

::*How do I get to the other captive?*::

Searlait's sword slashed though his vision. ::*Yer guide an' I shall make a way fer ye through the wall... a portal of sorts. That magic hasna been warded against. Then Catori shall drum the pathway fer us. 'Tis the only plan we have.*::

::*Then that will be our plan. I'll be ready.*::

::*Aye. I ken ye shall.*::

Bard felt the warmth of her smile and a feather-light touch brushed his cheek. Then Searlait was gone and his inner vision fell dark.

Slowly, Bard opened his eyes and sighed. Searlait had made the escape sound easy, but he knew it would not be simple. But what blockages, what dangers he would face beyond Feidhlim, he didn't dare contemplate. Instead, he leaned against the wall and thought of Kaelea and his love for her.

E leven weeks equaled seventy-seven days. Kae rolled her eyes at herself. Why did she continue to count time from when Bard disappeared? She should be counting forward, to the time of her child's birth.

She grinned and finished tying a fat bow on top of a package wrapped in baby style wrapping paper. Lara's due date had passed, so she would be giving birth to the newest family member any day now.

Kae patted the package and set it in a pile with other gifts-

-for Lara and her child. Then another two months and it would be Nanceen's and Carrie's turns. Kae hugged herself and sent loving thoughts to her own child. With the other births so soon, she was impatient, but knew she had to wait those long six months. She spent as much time as she could shopping and creating gifts for the new babies, but had insisted no one give her child anything yet--she didn't want to take away from Lara's or Nanceen's joy. And, definitely not from Carrie's tentative hold on happiness. The young woman still doubted the family would accept the child, despite repeated assurances. Kae supposed that was only natural under the circumstances.

If she was truthful with herself, she still expected to see Bard walk through her door. And she wanted to share every gift and every coming joy with him.

She wasn't fooling herself. She wasn't. He'd be back. She'd dreamed too often of purple, nothing but purple, the soulfire color she'd been told passed between them. If she dreamed of purple, then he was still in her life, her worlds, and would return.

Rubbing the tiny ache in her lower back, Kae turned to look out the window. Desert sand stretched to the horizon and disappeared into a white-hot haze. She should move back to the cabin in the Otherworld. She wasn't comfortable with the other librarians and caretakers, and without Gowthaman's assistance, there wasn't much more she could do here anyway. She could take the last few books with her. Even with the short passage through a portal, being in Faerie would keep her closer to her family. And when Bard returned, he'd be sure to look for her there if her house here was empty. And, she'd leave an obvious message.

Kae nodded to herself. Her mother had been wishing to coddle both daughters and she would be pleased. Kae glanced around the small space of her home away from home. She would miss the desert... but her Otherworld home called to her.

Once her decision was made, she started packing immediately. If she had everything ready, she should be able to talk Jayse into carrying the sacks and boxes for her.

As she packed, she reviewed the information she'd gleaned from the ancient book. Oberon had actually made the last entry. When she showed the passage to the boggart who originally taught her the fairy language, he taught her the magic to make the words speak in Oberon's voice.

Even now she paused and sighed. The beauty of the fairy king's voice, the tone and timbre, the flowing way he spoke the words with an exotic accent, would remain with her forever. If Titania had such a voice, they would have been a formidable pair. From all accounts, they were, together or separate.

During one of those separations Titania had a rare dalliance. Okay, so she was under the spell of some now unknown flower. Kae gave a wry chuckle. Even that part of Shakespeare's tale was accurate.

Oberon had cursed her to love the first being she set eyes upon when waking, and his son, the irrepressive Puck, had charmed a human, giving him an ass's head. Titania thought she loved the altered human, and a child was born of their union.

Oberon's telling of the tale had made her both laugh and cry. He was saddened and angered by Titania's pregnancy, yet didn't hesitate to continue his own affairs. People--both the gentry and human--hadn't really changed all that much.

After learning the half-human child's name, Kae worked backwards, tracing the descendants of that son. Until she reached the name she knew, the descendant sharing the current faerie generation,

She had laughed until tears came, then laughed more.

Her own family line had been of pure Faerie blood until Stephen found his way into the Otherworld and loved Kelene. Kae didn't begrudge her parents' love and was actually proud of her half-human blood.

But, the leader of the Nechtan-Cattee, the faerie who had long fought for the supposed purity of the Faerie race, was less pure. Less than her brother, the man he fought so hard to destroy. After generations of 'mixed breeding,' as close as she could figure it, Feidhlim had only about one-third pure Faerie blood.

Jaye sat in stunned silence when she presented her findings to the Queen's council. Then laughter had ruled the moment, until all remembered the leaking of Feidhlim's magic.

Despite his watered-down blood, Feidhlim was one of the most powerful faerie alive. Each time defeating him had taken the strength of more than one. Now the problem remained, how to defeat him, destroy him once and for all.

Kae glanced around and lifted her brows in surprise. Except for a small pile set in one corner, her packing was completed. She moved to the pile and knelt beside it. There, near the floor, and hidden by the other materials, she found a tattered, worn blanket. The pattern of the weaving was odd to her eyes and the rips and tears followed the weave rather than destroying the pattern. She clasped the blanket to her breast and freed her tears.

Bard's blanket. The one thing brought with him when he arrived in this world. She had forgotten it was still here. She swiped her palm over her face to dry the tears, then held the fabric to her cheek. Softer than it appeared, the touch comforted her as she nuzzled the blanket. Inhaling deeply, she caught a multitude of scents, but underlying them all was the essence of the man she loved.

He treasured this ragged cloth and wouldn't leave this world without it, for the blanket had belonged to his father-- and many fathers before him. Kae gave a teary sniff. And someday, the precious cloth would pass to his son. *Please, let him be here to wrap his son in this blanket. Oh. Please.* She didn't know to whom she sent the plea, but hoped the spirits watching over Bard would hear.

With gentle motions she smoothed the blanket and folded it carefully. She would carry this treasured item home and give it a place of honor until Bard returned to claim it.

. . .

F eidhlim reclined on a wide couch after sending his followers away. The latest return of magic weakened him strangely, though he didn't believe his demonstration on the librarian caused the weakness. He would rest before the next bit of him returned.

He felt like a puzzle with missing pieces that would fit together easily once found. Impatient for completion, he contemplated ways to speed the process. No new ideas came to him, so he told himself to be content with the flow of events.

He had gained useful information from the librarian, and would obtain more, from the human or from the usurper's sister when he bargained for the man's life. The bargaining would be--delicious.

He reached for the flagon at his side, took a long drink, then stared into the container with distaste. Water. How long had it been since he'd tasted fine ale? He licked his lips trying to recall the taste. Yes, delicious. One call to his followers and his flagon would be filled with the finest Faerie brew and he could again...

"No!" The flagon smashed against the far wall and water dripped down the gray stone. He would not succumb to the pleasures of drink again. Why was he cursed with an unfaerie-like inability to tolerate drink? He knew of no others who had a similar disability. It had taken him years while in the past to erase the effects of drink from his body and mind, though the craving remained. No. He would resist and be satisfied with water or the unfermented juice of the freshest of Faerie fruits. He would not fall into drink's trap and languish in the hazy half-world of drunkenness.

Despite the weariness of his body, he rose from the couch and began a series of fierce physical movements, continuing until he panted from the exertion. Then he called for juice on his way to the bathing chamber. Soon, more of his magic would return and he would be ready.

· · ·

Bemused, Bard watched his guide scratch at the mortar between the tightly fitted stones of the wall separating him from the other prisoner. The tiny animal had created a mess of loose dust and stone chips, but hissed at Bard when he moved closer to help. He shrugged to himself. The guide always had its own mind and ways of conveying its intent. But he wasn't sure how making such a small hole would help.

Although he didn't know how the other room appeared, he'd tried to form a portal through the wall, but the warding prevented his actions as it had when he'd tried portals to the human world and parts of Faerie he knew well. So now he sat and watched while worry ate at him.

It had been a long time since there had been sounds from the other room. The memory of the final scream still caused prickles of dread to crawl across the back of his neck. He hoped the captive was unconscious--not dead. The finality, the abrupt ceasing of sound, made him shudder. Urgency over-came the worry and he rose to pace the small space. There wasn't much time.

"Little guide," he whispered as he knelt beside the furi-ously working creature. "We shall begin when you have reached the other room?"

The rodent ran in a tight circle, a movement Bard now recognized as an affirmative answer. "Then, I shall disturb you no more."

With a tiny squeak, the guide dug at the mortar and soon nearly half of its body disappeared into the wall. Bard chuckled at the puffs of dust and debris flying from the hole. Trying to clear his mind of other things--of Kaelea--he returned to gaze out the window and focused on the escape. It would take the strength and ability of each of them to insure success, but he didn't know what part each would play.

And if the other captive remained unconscious...

Ah, precious Kaelea. I shall return soon. I give you this vow, the vow of my heart.

· · ·

K ae stepped into the Faerie Otherworld near her parents' clearing. Instead of sending a message ahead, she planned to surprise them with her decision to move home. With a large bag of personal items slung over her shoulder and Bard's blanket clutched against her chest, she glanced around and took several deep breaths of the clear Faerie air.

An amazing sense of homecoming filled her, then her stomach clenched as though she were being twisted in two.

As suddenly as the pain appeared it was gone, and Kae took a stumbling step forward. She'd have to limit her use of portals if it caused her baby such discomfort. Absently, she rubbed the blanket over her abdomen and wondered if that was how labor felt. Then she grinned. In any case, the discomfort would be a great excuse to use to get Jayse to bring the rest of her things from the desert.

The sounds of sudden activity burst from her parents' small house as she crossed the clearing. Stephen and Kelene rushed from the cabin and her mother rapidly formed a portal.

"Da? Mother?"

Kaelea's call stopped her parents from entering the portal and Kelene ran to embrace her. "Darlin', you're just in time."

"Time for what?"

"Lara's in labor," Stephen said as he took a turn hugging her. "We must hurry."

"Now? That's great." Kae took her mother's hand. Her homecoming surprise could wait, the birth of a great grandchild was much more important. She pulled Kelene toward the portal. "Come on, then. I can't wait to see my new great niece or nephew. Wish she could have told us which it was."

"Aye, daughter," Stephen laughed. "I just hope she doesna surprise us like the last time."

Kae froze, halting her parents as well. "You don't think she could have twins again, do you?"

He shrugged one shoulder then wrapped his arm about her. "Anythin's possible, darlin'. She has been complainin' that she's large as a house."

"Oh, no." Kae laughed. "I hope we've got enough welcoming gifts, just in case."

Stephen joined her laughter. "Never fear, Kae. There is plenty in this family fer all." He patted the slight rounding of her belly.

"Da." She hadn't realized how much she missed her father's teasing until that moment. It was good to be home. And happily, just in time.

From her place in the misty world between worlds, Searlait watched. In the human world, Catori was rested and waited within a circle she and her grandmother had prepared, her drum at her side.

Searlait angled to peer through the veil into Faerie and her eyes widened. The happy cries of new souls ready for birth tugged at the center of her chest. Her family, her charges. She closed her eyes and took a deep breath. She would never begrudge her duties to her charges, but now she was needed here. ::*Soon, little ones. Yer safe with the love of family surroundin' ye. Enter yer world wi'out fear. I shall be wi' ye soon enough.*::

Searlait turned again, this time to another area of Faerie, covered with a dark veil her sight barely pierced. The guide had nearly completed the first connection and Bard would rescue the other captive. Then... then, she was not sure. She only understood her part of the puzzle and sent a silent plea to those who held her within the world between worlds. Each of them must hold differing pieces that would, when brought together, make the whole. And escape would be possible.

She drew her sword and sliced the long blade through the air.

Then, she held the blade before her in readiness, calmed her mind and waited.

TWENTY-ONE

L ight, soft and comforting. Light drew him closer,
calling to a place within him that longed for the offered
peace. Light. With a starburst of color, the light
rejected him and sent him back to darkness. He fought the
rejection, clawing toward the light, but could find no hold, no
way to complete that journey. The light faded to dull gray and
as it did, pain returned.

Then realization he was alive struck Gowthaman with a
force that shuddered a thick moan from him. Disappointment
brought tears to his eyes that Feidhlim's torture had not. If he
had not died this time, how much more must he face? He
turned his head to one side and wept silently.

Feeling as though he was being watched, but no longer
caring who witnessed his pain, Gowthaman opened his eyes.
"You?" he gasped. A small desert rodent, the same animal that
had led him to witness Bard's disappearance, sat on its hind
legs, one paw stretched toward him. "How did you...?"

Speech was difficult and as he remembered the knife-like
pain from Feidhlim's power, he was amazed he could speak at
all. The animal ran in a tight circle then came closer and
touched his nose. In the confusion of his mind, Gowthaman
chuckled; it was a gesture of comfort--from a rodent. "'Tis not
safe here. Go."

The animal gave a shake of its head, but skittered away.

Gowthaman had no energy to watch or follow its path. He closed his eyes and longed for the light.

K ae glanced at the gathered family. The last time everyone had been together, Jaye shared her news of Feidhlim's heritage, and they had quickly dispersed to work on the problem of how to best use that information. No answers had been found and now they were together again. This time for an ultimately joyous occasion.

Iain was sequestered in the cabin with Lara and a single faerie healer. Their twins played with Bree and David under Allyn's watchful eyes. Kae chuckled. She knew her sister-in-law was anxious to be with her daughter, but Lara insisted that no one but Iain was allowed. Her insistence was easily adhered to after her vile temperament over the past month.

Seated on a blanket with Carrie, Kae waited impatiently for Nanceen's arrival. A faint concern hovered in her mind. It wasn't like Nance to take such a long time to arrive at a family gathering, although, her seven month pregnancy might be slowing her down some. And although Korin and Derrik had discovered a way to neutralize the portal's natural resistance to fairy magic, Korin still faced each passage with dread. They would be likely to come through one of the permanently open, safer portals and walk the short distance to Lara's cabin.

Kae wanted her sister and needed to talk with her. Carrie also sat silently, nervously twisting her hands together. Kae released a soft breath and covered Carrie's fingers with hers. "Wanna talk about it?"

Carrie glanced sideways at her. "You know."

"Yes, I do. And you know that your fears are unfounded. You had nothing to do with how your child was created--or who attacked you. I won't tell you to get over it, because I know that's impossible. But, Carrie, we love you. You and Bryce will raise a fine child, with no hint of the evil of the sperm donor."

"Kae... I..."

Kae lifted one hand to stop her, but before she could speak herself, a sharp pain rippled across her abdomen. "Oh."

"What is it?"

Kae waved away her concern as the pain faded. Interesting. She felt pain, but didn't believe it was her pain. That could only mean...

"I think I might be having sympathy pains for Lara." Kae chuckled and rubbed her belly. "What an odd feeling. Hope it means we'll get to see the baby soon."

Carrie finally smiled. "I hope so, too. Do you think everyone will be there when..."

"Honey, how can you think otherwise?" Nightshade lowered himself to the blanket and lounged next to Carrie. "Hi, Kae. Now, Carrie, honey..."

"You don't need to start, Nightshade." Carrie patted him on the shoulder. "I'm okay."

Kae studied Nightshade. When he adjusted his position, the hard outline of the gun pulled against the flowing material of his shirt. She worried about him, no matter what he said about knowing how to use a weapon. He just didn't seem the type for that kind of action. Then she grinned. Oh, well, Nightshade was Nightshade and there was really no figuring out the enigmatic man.

Another pain stabbed across her stomach. The birth better be soon, sympathy pains or not, she was becoming increasingly uncomfortable.

She squirmed, trying to discover a more comfortable position. When would Nanceen arrive?

T he guide leaped to Bard's knee and scratched at the denim, startling him from his meditative posture. Bard blinked a few times, then frowned at the small animal. "Is it time?"

The guide turned a tight circle on his knee then climbed his body to a position on one shoulder. Tiny claws bit through his shirt and prickled against his skin as the creature settled. Bard rose and stretched his cramped muscles. Then he faced the wall. The pile of dust and debris had grown; the wall must be thick. He'd thought long on what he needed to do once the guide had dug through to the other side. Hopefully his conclusions were correct.

Before beginning, he moved to the door and listened intently. No movement sounded from outside the room. He gave one sharp nod and whispered the words to form a portal. Focusing the energy to create a tiny, tiny portal, he positioned the magic over the guide's hole. Once the magical opening held steady, he slowly increased the size, letting the portal grow until, by stooping nearly double, he would be able to pass through to the neighboring room.

There. The captive lay with his back to the wall. Bard frowned at the crumpled form. There was something... Without further consideration, he bent, entered the cell, knelt and touched the man's shoulder.

"Gowthaman."

The faerie's eyelids twitched but he did not open his eyes. "Leave me be," he rasped.

"We're going to escape, Gowthaman."

"No. No escape. Do not torture me."

Bard eased his arms under the librarian's shoulders and legs and lifted him.

Gowthaman's eyes burst open and, he stared at Bard, wild disbelief filling his expression. "How?"

Ignoring the question, Bard said simply, "You are needed."

"No. No one needs me now. I... through me... the seeker..." Gowthaman turned his face away.

Bard made a harsh sound of disgust. "I met Feidhlim's seeker. Now, it is time to leave."

Gowthaman struggled weakly as Bard bent, carried him through the portal, and lowered him to the pallet. With a loose wave of one hand, he dissolved the small opening, then let his eyes close in sorrow.

The faerie had been viciously abused and it would take long for the physical wounds to heal. If the seeker had been successful in touching the librarian's mind, and he was sure she had, his mental healing would take even longer. Tortured as the librarian was by pain and obvious despair, he didn't believe Gowthaman would be able to contribute to their escape. Despite how the librarian might feel about him, Bard would not leave him to any fate at Feidhlim's hands.

He knelt at the librarian's side. "We're leaving this place."

"I do not believe I am able. You have to go without me. For Kaelea..."

Yes, for Kaelea. Bard nodded solemnly, though pain ripped through him at her name upon the man's lips. Yet, she counted this man as her... friend. "No. You'll not be left behind."

"I am... too weak."

"Then, I'll assist you. Listen, Gowthaman. I can't leave here alone and neither can you."

"If I die..."

Bard shook his head. "Then we are both lost."

"I... do not understand."

Carefully, Bard lowered the guide from his shoulder and the small animal crawled onto Gowthaman's limp palm. He narrowed his eyes.

"I know this creature."

The guide climbed carefully to Gowthaman's shoulder then remained still. Gowthaman watched with wide eyes as Bard explained. "It has been my guide since I came to your worlds. It also plays a part in our escape. Its actions allowed me to reach you. Now..."

A gray mist formed at the foot of the pallet. Gowthaman's eyes widened further and he cringed against the wall. A cloaked figure appeared and leaned on a long, silver sword. "At last, death comes...for me," he mumbled.

The figure tossed back its hood to reveal a long golden braid and she laughed silently. ::*I am nae death. But, I do come fer ye. An'Bard. 'Tis time.*::

Bard answered the unspoken fear in Gowthaman's eyes. "Derrik's cousin, Searlait."

"But, she was... banished."

::*Aye, but I am allowed to protect the clan of Jayezer. An' ye be named friend an' so under my concern. Come. Catori begins.*::

Brushing his hands together, Bard rose. "What do we do?"

::*Ye must form the portal. Gowthaman shall lend power--*::

"I have no power, lady. They... I... can not." He curled into a ball and angled to face the wall.

Searlait bent over him and touched her hand to his fore-head. He flinched but did not pull away. She smiled softly. ::*I am no seeker, but can show ye the power. Ye have great Alastriona talents, greater than ye imagine. Dinna worry. I shall keep yer secret. As will Bard. Ye must concentrate, Gowthaman. Lend Bard power, then block the path behind ye.*::

"I do not know if I can," he whispered.

Bard backed away two paces. "Then we are doomed to remain here. I can't do this alone. For Kaelea, for your friend-ship, you must try." He spread his hands in supplication. "I need your help."

Expression showing none of his thoughts, Gowthaman studied him for a few moments. The world stood still in an eternity of waiting for the librarian's decision. He would not force Gowthaman, and if the man's dislike of him were powerful enough, then they were both doomed.

The librarian pressed against the rock wall and struggled to stand. "I shall try. What... must I do?"

::*Guid. Ye shall know what to do when 'tis needed. We go.*::

Relieved, Bard released the breath from his lungs. Silent, he stepped closer and wrapped a supporting arm about the slender faerie's waist. Shock strained the man's face and he looked about to speak, but Bard shook his head, then nodded toward Searlait. She faced away from them.

::*With Gowthaman's help, ye shall open the portal. The drum shall draw the path fer ye. Follow yer guide and I shall protect ye. Dinna fear, fer though ye willna see me, I am here.*:: She stepped into the mist and the gray closed around her. ::*Now.*::

Shifting his hold on Gowthaman slightly, Bard formed a portal at the spot where the last of the gray mist hovered. Resistance, effects of the strong warding around the castle, bounced his words back to him. He fought for the magic, his body shaking as the wards stole power and will from him.

Gowthaman lifted a hand to his shoulder and a shimmer of power, hot and golden as the desert sands, poured into him. The magical opening formed easily but showed a noth-ingness of gray. Gowthaman shook his head and lifted his other hand as the guide jumped to the floor and raced into the portal.

The drumbeats grew louder, but not as loud as the pounding of footsteps upon stone outside the cell.

Bard grimaced. "Can you do anything?"

"I believe so." With a wave of his uplifted hand, Gowthaman slammed a blast of power against the opening door. Sweat beaded on his forehead as magic pushed against magic and the door eased open with short jerks.

"I can not... for much longer..."

"Then we go." Pulling Gowthaman with him, Bard stepped through the portal and into the world of gray. The portal snicked shut.

A shroud of silence wrapped tightly around them. No sound. No sight. Only gray. Indecision froze Bard in his place.

"Release me. I can stand alone."

Bard didn't believe Gowthaman would be able to do as he claimed for long, but took a single step to the side. He kept one hand on the faerie's shoulder and felt the trembling as he fought to remain upright.

"We are in the world between worlds." Awe filled Gowthaman's voice.

Bard strained to see through the gray mist. Where was Searlait? How would he know which way to go? Should he simply form another portal? He pictured the desert Sahara in his mind.

Swiftly, he created a portal--to another place of nothing-ness. With a frustrated growl, he waved the portal closed and tried again. And again. Where was his guide?

Gowthaman's hand on his arm stopped him from spinning in place as he created portal after portal. "Stop, Bard. Be calm. They will not follow. Listen." Then his eyes rolled back and he collapsed against Bard.

After lowering the librarian carefully to the ground, Bard sat and drew a deep breath. It would do no good to move if he didn't know where he was or which way to go.

Soft, barely audible, the hollow, muffled tone of a drum sliced through the gray mist. Catori.

He listened, waited. The drumming grew stronger, the beat a steady, insistent call. But the sound echoed around him and he was unable to pinpoint the direction. After time that dragged into a lifetime, the tiny form of his guide materialized from the mist. It ran back and forth before him, swirling the gray mist in waves with its rapid passage.

A faint light surrounded the guide then stretched from it in two thin streams of color against the gray, one pale orangish-pink, the other the deepest purple. The colors pierced the mist and, as the drum grew louder, swirled into small, parallel vortexes. From each vortex a wavering, window-like portal formed. The guide ran a circle before each one, then planted itself between them and hunkered down as if waiting.

Two destinations? Leaving Gowthaman, Bard rose and the powerful energy of the small portals tugged at him, each inviting him to enter. Now came the time for his decision, his choice, for he knew the two places he would be shown. The paler window held the promise of passage to his home world. He stood for a long time, peering into the stark environment. All he knew was there.

No, not all he knew. He side-stepped to stand before the other portal showing the deep, green oasis surrounded by the desert Sahara's golden sands. Here he knew love. Did he need more than that? Want more than that?

Bard glanced down at the guide. "You've been with me even when I didn't know you. Which pathway do I take, little guide?"

When the animal remained still, he sighed. "I know. This is my choice." He glanced back at Gowthaman. "If I take the portal to my world, what will become of him?"

::*He canna leave this place alone.*:: Searlait's disembodied voice thrummed through him. The drum called, the beats, loud when he looked into Faerie, faded to dull taps when he looked to his world.

Why did he believe there was a decision to be made?

A squeal from the guide jerked his attention back to the

small creature. Agitated, it bounced on all four stiff legs, baring sharp teeth.

::Ye must go. Now! Feidhlim's power comes.:: In the distance, but moving rapidly near, a bright orange streak cut through the mist.

Wildly undulating, it moved toward them with an intensity of mindless purpose. Hypnotic, the sinuous movements brought a shiver to Bard's spine, and chills broke over his body. Rumbling sounded behind him and the mists parted as he turned. No portal formed, but the shape of a figure appeared in the swirling mists.

Hands against its hips, the figure tossed back its head in a movement reminiscent of laughter. Catori's drum fell silent and no sound carried through the mist. Horrified, Bard watched the figure stride into full view. He shoved back a surge of helplessness.

Feidhlim.

Bard moved closer to Gowthaman as the librarian rose to sitting, cradling his head in his hands. Bard didn't know how to fight Feidhlim, but perhaps he could get the librarian to safety. Keeping his gaze fixed on the evil glint in Feidhlim's eyes, he bent to assist Gowthaman to his feet.

Gowthaman shoved his hand away. "No, Bard. Just go. My life is not worthy."

"So, you wish to be the martyr? Kaelea will be sorely disappointed if you don't return with me."

The evil joy of Feidhlim's laughter burst the mist and bit into Bard's resolve. How could they fight such power? Gowthaman expelled a soft moan as Bard dragged him to his feet.

Feidhlim angled slightly away from them and spread his arms.

Bard followed his hungry gaze to stare at the orange stream spinning through the mist. At his side, Gowthaman gasped, shrank back, then shook himself before standing tall and strong at Bard's side. "It is the return of a portion of Feidhlim's power," he explained then faltered for a moment.

"Somehow... somehow we must prevent the magic from reaching him."

Bard nodded sharply. Eyeing the advancing flow of color, he searched through the few things he knew about the evil faerie. But all reason was hidden from him in the face of failure. How would they stop such power?

The still gray mist parted before Feidhlim and he moved toward them. The hair bristled on the back of Bard's neck. Knowing Feidhlim would see the action as a sign of weakness, he fought the urge to rub away the prickly feeling. Laughter, chill as a snow-melt stream and hard as ice, echoed around him. While the mist muffled other sounds, Feidhlim's laughter was clear and the pure evil of his intent surrounded them.

The sound of Catori's drum sliced through the mist and the rattling like that of a stone filled gourd danced a counterpart to her call. The rattling confused Bard, but the familiarity of the rapidly changing drumbeats soothed the worry and he accepted the song as part of the newly formed puzzle.

::*Nay!*::

"Silence!" Feidhlim shouted, but the word echoed around him and the drumming continued. That simple fact, proof that denying him could be successful, brought a tilted grin to Bard's face and a fountain of hope to his heart.

"Dare you to laugh at me? Me?" The fire of Feidhlim's stare cut through the mist, but Bard simply shrugged. Perhaps they could use the volatile force of Feidhlim's anger against him.

"I dare much." Bard stepped slightly in front of Gowthaman, spread his legs, and folded his arms across his chest. He canted his head slightly to one side and watched Feidhlim. Bard's anger rose and simmered through him. He hadn't asked to be a part of evil's machinations. He hadn't even asked to be thrown into a strange world. He hadn't asked... but he had asked for a reason to his life. He held on to the intensity and strength the anger lent him, but loosed the anger itself into the gray nothingness of the world between worlds.

::*We dare.*:: Searlait's voice, sharp and cutting as the edge of her blade, sounded to one side and she appeared from the mist. With a swift, flowing movement, she cast her cloak aside and matched Bard's stance, holding the long sword loosely in one hand. The flash of her smile brightened the gray for a brief moment.

"Fools." Feidhlim nodded toward Gowthaman. "The librarian has witnessed the return of my magic, my powers." His eyes narrowed. "I will not be so... gentle... this time, librarian."

Bard's grin widened as, defiant, Gowthaman stepped forward. All they needed was--

He sensed the flow of power a moment before it surged over his shoulder. Searing flames of pain where the orange stream brushed against his skin nearly drove him to his knees. Gowthaman's hand touched his arm. The odd sensation of the faerie's power passed to him and Searlait's war cry straightened his back. He tensed, prepared to lunge at Feidhlim.

The silver sword slashed through the mist and Searlait stood between Feidhlim and him. ::*Go. I deal with this... filth.*::

Bard cast a quick glance over his shoulder. The windows into the other worlds had nearly faded from existence. If the magic disappeared, they would be trapped. Rough in his urgency, he grabbed Gowthaman's arm and backed away.

"You shall not escape me. I will have what I desire from you." A flaming orange sword burst from Feidhlim's outstretched hand. "I'll deal with her, then you, and finally have my revenge on the entire Zeroun clan. Each." He swung the sword to one side. "And." The sword sliced through the mist with an audible whoosh. "Every." Feidhlim arched his eyebrows. "One." He lunged but retreated before making contact with Searlait's weapon. "Of." Parry and thrust. "Them." He held the sword in both hands and pointed the tip at each of them in turn.

In a swift, arching movement, he lifted the sword to catch the first, faint glow from the stream of power. Orange wound around orange, caressing its way down the length of the blade. "Ah," he sighed and closed his eyes.

His eyes blinked open, shining with an unholy glow.

Bard took an involuntary step back, fought his fear, and

found the will to move forward. Despite the terror lodged in his throat, he wouldn't let Derrik's cousin face this menace alone.

She held one hand back toward him. ::*Nay, ye must go now. I canna hold the windows fer long. Ye must make yer portal while they remain. Or ye'll be doomed and held here as I am. Go. I shall manage this one.*::

Feidhlim laughed as the orange stream curled up his arm and wrapped tightly about him. Sparks flew from the contact, lighting the bleak, gray mist like swarming fireflies. Torn, Bard hesitated. She could not face Feidhlim alone and survive.

::*Aye. I shall. He is in my world now. Go.*::

Feeling the dying power at his back, Bard turned and, dragging Gowthaman with him, ran. He formed a portal without conscious thought and plunged forward. As their destination came into focus, the beating of Catori's drum echoed his footsteps. Fierce shaking of the rattle drove him forward. The resistance to their passage strengthened and the portal held them in a thick, sticky grasp.

Twisting and ripping at the fading power Bard fought until, with a final, resounding thrum of drum and rattle, he and Gowthaman fell forward. He rolled to his back and stared up at the blue sky. Warm sunlight bathed his face.

The tip of a sword pressed into his chest.

CHAPTER
TWENTY-TWO

J aye stood on the top step of Lara's porch and grinned at
the gathered family. Kae returned his smile. He was such
a proud granda. She took Carrie's hand and drew her
closer for the announcement.

Jaye lifted his hand into the air and after glancing at his
closed fist, lifted two fingers. Allyn joined him and he hugged
his wife to his side. "Two. Lara and Iain have another set of
twins. One of each."

While hugs and congratulations rounded the clearing, Kae
glanced about yet again for her twin. Where was Nance? She
should be here to share this moment. Another odd ripple of
pain bent her forward. Oh, no. How stupid could she be? This
wasn't a sympathy pain for Lara, this was her twins' connection with Nanceen. Her sister was in labor, too. And two
months early.

Not wanting to worry the family during the celebration,
she left Carrie in Bryce's embrace and circled the small clusters
of family until she found Derrik. She tugged on his sleeve. "I
need to talk to you."

They moved a few paces away. "I think Nance is in labor,
but I don't know where she is. We need to find her."

Derrik's golden brows lifted high on his forehead. Then he

concentrated and shook his head. "They're nae at home." He frowned.

"They crossed the portal into Faerie some time ago. Come, we shall find them."

Kae nodded. "Any clue to where..."

Frantic barking rose from the far side of the clearing. As Kae turned toward Noid's ruckus, Korin strode from under the overhang of lush branches. Curled in his arms, Nanceen pressed her face against his shoulder and wrapped her arms about her distended belly. Another pain ripped through Kae and she stumbled toward them.

The panic filling Korin's face faded as family gathered around him, but he wouldn't allow anyone to take Nanceen from his arms.

Kae touched his shoulder. "Korin? What's--"

Pain touched his silvery-blue eyes. "I did this to her."

Nanceen lifted her head and slapped weakly at his shoulder. "How many times? This is part of having our child. Our child, Korin. It's just--ooh... a bit early." She caught Kae's gaze. "Think we could go inside for this?"

"Yes, yes, come on. Hurry, Korin." Kae tugged on Korin's arm and he followed blindly. In order to distract them from the labor pains, Kae chatted gaily. "The healer will be able to help you now, since Lara's had her babies. Yes, babies. Twins, again. This is amazing."

Nanceen shook her head and gave a pain-filled chuckle. "Kae, are you talking for me... or for you? I'm gonna be okay. So's this baby. Oh, my gosh, twins? Again? She's gonna have her hands full."

"Happily so." Kae took Nanceen's hand as they climbed the porch steps. "I'm so glad you're okay. When I finally figured out the pains I've been having..."

"Sorry, Kae." Nanceen glanced at the family pressing behind them. "Uh, sorry. I'm gonna be like Lara here. Nobody but Korin and the healer." She gave Kae a strained smile. "Understand?"

She did, and nodded her assent. The birth of a child, while celebrated by the entire clan, was a private thing to be shared between the parents. Kae stroked the small bulge of her belly. Nanceen touched her cheek and gave her an understanding grimace. "Ooh, Korin. Hurry."

"Endearment," he whispered and hurried through the cabin door.

Sighing, Kae left the porch. As the rest of the family gathered around Jaye for further news of Lara's twins, she searched out Derrik again. Some feeling, unnamed and frightening, drew her to the defender.

A distracted expression controlled Derrik's face and his gaze darted about a small area. Even when Kae moved next to him, he continued his search.

"What is it?" Confused anticipation curled in Kae's chest. Something, somewhere, was happening. Something beyond the birth of her sister's child. Something... She rubbed at a spot over her heart. She hadn't had a feeling like this, such a sense of anticipation in a long time. Following Derrik's gaze, she tried to focus. *Focus! What is this?*

"I've called fer Macaire," Derrik stated softly. "I sense a portal, but 'tis nae portal. I sense..." He shook his head, sending his loose hair flying about his shoulders. "I dinna ken what 'tis I sense."

"I feel something, too."

"Aye. 'Tis verra strong, though the feelin' waxes an' wanes. Can ye feel it growing stronger now?" He took a single stride forward.

Kae followed, drawn by the sensations. "Yes. It's odd."

Both turned when a portal opened beside them and Macaire stepped through, expression alert, eyes intense, sword drawn. Before he reported to Derrik, another portal flashed open and two bodies exploded from the shimmering oval. Macaire leaped into action, towering over a figure lying on his back, sword pressed against the rapid rise and fall of the man's chest.

"Hold," Derrik cried and, startled, Macaire angled his face toward his leader.

Kae gasped for the breath fleeing her lungs. She had wished for this moment for three long months, and now, the disbelief of what she saw kept her rooted in place. It couldn't be.

A low moan pulled her attention from the man at Macaire's feet to the other prone figure. A soft cry burst from her lips. "Gowthaman?"

She rushed to him and fell to her knees at her friend's side. When he lifted his face to her, she cried out again at the pain straining his features. He turned his face from her. "Leave me be, Kaelea. Go to him... to Bard."

"But..."

Gowthaman held her gaze and she winced at the blankness in his normally expressive black eyes. "He shall need you, Kae."

"What about you?"

He gave a bitter laugh before touching her cheek. The trembling of his hand belied his words. "I am fine. Go to him."

She tried to speak, but he covered her lips with his fingertips and shook his head. So, she nodded, rested her hand on his shoulder for a moment then eased to her feet.

Macaire backed away and sheathed his sword. Derrik reached one hand to Bard and tugged him to his feet. Bard grunted his thanks and let his gaze stray past the defender's shoulder. His heart plummeted to the soles of his feet. Kaelea was at Gowthaman's side, touching him with the care he ached to feel himself. The memory of her touch burned just under the surface of his skin, igniting his blood. But, if she preferred another, there was little he could do. He closed his eyes against the sight of her with the librarian. Had he made the wrong choice after all?

Derrik clasped his shoulder. "Welcome, m' friend."

"Defender."

Derrik glanced back over his shoulder. "Dinna fasch yerself. He is her friend, but 'tis yer face she's longin' to see." Derrik stepped to the side. "We must speak, soon. First, ye must--"

"Perhaps, Derrik." Greedily drinking in the sight of her, Bard barely noticed when Derrik moved away. He wished he could hear the words Gowthaman spoke to Kaelea, and the sweet tone of her voice when she answered. Trying to ease the pain throbbing through him, he closed his eyes.

"Bard?" He held back a wince at the dulcet tone of his name. Only a week, and it felt a lifetime had passed since she'd spoken his name. He opened his eyes and the light of Kaelea's gaze fell upon him. He lost the ability to move. Now that she stood before him, he noticed a subtle difference hovering about her, something he couldn't name, but a thing that made her even more beautiful. Her eyes widened and he was drawn into the luminous depths. Shimmering tears gathered against her lower lashes, sparkling as a tentative smile brightened her face.

"Is it really you?"

It was a strange question, one that made him frown. Who else would he be? Perhaps she saw a difference in him caused by the strain of the past week. Her smile faded at his expression and his heart lurched in sorrow. How much pain had he caused her? How much more atonement must he face? Perhaps that was why she turned to another. Hoping for something he dared not name, he spread his arms slightly. "Precious Kaelea."

With a soft cry she stumbled forward and wrapped her arms about his neck. She sobbed into his chest and he held her tightly, stroking her back. All this emotion confused him. It was as if he'd left her longer than a simple week ago. He rested his cheek against the top of her head. They would sort this out later; now he would hold her and cherish the feel of her in his arms.

Her tears dampened his chest and he tightened his arms around her. The feeling of her lips moving on the skin exposed by his partially opened shirt careened through him, eliminating the doubt and fear. *This* was where he belonged.

Kae cleared her throat, leaned back to look into his face, and asked, "Where have you been all this time?"

All this time? Unless he had been held by Feidhlim longer than he thought, they had only been apart for six days. Then he sighed and stroked her hair. He counted those days as forever, and if she loved him--even with only a portion of the love he held for her--six days became an eternity.

There were no words he could find to say, so he touched her lips gently with his. After but a brief moment of tenderness, Kae captured his face in her hands and deepened the kiss until his body thrummed with the passion he'd tried to deny.

Though he physically ached to surrender to the passion and the woman clinging to him, an insistent tickle in his mind drew him from her lips. His precious Kaelea made a tiny sound of disappointment, clutched to his shoulder for a moment, then gave him a watery smile. He kissed the tip of her nose and tried to offer a silent apology.

"What's bothering you?" Kaelea frowned and rested her palm against his chest. "There's something going on, isn't there? There was a strange disturbance before you came through the portal. It wasn't how a portal usually feels."

"I..." Bard turned them so he faced the spot where they had been tossed into the Otherworld. "I must return."

She stiffened and pulled away. He realized what he'd said and let his shoulders slump as he gathered her close once again.

"No, precious one, not to my world. I am needed in the world between worlds."

"Where?" Her voice rose to a desperate shriek and she succeeded in jerking from his arms. "You can't go there. That's a place of banishment. You won't be able to return."

"I've just come from there. I've no wish to seek out the grayness, but I'm needed." He couldn't explain how he knew, but Searlait was failing in her attempt to contain Feidhlim. Just as the combination of powers had been needed for their escape; the pieced together puzzle would be the only way to defeat Feidhlim.

The sense of many eyes upon him made Bard turn to see the interest in the faces of the gathered family. He nodded an acknowledgement. These people and the acceptance he'd found here--this was why he fought. Jaye left the others and joined him.

A small white-blonde haired girl trotted behind Jaye, but she stopped beside Gowthaman. "Unca Jaye?"

"In a moment, Breanna."

"But..."

Gowthaman tugged the small girl to his side. "Quiet now, little missy. Your uncle has more important issues to deal with now."

"More important than you?"

"Yes."

Bard winced at the dull, empty tone of the single word, but had no time to concern himself with the librarian, for as Jaye moved beside him with a muttered denial, Derrik uttered a growl of challenge.

A vortex formed before them, a swirling tornado of gray and orange, twisting in tortured waves against itself. It grew large, bright, then faded to a size he could hold in his hand. At first predominantly gray, the orange blossomed, twining around and through the gray until the vortex shone with pale color. Growing again, gray slipped from orange until a double vortex formed and hovered in the air. One color advanced, then the other. Advancing, retreating, but no longer touching.

The vortexes indicated how Searlait fought valiantly, holding Feidhlim at bay--for the time being. As surely as Bard knew his love for Kaelea, he knew the outcome of the battle in the world between worlds if he did not return. He held Kaelea by both shoulders and made her look at him. She tried to watch the spinning vortexes so he curled one finger under her chin and held her gaze captive. "I must go."

"But, why? I don't understand."

"There is no time to explain. I must... Kaelea."

His kiss was urgent, probing, filled with the love in his heart and soul. The gift of her love returned to him shone vibrant purple behind his closed eyelids. The color lingered around them when he pulled away and stared down at her. She tried for bravery but her expression failed miserably. He loved her all the more.

"Go on then. But, don't forget to come back. Soon."

"I shall return, Kaelea. This is my vow to you."

She took his hand and pressed it over her heart. The warmth of her body, the strength of her love seeped into him, spreading belief and subtle power along every nerve, through every vein. Did she realize what she had given him? Eyes downcast, she let go of his hand and took a step back.

Before he turned to the vortexes, he leaned and captured her hand. "I love you, precious Kaelea."

"I... Bard, I love you. Come back to me."

"It is as I have vowed, my love." Anger and regret shot through him. He couldn't ignore the call of need from the gray world. *My love.* There was much to tell Kaelea and once he had returned, he would not leave her side.

Derrik and Jaye stared at the spinning twists of color, arguing in hushed tones. Bard stepped before them and easily formed a portal. With trailing colors whipping through the air, the vortexes zipped through the passage. He followed their paths until the faint shapes of the combatants showed through the wavering portal. Trying to steady the portal with a softly spoken command, Bard readied himself to return to the world of nothingness. Kaelea's love would lead him home again. Home, to her.

Derrik slapped one hand on his shoulder before he moved forward. "Ye shall nae go alone. I shall come wi' ye."

Bard turned his head to stare at the defender. With a fierce expression, he was so like his cousin that Bard had to smile. "If you can."

Derrik frowned in response, took the sword Macaire offered and strode into the portal. He stumbled back as though he had walked into a solid wall. With an angry growl, he tried again, and was again repulsed. He slashed at the magical opening with the sword, but other than the ringing vibrations of the sword blow, there was no effect.

"I didn't think you would be able to pass. I must go." Bard reached one hand out to the portal and pressed. The opening was solid, with not even the earlier stickiness to impede his entering. No! This can't be! He stepped to one side in surprise.

"Neither can you enter alone." Gowthaman's quiet words sounded close to his ear. "I must go with you."

Bard jerked to face the librarian. "You can't. You're too weak to return. Rest. I'll find a way."

"There is no other way. You could not leave the place of banishment alone, and it will not let you enter without my help. Or without the call of the drum. Listen. In the empty silence of my mind, I hear it."

Holding his breath, all Bard could hear were the soft sounds of Kaelea's weeping and the continued frustrated anger emanating from the defender.

"Listen, Bard, and you shall hear."

"You're still too weak. I wouldn't risk your life again."

Gowthaman gave a bark of bitter laughter. "What life? How much was stolen from me by the seeker? How much of what I now know is, in truth, my knowledge? What false memories may have been planted within my mind? I do not know. But, I do know this... I shall help you return to the world between worlds and together, somehow, we shall triumph over the evil one. Mayhaps then, I shall find peace."

"Your strength--"

"Enough has returned." A confused frown furrowed his brow. "The child... touched me. She has healed some of my injuries." He glanced back at the golden haired girl who blew him a kiss. "I do not understand."

Squaring his shoulders, Gowthaman shook his head. "There is much I do not understand, this is but a small part. Mayhaps I never shall. Now, we must go. The drumming in my head is loud. We are needed. Now."

"Come then. I don't hear the drum, but if Catori is with us in your mind, it should be enough." With Gowthaman at his side, he brushed past Derrik and faced the portal.

Hesitantly, he stretched out one arm and met the resistance. He could go no further until Gowthaman clasped his shoulder and the librarian's golden power flowed into him. He heard Derrik's gasp as they stepped together from Faerie into the gray nothing of the world between worlds.

TWENTY-THREE

"No!" Kae fell to her knees and reached her empty hands toward the portal that remained open but inaccessible before them. Empty. The world was empty with Bard gone. As empty as her heart would be until he returned.

"Sis?" Jaye knelt beside her and wrapped one arm about her shoulders. "Do you have any idea what's going on here?"

She shook her head and struggled to sniff back tears that would do nothing to bring Bard home sooner. "I don't. But, look. The portal's not closing. Do you think we can get through?"

As she asked, Derrik leaned his shoulder against the opening, straining to force his way through the impenetrable barrier. Even with Macaire muttering the strongest of power words, Derrik was denied access. Jaye drew and released a long breath. "Doesn't look like it. Kae, go back to the porch. Nance might need you."

Kae smiled at his concern. "She doesn't need anyone but Korin right now. You should know that. I'm okay. And I'm not leaving this spot until..."

"I'll wait with you then."

"Thanks, Jaye. Uh, maybe you should tell Derrik to stop before he hurts himself." The leader of the Alastriona threw himself against the portal repeatedly only to fall back and try again.

Jaye shook his head. "He'll stop soon. Did Bard say anything about those vortexes or the portal?"

"All he said was that he was needed. Like I don't need him here?"

"Did you get a chance to tell--"

"He was here barely five minutes, Jaye. How could I?" Her voice dropped to a whisper, "How could I?"

Breanna patted her cheek. "Don't worry, Auntie Kae. They'll be back. I promise."

Hugging the small girl to her, Kae took a deep breath. "You just keep believing that, darlin'. Okay?"

Bree nodded against her shoulder, then stepped back and entwined her tiny fingers through Kae's. "Come on, let's watch."

"Watch?" Jaye narrowed his eyes at the child. "What are you talking about, Bree?"

"The portal. We can watch 'em. I can see my Gowtham now."

After meeting her brother's wide-eyed gaze over Bree's head, Kae turned to the portal. She rose and let Bree drag her closer to the wavering images. Though the figures were faint and blurred by the gray surrounding them, by squinting she thought she could discern Bard and Gowthaman as they moved closer to a second pair of figures. It was like watching a movie through a screen smeared with gray oil.

Bree sat cross-legged on the lush grass and began patting the earth with her hands. She grinned up at Kae. "Do you hear the drum? It sounds like this." She demonstrated a simple rhythm and as she happily pounded the ground, the view through the portal grew clear.

"How's that, Auntie Kae? Better? See my Gowtham?"

"Yes, I see him, honey." But, she wasn't watching her friend, she was watching Bard stride confidently toward--

"Oh, my God," she whispered. "Feidhlim."

. . .

D epression seeped into his heart and mind, a gray to match the indistinct world around him. Bard slowed his strides, took long, deep breaths, and fought the debilitating sensation. Dragging his spirit down until he sank to his knees to accept a life of gray nothingness-- this had to be an effect of the world between worlds. He shook his head fiercely. Despite his loneliness and confusion while growing to a man, he'd never succumbed to depression. He wouldn't now.

He glanced sideways at Gowthaman. Strain tensed the lines of his face, drew tight, corded muscles along his neck. But a golden glow hovered about the librarian and his taut grin showed his determination. Bard peered at his own hands. The colors of magic amazed him. As individual as each wielder, so was the color associated with their talent. When he was thrown into Kaelea's world, he had discovered a magical talent within himself. What color of magic mani-fested within him?

"Purple." Gowthaman chuckled at Bard's surprise. "You were thinking about the manifestation of magic, were you not?"

"Yes."

"Your magic is purple, deep and pure. As is the soulfire of your love for Kaelea."

Bard searched for some mockery from the man he could easily count as a rival for Kaelea's love. The librarian's eyes held dull lifelessness, though his expression was serious.

"I don't understand."

Gowthaman chuckled again and clasped his shoulder. "You shall when you return to her."

"When we return."

A brief surge of power flowed to Bard from Gowthaman who stumbled and turned away. "Mayhaps."

A woman's war cry, a sound of challenge and elation, burst through the mist spurring them to action. The gray parted. Before them, in a small space cleared of mist, Feidhlim and Searlait faced each other in silent contemplation. Feidhlim wore a satisfied smile as he balanced forward on the balls of his feet. He held his flaming orange sword loosely, tossing it negligently from one hand to the other. Behind him, pressed against the edge of the cleared area, a twisting, writhing mass of orange hovered.

The evil one's magic. Bard sent a silent, thankful prayer to the Guardians. At least Feidhlim had not regained that portion of his power.

Searlait stood still, a half-smile tilting her lips. The only indication she recognized Bard and Gowthaman's presence was a slight rise in one eyebrow and the other side of her mouth lifted.

A slow, deep beat sounded from overhead. Expecting to see a drum descending upon them, Bard glanced up to nothing but a deeper gray. Squinting, he imagined faces in the swirling mist, watching, waiting... judging. He blinked, and the faces were gone and only mist--impenetrable, heavy, oppressive--remained.

Gowthaman made a soft sound of welcome, bent, and straightened with the desert guide in his palm. He held the animal up to Bard, then let the guide climb his arm to perch on his shoulder. Bard nodded. All the pieces of the puzzle were gathered. How did they fit to make a whole?

Feidhlim swung his sword above his head, leaped forward, and slashed through the spot where Searlait had been standing. From the far side of the cleared area, she laughed and Feidhlim whirled to face her. As though reaching for his magic, he strained back against the boundary, but could not touch the orange swirls. Silent, he narrowed his eyes and moved his angry gaze from Searlait to Bard and Gowthaman.

"What have you done? How do you hold my power at bay?" he ground out from between clenched teeth.

Searlait shrugged and adjusted her grip on her sword. "We have done nothin'. Mayhaps 'tis the Watchers of this place that keep it from ye. Mayhaps they dinna care fer yer presence here. Mayhaps--"

"Silence." Feidhlim drew deep, heavy breaths. Tense, his

body vibrated with anger that flowed from him in pale orange waves.

Bard drew a full breath of his own and prepared to enter the clear area. He didn't know how to help, but he would be there. If Searlait fell and he must take up the sword, then he would fight with the unaccustomed weapon. If he had to grapple with Feidhlim and subdue him with bare hands, he would. Perhaps that was the way, for magic had little effect on the faerie. He clenched then loosened his fists and flexed his fingers, imagining the satisfying feel of Feidhlim's neck in his grasp.

But when he stepped forward intending to enter the circle, he met with solid resistance.

"Bard?" Gowthaman whispered.

Suppressing a frustrated groan, he glanced at the librarian. "What?"

"I do not believe... uh..." Gowthaman slumped to the ground.

Kneeling at his side, Bard stared up at the mist-shrouded figure towering over them. "I won't let you harm him."

::*My time is not with him. He shall recover, more whole than he is now.*::

"What? Who are you?" Bard rested one hand protectively on Gowthaman's chest, relieved at the slow rise and fall of his breathing.

Gentle laughter curled around him. ::*I believe you might call me Guardian. However, I am one of the Watchers of the world between worlds. I have taken special interest in the woman and allowed her nominal access to the worlds from which she was banished.*::

"If you care, then stop them." Bard jerked one hand toward Searlait and risked a quick glance. Battle began in earnest, the ringing and clashing of swords muffled by the still mists outside the circle. "Or let me."

::*Your presence here is a mystery to us. You shall not interfere.*::

"What do you want of me?" If he wasn't there to fight or somehow strengthen Derrik's cousin... "Why did you allow us to return?"

::Curiosity. We did not know if you... or the gentle one here...would be willing.::

"If Feidhlim is not stopped, he will destroy the family of the one I love."

::Ah, love. Love brings with it a strange willingness, does it not?::

Bard rose to his feet and stepped over Gowthaman's prone form to stand between him and the strange figure.

::You will even protect one who may challenge for that love?::

"I will."

::Curious.:: The figure faded into a mist slightly lighter than the gray around them. Unsure whether to be relieved or angered by the strange interference then disappearance of the one who called himself a Guardian... Was this Guardian the same as the Guardians of his world?

::No, but we know of them and shall cooperate.:: The words rang through Bard's mind, followed by the bursting of anger at the intrusion on his thoughts. These Watchers were no better than Feidhlim's seeker.

::Do not equate us with such a creature. We do not steal your mind, but we do know your heart. We have witnessed your dreams. We... share in your pain. Watch. Rest your hands upon the boundary and lend your strength to the fighter of your choice.::

His choice? There was no choice. The Watcher reappeared and, though he could see no facial features within the deeply hooded figure, Bard felt the intensity with which the Guardian watched him.

The hood tilted slightly to one side. *::Which do you choose?::*

"The woman."

::And your companion there?::

Bard spared Gowthaman another quick glance. "His choice--the same as mine."

::Your conviction is strong.::

Not feeling a need to dignify the comment, Bard snorted.

The Watcher chuckled, then gave a low whistle. The desert rodent crawled from beneath Gowthaman's shirt and stood before the shrouded figure. Unmoving, the small creature stared up at the figure.

::You agree as well, little one?::

Harsh laughter burst from Bard as his guide circled in its affirmative answer. "We agree. As does the young woman whose drumming has cleared many pathways for us."

::So be it.:: The Watcher parted the mist with a pass of his hand, then lifted both arms above his head. The sense of a smile reached Bard. *::Are you prepared?::*

K ae shook away the irreverent thought that this was like watching a movie. The gray swirling mist gave the scene through the portal a surreal quality. If she didn't know those within the mist, she'd call what she was seeing nothing more than a dream. A very bad dream.

Behind her, the family gathered silently. Kae wished someone would say something--anything to break the tense silence. Fearful of the strong emotions careening through her, she didn't trust herself to speak. They couldn't hear anything from the portal, but if sound traveled to those inside, anything she might say could distract Bard.

Suddenly Gowthaman collapsed and a collective gasp filled the clearing. Derrik shook off Jaye's restraining hand and doubled his efforts to break through the portal.

"Oh, no," Kae whispered and gathered Bree close to sit on her lap.

Bree glanced up at her. "It's okay, Auntie Kae. Gowtham's just sleeping while Bard talks to the gray man." She turned her head and frowned at the portal. "Wish that fog would just go away." After she tapped an odd beat on Kae's knee, the view cleared nominally.

"That's better."

Bryce's daughter was exhibiting advanced talents and Kae made a mental list of what she'd seen to discuss with Bryce and Jaye. Later...

Happy for a less foggy view, she stroked Bree's back. "Good job, darlin'."

Still, no matter how hard she squinted, she couldn't see any gray man, although Bard did appear to be talking to someone. She spared a glance at the combatants set apart from the mist. She'd never seen Derrik's cousin, but the resemblance between the two left no doubt of their familial connection. The smooth, controlled movements of her attack and defense became a lively dance countered by the jerking, angry swipe of Feidhlim's sword. Kae shuddered and Bree patted her arm.

"Lottie's gonna win. I know it. Then everybody'll come home."

"I hope so, honey. I really hope so."

B ard flattened his hands against the barrier and stared through the triangle formed by his thumbs and index fingers. Searlait continued to fight bravely, but her movements had slowed. She was tiring. "Get on with this, Watcher."

::*Patience.*:: The hood shook back and forth and he waved an arm over Gowthaman. ::*You from other worlds have learned no patience. Rise, Gowthaman.*::

Gowthaman gasped as though taking a first breath. Wide-eyed and silent, he rose to his knees and pressed his palms to the barrier. The desert guide touched paws and nose to the space. The beating of Catori's drum resounded around them. Bard's heart matched the beat, throbbing against the walls of his chest. He wasn't sure he trusted this Watcher--or if he even should. But he knew of no other option.

He chanced a glance around at the gray mist. The shapes of faces and limbs, the hints of other figures pressed close, touching him with their cold, damp presence. Biting his lip concentrated his thoughts and he withheld a shiver. He would not show weakness before these creatures, any more than he would before the evil faerie who had held him. There was no sense of evil behind the misty Watchers, but no feeling of goodness either.

Sliding his hands along the barrier, Gowthaman rose to his feet but leaned heavily against the clear area. The librarian's strength and determination were nearly gone.

"Patience be damned. Get on with whatever it is you plan

to do," Bard ground out through clenched teeth. Being held as a pawn, knowing what must be done but not how, ate at him. Willing calm to his tensed muscles, he sought answers in the echoing drumbeats.

A sensation washed through him, cool yet not unpleasant, as if the entities joined in a collective sigh. The forms were clearer, yet had no discernable features except misty gray hands pressing, drumming against the barrier, taking up the rhythm of Catori's call. Tiny cracks radiated from each finger-tip, crawling across the surface in frenetic waves. Bard snorted with satisfaction. Good. He would be able to break through and...

A single high-pitched whistle stopped the drumming and the Watcher who had spoken to him disappeared. Two breaths later, his form materialized between Searlait and Feidhlim, one arm extended to each combatant.

::You shall hold.::

Searlait immediately lowered her sword and knelt, head bowed.

Feidhlim hesitated, then with a mighty roar, sliced through the misty creature. His flaming orange sword black-ened, dropped from his hands, and shattered. Holding his hands to his chest as if in pain, he shook his head and backed away.

The Watcher turned to face Feidhlim. He reached out and the thin, glowing strands of Feidhlim's magic oozed through the tiny cracks in the barrier and gathered in his hand. Soon the Guardian held the squirming mass of magic on his palm.

Arms outstretched, fingers clawed, Feidhlim leapt forward. "Mine."

With his free hand, the Watcher froze Feidhlim mid-stride. *::Think you so?::*

Cold laughter followed the Watcher's statement and Bard shivered. The benevolence that the gray being had shown toward them disappeared. The tone and stance of a harsh judge stood in its place. A flash of regret tinged with fear burned through Bard. Would the being remember his distrust, his defiance?

Comfort pressed against him, as physical as the touch of waves upon sand. These beings of the world between worlds were strange creatures.

::*Be at peace, Hisatsinom.*::

Before Bard could follow the imperious directive, the Watcher lifted both arms over his head and cradled the power mass between his palms. The voice boomed and echoed in Bard's head. ::*Desecration comes to many worlds with the presence of the one before me. For this, he shall be punished. He allowed magic to flow unfettered through the world between worlds. For this, he shall be punished. He dares to challenge one chosen of the Watchers. For this, he shall be punished.*::

Feidhlim's mouth moved silently and his face contorted with strain as he fought to reach his magic.

Still holding the power mass above his head, the Watcher pointed at Feidhlim with his free hand. With infinite slowness, the bundled magic moved toward the still faerie. A malicious grin stretched Feidhlim's lips.

Bard slammed one fist against the barrier. "No! Don't let him--"

::*Silence. You shall not challenge my actions.*:: Softer, the voice continued, ::*Searlait, you may join our... outworld visitors.*::

Searlait cast Bard a confused look then nodded, rose, and moved gracefully toward him. The barrier parted before her, disappearing completely into gray particles melding into the mist. After a quick glance, she slipped one shoulder under Gowthaman's arm and assisted him in remaining upright. She touched her fingertips to his lips and shook her head when he tried to speak.

Easing to the librarian's other side, Bard stood close enough to offer assistance if needed, but did not touch Gowthaman. The man held great pride and Bard would allow him all he was able.

Feidhlim cried out in silent glee as the magic neared him, separated again into thin strands, and encircled his body. The glee was cut short when the Watcher clapped his hands together, then twisted his clasped fists until one hand lay over the other. The magical bonds tightened around Feidhlim.

Ready to leap forward, Bard relaxed back on his heels as the entity twisted his hands. The orange bands tightened and Feidhlim's agonized cry echoed through the mists. Why were the gray beings returning the evil one's power? They needed to keep magic from him, not surround him with additional power.

::*Do not worry needlessly, visitor from the outer worlds. We do not return his power. Watch... see how the magic brightens. What has already returned to him now drains away. Becomes ours.*::

Feidhlim struggled violently, mouth moving in silent curses, eyes burning with frustration and a hatred so powerful, Bard took a short step back.

::*Ours to do with as we wish. Ours... to destroy.*::

With one hand opened, the Watcher held his palm to the side. A gray-black tunnel, darker than the mist around them, burst from his hand to consume the barely visible path Feidhlim's magic had cut through the world between worlds in the mindless search for its master. The Watcher slowly closed his hand, one finger at a time, folding into a loose fist. He slashed his fist toward the gray earth.

The tunnel shattered with a heavy tinkling of tiny orange particles drifting into the mist. Feidhlim's pain found voice. The mixture of rage and agony brought intense satisfaction to Bard. This was no more than the evil one deserved-- retribution for the pain he caused Kaelea's family.

Bard closed his eyes. No, not retribution. Retribution and revenge led only to an endless cycle of the same. It had been so in his world, and he was sure if he studied the histories of Kaelea's worlds, revenge would be a strong factor for war and disagreement. If Feidhlim were unable to exact his own retribution, his followers would take up the cause, naming him martyr. Effective punishment, nothing more, would be sufficient.

::*Good. I feared the touch of evil upon you was too great, Hisatsinom.*:: Bard experienced laughter in the Guardian's voice. ::*Think you the loss of what he values most to be punishment enough? That, and an endless time within the world between worlds to contemplate his... misadventures?*::

A soft snort escaped Bard. Misadventures? A mild word for the damage Feidhlim had done to both the Faerie and the human worlds. "Hold him here and I am satisfied."

::*Our time is nearly complete. Soon, this one shall contain no magic. His magic is destroyed. He shall never find power again. He shall remain here.*::

The Watcher slashed his hand before his chest. Brilliant orange sparkles rose from Feidhlim's body and exploded around him, falling into the swirling mist. Finally, with a third slash of his hand, the magical bindings holding Feidhlim dissipated into faint streams of smoke.

Wailing, Feidhlim collapsed and, covered by a roiling wave of mist, disappeared. The wave surged toward Bard. He bent to scoop the tiny guide into the protection of his palm, then stood before Gowthaman and Searlait and turned his back. Hot, cold, alive, the mist surrounded them, stole the ground beneath their feet and tossed them, flailing, into a bright light.

T he sparkling appearance of Feidhlim's magic drew the Zeroun clan closer to the portal. After learning of the commotion and insisting she was fine, Iain carried Lara from the cabin and she rested in a chair, her newborn twins in woven baskets at her sides. Not to be left alone, Nanceen had joined them, a tiny girl child cradled against her breast. Kaelea left Bree to her father's care and stood next to her sister, one hand protectively on her shoulder.

"Is that really his magic?" Nanceen asked in an awed whisper. "What are they doing to it?"

"I don't know." And she didn't really care. Kae watched Bard avidly, as if by keeping him centered in her vision, she could protect him. "Isn't that the color the Alastriona say is leaking from the urn?"

Nanceen shrugged and caressed her daughter's soft, rounded cheek.

"She's beautiful, Nance." Kae spared a glance at the tiny child. Fine red hair streaked with brilliant gold curled over her head. Bright blue eyes watched her for a moment, then the baby sighed and closed her eyes.

"Yes, she is. She looks like her father." Nanceen reached an arm to Korin and he bent to kiss her cheek.

"Endearment," he whispered.

Kae bit back a grin and took a few steps away from the loving demonstration. She smiled for her sister, but wept inside for herself and her own child. She stroked her belly and sent vague promises to the life inside her.

A flash of movement drew her once again closer to the portal. Feidhlim writhed in torment. Good! She wanted to wish the worst for him, to make him suffer as her family had suffered since before she was born. She glanced at the three newest members of the clan and sighed. What was the worst? Enacting such revenge would make her no better than Feidhlim. The thought settled like lead around her heart. How would they find a balance between revenge and rightful punishment?

An Alastriona warrior appeared through a portal and whispered urgently to Derrik, whose frown deepened. After the warrior disappeared the way he had come, Derrik turned to Jaye, but spoke so that all in the clearing could hear.

"The urn containin' Feidhlim's magic shattered. But, there's nothin' inside. Nae even a remnant of power. The Alastriona sense nothin'. No magic. No lifeforce. 'Tis as though Feidhlim ne're was."

Kae didn't think that was such a bad thing. However, the urn had once contained the magical powers of an evil faerie. Where had the evil gone? She turned back to the spectacle beyond the strange portal.

Sparkling shattered bits of orange light floated through the misty gray. Orange lights winked out like the deaths of fireflies. A sense of loss overcame her, as if part of her world disappeared with each tiny light. She jerked her gaze to Bard, but he was still there. Taking a deep breath, Kae hugged herself.

A sudden wave of mist overcame Feidhlim then moved toward Bard. Kae cried out. Gray exploded from the portal with a gale force that toppled her to her bottom. Expelled upon the gray wave, three figures shot from the portal and tumbled across the Faerie clearing.

Wailing, the voice of ultimate pain, drew the wave in upon itself and retreated into the world between worlds. The sound of stone closing upon stone ground through the diminishing portal. With a final snap, the portal was no more.

TWENTY-FOUR

Bard opened his eyes to the warmth of bright sunlight upon his face. He glanced at his chest and released a sigh. No sword held him in place. He rolled to his side, then rose to his hands and knees and looked around him. Statues, frozen in aspects of fear and surprise, stared at him.

Sitting back on his calves, he checked for his companion. Gowthaman had also risen to sit and held the desert guide, touching the small animal as if looking for injury. Continuing to scan the clearing, Bard discovered a gray clad form curled next to a tree, unmoving except for the rise and fall of breathing. Searlait had been expelled with them?

With a suddenness as explosive as the force that had thrown them back into the Faerie Otherworld, the statues came to life and rushed toward him. While happy to be surrounded by the gathered clan, there was only one who he wished to see.

Then she was on her knees before him, seemingly the answer to his unspoken summons. More beautiful with her tear-stained face than he could have thought possible, he drank in her appearance. The trembling of her hopeful smile. The mixed lights of fear, confusion and love in her eyes. The delicate way she tried to sniff back further tears.

She lifted her arms to him. He rose to his knees and collapsed into her embrace.

He was home.

Kae held tightly to the man in her arms, stroking her hands over the shaking of his shoulders, pressing to the heaving of his chest. The silence between them was profound, all the words she'd wanted to say to him captured in the moment--unneeded, unwanted.

When he drew a heavy, shuddering breath, she arched back slightly to look into his face. With a soft cry, she pressed her cheek to his, mingling their tears. He wove his fingers through her hair, cupped the back of her head, and kissed her with a reverence she felt clear to her toes.

She let her eyelids drift closed, but instead of darkness, a bright, blinding purple surrounded her, throbbing with the beating of her heart. A second beat--Bard's heart--danced with hers. Kae sighed into his mouth as their kiss deepened.

Bard was home.

J aye surveyed the excitement as small groups surrounded Bard and Gowthaman. Although Gowthaman's injuries concerned him, both men appeared out of danger. He grinned for a moment. If the soulfire surrounding Bard and his sister were any indication, Bard was in good hands.

He turned his attention to the third figure thrown from the world between worlds. Derrik had shoved Macaire away and now stood over the gray-cloaked woman, eyes narrowed, his face a chiseled study in disbelief.

Jaye crossed the clearing to his friend. Derrik shook his head.

"Nay, I dinna... I canna..."

Kneeling, Jaye turned her to her back. Derrik dropped to the other side and gathered the still form in his arms. "Sear-lait," he whispered. "Cousin, wake."

Agony pulsed from Derrik in waves that touched Jaye with palpable sorrow. Tears filled the brave defender's eyes, pleading with him for assistance and assurances. Jaye gave a

swift nod, took a deep breath, and rested one hand upon Searlait's forehead. He focused his concentration, then shook his
head. "She bears no injury. As far as I can tell, she's sleeping."

Derrik's frown deepened as he brushed stray hairs back
from his cousin's face. "Searlait?"

At his call, her eyelids fluttered. She gasped and jerked
from his embrace then held her head between her hands.
"Nay, 'tis but a dream."

"Nae dream." Derrik rested his hand on her shoulder. With
the other hand he touched her hair, her shoulder and ran his
fingers down the side of her face. "Sweet cousin, yer home."

Refusing to allow himself to be moved to the shade of a
towering oak, Gowthaman sat in a patch of sunlight.
But the sun did little to warm the chill surrounding
his heart. Guilt over his part in the past events wrapped him in
an icy grip and even though he supposed he had assisted in
rectifying the situation, he still held blame as a thick knot,
tight within himself.

Derrik's cousin had been expelled from the world between
worlds with them. Another thing he didn't understand.
Banishment was to be forever. Yet, she hadn't truly deserved
banishment for her act. If she hadn't killed one of Feidhlim's
followers, both Jaye and Derrik would be long dead and this
family wouldn't exist.

It mattered to him that Bard and Kaelea were together,
though nothing else did. Their reunion filled the glade with
deep purple soulfire, but they remained oblivious to the effect
upon the family.

The beauty of their love threatened to melt a portion of the
ice around his heart. Gowthaman ruthlessly reinforced the
frozen barrier. Ah, but the aching of his soul far exceeded the
numbing pain of his body. If he could simply just slink away,
make his way back to the desert, and disappear... like the
wounded animal he was.

"Gowthaman?"

Trying to deny the child's voice, he shook his head.

"Gowthaman?"

Releasing a long breath, he lifted his head and tried to smile. "Yes, little missy?"

The golden-haired child patted his hand. "I'm glad you're home."

U sing gentle strokes of her soft fingertips, his Kaelea brushed the tears from his face. Bard took her hand and pressed a kiss to the center of her palm. "There is much I must say to you."

She nodded. "Me, too. Bard, I've missed you so much."

"I thought of you often this past week." Bard paused at the strange expression pulling Kaelea's lips to a frown. As tremulous as it may be, he needed to see her smile. "I love you, precious Kaelea."

"I love you, too. But, you only missed me a week?"

"Each moment... from the time I left your bed six days ago." Her hand trembled as he brushed his lips over her knuckles.

"Six days?" She angled her gaze past his shoulder as though searching for assistance. Why was she so concerned with the number of days he'd been gone? Mentally, he recounted the days. Or had it been seven?

"Kaelea, is something wrong?"

Startled by his question, she laughed nervously. He believed he had only been away from her for a week. But, how could that be? She knew from Derrik that he'd remained at his camp in the southwest for five days before disappearing. What had happened that last day--that sixth day?

She'd ask the simple questions first. "What happened? Why did you disappear?" Kae held her breath. Would he answer why he disappeared on the sixth day--or why he left her alone?

Bard remained lost in thought for a moment, then rose and held out his hand to assist her to her feet. "As I prepared to return to the desert Sahara, I was taken by Feidhlim's followers and held some place secreted here in the Otherworld."

He paused again when Jaye came up to him and extended one hand. Bard clasped his forearm.

"Welcome back, Bard." Jaye turned his face to Kae. "I think the whole family will wish to hear this. Shall we spare Bard multiple retellings and let him speak to us all? Although..." He gave Bard a wry grin. "...you'll have the chance to speak again before the Queen."

"The Queen?" he gulped.

Kae interlaced her fingers with his. "It won't be so bad."

"If you believe so." The doubt in his face caused her to rise on tiptoe and kiss him. He smiled. "Your encouragement means much to me."

"I can offer more encouragement. Later. If you'll come to my cabin."

His lips stretched in a tired, yet wicked grin. "I shall come."

J aye arranged his family comfortably around the glade, then nodded for Bard to begin. He spoke slowly, beginning with the moment Feidhlim's followers lifted him from the human world to hold him captive in Faerie. He told of Searlait's encouragement, of Gowthaman's courage and strength, of the drumming from beyond a dream realm. He wasn't ready to speak of, Feidhlim's seeker, nor did he tell of the window he'd seen into his home world.

Searlait answered the rare question, but Gowthaman spoke little.

Kae worried about her friend's lack of interest. The dull look in his eyes seemed to go beyond the burden of physical pain caused by the bruises and cuts covering what she could see of his body. When the telling was over, she'd make sure Jaye healed Gowthaman, no matter what arguments the librarian voiced.

Bard closed his tale. "I don't know why the Watchers of the world between worlds chose to free Searlait. Perhaps to honor her for the part she played in our escape and Feidhlim's defeat."

"The Watchers took his magic?" Jaye asked again.

Searlait answered. "Aye, an' more than that. Nae only taken, 'tis destroyed. Nothin's left of his power, except the memories to torment him through his time between worlds. He is mortal now. Nae amount of conniving by his followers can return what nae longer exists."

She slumped wearily and when Derrik caught her arm, she smiled up at him. "Cousin, I fear I must rest."

Jaye nodded and Derrik led her to a spot beneath a thick-trunked maple and assisted her in reclining against the rough bark. Turning to his clan, Jaye spread his hands. "I'm sure we all have many questions for these three. Today has been blessed many times over, and we're all tired. We shall meet again tomorrow at Stephen's cabin to continue."

He gathered Allyn to his side and they moved toward Lara.

Bard wrapped an arm about Kaelea's waist and tugged her to his side. Something was different, but he was too tired to sort through the feeling. Later. So much was relegated to later. Would there ever be enough time? For now, he asked, "Why is your family gathered now? I was surprised to land here the first time, surrounded by so many." He leaned close to her ear. "I would have preferred a small welcoming. Perhaps you alone."

"That would've been nice. But, you reentered the portal so quickly." She smoothed one hand over his chest and he caught his lower lip tight between his teeth. Kaelea glanced at him from under lowered lashes. "I'll give you a proper welcome later." She let joy fill her expression and smiled. "Speaking of welcomes--that's why we're all here. Lara's had her babies. Twins."

"Now? They are early, but that is not uncommon for twins."

"Actually..." Kae took a deep breath. This was where it was going to get tricky. How did she explain that while he thought only a week had passed, he'd actually been gone for three months? She didn't even understand how that could be--so how could she explain the anomaly to him? "Uh, actually, they're a little later than we expected."

"Later? I thought--"

"Bard, I don't know how it happened, but you've been gone three months. Not a week. Ninety days. Ninety long, lonely days."

"Months? I don't understand."

Gowthaman limped next to them and stood unsteadily, weaving slightly as he spoke. "Feidhlim bragged to me... somehow he and his followers discovered a way to bend time. So while only a short time passed for us while we were held captive, a longer time existed here in the rest of the Other-world. And in the human world."

"Months?" Bard scrubbed his hands through his hair. "I have been away for months?"

Kae tried to give him a reassuring smile. "Yes. For three months. But, you're back now. And I'm not gonna let you go away again."

Gowthaman touched her arm. "Good." Then he limped toward the small group gathered around Lara and Nanceen.

"We'll sort this all out later, Bard. You're exhausted. I'll introduce you to the three newest clan members then take you home."

He dragged her against his chest and kissed her. "Okay." As they turned back toward the others he stumbled to a halt. "Three? You said Lara had twins."

Taking his hand, Kae pulled him forward. "As they were coming here, Nanceen went into labor, too. Now, her child is early. About two months."

Nanceen grinned up at her. "Gowthaman was just telling me that he'd read in some fairy herbal that the wee folk..." She gave Korin a teasing arch of one eyebrow. "... have a gestation of only seven months. If that's true, then this little one was right on time."

After Bard was introduced to the three babes held snuggly in their mothers' arms he glanced sideways at Kaelea. Perhaps... someday...

In the recesses of his memory he heard his grandmother's admonishment, *'Isn't there something you must do?'*

Yes, there was. He brought a vision of his grandmother to his mind and silently thanked her. Clearing his throat, he faced the parents. "I would ask of you... in my world... a blessingway is offered to a newborn child. I would be honored if I could offer the blessingway to the children born this day."

Kaelea clapped her hands together. "Oh, Bard, after all that's happened, that sounds wonderful. Please. What do we need to do?"

"You need do nothing but offer your hopes and wishes for the children. If I may hold them?"

Nanceen cast a quick glance at Lara before they both glanced at their husbands. Together they smiled and nodded.

First he gathered Lara's twins in his arms. Born of the same time in the womb, they would receive the blessingway together. Cradling the babes in his arms, he turned in a slow circle, acknowledging the cardinal points. He paced the slow circle twice, the first time starting with the south and the rising sun of his old world.

Then, he began in the east, honoring the rising sun of his new world.

At each compass point he whispered a prayer for the babes.

Finally, he closed his eyes against the brightness and held them high in the light of the yellow-white sun. A chant of praise, of blessing, of vital wishes rumbled from his throat. Before he returned the tiny twins to their parents, he opened his eyes and placed a kiss upon each small head.

Then he turned to where Nanceen rested against a wide tree trunk.

Reverently, Bard unwrapped the child and lifted her from Nanceen's embrace. The girl-child was so small she fit upon his hand, and he carefully positioned her so she lay with her belly against his palm. One of her hands opened and wrapped around his little finger. A band tightened around his heart, filling his chest with longing to offer a blessingway for one of his own, for his own child. A sideways glance at Kaelea showed her watching with rapt attention, her hands clasped between her breasts. A faint lavender glow surrounded her clasped hands.

Again the sense of some difference in her shot through him. It was a physical difference, and more than physical. He hadn't thought that a mere week away, when he'd thought of her more often than he should, would distort his senses so strongly. But, she said it hadn't been a week. By some evil magic, he had been held away from his love and his friends for three months. Three months, he struggled to accept the fact.

Bringing his mind back to the blessingway, he slowly retraced his steps in the circle, offering prayers for the tiny girl child in his hand. After lifting her to the sun, he stroked one finger over her fine red and gold hair. This child's world was his new world... if Kaelea would have him.

He gazed into the forest and met his guide's intelligent gaze. The rodent ran in a tight circle--once, twice, then a third and fourth time. Bard smiled. Finally, he had made the decision. The correct decision.

The child squirmed against his palm and he cradled her close to his body as he turned. He placed a second kiss on her head, but before he returned the child to Nanceen's outstretched arms, he froze. His jaw dropped.

Kaelea hurried to his side. "What's wrong?"

"I... look..." He nodded toward the child.

Two lumps formed under the pale, pink skin on the child's back. Movement rippled under the skin. Carefully, Bard sat next to Nanceen and Korin but continued to hold the child, afraid that to move her would cause harm. The adults watched in silence. The baby gave one sharp, gasping cry and the skin split in two long stripes. Soft, velvety protrusions, the color of turquoise stones laced with silver eased from her back then slowly opened to reveal large, damp butterfly wings. The wings fluttered slowly as they dried in the light breeze, then folded easily against her back. The baby sighed and snuggled into Bard's palm.

Nanceen punched Korin playfully on the shoulder. "Well, no doubt about it, she is your daughter."

· · ·

Gowthaman watched the unfolding drama of Bard's blessingway and the girl-child's unfolding wings with speechless awe. The young, golden-haired girl had plopped herself in his lap after he sat and showed no inclination to move. She watched him with a frown upon her pretty face.

Now that the fairy child had been returned to her parents, he hoped Kaelea and Bard would find time for themselves. On the morrow, he would ask forgiveness from them both.

"Somebody hurt you, didn't they?" The cherub's voice intruded on his thoughts.

"Yes, little missy, someone did." Why deny it, when the marks upon his body vividly showed the physical abuse? With luck, none would know of the rape and torture of his mind.

"Here, too." She touched his temple and a cool wave of comfort eased into his mind. Still, he tensed at the invasion and she jerked her hands away. "I'm sorry. I'm not supposed to do that without asking you first if it's okay. But, you hurt so bad."

He frowned. The child could not know of that pain. At her serious expression, he attempted a smile. "Do not worry about me, little missy."

She giggled and patted his cheek. "Why d'you call me that?"

"Because you are so young, but still I honor you."

"Oh, like you're old." She giggled again.

"But, I am, little missy." He couldn't help but smile at her. "Older than you can imagine."

"But, you're faerie, so you'll live a long time."

A wish that the fact weren't true coursed through him. Could he live with his actions, and those of Feidhlim and the seeker, for the length of a Faerie lifetime? Did he wish to? He had no choice. "Aye, that I shall."

"Don't be sad. I'm gonna marry you when I grow up."

A surprised chuckle broke from his lips. "Are you, now? Why would you want to marry an old librarian like me?"

"You're not old. And because that's what people who love each other do. Just like Daddy and Mommy."

The tall Alastriona moved closer, and Gowthaman fought not to shrink from his powerful presence and piercing gaze. He had exposed some of his talent to the defender when he and Bard returned to the world between worlds. Now that his secrets had been thus exposed, probably to the evil one's followers as well, he would not be able to hide his abilities any longer. Was there even any reason?

A fresh concern grew within him. After all that had transpired, would he still be allowed guardianship of the library? If that were taken from him as well, there truly would be nothing left.

Derrik crouched at his side and Bree frowned at him. "Granda, Gowtham's hurt bad. But, I can fix him."

Gowthaman stared at the young girl. None had used a shortened form of his name, not since he had been a young faerie, not much larger than the child was now. Warmth filled his chest. She was a...peculiar child.

"Did you ask him, Breanna? What did yer da tell ye?"

Counting on her small fingers, she answered as if by rote. "Don't heal without permission. Don't heal when people who don't understand are around. Faerie healing--"

"Aye," Derrik laughed. "Ye remember well. So, did ye ask him?"

She turned a crystal blue-green gaze on Gowthaman. Her earnest expression returned the smile to his face. What harm could there be to humor her? Her fledgling talent had earlier eased some of his physical aches.

"Gowtham, may I heal your hurts?"

After a quick glance at Derrik's tolerant grin, he nodded. "As you wish, little missy."

Bright joy suffused her face and she shook a finger at him. "My name's Breanna, silly."

Pressing her hands to his chest, over his heart, Breanna closed her eyes. The calm, cool waves engulfed him, easing the burning pain. One by one, he watched as his bruises healed and the skin knit over cuts and scrapes. This child had more than a fledgling talent. A pale pink glow surrounded her hands. Tinged with deep red and gold, the glow pulsed softly with the beating of his heart.

No. How could this be? Soulfire never appeared in one so young, despite her foolish claims she would marry him. The haze must be a remnant of confusion within his tortured mind.

Breanna opened her eyes and the brilliance of her smile held him still as she lifted her hands and touched his temples softly. He opened his mouth to beg her to stop, for he could not pull away from her touch.

::I'm not gonna hurt you, Gowtham. I'd never hurt you. See, let me show you.::

The pink entered his mind, hovered in the darkness of his abused memories, then took the form of small hands that lifted bits of his protective mental wall and pieced them together, slowly rebuilding his shields. Finally, with a touch as light as the kiss of innocence, she retreated.

In the physical world, Bree patted his cheek softly, then pressed a rosebud kiss to his forehead before she stepped away. Feeling whole and unabused, Gowthaman stared into Derrik's face. Confusion and surprise he knew mirrored his own expression, widened the defender's eyes.

Bree wrapped her arms about Gowthaman's neck and giggled. "See, Granda. I told you I could fix him."

TWENTY-FIVE

B efore Kae could tell Bard of his child, he fell asleep with
his head resting on his crossed hands on the table. She
smiled indulgently, stroked his shower-damp hair
back from his face, and shook his shoulder. "Go to bed," she
whispered when he lifted his head and tried to blink the sleep
from his eyes. "We can talk later."

"But, I want--"

"I want that, too. Not until you've had some sleep."

A yawn answered her.

"Go on now. I'll be here when you wake up."

Bard's eyes dimmed. "I should never have left you. My
quest was within myself, and I could have done that at your
side as well as alone."

"No, I don't think so. As much as I hated it, and as angry as
I was with you, we both needed the time apart." She ducked
her head. "I really hated it."

With a slight tug, Bard pulled her down onto his lap. She
wrapped her arms about his shoulders and rested her forehead against his. "I don't ever want to feel that way again."

"With all my heart, I will protect you from being alone.
There will be times when we must be separated, for that is the
way of any world, but I vow, you shall never be alone. Precious
Kaelea, you hold my heart, my love, within you."

As well as his child. She should tell him now. But before she could say the words, he covered his mouth and yawned. "I'm sorry."

She kissed the tip of his nose. "Go to bed."

"Will you..."

She nodded then gasped as he rose and easily carried her into her bedroom. Laying her on the bed, he stared down at her. Heat and longing filled her. He stretched out beside her and groaned in bliss when his head sank into the thick pillow.

Kae chuckled and kissed his cheek. "Go to sleep, Bard. I'll be right here."

She watched Bard until his peaceful slumber had lulled her to join him. Night surrounded the cabin in moonless dark when she woke.

Kae rolled to one side and lit a fat candle on the bedside stand. When she faced Bard, candlelight glittered in his black eyes as he watched her.

"Kaelea?"

Silent, she reached for him. She didn't need words to love him, didn't need words to make love with him. Slowly, carefully, she touched his face, smoothing her fingertips over his closed eyelids and along the seam of his lips. He sighed and rolled to his back, inviting her to continue touching him. She did so gladly, taking time to memorize each inch of his face, from the high arch of his forehead to the shell of his ears and the hard, moving lump of his Adam's apple.

"Your shirt's in the way," she mumbled.

Bard swallowed heavily and she hummed at the rise and fall of his Adam's apple beneath her mouth.

Bard jerked from under her sensual attack and stood at the side of the bed. Panting, his gaze bored into hers and he ripped at his clothing.

Kae stretched, arching her back. The light in Bard's eyes brightened. "Your clothing?"

She affected an innocent expression. "My clothes?"

Gloriously naked, Bard towered over her. She reached out and stroked his leg, sighing as the soft hairs tickled her palm. His skin quivered and she inched her hand higher.

Suddenly, he stepped back.

"Oh, Bard," she crooned.

"I shall not return until... Kaelea."

The pain of longing in his voice couldn't be ignored. She slipped from the opposite side of the bed and soon her clothes lay in a heap at her feet. When she turned back to the bed, Bard lay on his side, studying her.

Bard's pulse pounded through every vein, every cell. He wanted her, needed her with an overwhelming fierceness. The urgency to be within her, her body surrounding his, thrummed through him. Despite the aching, undeniable needs of his body, he would not take her without preamble, without knowing she wanted him as strongly.

He waggled his fingers at her but the worried, half-grin remained on her face. He patted the mattress at his side, then held out his hand to her. Finally, the glint of passion filled her eyes and she returned to the bed, pressing her body along his.

"Bard, there's something--"

He smothered her words with a kiss, then lifted his head to gaze into her face. "No talking... unless it is to tell me what you desire."

"But, before--"

He'd meant the taking of her lips to be gentle and teasing, but her surrender drove him to taste her deeply, to dance his tongue along hers, to drive the breath from his lungs. Her kiss was sweeter than the red and white swirled candies, her mouth warm, inviting, pleasing. He could, he would, spend long hours worshiping her in this way.

She squirmed beneath him, rubbing her firm nipples against his chest. He smiled against her lips; she didn't need to speak to tell him what she wanted. Never pausing in the delights of kissing her, he stroked one hand over her shoulder and up and down her arm.

Pushing against the weight of his chest, she tried to angle her upper body so his hand brushed the side of her breast.

With a rough chuckle, he gave in to her desire and cupped the fullness of her breast in his palm. Brushing his thumb over her nipple caused her to gasp and arch high into his hand. He allowed barely enough space to come between them to trail his fingers through the valley between her breasts and repeat his actions. The soft weight filled his hand--a dim thought tried to surface through the thick haze of desire. Heavier, fuller--her breasts were larger.

The thought faded rapidly, chased by her vocal responses to his touch. By the Seven, he loved this woman.

Moving his hand from her breasts brought a soft denial that turned to a sigh as he stroked his fingers around her navel and over the firm, rounded lump below the indentation.

He froze, his palm flat against her lower abdomen. Slowly, he lifted his head and stared down at her. Kaelea's eyes were wide, the passion overtaken by... fear. Without moving his hand, he eased back.

"What is this?"

"I... I tried to tell you."

A thousand possibilities streaked through his mind, each more ominous than the last. "You are ill?"

Her eyes opened wide and after a moment, she laughed. "Not...since last month."

"Kaelea, precious one, what has changed your body in such a short time?"

The touch of her palm against his face was meant to be comforting, but only increased his confusion. He fought the rise of fear. Why didn't she say something? Why was she hiding an illness? She wouldn't die... would she? Beseeching the Guardians of every world, Bard closed his eyes.

"Bard, look at me."

He shook his head. He didn't want to see the sorrow in her face, wouldn't hear what he feared she would say.

"Bard." She lifted her other hand and held his face captive. "Open your eyes and look at me." She waited in silence until he reluctantly did as she ordered. "When you left three months ago... you left something within me."

No, that couldn't be. Had he carried some wasting disease from his world and given the illness to his Kaelea? "I... Kaelea... is there no cure?"

"Cure? What are you talking about? Bard--no, you look at me--Bard, you left me with a child. Your child. I'm pregnant."

Child? "I don't understand."

Kaelea chuckled, a light sound that shattered his fears. "You don't understand how babies are made?"

"No... Yes, I understand that." He flopped to his back and stared at the ceiling. "I was only parted from you for a week. But, I return to discover in this reality three months have passed." The bed lurched as he jerked to sit. "Three months... my child?"

Patient, Kae sat beside him, took his hand and rested it over her womb. "Yes. William Bard Stonefeather, you are to be a father."

Delighted, she watched as full realization dawned on him. The tense muscles in his neck and jaw relaxed. The thin line of his lips softened to a smile.

"You truly are not ill?"

"Nope. The morning sickness ended about a month ago. I feel wonderful. And even better now that you're home." She winced at the questioning tone of the word home.

"We are to have a child?"

"Yes, Bard."

Tilting his head back, a warbling call erupted from him and he lifted both hands high into the air. Then he turned his face to her.

"What was that?" she asked as the sound faded.

He angled his body so that when he lowered his arms, he surrounded her in his embrace. "A call to the Guardians of my people praising the new life that has been granted to us. To love, to cherish, to bring into this... this world. Kaelea, I'd not thought my love for you could grow stronger. Yet, it has. It will continue to grow as each day passes."

"I was worried."

Bard held her close and she rested her head against his chest. The rumble of his words soothed the last of her concerns. "That I would not accept our child? Foolish thoughts, precious one. This child is a gift, a blending of our worlds." He paused, then held her slightly away from himself and tipped her head with a curled finger until he looked into her eyes. "I would join with you, become your life's partner, your mate, in whatever way such things are done here."

"Are you asking me to marry you?" She knew he was, as surely as she knew her answer.

"Yes."

"Then, yes. I will. Oh, Bard. I love you."

"As I do you. Uh, Kaelea... precious... can we... is it... okay?"

She drew him down on the bed. "More than okay. William Bard Stonefeather, make love with me."

TWENTY-SIX

Together they planned the celebration of their marriage, a combination of Faerie, human, and traditions from Bard's world. Anxious as she was to make their union official, Kae put off choosing a date. In the quiet of the night, wrapped in the security of her lover's arms, insecurity reared an ugly, disgusting head.

Would he really stay? The distant look that often filled his eyes concerned her. What was he seeing when he looked at nothing? But when she'd draw near, he'd blink, smile, and it was as if all his attention were focused continually upon her.

Solicitous and caring, he spent part of his days with her, then left to train with Derrik in the ways of Faerie magic. And often he'd return to the human world to visit the young woman who he claimed had drummed the path to lead him home.

Okay, Kae told herself, *I'm jealous.* Though she knew there was no reason, she couldn't seem to help herself.

"Kaelea?" Bard's sleepy voice sounded close to her ear. "Stop worrying and go to sleep. You need rest to grow our child." He tucked her close to his side and brushed the hair back from her face. "Sleep now. I have something important to tell you in the morning."

She twisted until she faced him. He would tell her he was... no, she wouldn't think such things. "What is it?"

His eyes twinkled in the dark, promising a pleasant topic for the morning's discussion. "In the morning, precious one."

"You're mean, teasing me like this."

"No, just tired. Go to sleep." After a soft, lingering kiss, he lay back and closed his eyes.

There would be nothing further from him until morning. Kae blew out a frustrated breath and watched a tiny grin tug at one corner of his mouth. "Oh, you. Okay, I'll wait. But, this better be good and worth waiting for."

"Sleep, Kaelea, and the time will pass quickly."

"Over the past weeks, I have taken many drum journeys with Catori's assistance." Knowing that he would see a flare of jealousy in Kaelea's eyes when he spoke the young woman's name, Bard stroked the back of his knuckles along Kaelea's jaw. Then he rested his palm flat over their child and smiled when the babe confirmed its presence with a firm kick.

"Ow," Kaelea grumbled good-naturedly. She rested her hand over his. "Baby's active this morning."

The lavender glow, the baby's soulfire, deepened, encompassing their hands, then fading to a few tiny sparkles. "This is why I have undertaken the journeys."

Kaelea's brow wrinkled but she remained silent.

"As you wished to give others in your family a sense of their history, the knowledge of their ancestors, so I wished this for our child." He shrugged one shoulder. "My lineage... Although Grandmother claimed to come from another place, I didn't truly believe her tales, even when she showed me her precious book of Shakespeare's tales. Through my dream journeys, I now understand."

"Tell me." She patted the couch next to her and he moved from his place on a cushion at her feet. Angling so they faced each other, Bard took Kaelea's hand and held it between his palms.

"At a place one time sacred to the indigenous peoples of the Southwest there is a cave with a spiral carved deep into the floor. A natural stone arch stands before the cave. At certain times, the moon rises and the light shines through a narrow crack in the arch and follows the path of the spiral."

Kaelea nodded. "Some sort of astronomical, worship kind-a-thing?"

"So it would appear. My grandmother discovered this place and when the moonlight completed the spiral, a window formed within the arch--a window showing her the world I come from. Looking back at her through this window was a man. My grandfather. As I loved you from the moment you rose from the oasis pool, they loved each other immediately."

Pink flushed over Kaelea's cheeks and he leaned closer to press his lips against the heat. "As I love you, precious one. My grandmother vowed to find a way to be with the man she had only seen, but discovered that the moonrise that opened the portal occurred in intervals of about eighteen years. She didn't wish to wait that long."

"If she felt half of what I feel for you, Bard, I can sure understand. So, how did she find a way there? You know there's no evidence of a faerie portal."

"There are other means of movement between worlds. The drum journey is but one way."

"You've returned to your world on a drum journey?" Panic filled her eyes and she snatched her hand from his gentle grasp.

Bard calmly took her hand, kissed the palm, then captured it again between his own. "I was saying the drum journey is but one way to view another world. However, it's like a dream. I can almost feel a substance, like the ground beneath my feet, but when I consciously attempt to feel, there's nothing there. It's difficult to explain."

Watching as she absorbed his words, Bard paused before continuing. Though she had not yet spoken the words, she feared him leaving. How could she not know, not understand the depths of his love? He held back a deep, resigned breath. Had he not left her alone, with no explanation, after the night their child had been conceived...he still had to atone for much.

Finally, she nodded, then tipped her head to one side. "I think I understand. So, she could see where she wanted to be, but not get there."

"Exactly. During this time, she and Grandfather came to know each other, for their spirits were able to communicate during their shared drum journeys. It was then she discovered something amazing, a tale that has been hidden from both our worlds."

"A common tale?"

Bard grinned at the interest sparking her dark eyes. He'd counted on her love of history, of learning the secrets of the past. Because of this aspect of her nature, she would accept the rest of his tale. "The history of my world goes back comparatively only a short while. None speak of the time before, and while the knowledge may have been hidden at one time, I believe the extent of the knowledge died with Grandfather." A wash of shame burned through him. "I should have continued training with him."

After tugging her hand from his, Kaelea touched his cheek. "We all have regrets and wonder how our lives would be if we'd made different choices. If you had completed training as a shaman, would you have needed to seek answers as you did?" She sniffed and a single tear trailed over her cheek. "Would you even be here now?"

"Never doubt, Kaelea, that in some way, I would have found you. Doesn't the soulfire show how we belong to each other? But, yes. I do have regrets of my past."

"And now?" She sniffed again and glanced away. "Darn hormones."

He pulled her closer and kissed her deeply. "No regrets, precious one."

She struggled to ease away, but he held her tight. Finally, she rested her head on his shoulder. "Go on."

Bard chuckled. Curiosity once again overcame her insecurities. "There is a place in the Southwest, ruins on a high plateau. I felt called to that place and for those first days we were apart, built my camp near there. Do you know much of Native American history?"

Kae shook her head. "No. Actually, I've not studied much human history except for when it relates to the family."

When she lifted her head, he gave her a wide smile. "We shall have to ask Gowthaman if he knows of any reference materials on the Anasazi."

"Who? Oh, good. That'll give him something to focus on." She worried about her friend. Breanna had healed his physical and mental injuries--an amazing feat for one so young--but he was still oddly distracted.

"Why the... Anasazi? I don't remember ever hearing anything about them." Admitting to a lack of knowledge was difficult for her and she ducked her head.

Bard caught her chin with a curled finger and lifted her gaze to his. "Because I am descended from those peoples."

"How? You're from another world. Oh, you're saying there have been others who passed between the worlds?"

"Other than Grandmother and myself? None since hundreds of years ago when the Anasazi built their home in the cliffs of the desert."

"Um, I've seen pictures of those."

"Jayse has a book showing the mesas. That book lead me to that area and a place now called the Sun Temple. Long ago there was a drought--or perhaps it was warfare that caused those of the mesa to disappear. No one is sure of the exact reason. However, some of the ancient ones moved to other, more prosperous areas and became members of established tribes while others discovered a new life in a new world. Through a passage created at the Sun Temple."

"To your world?" This was amazing. Imagining the disbelief that would fill the faces of human historians, she chuckled. "This sure would change many beliefs about the past."

"As it has changed mine. Somehow Grandmother discovered the way. Perhaps the Guardians of my world assisted, or those who call themselves Watchers in the world between worlds intervened."

Kae waited as he paused. The pulse point just below his ear

throbbed. He struggled with a strange, sad anger directed toward those who inhabited the world between worlds. Wishing he would talk more about his ordeal during the time spent within the gray mists, she didn't believe he understood the anger. But, as with Gowthaman, it wasn't yet time to press the issue.

After a deep breath, his smile returned and he continued. "Once she knew the way, she crossed into her new world, leaving everything behind but the book of Shakespeare she had been reading within the Sun Temple grounds. I don't believe she ever regretted her decision."

Did he? Kae scolded herself for continually doubting Bard's insistence he would remain with her. Maybe she should finally set the wedding date. Maybe that would bring closure to her doubts.

"It's an amazing story. I'm sure Gowthaman will be happy to help with the research."

"Good. I look forward to speaking with him soon."

Relieved, Kae released a long breath. She feared the two men would stand before her as rivals, but Gowthaman had readily blessed her relationship with Bard. Something changed her friend in the months Feidhlim held him. Or, perhaps it was during the time spent in the world between worlds.

Bard turned his head to peer out the window. "Ah, we have company."

He rose in a fluid movement and held out his hand to her, giving her fingers a quick squeeze before tugging her to her feet. "It would appear your parents have brought a gift."

Kae rushed to the door, opening it just as Stephen lifted his hand to knock. "Da. Mother."

"We've brought something for our grandbairn." Stephen stepped to the side to reveal a hand-carved cradle wrapped in ribbons and a huge bow. Kae dropped heavily to her knees beside the wooden baby bed and ran her fingers over the finely carved flowers and tiny animals.

"This is beautiful." She touched the side and set the piece rocking smoothly. "Where did you get this?"

"It's yours, darlin'," Kelene answered.

"Yes, thank you. But where did it come from?"

Kelene knelt beside her daughter. "No, you don't understand. This is your cradle. Your Da made it just after you were
born." She ducked her head as if embarrassed before lifting a
smile to Kae. "We just took Nanceen's cradle to her. Her
daughter is yet so small, she will fit within the cradle for many
months. I fear we had stored them away and only now found
them when searching for another something."

Kae hugged her mother. "That doesn't matter." She smiled
up at Bard. "Can you believe I used to sleep in this?"

"Then it shall be a safe and happy bed for our child. I'll
bring it inside, if I may."

Stephen nodded. "'Tis not the lightest of things. I am
wearied from the long journey here with it in my arms."

Laughing, Kae rose and hugged her father. "Da, I'll bet you
could have carried both cradles without any trouble."

"Mayhaps, daughter. Still, these old bones could use a bit
of rest and some fine conversation with one of m' two favorite
daughters."

Bard lifted the cradle easily. "I shall invite you in, then,
since Kaelea hasn't seen fit. Perhaps she could be persuaded to
prepare some juice for you--or some of that coffee you seem to
prefer?"

"Bard." Sometimes he teased her as mercilessly as her
Da did.

"Precious one?"

"Oh, never mind. Will you put the cradle under the front
window for right now?"

He inclined his head. "As you desire."

Desire. She loved when he said desire in that way. The
rumbling purr of the word sent sparks shooting through her.
She loved--and hated it because she always lost her train of
thought. Desire.

Chuckling, Kelene took her daughter's arm. "Come along
then, darlin' and I'll help you with the refreshments."

Heat burned across her cheeks. She had to get her

emotions under control. She couldn't always blame hormones--could she?

Bard placed the cradle where she requested then joined them in the small kitchen area. "If you will excuse me, I must leave for a short while." He kissed her mother's cheek then clasped Stephen's shoulder. "We'll long cherish the fine gift you've brought us this day."

Kae pouted. He was going to leave and not say goodbye to her? She turned away and reached for the coffeepot. Suddenly, hands on her shoulders spun her around and pulled her against Bard's firm chest. He arched one eyebrow before kissing one corner of her lips. "I love you," he whispered. The second kiss, pressed to the other side of her mouth was more insistent. Finally, with a sigh of pleasure--hers or his, she didn't know, didn't care--he teased her mouth open with a kiss that curled her toes.

She stumbled forward when he moved away, so he steadied her with a hand against her side. A deep chuckle rumbled through him and he kissed the tip of her nose before leaving.

The door closed behind him and she turned back to her parents. Stephen and Kelene sat at the table, wide smiles belying the innocent way they studied the bowl of fruit centered on the polished wood.

B ard stepped through the portal into the heat and bright sands of the desert Sahara. He jogged over the sand, now enjoying the way the sand shifted beneath his feet. Slowing, he entered the oasis and strode quickly toward the pool and the figure seated at the water's edge.

"Gowthaman, how fare you?"

"I am well."

Bard scrutinized the librarian. From his outward appearance, all did seem as he said, but Gowthaman was unable to hide the deep pain lingering in his eyes. "How are Kae and the babe?"

"Both are fine. I was delayed because Kaelea's parents brought her cradle this morning."

"Good." The dull tone of the word fell heavily in the oasis.

"I have a request of you."

"You have but to ask."

Bard made his request for information on human history. Returning life to his face, interest sparked in Gowthaman's eyes. Glad he'd brought his request to his friend, Bard knelt beside the pool and touched a few of the stones edging the water. "A second request?"

"Yes?"

"May I remove one of these small stones?"

Gowthaman laughed. "You wish a stone? For what purpose? As long as you do not harm the oasis, you may do as you wish with what you find here. I have no control over the oasis, only the library. For the time being." His words faded into bitterness.

"The Alastriona will not remove you from the library, Gowthaman. I have heard Derrik recommend your continued guardianship."

"The defender has been... understanding." Gowthaman smoothly turned the conversation. "How fares his cousin?"

Bard sorted through the stones he'd gathered. "Well." Bard chuckled. "Derrik is able to spend little enough time with her, though his second, Macaire, is seldom far from her side."

Gowthaman nodded and rose. Brow furrowed, he looked down at Bard's pile of stones. "Why do you wish a stone?"

"For Kaelea. To remind her of the place we first met. She has a large collection of stones, and knows the meaning and importance of each. Until now, she has no stone from me."

"It is time then. I must return to the library. I shall notify you when I have discovered what you wish."

"Could you bring the information to us? I don't wish for Kaelea to use the portals too often. She's told me many times that portal travel is safe, but I prefer to take no chances. Besides," Bard glanced sideways at Gowthaman, "Bree asks to see you."

Gowthaman's frown deepened, then his face relaxed.

"Then it shall be as you say." He turned and, shoulders drooping, ambled away. Bard watched a few moments, then returned his attention to the stones.

Selecting a smooth oval stone sparkling with a myriad of crystals, he rose and returned to the edge of the oasis. His portal transferred him from the desert Sahara to the dry world of Catori's reservation.

TWENTY-SEVEN

After her parents left, Kae puttered around her home, always seeming to find herself at a window watching for Bard's return. Bard's ancestral blanket looked perfect when she smoothed it over the cradle's silk covered mattress, but she still took a long time fussing with it, trying the stripes first one way then the other. Then she leaned against the window frame and stared unseeing at the trees surrounding the clearing. One by one, she touched the stones lining the sill. Would she ever be rid of the doubts or the fear that one day he would walk away and never return?

The child moved within her and a sense of comfort radiated from her womb. "Thank you, little one. I know I shouldn't doubt."

Yet, she did. And this time there was only one cure. Kae rushed from the cabin. A twinge of guilt surfaced when she formed a portal, Bard didn't want her using the magical conveyance unnecessarily. She shook her head. Right now, nothing was more necessary.

She exited at the Fey library gates. Hopefully Gowthaman still allowed her access. She held her breath and touched her toes to the first riser. No warding tingled along her skin so she hurried down the sandy steps and turned toward her friend's favorite workspace.

He hunched over a book, his back to her. A tall stack of volumes sat next to his elbow. She watched him set the first book aside and take another from the pile. Quietly, she moved closer.

"Gowthaman?"

His back straightened and he held himself stiff. "Kae?" he asked without turning.

"I need your help."

The square set of his shoulders slumped and he turned slowly to face her. "This appears to be the day for such requests."

"Oh, then I don't want to bother you for long. I just... don't want to ask Derrik. He'll give me a lecture." She rolled her eyes at herself--sounding like a scared schoolgirl. "I know you don't want to--"

"What is it you wish of me, Kaelea?" The harshness of his voice forced her to take a step back. Immediately, his expression softened. "I shall do what I can, you know I can deny you little."

That little hint of the Gowthaman of before--before the world between worlds--gave her hope. She moved closer and rested her hip against the table. "I need to know where Bard is."

"Kae? What is it you ask of me?" The harshness returned to his voice.

Would he accept her request? She hesitated then plunged ahead, speaking rapidly. "I know you can follow his route through the portals."

Gowthaman clutched her elbow and hissed her to silence. He glanced around, worry filling his expression. She followed his gaze but no movement indicated they had been overheard. "I can not."

"You mean you won't."

"Kae, I can not. To do so would be a breach of trust."

Tears burned behind her eyes. "I've got to see him. Gowthaman, I'm frightened he'll leave me."

The librarian sighed and wrapped his arms about her. She

accepted the comfort of a friend as she fought the tears. "I know I'm being silly. I just have this feeling..."

"How can I resist your tears?" Kae glanced into Gowthaman's sincere expression when he stepped away from her side. Concern covered the usual dullness in his eyes. "Come, we shall go to the pool. It shall be easy to follow him from there."

"Follow him? He was here?"

Giving a chuckle Gowthaman swept his arm over the table, indicating the piles of books. "I did not exaggerate when I said today was a day of requests. He has asked me to research an ancient human tribe, the Anasazi. There's an amazing amount of information in Faerie histories, beliefs and ideologies that I do not believe would be found in human texts. An interesting people."

"They're Bard's ancestors."

"Ah." Gowthaman wrapped an arm about her shoulder and led her from the library. "That explains much."

"What does it explain?"

"When I complete my research I shall be pleased to expound upon my theories. Until then, you must wait. Unless you wish to forgo this foolishness of yours and stay for a time to assist me."

"Oh, that would be fun. It's been a long time." The temptation of scholarly pursuits, especially concerning Bard's ancestors, was strong and she nearly turned them back to the library. Until the tiny voice of her fear grew loud and strong within her. "No. I have to find Bard."

"Then I shall create the portal for you." He pressed a cool kiss to her forehead. "Soon. I shall see you soon. And, Kae, your fears are unfounded. The love Bard bears for you--"

"I know. But, I have to. Please?"

Gowthaman gave her one of his sad smiles. "Be careful, Kae. Hold fast to belief and trust. And love." A portal formed behind her but before she could thank him, he had turned and walked away.

. . .

C atori stood at Bard's side staring through a small, window-sized portal. "This is amazing. I've seen this place, the peachy sky, the bleak landscape so like ours. This is your world?"

"No. This is the world where I was born, where I grew to a man. But no longer my world. My place is here with Kaelea. With our child, our children. Here, with you, I can continue training in the shaman's way. I regret denying my grandfather the chance to go further with my training, however, had I not been questing, I would not have been thrown into this world."

"Have you told Kaelea that?"

"Many times and in many ways."

"But she still believes you'll return there?" Catori pointed at the portal.

"Yes."

"You know she's here, watching us from the rocks." Catori angled her head to the side to indicate direction.

"Yes, I know. I felt the portal when it opened. I wonder how she convinced Gowthaman..." He gave a rough chuckle. "It doesn't matter. Now she knows the kind of world I came from."

"You've never shown her your world before?"

Bard shook his head.

"Foolish man. That might be why she's been so afraid. She thinks you're hiding something from her. And here you are. Now, when you stand here with me, looking at what she's never been allowed to share, she's got to be thinking the worst. For her, the worst would be for you to return to that world."

"Have I been a fool?"

Catori laughed and moved across the stone circle to sit cross-legged beside a pack and a long pole. "You're a man. Of course you've been a fool."

. . .

T he young woman's laughter rang over the rocky
ground and Kae clenched her teeth in response. When
Bard joined in the happy sound, Kae sank to the
ground and covered her face with her hands. Why had she
done this? Why had she followed him? She should have
known that she'd feel even worse than she had before learning
where he went.

Lowering her hands, she stared through the small portal
that still hovered at eye level to one side of a wide, stone lined
circle. That had to be Bard's home, the world he said he left
behind when he found her in the desert. But, if he'd left it
behind, why was he here, with that--other woman--laughing.

Oh, she was such a fool. First a fool for falling in love with
him, then for believing he loved her enough to give up his
home. She should leave. Now. She should--but she couldn't.
Awkwardly, she rose to her knees and turned her attention
back to Bard and the woman.

"Y ou have completed the journey pole?" Catori asked.
Bard grinned. "I have. And I have not. My life will
be a constant journey of discovery. Much will be added
to the pole in the future. Something for the births of my children, memories of adventures with Kaelea, reminders of the
truths I discover as I learn more of the shaman ways. This is
both my history and my future."

"Good. Too many believe a journey pole can be completed.
Even as we meet death, it is only a new journey." She chuckled.
"One you won't have to worry about for a long time. What will
you do with the pole?"

"I shall ask Kaelea. Perhaps there is a similar Faerie tradition. Or, perhaps we'll start a brand new tradition."

"What a wonderful idea. Blending of cultures, of lives, of
love." Catori clasped her hands at her breasts.

Bard turned toward his window-portal. "This is the last I
will view that world."

"You should see it once more. With Kaelea. So she will know of that world and accept your decision to stay."

He glanced back at Catori. "This world and Faerie are my worlds. I need no other."

She nodded, but gave him a look that once again proclaimed him a fool. "Close the window."

With a wave of his hand the portal snapped out of existence. "There's a question I've meant to ask for some time."

"Ask away, Bard."

"When we were in the world between worlds I heard a rattle along with your drumming."

"A rattle? Interesting. I had no rattle."

"How then?"

"A question for a drum journey. Though I would suspect that many worlds converge at the place you call the world between worlds. Maybe the rattling came from one of these other worlds."

"Hmm, a possibility. I will think on it. I must go. Kaelea will be impatient."

"I'm not sure impatient is the emotion she's got to be feeling right now. But, yes, you need to go. I have something for you first." Catori reached into the pack at her side and withdrew a small hoop wrapped with leather dyed a deep purple. Feathers and beads hung from the bottom. Within the circle, a thin strip of sinew wrapped over and around itself, creating a design with a small hole in the center.

"This is a blending, like your life, in your worlds. The dreamcatcher is not a part of my people's tradition, but really I like the idea. Hang this over the bed and the web will catch bad dreams and let the good dreams through the hole to bless your sleep. This took me a long time to create because the design of the web isn't traditional. At least not traditional Native American."

Bard took the dreamcatcher and studied the weaving. "No, this looks like designs Kaelea's sister by marriage creates. A Celtic design."

"Oh, good. Then I did it right."

"Catori, this is a beautiful gift. I shall hang it above the cradle to give my child happy dreams. I'm not sure how long it will be before I am able to return to my training..."

"When you're able. I know there are issues you must deal with first. I'd be disappointed with you if you didn't. Go on, now. Go home and convince Kaelea of your decision."

Bard bent to retrieve his journey pole, but before he straightened he pressed a kiss to Catori's forehead. "She is jealous of you," he said.

"Me? You've really got your work cut out for you, William Bard Stonefeather. Now, get going." Catori shook her head and stared into the sky. "Men... fools and idiots."

Laughing, Bard turned from the drum circle and made his way silently toward the rocks hiding Kaelea.

K ae thought she was handling things fine and had control of her emotions when the young woman handed something to Bard. But when he kissed her forehead, Kae sank behind the rocks. She couldn't watch, couldn't bear to see more. When Bard laughed, she covered her ears.

She would go home, but she'd never be able to act like nothing had happened. There had to be a confrontation. Bard had to make his choice. His world or hers. Her or the young woman. Their son or...

Kae pressed the heels of her hands against her temples. She had to stop thinking or she'd dig herself into a pit so deep she'd never be able to find her way out.

After long minutes of silence, she peeked over the top of the rocks. The stone circle was empty. She closed her eyes. Where had they gone? Where had Bard gone?

"Spying on me. Kaelea?"

A scream ripped from her throat and she whirled to face Bard. His stern expression faded at her fright and he gathered her in his embrace. She melted against him then drew back and slapped his chest.

"You scared me to death."

"You shouldn't be here."

Kae wrapped her arms about herself. "Boy, you've got that right."

He tried to take her hand. "Let's go home."

The rock halted her backward steps. "I'm not going anywhere with you until I understand a few things."

Bard laid the pole he carried against a stone and scrubbed his hands over his face and hair. "I ask you to forgive me."

Suspicious, Kae narrowed her gaze at him. "For what?"

He pointed toward the circle. "The small portal you saw-- that was the world I came from."

Slumping against the sun-warmed rock, Kae clutched her throat. She couldn't breathe. "Then... then you're going home?"

"Home? Yes."

Tears slipped from behind her closed eyelids. She couldn't look at him. His fingers brushed over her cheeks and wiped the tears from her lashes. Then he kissed her eyelids. "I'm going home to the Faerie Otherworld. Kaelea, my home is with you. Nowhere else. I should have shown you my world long ago, let you share my thoughts as I made my decision. I was wrong to exclude you. Today was the last time I will see the place of my birth unless you are at my side. From this moment--Kaelea, precious, open your eyes and look at me."

Shaking her head she tried to turn from him. She couldn't bear to see what his expression might truly reveal.

"Yes. Look at me."

When she didn't open her eyes, he made a frustrated noise in his throat and scooped her into his arms. Leaning her slightly to one side, he growled, "Please bring the journey pole."

Barely raising her eyelids, she found the pole he indicated, took it in her hands, and squeezed her eyes shut. The magic of a portal curled around her but still she refused to look.

"Kaelea," he whispered as he set her feet on the ground. "Look around. This is the only world I desire."

The sensual trembling low in her belly, beneath the calm presence of their child, made her sigh. That word again. Giving in, she opened her eyes.

They stood before her cabin. The late afternoon light of the Faerie sun sparkled on the window panes and highlighted the doorway. Bard pointed at the door. "This is my home. If you will still have me as your life mate. As Catori has told me--"

"Catori?"

"--I have been extremely foolish. If you wish to begin again, then we shall. If you can forgive me now--"

She dropped the pole and threw her arms about his neck. "Oh, Bard. I'm the one who's foolish. To doubt you and your love. To doubt myself. Will you forgive me?"

"'Doubt thou the stars are fire, doubt that the sun doth move, doubt truth to be a liar, but never doubt I love.'"

"Shakespeare, William Bard Stonefeather?"

"Shakespeare, precious Kaelea. Shall we... go inside?"

Kae snuggled against him, then patted his shirt pocket. "What's this?

"Catori created it as a gift for us, for our child. I thought to put it above the cradle... if you approve."

"What's it for?" She turned the feather-bedecked circle over in her hands. "This Celtic weaving is very well done."

"It's a dreamcatcher. The weaving catches bad dreams and the good dreams..." he stuck the tip of his little finger through the center hole, "...go through here to bless the dreamer."

"That's a beautiful idea." Kae kissed him, then climbed the porch steps. "Let's hang it up right now. Oh, don't forget your big stick."

She winked and entered the cabin.

Bard shook his head and grinned. Life with his precious Kaelea would be interesting. When he entered the cabin he propped the journey pole in the corner by the cradle and reached into his pocket for the small stone.

"I chose this for you from the oasis pool as a remembrance of when we first saw one another. When I first loved you."

Kae oohed and ahhed over the stone, set it centered on the window sill, and stood back. Sunlight twinkled across the crystal flecks. Lights danced about the cabin, highlighting the cradle. Bard took her in his arms and kissed her soundly.

"The blanket of my fathers and the dreamcatcher will

protect our son. He'll grow strong and happy knowing his place in his worlds."

"Umm. Aren't you going to hang the dreamcatcher now?"

Bard took the leather circle from her and tossed it into the cradle. "Later," he whispered and swept her into his arms. "For I have already caught my dream."

DEAR READER

Thank you for reading this tale. Bringing stories to life is one of my greatest delights and I hope you enjoyed your time in one of my worlds. Readers like you spark the energy needed to tell these tales. Again, thank you.

With today's world of vast reading choices, word of mouth is the best advertising. So please let others know about this book. Tell your friends, relatives, acquaintances, the dog next door (hey, you never know...). And please consider leaving a review at your favorite retailer or review site.

To keep up with new releases, sign up for *Starr Words*. Yes, it's a newsletter, but will appear in your email only occasionally. Your email is safe with me, will never be shared, and you can, of course, unsubscribe at any time. You can find the link on my website www.lizziestarr.com

Next, there's a bit about each of my books. Enjoy the love and discovery! Happy reading!

NEXT IN THE SERIES

(Author's note: This story takes place between books 5 and 6 of the *Double Keltic Triad* and introduces the heroine of book 6. While it's not necessary to read *Prince of Dark Ness* here, it does give background into Lucidea's life prior to meeting Jaysson.)

Prince of Dark Ness: Keltic Mulitverse

An ill-prepared Alfar-Sindhu prince struggles to protect two worlds from an ancient fire elemental.

Will Morghan's two worlds be lost if he chooses family and Coralie over battle? Or will his actions doom a multiverse of worlds to fiery destruction?

A Faire Keltic Renaissance: *Double Keltic Triad 6*

It ain't easy being fey... and the subject of prophecy

Three worlds are in peril. A pieced together ancient prophecy might defeat the separate evils, but will it also bring them love?

KELTIC MULTIVERSE: DOUBLE KELTIC TRIAD

By Keltic Design: *Double Keltic Triad 1*

It ain't easy to be fey when you don't believe in fairy tales.

In the fey Otherworld, a half-faerie child is born. To protect him from evil's crusade to ensure the purity of the faerie race, he is abandoned in the human world, never to know of his magical heritage.

Now Jaye Zeroun is a successful businessman, rooted in reality. Fantasy is only something from an undisciplined imagination. Until he meets Celtic artist and friend of Faerie, Allyn Keeley.

Allyn has found the man she can love but fears their age difference and the overwhelming task of helping him realize his destiny will tear them apart. But Allyn knots her way around Jaye's heart and fills his life with a fantasy he refuses to believe.

Until danger threatens their love, forcing him to either accept a deadly battle or lose the very things he never planned for in his life' a family and a love beyond his wildest imaginings.

Fires of a Keltic Moon: Double Keltic Triad 2

Can love find a way through time?

Lara Zeroun needs an adventure, so she opens a portal in time and travels to the ancient Scottish Highlands. She meets two mysterious men but dares not trust her heart with either.

Under a matriarchal line of succession, Iain is unable to claim his father's holdings--his home. With no lands or possessions, he fights the temptation of a golden-haired woman who came to the manor on the arm of a wandering storyteller.

The storyteller's deceptions bring danger in Iain's time and threaten the destruction of Lara's present. Will Lara and Iain defeat the power of this growing evil and find their ways through time to the love they both desire?

Keltic Flight: Double Keltic Triad 3

What does she need to believe in love?

Even as a mythical faerie, Nanceen doesn't believe in the legends of tiny winged fey. Until a soft voice compels her to search... for love. She doesn't know what she believes but what she discovers changes everything.

Korin Goodfellow has loved the gentry maid from afar. But showing himself to her is forbidden by the fairy king, until using deceptions hidden by dark plans, the king forces Korin into an agreement with seemingly impossible conditions. Fueled by his pure emotions, Korin appears to Nanceen as a wingless man. One she can see. Touch. Believe in.

The evil fairy king keeps Korin's heritage hidden, warping the conditions to force Korin into battle after battle until he discovers his true place in the fairy world. Will Nanceen stand at his side as he risks everything for love?

Wild Keltic Carouselle: *Double Keltic Triad 4*

Falling in love is easy, the possibilities endless.

After months of searching, Bryce accepts he'll never find the masked dancer who captured his heart. Time to get on with life. But when his darlin' daughter climbs onto the lap of a captivating woman in a coffee shop and calls her Mommy, he certainly wouldn't mind exploring the possibility.

After a lengthy vacation, Carrie dreads returning to the job she once loved. Especially when a blond-haired cherub insists on calling her Mommy. The tiny girl's father is intriguing, and Carrie believes she's ready for a real relationship. But memories of a horrific attack surface making her doubt and fear a happy future.

Although he's human, Bryce's family ties are to the Faerie Otherworld, so when one of his fathers is kidnapped, no one knows if the abduction was of human or fey origins.

Falling in love was easy. Telling Carrie about the Otherworld risks that love. But demons resurfacing from both their pasts and evil-doers intent of destroying the present are intent on tearing them from their newfound love. Will their love survive a world of deception, lies and revenge?

Keltic Dreams: *Double Keltic Triad 5*

Passion blazes hotter than the desert sun.

A spiritual quest throws Bard, naked and alone, from his world to the desert Sahara. In search of answers, each grueling step through the shifting sands only adds to his questions and confusion. What did the seven Guardians mean for him to learn in this strange place?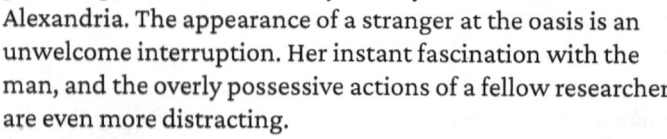

An ever-present evil continues to stalk her family, so Kaelea researches possible protections at the Fey Library of Alexandria. The appearance of a stranger at the oasis is an unwelcome interruption. Her instant fascination with the man, and the overly possessive actions of a fellow researcher are even more distracting.

Time alone might bring solutions to Bard's quest. But will unknown danger and the search for knowledge drive a wedge between him and Kaelea? Will they survive a passion that burns hotter than the desert sun?

*(**Author's note:** The action of the book *Prince of Dark Ness* takes place between Triad books 5 and 6. While it's not necessary to read *Prince of Dark Ness* here, it does give background into Lucidea's life prior to meeting Jaysson.)*

A Faire Keltic Renaissance: *Double Keltic Triad 6*

It ain't easy being fey... and the subject of prophecy

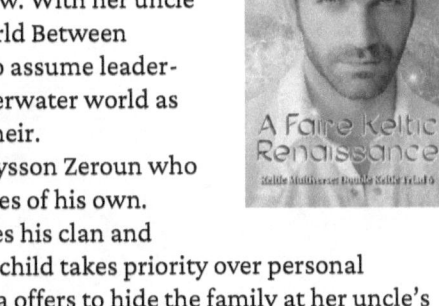

Lucidea had no idea her father wasn't human—until a chance assignment as a forensic artist leads her to Scotland and a family she never knew. With her uncle imprisoned in the World Between Worlds, she's forced to assume leadership of a parallel, underwater world as his half Alfar-Sindhu heir.

Then she meets Jaysson Zeroun who has Otherworldly issues of his own. Once again evil plagues his clan and protecting a newborn child takes priority over personal dreams. When Lucidea offers to hide the family at her uncle's manor, Jayse accompanies them to Scotland. He's falling for Lucidea, but he fears how she'll react to the fact he's part Faerie.

Three worlds are in peril. A pieced together ancient prophecy might defeat the separate evils, but will it also bring them love?

KELTIC MULTIVERSE: OTHER TALES

Prince of Dark Ness: Keltic Mulitverse

(Author's note: This story takes place between books 5 and 6 of the *Double Keltic Triad* and introduces the heroine of book 6.)

An ill-prepared Alfar-Sindhu prince struggles to protect two worlds from an ancient fire elemental.

Torn between duty and love, Morghan stands alone to protect both his Alfar-Sindhu underwater world and humanity from an ancient fire elemental bent on escaping the World Between Worlds. While he's loved Coralie long upon long, he never acted on his desire.

Raised in the royal household, Coralie has remained steadfast at Morghan's side through long human years. She's hidden her true feeling for him, even from herself.

A forensic artist from America, Lucidea Galvagin travels to Scotland to determine the identity of a skull found on

Morghan's land. What she discovers changes her life and possibly the fate of two worlds.

Will Morghan's two worlds be lost if he chooses family and Coralie over battle? Or will his actions doom a multiverse of worlds to fiery destruction?

Blue Keltic Moon: Children of the Triad 1

Love and redemption? Only under the blue Keltic moon.

It's been twenty years since Morghan, leader of the Alfar-Sindhu, was trapped in the desolate World Between Worlds. Now blue moons are aligning in a multitude of worlds, signaling a magical opportunity.

Devoting his life to the Fey library hasn't saved Gowthaman from the agonies of his past, and the long moments he spent in the World Between Worlds. Now, the woman he loves stands ready to lead others into that cursed place. Only he holds the knowledge enabling them to enter. And with luck, safely return with the prince. The risk to his mind doesn't matter, as long as he keeps Breanna from harm.

A competent warrior, Breanna sets aside her personal desires to lead the rescue mission, facing the unknown to bring Morghan home. While she's loved Gowthaman forever, he claims their age difference is too great. But she's seen their soulfire and knows he loves her as well.

Together they must face the World Between Worlds. Can a place filled with despair and loss also be a discovery of love and redemption? Perhaps... only under the blue Keltic moon.

Candy Guy and the Chocolate Brownie: *Keltic Mulitverse*
A short story

Who better to assist a struggling chocolatier than a Brownie?

Candy Guy is in trouble. Winning a design contest will prove his abilities as a chocolatier, but creativity eludes him. An enchanting intruder invades Trace's workspace. She may be real, or she might be a dream. It doesn't matter. Desire consumes him at her lingering touch and the deep chocolate flavor of her kiss.

Deleesi hopes to end the ancient fey curse haunting her family, but the handsome wisher defies her sleep-inducing magic. Something about this human calls to her soul, and, unbelievably, to her heart. The sensual distraction proves impossible to ignore, even while granting his unspoken wish.

By the end of the rainy afternoon, Trace has his inspiration. But will he ever again see the tiny woman who captivated his heart and became his muse?

THE ASPEN GOLD SERIES

The Aspen Gold Series

The Aspen Gold Series is a multi-author series set in the small, but affluent tourist town of Spenser, Colorado. I'm delighted to join with these six fantastic authors to bring you these tales. Find out more about the entire series at www.aspengoldseries.com.

These are my contributions to the series... so far.

Ryder's Heart: *Aspen Gold Series Book 3*

Ryder discovers an intriguing woman in his bed...

Five celibate years in Hollywood didn't ease Ryder Barlow's guilt over his father's death, and now he's coming home to Spencer with a new purpose—to create a camp specializing in equine therapy. When he discovers a beautiful woman in his bed, his plans aren't exactly derailed, but definitely knocked off kilter.

Escaping her past hasn't been easy for Vianna Harrison, but she thinks she's found a welcoming home in Spencer—as long as she can keep her ability as a psychic medium hidden. Not an easy task when spirits need to speak of forgiveness and joy to so many loved ones. Or when the owner of the exquisite cabin she's been allowed to live in comes home unexpectedly.

Neither can start a new chapter in their lives until they stop rereading the old ones. Will acceptance overcome their secrets and show them their Rocky Mountain path to love?

For Keeps: *Aspen Gold Series Book 4*

Hiding the truth is like denying the sun.

Widow Kate Michaels kept a secret from the man she loves, and from the entire community of Spencer, Colorado. She's content running her bookstore and life is good. But in order to pay for his medical care, she must sell the ranch that was her father's dream, and in doing so disappoint her 8-year-old, horse loving daughter. Madison makes an unlikely friend in someone Kate would rather forget.

Veterinarian Jackson Samuels is intrigued by the charming girl, and occasionally lets her shadow him in his nearby clinic. He's enamored with the child's mother, but her defenses are so sturdy, not even his charm or their shared past can make a dent. When Jack uncovers a family secret, the truth makes him question who he thought he was.

Will two people who once shared a heartfelt love, allow their lonely secrets to consume and define them? Or will they help each other, forgive each other, and build a future together —For Keeps?

(Author's note: Barbara Gwen was one of the original authors who created the Aspen Gold Series. When I joined the group and planned my own story, we discovered our heroes were best friends. When Barb left this world much too soon, how could I not finish the book of her heart. **For Keeps** is by her and for her.)

Speechless: *Aspen Gold Series Book 8*

How many peonies does it take to get married?

It's a beautiful day in Spencer, Colorado, and the peonies are in bloom. A perfect day to gather for a wedding, filled with love, traditions, fun, and maybe even a prank or two.

Vianna Harrison and Ryder Barlow would love the honor of your presence as they celebrate their marriage.

Fortunate Cookie: *Aspen Gold Book 11*

This woman. Wearing Frosting. And nothing else...

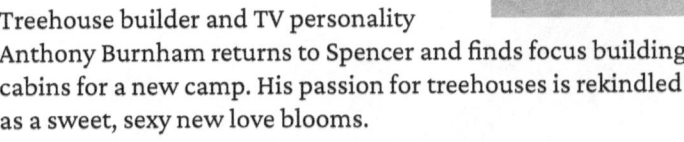

Cookie Lamont owns a successful cupcake shop in Spencer's trendy tourist center. Life would be perfect if not for the escalating unwanted attention from a self-important town trustee. She has everything she needs—and a man is the last thing on her mind.

Until he walks into her shop.

Treehouse builder and TV personality Anthony Burnham returns to Spencer and finds focus building cabins for a new camp. His passion for treehouses is rekindled as a sweet, sexy new love blooms.

But the past haunts his steps and threatens his growing relationship with the alluring baker.

Some Days are Diamonds, is a short story included in:
Yesterday's Promise: *Aspen Gold Series Book 16*

A high-stakes poker game, first meets, a dog rescue, loves lost and rekindled, and life-altering choices fill the history of Spencer, Colorado. Discover the challenges faced in these heartwarming stories crafted by the multiauthor group who brings you romantic fiction at its finest in The Aspen Gold Series.

This collection includes:
The Card Game~~ M.A.Jewell
Some Days Are Diamonds~~ *lizzie starr
Ah, Venice ~~ Debra Hines
First Chance ~~ Donna Kaye
Racing Hearts~~ Bernadette Jones
Rescue Me ~~ Cheryl St.John

FANTASY ROMANCE

Double Moon Destiny

On the night of the Double Moon a child
is born, and the destinies of an acolyte
and a rebel are changed forever.

Jermanah, acolyte of the religious
Compound, has never been given the
opportunity to make her own choices.
Although she accepts her way of life and
yearns to rise higher in the order, she
learns ancient, forbidden healing from
the Seer. On the night of the Double
Moons, a child is born and given into
Jermanah's care until the boy is taken to the king.

Kierigh was born moments before the rising of the Double
Moons, but his twin brother wasn't so lucky. Rumors flow
from the Stronghold—following an ancient prophecy, the king
sacrifices the baby boys to increase his power. But Kierigh
senses that even after five cycles, his brother still lives.

When Kierigh's rebels attack the procession, he takes the
babe, and Jermanah, to his hidden camp. The captivating
acolyte disrupts Kierigh's ordered and simple life. He opposes
her religion and all the Compound claims to stand for. She's

everything he doesn't need in his life. Yet she is everything he desires.

No longer considering herself one of the Compound, Jermanah discovers freedom, and truths she finds difficult to believe. But when the babe is taken from the forest, she will do anything to save the child, including face the leader of the Compound—and the king.

Can a rebel and an acolyte set aside pride and differences to find a lost brother, defeat evil, and discover their prophecy fulfilling destinies?

CONTEMPORARY ROMANCE

Birds Do It!

A search for truth, switched babies, and a threat from the past...

Macaws as lovebirds?

An avian expert, Birdie Simons is called to help control a cantankerous hyacinth macaw during a young girl's birthday party. Inexorably drawn to each other, she and single father Garr Logan share an afternoon of joy and bittersweet memories, for Garr's wife died the same day as Birdie's newborn child.

Something about Rachelle makes Birdie wonder if the golden-haired girl is her daughter, switched at birth. Then her child's father returns, dogging her search for understanding and throwing her deeper into fear and confusion.

Ready to move on after his wife's death, Garr wants the intriguing woman, but Birdie keeps the search, threats, and hidden relationships to herself, driving a wedge between them.

Will discovering the truth from nine years ago bring them closer, or forever tear them apart?

SHORT STORIES

Written in Stone: *'Structs in the City 1*

Fantasy Romance

Undercover agent Stone Mason must find a data-link before a demonstration for underground bidders leads to mass destruction. His search of a posh hotel is risky, but time is up.

Monika Linberg returns to her hotel room after her boss dumps her and assumes the striking, robotic sex-struct is her consolation prize.

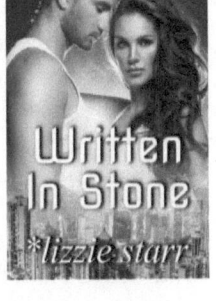

Stone is no construct, but a living, breathing man whose touch and need for information and assistance turn her world upside down. Will working with the sexy agent to keep the city safe be too dangerous for her heart?

Dead Lily Blooms: *At Death's Gates 1*

Fantasy Romance

For ages uncounted, Master Death has assisted souls in transition. But what happens when love gets in the way?

Someone wants vampyre Lily dead, and a bargain with Death has been struck. Death sends servant Agaar to bring Lily to him, but the task becomes more complicated than either Death or Agaar anticipated.

This short story originally appeared in the anthology **Tales From The Mist**. *This re-release has had minor corrections from the original edition.*

Death and the Dryad: *At Death's Gates 2*

Fantasy Romance

For ages uncounted, Master Death has assisted souls in transition. But what happens when love gets in the way?

What's Death to do when a dryad appears at his gate without her soul? She can't move on, nor go back. Will Death find a place for her--at his side?

This tale appeared originally in the **Martini Madness** *anthology and this re-release has had minor corrections and additions from the original.*

FUN STUFF

*lizzie also enjoys creating journals and guided workbooks for authors and other creatives. Look for them on her <u>website.</u>
www.lizziestarr.com

ABOUT THE AUTHOR

*lizzie always made up games and stories to keep her
company. So, a cunning witch lived in Grampa's weather
research station and was only held at bay by waving a certain
weed. An ancient road grader morphed into a boat carrying
wild adventurers to islands filled with fierce lions and
dangerous cannibals, which really looked a lot like sheep.

Now filled with fantasy, love, and romance with a
sparkling twist, the stories of her imagination swirl their way
into the mundane world.

*lizzie recently retired from her more routine life of being
the Lunch Lady at a private school. According to the kids,
she was 'the best cooker!' Yes, she misses the students and
teachers, but is delighted now to start her days by telling

stories rather than opening cases of chicken nuggets and counting milk cartons.

Her tag line of *Author and lunch lady~~what a combination!* no longer holds true (which makes her sad because she really liked that one).

Now you'll know *lizzie by her tales of...
~~Romance with a sparkling twist~~

Want to keep up to date with all of *lizzie's worlds? Sign up for her newsletter on her website:
www.lizziestarr.com

facebook.com/authorlizziestarr

twitter.com/lizziestarr

instagram.com/lizistarr

amazon.com/*lizzie-starr/e/B003F33Y0W

bookbub.com/profile/lizzie-starr

goodreads.com/lizziestarr

pinterest.com/lizziestarr

tiktok.com/@authorlizziestarr